PRAISE FOR
FANG FICTION

"*Fang Fiction* isn't just a totally delicious escapist romp for vampire romance fans—it's also a delicate and thoughtful exploration of the power of fandoms, friendships, and survival. Brimming with sparkling banter, high fashion, pop culture references, and simmering sexiness, it'll sweep you off your feet and make you wish the *Blood Feud* books—and the vampires in them—were real."

—LANA HARPER, *New York Times* bestselling author of
the Witches of Thistle Grove series

"*Fang Fiction* is the first book I've ever read that asks the brave question we've all wondered about (or at least, that *I've* wondered about). Which is: What would happen if the fictional characters you've obsessed over for years in secret and in online fandoms were *real*? The answer, it turns out, is a delightful romp that's as much a story of self-empowerment as it is sweet and hilarious. Oh—and also, there are a lot of sexy vampires. This book is cracky in the best possible way and full of delirious surprises. I loved every word!"

—JENNA LEVINE, *USA Today* bestselling author of
My Roommate Is a Vampire

"This is a thoroughly delightful, entirely unpredictable supernatural romp. Kate Stayman-London has put a fresh twist on vampires and the power of fandom, and readers will be rooting for our heroine, Tess, from page one. It's perfect for those who love their romance with a side of danger, adventure, and, yes, vampires. *Fang Fiction* is a bloody good time."

—ELISSA SUSSMAN, bestselling author of *Funny You Should Ask*

"*Fang Fiction* is totally unique and utterly captivating. Kate Stayman-London expertly blends atmosphere, nostalgia, and a distinctive premise wrapped in a journey of healing, growing, and revival. The result is a fantastical vampire story that feels deeply and profoundly human."

—LYLA SAGE, bestselling author of *Done and Dusted*

"Propulsive, hilarious, and unique, this is Kate Stayman-London at her best. She once again masterfully explores the allure of fandom, but this time, it's with a dash of vampires. *Fang Fiction* is a witty, bighearted tribute to those of us with one foot in the real world and the other drenched in a fantasy universe. And maybe some blood too."

—KATE GOLDBECK, bestselling author of *You, Again*

"*Fang Fiction* expertly blends romance, worldbuilding, wit, and fandom deep cuts to deliver a paranormal adventure that will leave you breathless! Fast-paced and immersive with a killer (pun intended) ensemble, I couldn't flip the pages fast enough. This one is for the #Spuffy fans!"

—ROSIE DANAN, *USA Today* bestselling author of *Do Your Worst*

"I absolutely devoured *Fang Fiction*. This book is for anyone who's ever fallen in love with something fictional and wished they could disappear into it. Kate Stayman-London is so deft at making you laugh, swoon, and feel big feels—sometimes all in one go. Readers will love sinking their teeth into this one."

—AMY SPALDING, bestselling author of *For Her Consideration* and *At Her Service*

"Calling anyone who has ever found comfort in fandom: Kate Stayman-London has given us a new world over which to obsess. *Fang Fiction* combines dazzling vampires with an emotional story of friendship and healing. Once you sink your teeth into this richly imagined, swoony, and hilarious novel, you won't want to let go."

—Laura Hankin, author of *One-Star Romance*

BY KATE STAYMAN-LONDON

One to Watch
Fang Fiction

FANG
FICTION

FANG FICTION

a novel

Kate Stayman-London

THE DIAL PRESS

NEW YORK

A Dial Press Trade Paperback Original

Copyright © 2024 by Kate Stayman-London
Dial Delights Extras copyright © 2024
by Kate Stayman-London

Published in the United States by The Dial Press, an imprint of Random House, a division of Penguin Random House LLC, New York.

THE DIAL PRESS is a registered trademark and the colophon is a trademark of Penguin Random House LLC.

DIAL DELIGHTS and colophon are trademarks of Penguin Random House LLC.

LIBRARY OF CONGRESS CATALOGING-IN-PUBLICATION DATA
Names: Stayman-London, Kate, author.
Title: Fang fiction: a novel / Kate Stayman-London.
Description: New York: The Dial Press, 2024.
Identifiers: LCCN 2023059402 (print) | LCCN 2023059403 (ebook)
| ISBN 9780593729120 (trade paperback; acid-free paper) |
ISBN 9780593729137 (e-book)
Subjects: LCGFT: Vampire fiction. | Romance fiction. | Novels.
Classification: LCC PS3619.T39 F36 2024 (print) | LCC PS3619.T39
(ebook) | DDC 813/.6—dc23/eng/20240117
LC record available at https://lccn.loc.gov/2023059402
LC ebook record available at https://lccn.loc.gov/2023059403

Printed in the United States of America on acid-free paper

randomhousebooks.com

2 4 6 8 9 7 5 3 1

Book design by Alexis Flynn

For Rebecca, Rob, Zoe, and Jessica.

Even if we were trapped on a mysterious island with no daylight, you would still be my California sunshine.

"I know that I'm a monster, but you treat me like a man."
—*Buffy the Vampire Slayer*

Fetch the bolt cutters—
I've been in here too long.
—*Fiona Apple*

Author's Note

Dear reader,

Before you dive in, you should know that *Fang Fiction* tells the story of a sexual assault survivor who begins to heal from her trauma in the usual way: love from her friends, support from her community, and a magical adventure with very sexy vampires. I've taken care to avoid any graphic descriptions or triggering language, and my hope is that this will be a joyful and empowering read. All the same, if you're in active trauma, you may want to proceed with caution.

If you need support, you can call the National Sexual Assault Hotline for free, confidential counseling anytime at 1-800-656-4673 (other resources are available at rainn.org), and *Psychology Today* has a very good directory of therapists who specialize in trauma counseling. No matter your situation, I strongly urge you to learn more about resources in your community, donate to support them if you're able, and vote to elect leaders who are passionately committed to ending gender-based violence.

Okay, now let's get to the vampires, shall we? I hope you have a fabulous time reading *Fang Fiction*—and remember, never be ashamed to ask for what you need.

All my love,
Kate

FANG
FICTION

Prologue

After her first two weeks as a PhD student at Columbia University, Tess Rosenbloom was absolutely certain of exactly one fact:

Coming here was the best decision she'd ever made.

Everything about this place was stupidly intimidating, but she loved it anyway. The campus, with its marble rotundas and twisted iron gates, Rodin sculptures casually dotting the manicured green quads. New York City itself, a place that moved so briskly Tess could barely keep pace; no matter where she was or what she was doing, she always seemed to be in the way of someone in a terrible hurry, and she was always curious about where they were going and why it was so important to get there as quickly as possible. The professors in the Comparative Literature department moved even faster, from Whitman to Morrison to Chaucer in a single breath, expecting every student to catch the references and lob back opinions of their own.

Her fellow students, if Tess was honest, had been the least excit-ing part of her adventure—at least so far. They regurgitated other people's takes on the literature at warp speed, tying everything to schools of thought, postmodernists and neo-traditionalists and fourth-wave queer feminists, every sentence so scrambled that you barely had time to notice they didn't contain a single original idea. As if everyone were out to prove that being well-read was the same as being insightful.

It wasn't like Tess hadn't read all the same books they had—she'd just rarely been in classes or seminars with anyone else to discuss them. Tess's parents were nomadic artist types, and she spent her childhood constantly on the move—a summer in a commune in Vermont, a winter staying with some friend of a friend on the Olympic Peninsula, hiking in moss forests so thick and wet they almost never saw the sun. Tess was shy, a constant reader (especially of all things spooky), dreamy and romantic and a little bit goth, attaching her literary fantasies to her latest crushes. It never mattered much when they failed to live up to them because she'd be moving soon anyway. College was much the same: Tess got her GED and bounced between community colleges, wherever she could find work, until her Shakespeare professor recognized her potential and encouraged her to consider a career in academia.

Tess had never given much thought to what she would do with her life; she was always so consumed with figuring out where she would be next week or next month that concepts like "five years from now" felt too abstract to merit consideration. But Tess's professor helped her transfer to a four-year school to finish her BA, then apply for doctoral programs in comparative literature. Tess wrote her admissions essay about the witches from *Macbeth,* and the way supernatural beings are so often used in literature to externalize human fears and failings, arguing passionately for the need to study Shakespearean portrayals of the supernatural in a contemporary context.

Tess could see herself at a number of schools, but Columbia was her dream—she was so taken with the notion of a gothic campus in the middle of New York City. As Tess thumbed through a glossy brochure, a slideshow of images ran through her mind: Endless days poring over books in libraries so cavernous and reverent they felt more like cathedrals. The thrill of a new folio coming in, putting on gloves to protect the yellowed pages, the soft sounds and dusty smells as intoxicating as any cocktail. Walking across a stage in sky-blue velvet regalia, becoming a celebrated professor traveling the world to lecture eager students, working with Shakespearean theater companies and wearing glamorous gowns to their opening galas. Meeting a lover—or maybe even a great love?—who was as passionate about literature as she was, spending their days arguing about poetry and their nights in a satisfied tangle of limbs.

The day the thick white envelope arrived bearing news of her acceptance, Tess cried. She could feel the pictures in her head growing crisper, more vivid—not just fantasies, but possibilities within reach.

Tess was a little disappointed she hadn't yet made any friends in her program (let alone found the love of her life), but she wasn't going to let that derail her excitement. She loved being here. She loved doing this. And she'd been a loner for as long as she could remember! Maybe that was just the sort of person she was always going to be.

So she had no intention of going to the mixer the department was throwing to celebrate the end of their first full week of classes—until she heard there would be sandwiches. Most of these events had pizza, and while Tess was always thrilled to enjoy a free slice or three for dinner, there was no convenient way to snag leftovers to bring home. But wrapped sandwiches? If they were big, and Tess was lucky, she could eat for the entire weekend. She didn't bother to change out of the jeans and black tee she'd worn to class that day, but she did bring her roomiest tote bag.

The mixer was an uninspired affair, held in the department lounge, well-attended on account of the sandwiches and cheap bottles of pinot noir and chardonnay. Tess made a half-hearted attempt to join a group chatting about Dickens, mostly because one of the guys was pretty cute—his name was Rick, and Tess often dazed off in their romantic poetry seminar imagining how it would feel to run her fingers through his soft brown hair. But after eight minutes exactly (she glanced at the clock on the wall often enough to know), she'd had her fill of ostentatious opinions and decided it was time to grab her sandwiches and get the hell out of there.

Only one other girl was by the sandwich table; most everyone had already gotten their firsts, and it was too soon to politely go for seconds. She looked around twenty-four, same as Tess. She was tall and gawky, Indian American, with deep brown skin and long black hair, wearing cutoffs and a faded green tee. Her body was all angles, sharp elbows and hips and knees, but her face was full of curves— big lips, a prominent nose, and wide eyes. Tess had seen her at orientation, but they didn't have any classes together, so they didn't know each other at all.

"Turkey or ham?" she asked Tess.

"For now or for tomorrow?" Tess replied. This girl had brought a tote bag too.

"Oh, *great* point," she enthused. "I feel like ham won't keep—it gets that sheen to it, and no one wants to eat a shiny ham sandwich."

"But if you want tuna, it's now or never," Tess countered. "Definitely not taking chances on anything mayo-based in this heat."

"Okay, okay." The girl nodded, formulating a plan. "So we do tuna right now—and I'm gonna say that pairs with white wine, right? Fish and white? That's a thing?"

"I'm not sure either this fish or that wine is good enough to worry about pairing, but I'm always down for a bottle of white." Tess laughed.

"Excellent. Then we take take turkey for tomorrow . . ."

"And the BLT for Sunday," Tess finished.

"Oh my god, *yes*." The girl grinned. "It's gonna be so cold and salty, we won't care at all that it's two days old. You're so fucking smart. I'm Joni, by the way."

She was already shoveling sandwiches into her bag, not bothering to be stealth about it—Tess absolutely loved her style.

"I'm Tess." Tess grabbed some sandwiches of her own, plus a couple little bags of chips, two apples, and some chocolate chip cookies in Saran Wrap.

Joni glanced at the wine and furrowed her brow.

"I don't think I have a corkscrew, do you? Should we steal one of those too?"

"I have one," Tess said and laughed.

"Great! We'll eat at your place. Oh my god, is that *Blood Feud*?!?!" Joni pointed at the worn paperback in Tess's overstuffed tote. "I'm obsessed with those books!"

"Seriously??" Tess had felt certain that not one of the snobs in their program would be into her favorite vampire novels.

"*Yes!* Omg, how hot was it when Callum and Isobel have sex in the middle of the moonflower meadow?"

"Not as hot as when she and Felix have sex in the milky jade pools after their battle with Tristan!"

"Do not even *tell* me you're a Felix girl, he's so boring!" Joni protested, but she was grinning.

"Who's your favorite then?" Tess goaded her. "Callum? The bad boy? Ooooh, how original."

"Puh-lease, it is so obviously Octavia!" Joni shrieked. "By the way, did I not mention I'm a big giant lesbian? Anyway, Octavia rules, everyone else drools, when I turn twenty-nine I'm throwing a *Blood Feud*–themed party just like the ball Octavia had for her twenty-ninth birthday."

"That's *genius*," Tess gushed. "You could do Victorian decorations, make your place into Konstantin's townhouse with the blood punch and everything."

"The *blood punch*, oh my god, yes! With cranberry juice! Or actual blood!"

"Or both!"

By this time, they were both doubled over laughing, and the rest of the mixer had gone more or less silent as everyone turned to gawk at them. But Tess found that as long as she was standing with Joni, she absolutely did not care.

"You ready to go?" Tess asked.

"Boy, am I!" Joni grabbed an unopened bottle of chardonnay, and they both waved jovially to the group as they strode out of the room.

Within two weeks Joni and Tess were best friends, and by spring semester they were living together in a grimy basement apartment a few blocks from campus, a place filled with cheap furniture scrounged from Housing Works, daring experiments in homemade frosé, Harry Styles dance parties, and online quizzes about which vampire from the *Blood Feud* books you should marry. The year Tess spent living with Joni was the best year of her life.

Until Rick's Valentine's Day party.

And the panic attacks. The nightmares. The insomnia.

And then Tess moved out while Joni was away on spring break without ever telling her why.

Back at that first mixer, Tess never could have guessed that she'd be dropping out of Columbia in just eighteen months, leaving behind her best friend, her career, and all her dreams.

It wasn't personal. It was just what she had to do to survive.

Chapter 1

Five Years Later

Cat: Hey, this is Cat Koorse!

Ruby: And this is Ruby LaBruyere.

Cat: And this is *Here to Slay,* the podcast where we bring you *biting* commentary on all things vampire.

Ruby: Oh my god, Cat, you said you weren't going to do the bite joke.

Cat: Sue me! I lied!

Ruby: Okay. Anyway, big news this week—the long-anticipated *Blood Feud* movie has officially been green-lit! Guy White-man is writing and directing, with Henry Golding and Gemma Chan set to star as sexy-evil vampire twins Callum and Octavia Yoo—

Cat: Aren't those characters supposed to be British Korean? Neither of those actors is Korean.

Ruby: This is Hollywood, let's be glad they're Asian at all. The biggest news is Timothée Chalamet himself is playing heartbreaking hero Felix Hawthorn! Truly the most perfect casting I could imagine—I can't wait to see Timmy bring that fabulous mop of hair to sweet, charming Felix.

Cat: Oooh, the Chala-mop.

Ruby: I prefer Chala-mane.

Cat: So today, we're going to dive into some of the controversies surrounding the *Blood Feud* novels and speculate about what they might mean for the film.

Ruby: I've read all the *Blood Feud* novels—

Cat: And I've read none of them.

Ruby: So let me take you through some of the basics. *Blood Feud* follows the story of two warring clans of vampires trapped on a mysterious isle that looks a lot like Manhattan, but with more magic and stuff.

Cat: What kind of magic?

Ruby: Okay, so like, you know in most vampire stories the vampires can glamour people?

Cat: Like when the vampires look into your eyes and you fall into a trance and do whatever they say?

Ruby: Exactly! Well, on the Isle, there are no people, but the vampires who live there can glamour their surroundings instead, like make fabulous castles and stuff.

Cat: Oh wow, it's like vampire HGTV.

Ruby: You got it. Otherwise the *Blood Feud* novels mostly adhere to regular vampire rules. You can only kill them by chopping off their heads, driving a wooden stake through their hearts, or setting them on fire. They sire new vampires by draining a human's blood and then the human drinks the vampire's blood instead, the usual.

Cat: Do they glitter in the sunshine like the vampires in *Twilight*?

Ruby: Nope! They burn to death in a spectacular blaze of violence.

Cat: Copy that.

Ruby: There are three novels so far, and they've sold upward of ten million copies worldwide—fans are absolutely rabid for the fourth, but we have no idea when, or if, it's coming out.

Which brings us to our first controversy: Who is August Lirio?

Cat: I know this! August Lirio is the author of *Blood Feud*!

Ruby: Yes, well done. But who are they? August Lirio is a total recluse: We have no idea what gender they are, how old they are, where they live, what they look like—absolutely nothing.

Cat: Wait, they don't even have an author photo?

Ruby: No! Rumors have swirled that "August Lirio" doesn't exist, and the name is just a pseudonym for another famous author.

Cat: Like who?

Ruby: Oh my god, you name it—George R. R. Martin was a popular one because Callum and Octavia are biological twins, plus they have the whole twin sire bond thing, but they've never had sex, so that doesn't seem like George.

Cat: I'm sorry, the twin sire what?

Ruby: So in the *Blood Feud* books there's this thing called the twin sire bond, where Callum and Octavia were sired and reborn as vampires in the same grave on the same night, which gives them special powers, like they're especially fast and strong and stuff. But *that* is not what's controversial about them.

Cat: What's controversial about them??

Ruby: People think they're real.

Cat: I'm sorry, what?

Ruby: Okay. So members of the *Blood Feud* fandom call ourselves Feudies, and certain corners of the Feudie fandom believe that the characters in the books are, ya know. Real vampires.

Cat: Ruby, are you a vampire truther??!?!

Ruby: I would say I'm vampire-truther-curious.

Cat: Wow. Wow.

Ruby: Have I shocked you?

Cat: You know, I think it's a good thing. We've been friends for a decade, we have two podcasts together, and you still find ways to surprise me. I think it's nice. Okay, so say you're interested in these vampire conspiracies. Where would you go to learn more?

Ruby: Tumblr, reddit, the usual. FeudieTok, obviously.

Cat: So, are there . . . a *lot* of people who think vampires are real?

Ruby: Listen, what we lack in numbers we make up in sheer unhinged fortitude. No, but really, I've met some awesome people in the Feudie forums. One truther was a PhD student at Columbia, she wrote a really thorough essay explaining the theories that went viral after it got picked up by *BuzzFeed* last year.

Cat: Oh shit, I think I remember that!

Ruby: Anyway, we're going to get way more into the vampire-truther conspiracies in a minute, but first, if you're feeling like a vampire who can't get any sleep, you might benefit from SheCalm, which are medical-grade, all-natural CBD gummies clinically proven to help with relaxation and insomnia, specifically formulated for women.

Cat: How is it different from CBD for men?

Ruby: It comes in a pink bottle.

Cat: Can't argue with that! We'll be back right after this.

—Forwarded Message—
From: Joni Chaudhari <jc718@columbia.edu>
To: <recipient list unspecified>
Sent: August 6, 11:26 AM
Subject: *~invitation~*

You are cordially invited
to Joni Chaudhari's
TWENTY-NINTH MOTHERFUCKING
BIRTHDAY!!!!!!!!!!!!!!!!!

The theme is *Blood Feud,* so come dressed in your most fabulous vampire attire! Even if you think it's lame, just do it anyway, stop taking yourself so seriously and I promise you'll have fun.

The deets:
Joni's place
Saturday night, 6 P.M.
Don't be cheap, bring nice booze
(we will have ~blood punch~ but the rest is up to you!)
Hope to see you then!!

—**Forwarded Message**—
From: Professor Lareina Vázquez <lv553@columbia.edu>
To: Tess Rosenbloom <tess.tament@gmail.com>
Sent: August 8, 3:01 PM
Subject: Question

Hi, Tess—it's been a long time. Joni mentioned her vampire party the other day and it made me think of you; I asked how you were doing, but she didn't know. In any case, the timing was fortuitous. One of my researchers just informed me she'll be transferring to UC Boulder this semester, which means I have some unexpected additional PhD funding, and I thought of you—any chance you'd consider returning to the program? Let me know if you're interested and we can discuss next steps. Thanks—speak to you soon. Hope you're doing better. LV

e can't do this." Isobel glowered at Callum.

"Why not?" he snarled.

He took another step toward her, and she felt overwhelmed,

her senses flooded with every aspect of this hulking brute of a man. He was easily a foot taller than she was, thick with muscle, and he smelled of pine and musk, like he was the essence of the Isle itself. She didn't know how he tasted . . . but god, she wanted to.

Desperately.

"You know exactly why not!" Isobel flailed. Above them, giant moonflowers grew tall and twisted, their blue and purple petals glowing in the starlight, casting Callum's face in soft prisms. Try as she might, Isobel couldn't get the image out of her mind of Callum pressing her against one of those thick moonflower stalks, his hands roving roughly down her dress as she moved her body against his, savoring the delicious friction—no. No! She couldn't do this! *They* couldn't do this.

"If Felix finds out . . ." she whimpered, unable to finish the sentence. *He'll kill you, Callum.*

"I'm not afraid of Felix." Callum's British accent was gruff, his voice low and graveled—just the sound of it sent rumbles through Isobel's core. "He's wanted me dead for a century, and he's never managed it yet."

"He's my lover." Isobel's voice broke. "I owe him everything."

"You owe him your freedom?" Callum challenged. "Your autonomy?"

"No," Isobel conceded. "But I do owe him my loyalty."

Callum leaned close to her, his breath tickling her neck as he spoke softly against her ear.

"I've spent months imagining this moment," he intoned. "The way I want to touch you, to make you scream. I've considered every angle, every detail."

"Why are you torturing me like this?" she pleaded. "You're my lover's sworn enemy—"

"That's his choice," Callum said firmly. "And this is yours. You know what I want. And I know what you want. The question is whether you're going to take it."

"I . . ." Isobel gasped for breath and faltered for words. Her small body heaved beneath her silky black peignoir as she filled her lungs, trying to convince herself to run, to leave, to go back to Felix's castle, to go *anywhere* outside the presence of this devastating man, anyplace that would make her forget how badly she was burning with desire.

"You what?" he prodded. He leaned a little closer, so she could feel his chest brush against hers, and that was it, she couldn't take it anymore—she grabbed his collar and yanked him toward her, and then his mouth was hungry against hers, kissing her so intensely she felt she might black out. Callum expertly untied the bows at her shoulders, and shivers ran through her as the chill mists of the meadow whispered deliciously against her skin.

"Please," she rasped. He pulled her close as he straightened up, and his hardness pressed against her. The feel of it sent a knee-shaking twist of desire through her center.

"What should we do next, pretty Isobel?"

His teasing voice tickled at her ear, but she couldn't form words—she could only kiss him again and again. He picked her up as if she weighed no more than a pile of blankets, laid her down on a bed of moss as he began to strip off his clothes. She knew the moment was close, that she was about to experience the exquisite agony of him inside her, that in just a few seconds—

"Tess! Thank god I found you. There's a total crisis downstairs."

Tess looked up from her *Blood Feud* paperback with a hardened stare. It was six P.M. on a Saturday night, and she wasn't scheduled to work until eleven. She was availing herself of one of her favorite perks of employment at The Georgia Hotel in Williamsburg: a fantastic terrace pool and tiki bar with a view of the Manhattan skyline. Tess could hole up reading for hours, escaping her own mundane world to visit a mysterious island filled with romance and adventure, with absolutely no one to bother her.

Except for now, apparently.

"Can't Taylor deal with it? I'm not working yet." She nodded meaningfully toward her book, but Willie—a scrawny bellhop with very anxious energy—was undeterred.

"I talked to Taylor, but she's already handling a whole thing with a wedding in the solarium where a bunch of bees got loose? So she said to come get you for Mrs. Harriman at the front desk."

"You've gotta be fucking kidding me," Tess grumbled and pushed off her barstool. Elaine Harriman was one of the hotel's most important guests—she frequently dropped by for last-minute stays in their rarely booked, dramatically overpriced penthouse suite—which explained why everyone was expected to put up with her every grievance, no matter how unreasonable. And in Tess's experience, Mrs. Harriman's complaints rarely adhered to anything that could be considered within the bounds of reason.

The Georgia was owned by a pair of eccentric lesbians and inspired by Georgia O'Keeffe; the lobby was decorated in desert hues of sage, rose, and terra-cotta, dotted with soft leather couches and vivid green cacti. A giant O'Keeffe print hung prominently near the entry, with their favorite O'Keeffe quote inlaid in a tile mosaic beneath it: *I have done nothing all summer but wait for myself to be myself again.*

Mrs. Harriman was standing at the blond wood front desk, dressed in an impeccable cream cashmere suit, her white hair coiffed and her face tomato red as she huffed out a stream of criticism at Mika, the front desk worker. Mika was dry and fun and always kept her cool with guests, but it was obvious that Mrs. Harriman was seriously trying her patience.

"Mrs. Harriman, such a pleasure to see you again. I'm Tess Rosenbloom, one of the managers here," Tess interjected, to Mika's visible relief.

"Really?" Mrs. Harriman peered at Tess. "You don't look like you work here."

Tess usually dressed for work in faded linen slacks and blazers to match the vibe (the staff had uniforms, but not the managers). But tonight, Tess was stopping by a *Blood Feud*–themed party before her shift, so she was wearing a silky black slip dress that clung to her size-sixteen curves, the low V-neck perfectly suited to show off her cleavage, and a floaty chiffon peignoir trimmed with delicate lace accents, mimicking Isobel's outfit in the scene Tess had just been reading. (She'd been tempted to go for a full corseted gown for the affair, but even a party based on her all-time favorite novels couldn't convince her to wear velvet in August.) Her wavy auburn hair fell in tumbles well past her shoulders, and she wore a fresh face and a bright red lip, accenting her round cheeks with dewy pink blush and her wide hazel eyes with shimmery shadow and dark mascara. Tess's skin had always been pale, but never more so than the last three years working the night shift. Never seeing the sun wasn't ideal for life, but it was kind of perfect for a vampire party.

"I was actually just on my way out, but I wouldn't *think* of leaving without helping you." Tess gave Mrs. Harriman her most understanding smile.

"Oh, if you have plans—I don't mean to interrupt, it's just that I was absolutely *terrified*."

"Terrified?" Tess raised an eyebrow; she had never known Mrs. Harriman to be intimidated by any person or thing.

"Wouldn't you be?" Mrs. Harriman shot back. "If you opened the door to your room and found a *stranger* on your bed?"

Tess exchanged a look with Mika. The fuck?

"I was just saying it was probably a member of our cleaning staff," Mika filled Tess in.

"But they weren't in a uniform!" Mrs. Harriman was indignant. "And are you honestly saying that this hotel allows cleaners to sleep on guest room beds?"

"Of course not, Mrs. Harriman," Tess said smoothly. "What were they wearing? Did you get a look at their face?"

Mrs. Harriman shook her head, as if trying to remember.

"I couldn't," she said softly. "They moved too quickly."

"We sent security up to the suite right away, but there was no sign of anyone having been there," Mika muttered to Tess. "The bed was made. No one had been in it."

"They weren't *in* the bed, they were *on* the bed," Mrs. Harriman insisted.

"Okay, Mrs. Harriman, here's what we're going to do—if you want to change rooms, of course we can give you a new one. We have our cabana suite available—that one opens right onto the pool! But if you'd rather stay in the penthouse, we can perform a full security sweep and issue you a brand-new key to ensure no one else can get in there. What would you prefer?"

Mrs. Harriman looked shrewdly at Tess. "If I go back to the penthouse, will you knock a night off my bill?"

Tess smiled thinly. "It would be my pleasure."

After Willie the bellhop got Mrs. Harriman back onto the elevator and out of sight, Mika burst out laughing.

"What a fucking fraud!" Mika shook her head with grudging respect. "Staging a meltdown to get a free night. Like she even needs the discount!"

"No, she's not a fraud. She's just—I don't know. An opportunist." Tess couldn't help laughing too. "How's the day going otherwise?"

"You heard about the wedding with the bees, right?" Mika cocked her head and leaned in for gossip. "Joey the bee guy obviously wasn't supposed to be here today to pollinate the flowers in the solarium, but he got the days mixed up, and the bees got loose, and apparently the groom's nephew is allergic, so the bride lost her shit and swore she was getting hives, and the bride's mother said it was just a panic attack and she'd freak out too if she was about to marry that guy, which set the groom's mother off, so they're screaming and yelling, the bride's crying, the nephew is curled up in a corner hiding from the bees. Meanwhile, the best man has been plastered since breakfast, knocks over a giant floral arrangement, gets stung like sixteen times."

Mika exhaled with satisfaction, and Tess grinned. "So you're saying Taylor's going to be in the lobby bar drinking herself into oblivion the second her shift is over?"

"Exactly," Mika laughed. "Do you really have plans, or were you just trying to get away from Harriman?"

Tess suddenly felt a twist of nervous energy. "My old roommate's birthday. Gotta get to her party in Morningside Heights and back by eleven."

"That far uptown?" Mika looked skeptical. "Must have been a good roommate."

"Yeah." Tess forced a smile. "She was the best."

Tess took the L west to Manhattan with some regularity, but transferring to the 2/3 at 14th Street and heading north felt more like time travel than riding the subway. After Tess unceremoniously moved out of their apartment while Joni was out of town, they didn't speak for months. Joni was hurt, Tess was ashamed, and back then, Tess's panic attacks were still so regular and so debilitating that she could barely make it through each day—an emotionally fraught conversation was out of the question. Eventually, Tess and Joni had intermittent text exchanges, but they were always awkward and stilted. Tess and Joni had never been able to get back the easy connection they shared when they were living together—closer to each other than Tess had ever been to another person.

Then Tess got a night job at The Georgia, which was great since Tess hadn't been able to sleep at night since Rick's party, but it didn't make it easier to get together with Joni. Between their opposite schedules and living at least forty minutes apart, there was always an excuse to put off making plans, to cancel and reschedule, and now it had been more than three years since they'd seen each other. Tess was honestly a little surprised she was invited to Joni's party; Tess hadn't invited Joni to her last birthday. Not that she'd done anything big, just went to a chintzy bar with her friends from the hotel. She didn't want to have to deal with the awkwardness of introducing Joni to everyone, of making flimsy excuses for why she'd left Columbia—a topic she'd barely addressed for herself, let alone with Joni. She'd worked hard to move past all that; she didn't see the point in dredging it up again.

But Tess was doing better now. She slept a solid five hours during the day, sometimes six. She'd been promoted to night manager, which meant she could afford to live in a "junior one-bedroom" near the hotel—i.e., a cramped studio with a closet large enough to fit a double bed, which, it turned out, was extremely practical for someone who slept during the day. She could buy nicer clothes and take herself out to dinner before work. She'd downloaded one of those apps where you could text a therapist—which hadn't been all that helpful, but she thought it showed pretty good progress that she'd installed it in the first place. And she liked the mindfulness meditations that came with the app, coaxing her in soothing tones to name five things she could see right now. Sometimes she listened to them as she wandered through Marsha P. Johnson Park, drinking cinnamon cortados and watching the churn of the river.

And now, her adviser had emailed her about a chance to come back to Columbia—and to Tess's absolute shock, she was actually considering it. She wasn't sure whether she wanted to go back, but she liked feeling strong enough to know that it could be a possibility. She was thinking of this party as a way to test the waters, dipping her toes back into the world she'd loved so much until she'd had to leave it so abruptly.

It was both familiar and bizarre to get off the train at Cathedral Parkway, to see the same tiles spelling out the words that used to mark the way home. There was the bodega where she and Joni would get chopped cheeses at two A.M. when they still had piles of papers to grade, the weird natural wine store where they pooled their meager spending money for a bottle of something effervescent, the diner where they ate mountains of scrambled eggs and crispy hash browns smothered in ketchup and Tapatío on mornings after gathering with other people from the program, arguing about Dostoyevsky and pounding bourbon.

They used to get out pens and paper napkins and divide their various crushes into two columns: For Fun and For Real. Joni's crushes were almost never in the For Real column; Tess's almost always were. Tess was an optimist back then—she'd spent her life reading earth-shattering love stories, and she believed that someday she'd meet someone special enough to be in one of her own.

Stupid, she thought, reflecting on her past naïveté. She looked for the good Chinese place where she and Joni always got the spicy sesame noodles, but it wasn't there anymore—it was some corporate frozen yogurt chain instead. After a lifetime on the move, Tess had been in New York for almost five years, by far the longest she'd ever lived anywhere. She liked that you could stay in one place, and the city would keep changing around you. The constant flow of guests and workers at the hotel, shops and restaurants coming and going like seasons, New York made Tess feel grounded but not suffocated. It had been years since the impulse to pack up everything and *go* had taken over her senses, invading her thoughts until she had no choice but to run.

It hadn't happened, in fact, since she lived in this apartment.

The building looked the same as ever: a brownstone that had seen better days, a permanent layer of soot coloring the stones a dingy gray. A couple of people Tess didn't recognize were smoking on the stairs. She walked past them to the little doorway on the lower left into the "garden" apartment—but since there was no garden, she and Joni had never harbored illusions that they were living in anything but a basement. This didn't bother them; it was the only way they could afford to live so close to campus without staying in student housing. Joni had been desperate to find a place that felt like her own, that made her feel like a grown-up. Tess didn't care as much, but Joni was so magnetic, so much fun, that all Tess wanted was to be wherever Joni was.

Tess could hear ABBA blaring as soon as she walked through the door. It was just after eight and not even dark, but the party was already in full swing, people dancing and drinking and spilling into the hallway. Tess fluffed up her hair and smiled wide as she stepped into her former apartment.

"Tess?! Oh my god!" Joni rushed over, clearly tipsier for wear, and pulled Tess into a vise-grip of a hug. "I can't believe you came."

They had talked about this party countless times, even the first time they met. Joni had planned to dress as Octavia Yoo, the most fashionable character in *Blood Feud,* who was turned into a vampire on her twenty-ninth birthday. Tess smiled to see Joni looking absolutely perfect in an ice-blue fringed mini and a fabulous rhinestone tiara.

"Of course I came," Tess assured her. "I wouldn't miss your *Blood Feud* birthday!"

Joni pulled back and gave Tess a skeptical look.

"If you say so." She laughed awkwardly. "But whatever, I'm so glad you're here!"

"Me too." Tess brushed past the weirdness. "And wow, this outfit, you look incredible!"

"You like?" Joni did a little twirl. "And omg, of *course* you're Isobel—please don't tell me you're still in your Felix era!"

"You mean my kind, charming, brave romantic hero era?!" Tess scoffed, and Joni laughed. "You're the perfect Octavia, though."

"Fran and Nasser are both dressed up as my Callums, we have to show you—they're around here somewhere."

"So it's going good? Living with them?" Tess pushed down the twinge of jealousy, tried not to imagine Joni and their two lovely weirdo theater arts friends spending hours on the couch together watching music videos and bad TV.

"Oh yeah, it's been really great." Joni smiled wide, in that way where Tess knew she wasn't saying something. "But I've been so busy lately, it's not like we see each other that much anyway. I'm finishing my dissertation, and there's an opening for a tenure-track job in the department, which is kind of crazy, so I'm applying for it."

"Oh my *god,* seriously?!" Tess squeaked. "Joni, that's amazing!"

"I totally have no chance—"

"Stop that, yes you do! It's obvious to everyone you're a star." Tess nudged Joni, genuinely proud of her friend.

"I don't know about that." Joni flushed, but Tess could tell she relished the compliment. "People are applying from all over the country, but I dunno, they say they would love to give it to someone in the department? Promote from within or whatever? But even if they do, you know Rick Keeton will probably get it anyway. Fucking golden boy."

Joni rolled her eyes, and Tess froze.

She just mentioned his name. He isn't here. This doesn't matter.

Joni was still talking—Tess forced herself to focus back in on their conversation.

". . . so annoying that he's such a nice guy, you know? Otherwise I would totally hate him."

Tess nodded numbly. Nice guy. Sure.

"Anyway, enough about me!" Joni grinned. "How are you? How's everything at the hotel?"

"It's good!" Tess swallowed hard. "I forget if I told you I got promoted, so that's been good, I guess."

"I saw on Insta." Joni's voice was clipped.

"Right," Tess faltered, then forced a smile. "Um, anyway, here's this!"

Tess held out a shiny gold gift bag she'd brought from Brooklyn, and Joni perked up—she loved presents.

"For me? My stars!" Joni affected a blushing belle. The bag held two bottles—Joni pulled out the first and cracked up laughing. "Oh my god, Party Girl Frosé™! The literal worst bottle of alcohol we ever consumed! Where did you even find this? I thought they recalled it!"

"Oh, they did, you absolutely can't drink that," Tess deadpanned. "I had to promise the guy at the shadowy warehouse I would never tell anyone he smuggled this out for me."

Joni opened the little card tied to the bottle's neck.

"For fun," she read aloud, then reached into the bag to pull out the other bottle. "Which means that this one is . . ."

"For real," Tess finished the sentence as Joni extracted a gorgeous bottle of Perrier-Jouët rosé champagne, painted with pink anemones.

"Damn, Tess." Joni looked up at her. "This is like, a really good bottle."

"Well, you're like, a really good friend." Tess tried to hold Joni's gaze, but her emotions were too intense. After a moment, she looked away.

"Hey, you need a drink!" Joni enthused. "You have to have some blood punch—that was your idea, remember? Nasser found this recipe for sparkling tart cherry punch on Martha Stewart, he's like totally obsessed with it, it looks so bloody and gross. I can't tell him how much I love it because he already won't shut up about how great it is."

"It sounds delicious." Tess laughed, but she stopped short when she saw the glass punch bowl on the counter.

"Is something wrong?" Joni asked.

"No, I just—the punch is just sitting out," Tess said stupidly, not knowing how to explain the way her insides were currently seizing up.

"Yeah, it's punch, it kinda has to be in a bowl?" Joni said, obviously confused. She ladled some punch into one of those clear plastic cocktail cups. "Try it, you'll love it."

"Oh, thanks." Tess held the cup, stared at the little bubbles fizzing at the surface. This wasn't a problem. It was ridiculous to act like this was a problem. But she couldn't make herself take a sip of that fucking punch. She put her cup down on the counter.

"Tess?" Joni asked. "Are you okay?"

"Yeah!" Tess cleared her throat. "Totally. I just—you know what? It was a really long train ride. I have to pee."

"Okay . . ." Joni said warily. "I assume you remember where it is?"

"Yeah, yeah of course." Tess smiled too broadly. "I'll see you in a few, okay?"

But Joni was already being pulled aside by some new group of friends walking through the door and screaming happy birthday. Tess marveled at how many people were here—when she and Joni lived together, it was mostly just the two of them. They went out with people from their cohort often enough, but they never came close to liking anyone else as much as they liked each other. But now Joni was well on her way to finishing her dissertation and graduating, surrounded by people who adored her. Maybe this was the way things were supposed to work out, Tess thought. Maybe it was for the best she'd left when she did.

"Tess? Is that you?"

Tess turned to see Oscar Matson, a quiet guy from her cohort whom she'd never gotten to know all that well. Oscar was Black and chubby with a warm, kind energy; he wore soft gray jeans, a white button-down shirt under a Fair Isle cardigan, and round thin-rimmed glasses that looked like he'd borrowed them from someone's dad in the '70s.

"Hey, Oscar." Tess peered at his getup. "Is that . . . a vampire outfit?"

"I'm Guillermo from *What We Do in the Shadows*," he said shyly. "I know he's not technically a vampire, but he's my favorite."

"He's *awesome*." Tess smiled brightly, feeling grateful to be in less complicated company.

"So how have you been?" he asked. "We've missed you at school. What have you been up to?"

"Oh, um, nothing that exciting. I moved to Brooklyn, I've been working for a hotel. The Georgia? In Williamsburg?"

"Oh yeah? I went there for drinks once, that's a really cool spot.

Makes sense they'd hire you." Oscar took a sip of his beer, and Tess caught a bit of a flush creeping up his neck. It was absolutely news to her that Oscar had ever noticed anything about her, let alone that he'd formed an opinion on her level of coolness. He looked up at her. "Have you been reading or writing at all?"

Tess laughed. "Only if you count getting into fights on reddit about *Blood Feud* conspiracies."

"Wow, so you're really into this vampire stuff, huh?"

"Oh, yeah. They're like my brain candy, you know? Total comfort food."

"Definitely," he agreed. "And what are the conspiracies? Are the vampires secretly gnomes or something?"

"Oh my god, this is gonna sound so stupid." She grinned. "Promise you won't laugh at me?"

"I guess that depends on what the conspiracy is and which side you're arguing."

"Okay, so, some people—I'm not saying me necessarily, but some people—think the vampires in *Blood Feud* really exist."

"Shut up, no they don't." Oscar's eyes went wide. "*You* think this? You think this and argue with strangers about it on the internet?!"

"And occasionally write essays about it that go viral and get picked up by *BuzzFeed*?" Tess flushed with embarrassment—and also a little bit of pride.

"No fucking way." Oscar guffawed. "Stop talking, I'm googling that immediately."

"Don't!" Tess protested playfully. But it gave her a thrill to imagine Oscar reading her work, nodding with pleasure the same way her professors used to when she made a particularly subtle argument.

"You're right, it would be rude to google at a party," Oscar agreed. "Give me a preview?"

"Oh, well, basically—myths of vampires have persisted for thousands of years, across all different cultures that had no possible way to communicate with one another. People in ancient India and the Scottish highlands and the Philippines all have their own distinct vampire folklore. Homer even talks about vampires in *The Odyssey*."

"No shit, did he really?"

"Yeah!" Tess pushed her hair back and beamed. "So I mean, isn't it possible the reason these stories are so popular across all different places and time periods is that there's something about them that's rooted in truth? Or at least, isn't it worth considering that they might be?"

"I hadn't thought about it like that." Oscar laughed, but Tess could tell he was being sincere.

"So if you're willing to accept the basic premise that vampires *could* be real, then there's, like, all this evidence. About the vampires in *Blood Feud* specifically."

"Evidence? As in clues?!"

"Enough for an entire Poirot novel." Tess couldn't help getting excited—she loved talking about this stuff. "So there are these two characters in the books, Callum and Octavia Yoo, and there were two people really named that in Victorian England, which is where the characters are from too."

"So you think the author based those characters on the real people?"

"Definitely, but here's where it gets weird." Tess dropped her voice for dramatic effect. "They were a really striking pair—they're British Korean twins and both gorgeous—and people have found photos of them from all different time periods. Victorian England, but then also Paris in the twenties, at an Andy Warhol Factory party in the sixties. They popped up on Facebook in the back of someone's vacation photos from Jeju Island in Korea in 2006, people went fucking nuts when they found that one. People have found photos of the 'real' versions of other characters too, but they're harder to track. Callum and Octavia are easier because they're so often together. But then—remember eleven years ago, when there was that fire at that nightclub in Prague, and all those people had bites on their necks, and the authorities thought it must have been some kind of wild animal?"

Oscar nodded. "Sort of."

"Okay, well, after that, there aren't *any* more photos of Callum and Octavia—or any of them, you know? So the theory is that the attack at the nightclub was really vampires, and they were all sent to the Isle as some sort of punishment. And maybe it's all a total reach and absolute nonsense, but it's, like, *fun,* you know? Just to imagine that any of it could be real."

Oscar gazed at Tess with a sort of wonder.

"What?" she asked, mildly unnerved.

"Nothing, sorry." He scratched absently at the back of his head. "I just forgot how much fun it is to listen to you talk."

Someone pushed behind him to get to the kitchen, moving him closer to Tess. He smelled nice, fresh, like soap and cedar.

"Hey," he said quietly, close enough that he could almost whisper and still be heard.

Tess felt suddenly tense. Was he going to touch her?

But he just nodded toward her empty hands. "You don't have a drink. Can I get you something?"

"Oh!" she sputtered. "Sure! Sure. Maybe a beer? If they have one? Like in a can? You don't have to open it, I can open it."

He gave her a perplexed smile that said something like *I'm not sure what your deal is, but I'm interested in finding out.*

"One beer in a can, coming right up."

He disappeared into the kitchen, and Tess exhaled and made her way toward the bathroom. This was going well! Not that she thought it wouldn't, necessarily, but obviously it could have been super weird to see Joni for the first time in three years. It could have felt like a nightmare to walk into her old apartment, to see her old classmates, to get sucked back into how bad things had gotten in those last weeks before she left the program.

And okay, so maybe Oscar had been trying to flirt, and that made her feel more than a little uneasy. Sometimes she wondered if waiting so long to try dating again would put an outsized burden on whomever she dated next—a burden so large there was no possible way for a stranger to carry it. Then again, Oscar wasn't a stranger. She could have a beer with him, and relax, and see what happened. She'd tell him when she had to leave for work, and maybe he'd offer to walk her to the subway, and they'd kiss softly, briefly, on a well-lit corner where nothing more could happen.

No—she shook off the image. That would be too much; she wasn't ready. But still, it was nice to think that someday she could be.

She reapplied her red lipstick in the bathroom mirror, then blotted it carefully so it wouldn't smudge across her face when she took a sip of beer. She smiled at her reflection, took a deep breath, and opened the door to go back to the party.

"Rosie? Oh my god, I didn't know you'd be here."

Tess stopped short. This wasn't happening. He couldn't be here. Why would he be here? Joni and Rick had written one article together, but they were never *friends*. What the hell was he doing here?

"I . . . I'm still friends with Joni," Tess choked out. He was standing right here, with his easy rich-guy clothes, khaki shorts and a soft linen button-down, not even bothering to pretend to dress on-theme, with his full lips and crooked nose and floppy curls. But he was also in his apartment on Valentine's Day, snow falling over the Hudson. Rocks glasses made of cut crystal, the whiskey his dad brought back from Japan. Their clothes piled on the floor. Her foggy memories.

"Oh yeah? That's so great." He smiled. "Joni's the coolest, who else could get our whole department to dress up as vampires?"

"Right, totally." Tess mumbled her agreement, and she felt crazy, like she was choking on poison fog, because he was acting like this was a normal conversation and she could still feel his hands covering her mouth.

"So how have you been, Rosie? Is everything good? It's really nice to see you."

He called her Rosie because of her last name, Rosenbloom. She mentioned once in class that she loved blue roses because of *The Glass Menagerie,* how the gentleman caller always called Laura "blue roses" because he'd misheard the word "pleurosis." Rick said it was funny, because a person could mishear Tess's last name as "rose in bloom." He only ever called her Rosie after that. She used to love it. She used to live for hours, days, on the memory of the last time he said it. The hope for the next time he'd say it.

"I have to go to work." The words fell out of her mouth in a torrent, the syllables eliding like she was drunk and slurring, her brain lacking the control to make the sounds into cogent speech. All her energy in that moment was focused on her feet, because she had to leave, she couldn't wait another second, she had to fucking *go*.

She walked away from Rick and shoved through the mess of party-goers, not looking back to see who was pissed at being jostled or having their drink spilled. They probably thought she was an ass-hole, same as Joni did, and it didn't matter, and she didn't care, because all of it was fine as long as she could not be here anymore. She saw Oscar craning his neck to look for her, two beers in hand, but she turned away before he could see her face. She barely knew him, she was already a disappointment.

She pushed through the front door into the hall and stumbled into the street. The air was thick and hot, the sun had only just gone down. Tess paused to lean against the stone banister that led up to the rest of the building, breathing hard. She was out of there—and the idea that she could come back to this world, to Columbia, to a campus and meetings and parties that included Rick, was laughably out of the question.

But as she took deep breaths and her heartbeat steadied, she decided she wasn't going to wallow in her panic either, not again. This wasn't three years ago. She could get on the train and cross the river and not look back. Better yet—she'd go even farther: quit her job, leave New York. She had a marketable skill now; she could go work at some other hotel in some other country, anywhere in the world.

Five years was long enough to be trapped in the same city as a monster like Rick. It was time for Tess to make her escape.

"Tess?"

Tess looked back—Joni was there, shadowed in the doorway, hurt and confusion clearly legible across her expressive face. "You're leaving?"

"I—yeah, I'm sorry, I'm working tonight, so . . ." Tess could feel sweat beading at her hairline. "I'm sorry to leave so early."

"Without saying goodbye?" Joni stepped out of the doorway and into the light. "Tess, it's my *birthday*."

"I know!" Tess sputtered lamely. "It's just—work."

"I don't understand." Joni's voice broke.

Tess felt her lungs contracting in pain—she couldn't get a clean breath. Everything felt ragged.

"I'm sorry," she whispered. "I have to go."

Chapter 2

Excerpt from *Blood Feud*
(book three, chapter nine)
BY AUGUST LIRIO

Callum grinned at Octavia, blood dripping from his fangs. He was soaked from the fight, his shirt gleaming crimson, a look of savage wildness in his eyes.

"Oh my god," Octavia sputtered. "You *liked* that, didn't you?"

"'Course I did." Callum slicked back his hair with bravado. "Spot of violence, adrenaline going, what's not to like?"

"Aren't you sick of fighting Felix after all this time?" Octavia pleaded. "Konstantin is long dead, what does it matter anymore which of you was his favorite? We're all trapped on this stupid island—"

"And I'm making the most of it!" Callum shot back. "Look, you've spent years trying to find a way out of here, and where has it gotten you? Exact same place as me, innit? Except instead of wasting my time wishing I were somewhere else, I'm actually enjoying myself. And don't tell me you aren't capable of joy here. I saw the look on your face when you shoved your stiletto through that goon's eye socket. You were happy, Vee. It was like old times."

"Happy? Happy?!" Octavia's laughter bordered on manic.

"*Happy* is lobster thermidor from room service at The Carlyle, with a cheese soufflé on the side and the bellhop's neck for dessert. Happy is the opening gala for a new exhibit at the Leeum Museum, or sitting front row at McQueen in Paris, my pick of the gowns, bodies draped in sequins."

"You can have lobster here! Or art or sequins or soufflés or whatever the bloody hell else you like," Callum argued.

"It's not the same!" Octavia snapped. "All our glamours here, they're just memories made manifest, shadows of the lives we used to have. I miss travel and parties, meeting new people, tasting new blood. I miss *living,* Callum. We've been here for years already, and I don't know how much longer . . ."

"How much longer what?" Callum stepped toward her. "What are you saying?"

Octavia closed her eyes. She felt like she was suffocating on this island, her brain slowly giving way to madness. She thought about how it would feel to leave this place. To step onto the crystal bridge that left the Isle, to feel the warmth of sunlight erupting across her skin.

Maybe she'd burst into flames like every other soul who'd been desperate or stupid enough to walk into the sun, charred into a pile of ash.

Then again, Octavia had always been different. She suffused everything she touched with her own particular brand of glamour. Maybe when she stepped onto the bridge, it would be like a glittering dance sequence in an Esther Williams movie, splashes of water and sparkles of light, a glorious sight to behold as she crossed over to Bar Between, the way station between worlds that could lead her back to New York.

But the beauty of her fantasy faded as she opened her eyes and focused back in on Callum, his brow lined with concern. She'd been with him since before they were born, and for more than a hundred years since their deaths. She couldn't leave him now.

As much as she hated this island, she loved her brother more.

She needed him as much as he needed her—and she knew that to be separated from him would be worse than splitting her own body in half.

"Vee?" he said softly, using the pet name he'd had for her since they were children in London, bratty orphans with naughty smirks and coal-smeared faces. "You won't leave me, will you?"

"Never." Octavia took his hands in hers. "I swear it."

It took Tess nearly an hour to get back to Williamsburg after she left Joni's party. She spent the train ride with her eyes glued to her copy of *Blood Feud,* getting lost in a scene she'd read a million times before, going through the words over and over until she settled into the world of the Isle, traveling along the characters' emotions like grooved tracks. Ever since leaving Columbia, Tess found her life was easier if she didn't think too much about her own feelings. Her emotions were too overwhelming, too painful and unwieldy. She tried to keep the volume turned down on her own life, to keep her daily existence muted and manageable.

But in *Blood Feud,* everything could be big without being scary. The ruthless violence, passionate sex, devastating betrayals—Tess could feel all of it, because none of it was happening to her. The deeper she let her mind sink into the world of Callum and Octavia, Felix and Isobel, the farther away she felt from Joni's apartment. And from Rick.

The loud rumbles and metallic screeches of the subway, the hum of people shuffling on and off the train, all of it felt like a rhythm that lulled Tess back into a calmer state of mind. The vampires in *Blood Feud* were trapped on an island, but Tess didn't have to be. Once she found a new job, she'd be behind the desk of a cozy inn in the Cotswolds, thrilling guests with little tidbits about Agatha Christie mysteries set in the area; or perhaps she'd go to Paris, or Bali, or Big Sur. She could feel the tension in her shoulders unspool as she walked out of the subway and imagined the possibilities, traveling the world by night like Callum and Octavia, each new chapter bringing another glamorous adventure.

By the time Tess walked into The Georgia, she almost felt like herself again—until she saw Rick sitting at the lobby bar.

No, not Rick. Just some guy with blond hair—they didn't even look alike.

"Shit," Tess muttered, willing herself to keep it together.

Mika eyed her from behind the front desk. Mouthed, *You okay?*

Tess nodded apologetically, but before she could go talk to Mika, Taylor, the hotel's afternoon manager, rushed over, looking like she'd just been through a very fancy war.

"Where have you been?" she rasped. "The fucking bee wedding finally got started three hours late—they're gonna be here until three A.M. instead of midnight."

"What?!" Tess yelped. "But the staff—all that overtime—"

"I know." Taylor gave Tess a dark look. "But it was our fucking bees that caused the delay in the first place, so I couldn't exactly say no, could I? They were already screaming about a lawsuit, but hopefully if we just get them absolutely plastered, they'll forget about it."

Taylor was the most competent and organized person Tess had ever met—if she was this frazzled, the wedding must really have been a disaster.

"You go home," Tess told her. "I've got this."

"I can't! What if something goes wrong and they all start fighting again? They yelled so much," Taylor whispered, looking near the point of tears.

"I'll go down to the reception myself and make sure everything runs smoothly. Look!" Tess gave her silky dress a little swish. "I'm even dressed for a party."

Tess thought Taylor might argue further, but instead she collapsed into a grateful hug. Tess promised it would all be fine and headed down to the wedding. She was a little bummed she wouldn't have time to start looking for new jobs, but on the other hand, it was probably for the best to have a distraction tonight.

The hotel's primary wedding venue was an indoor-outdoor space on the garden level. Smaller events could be held on the pool deck, but for a party of two hundred, it had to be the big, airy ballroom with whitewashed brick, rafters strung with lush vines and vintage fairy lights, and a wall of glass doors that opened out onto a cobblestone patio. By the time Tess walked in, the food and cake had all been cleared; drinking and dancing were the only items left on the agenda, and the guests were excelling at both.

Everything seemed to be going fine, with the possible exception of the best man, whose head was now mightily swollen from his many bee stings, and whose colossally drunken dance moves seemed likely to result in injury either for himself or someone else.

"Sorry you have to deal with that until three A.M.," Tess said to Patrick, the hotel's dapper bartender.

"Oh pish, it's no problem—the rave I'm going to later doesn't start until four. You want to join?"

"My shift isn't over till seven." Tess laughed.

"Perfect! The party will just be getting good." Patrick sighed wistfully. "Aren't you grateful we're not as boring as the so-and-sos waking up at dawn, getting ready for another day? We're unbound by time!"

Tess told him she'd think about it, then continued making her rounds. As she scanned the room to make sure everyone seemed happy, her eyes fell on one guest who seemed woefully out of place. She was staggeringly beautiful, leaning against a wall, sipping a glass of champagne: at least six feet tall in heels, possibly of Eurasian descent, with wide eyes, apple cheeks, and glossy black hair that framed her face in chic layers of fringe, stopping bluntly just above her shoulders. She wore a strapless black cocktail dress that hugged her body with elegant drapes, accentuated by an oversized fabric flower at her hip made of shimmering white velvet, and barely-there strappy silver sandals that would have caused Tess to break an ankle in approximately seventeen seconds. Her makeup was minimal, just a cat eye and flushed cheek.

In New York, it wasn't uncommon to see stunning women at any given restaurant or party; hell, in Soho, runway models roamed the streets in vaguely unsettling packs, looking like sculptures constructed with wire hangers. But there was something different about this woman. Even in the relative darkness of the room, her skin was so pale it almost glowed.

Tess flushed with embarrassment when the woman looked over and caught her staring. Tess looked away quickly, but to her surprise, when she glanced back again, the woman was still gazing right at her. The woman gave a little wave, and in an exquisitely cringey moment, Tess actually glanced over her shoulder to see if she might be waving at someone else. The woman snickered and walked over to Tess, standing beside her at a little high-top bar table made of wrought iron and glass.

"I know the wedding started late, but arriving at eleven-thirty? Exceptionally New York of you." She spoke in a crisp British accent, her voice rich and clear and dripping with money.

"I'm not a guest," Tess clarified. "I work here at the hotel."

"Do you?" the woman eyed her with interest.

"I'm the manager," Tess stammered, unsure why she felt the need to explain herself. "Just here to make sure everything's going smoothly."

"Ah, a woman in charge." Her lips curled deliciously, like she was savoring a secret. "In that case, I don't suppose you could give yourself permission to join me for a dance? Since you are the boss and all?"

Tess opened her mouth and shut it, neither wanting to look like a vacant goldfish nor having the faintest idea what to say—she wasn't exactly accustomed to being hit on at all, let alone by arguably the most beautiful woman she'd ever seen.

"I, um, sorry, I'm not even sure if you're asking me to dance, in like, a romantic way, but I'm actually straight?" she sputtered, wondering if any person had ever embarrassed themselves more than she was in this moment.

"How completely dull." The woman's dark eyes glittered with amusement. "No matter. Let's dance anyway so you can reassess."

Without waiting for a response, she circled her fingers around Tess's wrists and pulled her onto the dance floor. Her hands were shockingly cold, and Tess had to shut her mouth not to gasp in surprise. Sade's "Smooth Operator" flowed through the room, and between the music, the liquor, and the throng of swaying bodies, the mood on the dance floor oozed sex.

The woman moved her body in time with the music, close to Tess but not touching her. Tess couldn't remember the last time she'd been dancing—maybe Joni's last birthday before she'd moved out, the one at a kitschy disco bar in the West Village? Back before Joni hated her, back when she used to light up at the sight of Tess instead of glaring at her with anger and hurt.

"What's wrong?" the woman asked, peering at Tess.

"Oh, sorry, nothing. Um, I love your dress."

"This? Miss Sohee, her work is divine. I've been gone so long, I have so much fashion to catch up on."

"Gone?" Tess furrowed her brow. "Gone where?"

"The place you'll be going. The place you've dreamed of," she murmured. She moved closer to Tess, resting her arms on Tess's shoulders. Tess felt confused, and claustrophobic—what was happening here?

"What does that mean?"

She leaned close enough to Tess to whisper in her ear. "The Isle."

"What?" Tess tried to jerk back, but the woman pulled her closer. "What are you talking about? Who are you?"

"Come on, Tess." She grinned. "You know who I am."

"Wait—how do you know my name?" Tess was breathing harder now, but all around her, people just kept dancing, too caught up in their own moments to notice hers.

"Because I came here to find you." The woman looked more serious now, her gaze intensely focused on Tess. "Because I need your help, Tess Rosenbloom. And because you've been dying to meet me."

"I don't even know who you are," Tess protested, but her voice was weak as the pieces started to click together.

"Tess, look at me," the woman ordered.

Tess did. The woman was a solid six inches taller, so Tess was more or less eye-level with her lips. Tess watched as the woman smiled widely, then went frozen with wonder and terror as the woman's canines elongated into dagger-sharp fangs.

"What the fucking fuck," Tess blurted, her voice barely above a whisper. Had she well and truly lost her mind, and this was just an exceptionally vivid hallucination? Was she a walking twist in an M. Night Shyamalan movie?

"See?" The woman leaned in. "You know who I am—and what. You've seen my photograph. You know what I can do. And you know my name."

Tess looked at her, knowing the answer, but too shocked and confused to speak the words.

"Go on," the woman prodded. "Say it."

"You're not . . ." Tess whispered. "I know you're not . . ."

"Who, Tess?" She ran an ice-cold finger along Tess's jaw.

Tess closed her eyes.

"You can't be Octavia Yoo."

Chapter 3

Hi Troi! Longtime reader, first time submitter—and needless to say, ANON PLEASE! Okay, so here's the tea: I work the front desk at The Carlyle, and last night, this woman comes in, absolutely stunning, wearing a killer green cocktail dress, but she doesn't have a purse, a wallet, no luggage, nothing. She comes to the desk with the poshest British accent you've ever heard and tells me she has a room booked under the name Octavia Yoo. All right, people book under fake names all the time, so I don't think anything of it, I just laugh and ask her if she needs rollaway beds for Hermione Granger and Bella Swann, but she doesn't smile back, like, at all. So of course I don't have anything booked for her, but she insists I do, and then she starts glaring into my eyes in this funny way, and I'm like bitch are you trying to glamour me? Like does she seriously think she's a vampire right now? So I tell her hey, I love *Blood Feud,* Octavia is obviously my favorite character—I'm a homosexual who lives in Chelsea, like duh I'm obsessed with her—but I can't give her a room unless she gives me a credit card. And then she looks, like, scared? And asks me what *Blood Feud* is? So at this point I'm like, lady, snaps for your cosplay, but I'm at work, okay? Time to take your performance art elsewhere. Then a security guard came over and she physically *ran* out of the hotel without another word. So anyway Troi, just thought your readers should know: Either the best Octavia Yoo impersonator in history is roaming around New York, or vampires are real.

⁂

"Right in one guess." The woman smiled wider, her fangs gleaming in the candlelight. "Not bad for a human."

"No." Tess shook her head. "No, this is—I don't know, a trick. You're not—you can't possibly be—"

"A vampire?"

"Vampires don't exist!" Tess insisted.

"That's not what you said on *BuzzFeed*."

"God, that fucking essay." Tess exhaled. "So you read it, and you came here . . . why? For a prank? To get money or something? The Nigerian prince scam, except you're a fake vampire instead?"

"You work in a hotel and you're wearing that dress." The woman's expression was somewhere between disdain and pity. "And you've come to the conclusion that I'm after your money?"

"Hey, you're hot," a drunken voice interrupted. They turned to see the best man, his body swaying and his speech slurred.

"Thank you for that unprompted assessment, but we're in the middle of a conversation," Octavia snapped.

"No, we're not." Tess took the opportunity to back away. "I need to—excuse me."

She turned and hurried toward the ballroom exit. Whoever that woman was, whatever racket she was running, Tess wanted no part of it—this night had already been enough of a disaster without adding a fanged con artist into the mix. Tess let out a sigh of relief when she pushed into the empty service stairway. Everything at the wedding was fine; there was no reason she shouldn't head back up to her office and start looking for a new job—preferably one that put at least one ocean between Tess and everyone she'd seen tonight.

She heard the door to the stairwell open behind her, and her body tensed up. Was the woman following her? Were they going to have some kind of unpleasant confrontation?

"Why did you leave? We were talking."

Tess froze. That wasn't the woman—it was the best man.

"Um, I'm working!" she called down to him. "Have a nice night!"

She kept walking up the stairs, hoping the excuse would deter him, but she heard heavy footfalls, and in a few seconds he was beside her.

"Working?" He gave her a lopsided grin. "It's midnight."

He was big—like, linebacker big, with close-cropped hair and watery eyes—and something about his expression made Tess's blood run cold. She wanted to get out of this stairwell, but he was blocking her path.

"I'm the manager of the hotel," she explained, smiling pleasantly. "And this area is really only for employees. So if you'll just head back down to the ballroom—"

"That doesn't sound fun." He slumped toward her, bracing himself against the wall so he loomed over her.

"Are you staying with us at the hotel?" Tess's heart was thumping. "Perhaps I can send you up some complimentary room service, or call you a cab . . ."

"What's wrong with right here?" He gave her that grin again, and Tess knew she should get the fuck out of this stairwell, but she was afraid that any movement might make him pounce. She frantically ran through options in her mind: If she screamed, would he startle? If she pushed him, would he fall?

But before she could do anything, the stairwell door opened again.

"Oh, *there* you are, I've been looking everywhere, naughty Tess." The woman from earlier slipped in beside them, weaving her arm around Tess's waist. Tess gave her a panicked look, but the woman seemed entirely unbothered.

"You . . ." The best man looked from the woman to Tess, his face somewhere between titillation and complete bewilderment. "You two are . . . you two?"

"Yes, well spotted, we usually do keep it to the two of us." She kissed Tess's cheek, and Tess's face warmed. "Unless . . . darling? What do you think? Should we invite him to join us?"

"I . . ." Tess was the bewildered one now. "I don't know?"

"Come on then, let's give it a try." She flashed them both a dazzling smile, then turned to the best man. "What do you think, mate? You up for a little play? I hope you like it rough."

The best man chortled, like he couldn't believe his good luck. The woman repositioned herself so his back was against the wall, and then leaned in to kiss him . . . moving slowly . . .

Until the very last second, when she tilted her head to the side and sank her fangs into his neck instead.

"Oh my god!" Tess screeched.

The best man's eyes shot open and he tried to shove her off, but her grip was strong—he was already sluggish from all the booze, and within a few seconds, she'd drunk so much blood that his neck lolled to the side and he slumped to the floor, completely unconscious.

"Damn," the woman muttered as she wiped her mouth. "I think he got blood on my dress."

Tess was shaking—she felt like her brain had short-circuited, completely unable to absorb what she'd just seen.

"You—" Tess sputtered. "You—you—"

"Yes, like I said." The woman sighed and tidied her hair. "I'm Octavia Yoo, and I'm a vampire. Believe me now? You're welcome, by the way."

"Welcome?"

"For dealing with that." Octavia nodded at the man heaped on the floor. "I should probably kill him. Do a service for womankind."

"Don't!" Tess yelped. "I mean—the police, the hotel, I work here—"

"Take it easy, I was just having a laugh! Humans get so serious about death." Octavia peered at Tess with concern. "Goodness, you've gone pale. Do you need a water or something?"

For some reason, this struck Tess as unbelievably funny.

"Oh sure! Sure, Octavia Yoo, pretend vampire from my favorite books, will you run down to the bar and grab me a Dasani?"

"What's that?" Octavia wrinkled her nose.

"It's a—never mind—what the fuck is going on right now?"

"In the first place, I'm not pretend, as you've previously argued and can plainly see. In the second place—I'm sorry, but must we have this conversation in a stairwell standing over an unconscious man? It's so . . . déclassé."

"What conversation are we having, exactly?" Tess felt light-headed.

"The one where I explain that eight nights ago, I crossed over from the Isle to New York City with no warning or explanation, that I find myself utterly alone and completely without my powers, and that I've come here to ask for your help."

"How . . ." Tess shook her head. "I'm sorry, but you're an ancient vampire, and I'm the night manager of a hotel in Brooklyn. How can I possibly help you?"

"I need you to go to the Isle to deliver a message to my brother."

Tess looked at Octavia for a long moment, then leaned against the banister and sighed.

"I think I need a drink."

• • •

Ten minutes later, Tess had procured a bottle of red from Patrick the bartender, and she and Octavia were drinking it on a small outdoor patio adjoining the ballroom.

"I don't see why we couldn't go to the pool deck," Octavia groused. "The view up there is lovely."

"I literally just watched you drink a man's blood, and you think I'm going anywhere alone with you?" Tess shot back.

"I'm not going to hurt *you,* obviously," Octavia huffed. "As you may recall, I just protected you."

"And as *you* may recall, I've read, like, many hundreds of pages about how you and your brother are murderous villains!" Tess countered. The surreality of this conversation was way too much to process.

"Those infernal books," Octavia muttered.

"So . . ." Tess couldn't help feeling curious. "So you've read them?"

"Indeed." Octavia rolled her eyes and sipped her wine. "Finding out about them was quite the shock, really puts a cramp on being incognito when the entire bloody world knows your name. Not to mention the audacity of this August Lirio person, making millions airing my private conversations, then having the gall to call *me* evil."

"That's actually a really good point," Tess agreed—though she noticed Octavia hadn't refuted the "murderous" part of Tess's accusation.

"Besides, it wouldn't do me any good to harm you. I need your help, remember?"

"To go to the Isle." Tess echoed Octavia's words, still not fully believing them. "Does it really exist?"

"It does." Octavia nodded. "You were right, Tess. About all of it."

A thrill went up Tess's spine. Even though this was easily the strangest night of her life, it was still deeply satisfying to finally know that all those hours she'd spent reading and writing and arguing about *Blood Feud* conspiracies hadn't been for nothing.

"So how did you get back to New York?" Tess asked.

"I wish I knew." Octavia exhaled dramatically. "One moment, I was visiting an angel statue in the graveyard in the forest at the center of the Isle. I saw a flash of light, felt a buzzing sensation, and everything went black. Next moment, I was in Central Park, by the angel statue in the Bethesda Fountain, with no idea how I'd gotten there."

"And something happened to your powers?"

"Gone. Poof! Disappeared," Octavia said sadly. "No more strength, very little speed, and no ability to glamour. And everyone I've ever met is either dead or trapped on that island, so there's no one I can turn to for help. I've been skulking about like a common criminal, stealing clothes and sneaking into hotel rooms."

"Oh my god." Tess gasped, putting it together. "That was you in Mrs. Harriman's penthouse."

"Gave the old bat a proper scare." Octavia couldn't help chuckling. "It would be so helpful if you could book me into an empty room, just temporarily, of course, until Callum can figure out a way home. I think the reason I've lost my powers is because we're so far apart—our powers are tied together because of the twin sire bond, you know?"

Tess nodded—she'd read about the twin sire bond dozens of times in *Blood Feud,* the bond that supposedly gave Callum and Octavia stronger powers than other vampires.

"Callum and I have never been away from each other for more than a few weeks, let alone on entirely different planes of existence," Octavia went on. "That's why I need you to go to the Isle to tell him what happened to me. Obviously I'd go myself if I could, but the only way I know to get back to the Isle is through Bar Between. And if I go there . . ."

"Whoever sent you to the Isle will know you escaped." Tess knew from *Blood Feud* that Bar Between was something of a magical way station between worlds, and it was the only way on or off the Isle.

"Exactly." Octavia took a sip of wine, gripping her glass tightly. "I've been so frightened that someone will recognize me, that they'll send me back."

"Was it very bad?" Tess asked. "On the Isle?"

"I'd rather die than be trapped there again," Octavia said quietly. "Being stuck there for so long, I felt like the part of me that was *me* was—slipping away, somehow. Like I was watching myself float off to sea."

Tess thought back to her last weeks at Columbia, the nights when she would take half a dozen sleeping pills to try to knock herself out, how fuzzy and barren she felt. She would have done anything to escape that feeling—and she did. She gave up everything that mattered.

"Listen," Tess said softly. "I'd love to help you, it's just—wouldn't that be pretty dangerous? To visit an island full of very thirsty vampires?"

"Oh god no, you wouldn't actually be *visiting* the Isle," Octavia clarified. "That'd be suicidal. I'll just give you my scent vial so that Callum will smell me when you get to the crystal bridge that links the Isle to Bar Between. It's the only way on or off the Isle, and it's covered in sunlight—no vampire can touch you there. You'll stay in the light, give him the message, and be on your way, no worse for wear. Sound all right?"

"Oh." Tess felt relieved, but also strangely disappointed. "So you're saying—I wouldn't get to explore the Isle, see the places in *Blood Feud*? Like Nantale's compound or the moonflower meadow or the milky jade pools or whatever."

"You really do love those books, don't you?" Octavia's lips were thin.

"Yeah, guilty." Tess dipped her head and tucked her hair behind her ears. "And I guess, speaking of the books . . . Callum."

"What about him?"

"I don't need to be, you know. Afraid of him?"

Tess's heart beat faster—she thought of the disgusting best man in the stairwell, of Rick in the bathroom doorway, smiling affably, touching her arm. And those weren't even deadly vampires. They were just fucking guys.

"Look at me," Octavia instructed, and Tess obliged. "My brother is a good man. That's the worst part of being here—it's not about losing my powers, it's about being apart from him. For a hundred and thirty years, he's been my best friend, closer to me than my own skin, and now I can't feel him at all. Have you ever felt anything like that? Like the closest person in the world to you was just . . . gone?"

Tess closed her eyes, wishing she could picture anything but Joni's disappointed face. She nodded slowly.

"Then you know how it feels," Octavia said. "And you know me. That's why I picked you. Of all those people on your message boards, your—what do you call them? Friends?"

"Mutuals." Tess smiled at the absurdity of teaching internet parlance to a vampire.

"That's a stupid term, I'm not repeating it." Octavia sniffed. "Anyway, out of all of them, you seemed to care less about me as a character, and more about me as a person. And I thought, okay. If I can find her, maybe she can help. If I can find her, maybe I won't be so totally alone."

Tess looked out at the wedding, which finally seemed to be winding down. Groups of friends were sitting at tables, drinking and laughing; the bride and groom twirled slowly in the middle of the mostly empty dance floor. Tess thought about her friends at the hotel, all of whom were fun company, but none of whom really knew her. She thought of her parents, how her relationship with them was really nothing more than an occasional phone call. And she thought of Joni, of everything they used to have. How all of it was gone now. Maybe forever.

Ever since leaving Columbia, Tess had felt like a stranger in her own life, working at someone else's job, having someone else's conversations. She had no idea how many times she'd read *Blood Feud* in the past three years—a dozen? A hundred? But it meant something real to her that Octavia Yoo, a woman who had brought her so much comfort, was now asking Tess to be part of her story. More than that, Tess had the distinct sense that saying yes to Octavia could change her own story.

"It's funny," Tess said, though it wasn't at all. "For the past three years, I've been pretty much alone myself."

"Well then." Octavia lifted her glass. "It's a good thing we found each other."

Chapter 4

——Forwarded Message——
From: Fern Castillo <f.castillo917@gmail.com>
BCC: [COVEN DISTRIBUTION LIST]
Sent: October 1, 7:53 AM
Subject: Project Isle is a success!

Hi all,

I write today with excellent news: After months of arduous preparation, Project Isle went into effect at midnight last night. Below, please find a summary of previous actions and next steps:

- Three months ago, at our annual Summer Solstice Summit, our leaders proposed a motion to imprison earth's vampires in a shadow dimension to prevent the violence and mayhem that's been on the rise. The motion carried by a vote of 64–13, and work commenced to create such a dimension. That work was accelerated following last month's vampire attack in Prague.

- A group of highly advanced witches created the Isle, an island that shares roughly the same geography as Manhattan, though none of its infrastructure. The Isle exists in its own discrete dimension, and while there, vampires will have access to material magics (i.e., the ability to create their own homes and other objects, including food and drink). They will not retain access to these magics in any other dimension.

- The only way on or off the Isle is the crystal bridge which connects it to Bar Between. That bridge will remain covered in sunlight 24 hours a day, ensuring no vampire can cross it.

- Last night at midnight eastern time, representatives from thirty covens cast a successful global transport spell to send every living vampire to the Isle. No vampires will be able to leave the Isle until such time as a supplementary motion is passed by this body to permit their return.

- Per the terms of our previous motion, any human, witch, or magical creature will have permission to visit the Isle via Bar Between, assuming their own bodily risk. However, since the existence of the Isle is completely secret except to the witches on this distribution list, we don't anticipate that will be an issue.

Thank you for all your efforts to make this project an unqualified triumph. As ever, should you have any questions or concerns, please don't hesitate to contact me via email or telepathy (preferred).

Sincerely,
Fern Castillo
Coven Secretary/Treasurer

REVIEW: BAR BETWEEN—FOUR STARS
posted by user JustJeanne114 on yelp.com

Okay, so I've heard about this place forever, my cousin Nichole swears it's like the coolest place she's ever been, but you can never find it online? She says the location is always moving, but she's kind of a liar anyway, so I just chalked it up to an urban legend. But last week, I was with a couple of friends, and this cat came out of this bodega in Dumbo at 4am and started walking with all this purpose, and we were high as shit, so we were like let's follow that cat! And I swear to fucking god, the cat took us to this vacant lot in Vinegar Hill, except there was this weird like, little stone hut in the back? None of us had ever seen it before, but it's just some lot, so why would we have noticed? Anyway, the cat is all meowing and staring at us outside the door, so we go in, and I don't know if we were hallucinating or what, but it was the craziest night of my life??? The walls, like, touch you back? And the people had really weird necks and shit? It was like being in a maze of your own dreams, I don't even know how to describe it. We stayed a really long time, when we came out into the vacant lot, it was already the middle of the next day. We tried to come back the next night, but we couldn't find the hut, no matter how many corners we tried. Only reason I'm not giving it five stars is because I'm still not totally sure it was real. But I really respect that cat for taking us there.

"Couldn't you put me in the penthouse?" Octavia grumbled. "That rude witch checked out, didn't she?"

"No, she stayed, despite you scaring the shit out of her." Tess grinned. She'd checked Octavia in to the hotel's rarely used cabana suite, which was set right next to the pool and had two glass walls allowing for fabulous views of Brooklyn to the east and the Manhattan skyline to the west, but which provided almost no privacy (unless you kept the blackout curtains shut all day, thus depriving yourself of the views you were paying for). Since Octavia couldn't allow any sunlight into the room anyway, it was the perfect place to stash a vampire.

A vampire.

Tess glanced over at Octavia, who had changed into low-slung black trousers and a tight black crop top that showed off her sharp shoulders and unnaturally pale complexion. Even after watching her feed, Tess still kept expecting to wake up—at the hotel, in her bed, maybe in a hospital—to discover that all of this was nothing more than an exceptionally vivid dream. For the moment, Tess had told her assistant manager that she wasn't feeling well and needed to leave her shift early. And now she and Octavia were walking toward Vinegar Hill, where Octavia knew of an entrance to Bar Between.

"Let's run through the plan again," Octavia commanded. Between her stern bearing and staggering beauty, Tess thought this woman wouldn't even need to glamour someone to get them to do exactly what she wanted.

"I walk into Bar Between, I tell them I need to visit the Isle to deliver a message," Tess started.

"No," Octavia interrupted. "First you walk down the main hall, ignore all side rooms no matter how interesting they seem, and go directly to the bartender. *Then* say you need to go to the Isle to deliver a message. They'll make you a doorway and send you straight there."

"And after that . . ." Tess trailed off.

Octavia was wearing a few layered necklaces, and she tugged at one of the chains—it was delicate and silver and looked at least a century old. The chain was long, and dipped beneath the neckline of her crop top; when she extracted it, Tess saw that it held a tiny, intricately carved vial.

"Your scent vial?" Tess asked, and Octavia nodded. Tess loved when characters in old novels wore little vials of perfume, partly because it was romantic, and partly because it made her laugh to think of the lengths people went to to smell nice in the times before deodorant.

"Callum gave this to me when we were human, for our final birthday as mortals. I was wearing it the night we were reborn, and I haven't taken it off since." She lifted the necklace over her head and handed it to Tess, who stared with wonder. "When you get to the end of the crystal bridge, just open this, and he'll smell me and come straight to you. Tell him everything I've told you—about how I got to New York, how I lost my powers, how he needs to find a way back to me. Except, maybe don't mention the *Blood Feud* novels."

"Why not?" Tess frowned.

"I mean, it's kind of unbelievable."

Tess choked back a laugh—it was a bit rich that a literal vampire was telling her the existence of some novels would be difficult to believe.

Tess pulled Octavia's necklace over her head, and she felt the scent vial's cool weight thump comfortingly against her breastbone with each step. They passed some drunks and other late-night sorts as they walked south through Williamsburg, but once they reached the misty cobblestone streets of Vinegar Hill, the city was silent except for the clack of Octavia's heels. Tess loved this neighborhood; especially at night, walking through it felt like traveling back to the city's earliest days.

"How do you know where the entrance to the bar is?" Tess asked Octavia.

"I came here once with Callum, decades ago." Octavia waved her hand as if to dismiss the stretch of time between that moment and this one. "The key to finding the bar is that a silver birch tree with yellow leaves always grows in front—two trees with a connected trunk. Like this one."

"Oh!" Tess looked up with surprise—there was a birch tree, just as Octavia had described. But there wasn't a bar behind it, just an empty space between buildings, an overgrown vacant lot.

"Where is it?" Tess peered at the lot, and then at Octavia.

"It's here," Octavia replied, her voice steady. "Stand still. Don't you feel it?"

Tess stood very still, wondering how one might "feel" an invisible bar. She tried to open her senses, but after a few seconds she had to admit she didn't feel anything.

"Humans." Octavia sighed and shook her head. "You have the scent vial, correct?"

Tess nodded. While she wasn't totally sure how she was meant to execute any of Octavia's plan in a building that didn't exist, she was still starting to feel pretty anxious.

"Tess," Octavia asked carefully, "are you sure you want to do this?"

Tess started feeling dizzy as she accounted for all the possibilities—that a vampire would kill her, that she'd somehow fall into an interdimensional wormhole and never return, that she was talking with some random stranger in front of a vacant lot and none of this was real.

But she *wanted* it to be real. She felt the desire so keenly—for another world, a magical doorway, a fantastic reality. Even if she was only there for a few minutes, she had to see it for herself.

She turned to Octavia and nodded. "I'm sure."

"All right, then." Octavia dropped Tess's hand and folded her arms. "Time for you to take a walk around the block."

"Excuse me?" Tess peered at Octavia.

"Just a quick walk around the block, get your head clear, that sort of thing." Octavia gave her a little nudge. "Go on."

"I—okay," Tess agreed. "Which way?"

"Whichever way you like." Octavia smiled placidly. "See you soon."

Tess didn't look back as she walked north on Hudson. She turned east on Plymouth, where the wind rustled through the leaves of the many trees. Had it really been only a few hours since Joni's party, seeing Rick? It already seemed like another lifetime, like she could feel the strings of a new chapter gently pulling her away from the old one. She turned south on Little, and every step felt lighter than the last. A quick turn brought her back to Hudson, where she peered to make out the silhouette of Octavia waiting—except she wasn't there. Had she already left?

Tess walked quickly toward the spot where they'd just been, gathering speed. Was this really the end of the story? Just a strange interaction with a strange woman, and after all this, Tess was simply going to get in a cab and head back to work? Tess was nearly jogging by the time she got back to the vacant lot, except—

Except the lot wasn't vacant anymore.

Behind the silver birch tree, there was a small, igloolike building made of stone. And in the center of that building, there was a door.

"Holy shit," Tess whispered. She closed her eyes, wondering if this small gesture might make the building evaporate just as suddenly as it had appeared. But when she looked again, the dome was still there, and she could faintly make out a warm orange glow coming from behind the door.

She approached the building carefully, looking hastily around—someone was always awake in New York. Was someone looking at her right now? Could a restless woman in Vinegar Hill be sitting at her window, smoking a cigarette, watching Tess Rosenbloom walk through a doorway into another world?

As Tess got closer, she saw that the stones of the building were glossy and black, splattered through with splintery white patterns—obsidian, maybe. The door was ebony wood, carved with intricate patterns that looked to Tess like a series of ancient runes, but she couldn't be sure. The handle was wrought iron, a graceful arch finished with a small filigree.

Tess reached out and touched the handle—it was cool and smooth, and felt like any other door. She didn't know if she'd be asked for a token, or to answer a riddle, or otherwise interrogated by some sort of intergalactic bouncer. But when she pulled on the handle, the door opened, and Tess simply walked inside.

The first dome—because the "bar" was actually an interconnected series of domes, like a massive subterranean maze—was dimly lit. The warm orange light Tess had seen emanated directly from the walls, which had a mossy quality. The room was empty except for a bored-looking, androgynous person in a slinky outfit that looked like chain mail glimmering violet and red as it caught the strange light. They were lounging on a cushiony chair that looked like an outgrowth of the wall itself, paging through a paperback novel in a language Tess didn't recognize. They didn't even look up as they waved Tess through.

Tess walked slowly into something like a hallway—it had an arched ceiling, and it continued far enough that Tess couldn't see what lay at the end of it. Dark, vaguely electronic music pulsed through the space; it reminded Tess of Joni's Portishead phase. The hall was covered in the same mossy material as the entryway, but the lighting in here was deep blue-green, sparkling brightly through some spots on the wall that seemed more sheer than others. Tess wasn't sure if she should touch the moss, but her curiosity got the better of her and she laid a palm on it—it reacted immediately, pressing back against her hand with a gentle buzzing not unlike a purring cat. The sensation was intoxicating, and Tess had to fight a bizarre desire to lean her entire body into the moss. As she pulled her hand away and kept walking, she saw that some other patrons of the bar had not been able to resist that urge.

As Tess moved through the hall, she began to see openings toward other rooms, each one totally unique. One had walls that were slick and iridescent, as if they'd been covered in black oil, where half a dozen people dressed in spotless white nylon drank cocktails on high-backed sculptural chairs. Another room was nearly pitch dark, lit only by towers of glowing lily pads that people wandered around like a moonlit garden.

One dome was larger, filled with clear glass tubs that looked like they were floating in a night sky projected on the floor, walls, and ceiling. Tess couldn't resist wandering in for a closer look: The tubs were filled with something that looked like foaming bubble bath, but when one of the people in a bath moved, Tess saw the substance was more solid than any bath she'd ever been in—the foam was thick and crunchy, tinted in pastel pinks and blues, and seemed to coalesce around the bodies of the people bathing.

Tess understood why Octavia had told her to go directly to the main bar and not to waste time exploring Bar Between. She easily could have spent weeks in this place, visiting different rooms, asking the other patrons endless questions about where they'd come from, where they were going, and how they had ended up here. And while she didn't rush through the hallway, exactly, she also didn't linger. She didn't know how quickly time passed here—and besides, she'd be back soon enough once she successfully delivered her message to Callum.

At the end of the hall, Tess walked through a plain wooden door that turned out to be the entrance to the main bar. Given the varying sizes of the rooms she'd passed, Tess had expected it to be a cavernous space, the most spectacular setting of all. But it was the opposite—the closest thing Tess had seen to an actual bar in Brooklyn.

The room still had a vaguely rounded shape with a low, curved ceiling, but the walls were straight enough to hang paintings—dozens of them, oil portraits of all different kinds of people, some of whom Tess recognized from her walk through the bar tonight (like the white-nylon wearers), others more strange than anything she'd yet seen. The walls were a pleasant mushroom taupe, covered in a claylike substance, and the wood floors looked centuries old. The room was full of vintage, mismatched furniture: a velvet couch here, a leather wing chair there. Torches on the walls and a crackling fire in an iron hearth lit the space with a homey glow, and the music was both odd and comforting, muted pop electronica with a dash of jazz, or maybe funk.

There were only a few people in the room: two teens with green-tinged skin playing cards in a corner, a pot-bellied man in a fur coat dozing by the fire, an older woman with an extremely long neck wearing a dress trimmed with ostrich feathers, thumbing idly through a magazine. At the dark wooden bar, a woman in a gray skirt-suit was arguing with the bartender—their styles were radically different, so it took Tess a second to realize they were sisters.

"Honestly, Flora, I don't see why it's a big deal for you to make me a portal!" the skirt-suit woman said. "It's literally the only kind of magic you can do, so why not just do it?"

"Because you can take a cab!" the bartender huffed. "Or a train, or a private jet, or literally what-the-fuck-ever. I create portals between dimensions, not to make it easier for you to go to Boston."

The women both had dark hair and nearly interchangeable faces with wide eyes, button noses, full lips, and pudgy cheeks—but the similarities ended there. Where the skirt-suit woman was reedy and prim with a chic little pixie cut, the bartender was retro and goth, short and curvy, her hair styled in pin-up curls, eyes rimmed in black liquid liner. She wore a fitted halter dress that showed off the dozens of black tattoos snaking around her neck and down her arms, even onto her fingers, drawing Tess's eyes to her nails, which were painted black and filed into talons. If this was New York, Tess would have guessed they were both Dominican, but trying to narrow people down by ethnicity (or planet, even) in this bar seemed a bit reductive.

"In the time we've been arguing about this, you could have just done it already," skirt-suit huffed. "I'm going to be late to my meeting because you're throwing a tantrum about helping me when you're literally just sitting here doing nothing."

"I'm not doing nothing!" the bartender retorted.

"Oh, pardon me, you're making playlists and reading romance

novels, high-stakes stuff." Skirt-suit rolled her eyes. "I really am going to be late. Can I please go?"

"Fine." The bartender exhaled. "Go ahead."

Skirt-suit sauntered off without so much as a thank-you toward a door on the left side of the bar that Tess was pretty sure hadn't been there when she walked in. There was a faint flash of blue light as the door thwacked shut behind her, but the light faded almost instantly as the outline of the door melted seamlessly back into the wall. The bartender folded her arms and gazed sulkily after her sister, but she straightened and flushed when she saw Tess.

"Oh! Sorry, didn't see you come in. You want a drink?" She indicated one of the open stools; Tess was grateful the seats had backs and wide, supple leather cushions.

"I really like your playlist," Tess said as she sat.

"Oh yeah?" The bartender brightened. "It's Japanese city pop, I've been kind of obsessed lately—it's not a genre, more like a style? I love how it has this eighties synth sensibility, but it still weaves in elements of jazz and funk, and it can be almost kind of nostalgic, you know?"

"Yeah, totally." Tess nodded emphatically despite having understood at most twenty percent of what the bartender had just said.

"Anyway, hi! I'm Flora, and you are . . ." She peered at Tess, and Tess felt the most peculiar sensation of being understood very deeply by this perfect stranger. "Oh. Okay. Okay. Your first time here. What's your name?"

"It's Tess," Tess said quietly, somehow afraid of giving the wrong answer to a question as simple as her name.

"Right, Tess, but that's short for something, right?"

"Anastasia," Tess offered, the syllables feeling foreign in her mouth. Her given name was so stuffy and ornate; she'd always preferred the simplicity of her nickname. "Are you a mind reader?"

"Mm, not exactly." Flora leaned on the bar. "Portal magic is all about *desire,* you know? Understanding where someone wants to be—that's the connection between being here and being there. So when you tell me your name is Tess, I can feel the desire there—the desire to be seen one way, and not another."

"I don't know what your sister was talking about," Tess murmured. "Seems like pretty powerful magic to me."

"Fucking Fern." Flora rolled her eyes. "She actually *is* a super powerful telepath, runs around performing ultracomplex spells for the magical authorities, potion expert, gemology savant, thinks she's the world's hottest shit, and everyone treats her like she is, so why not? Anyway, look at me rambling and you have nothing to drink. What can I get you?"

Tess opened her mouth, but Flora cut her off.

"Wait! I'll tell you." She gazed at Tess again, then frowned in disappointment. "Really, Tess? A *beer*? I get that you don't want anything already open, but you're at an interdimensional bar between worlds! Live a little!"

Flora pulled out a crate from beneath the bar and deposited it with a thud on the credenza behind her. She rummaged through it, bottles clanking until she extracted the one she'd been looking for: It looked like a miniature wine bottle, sealed with wax and covered in dust.

"Is that port?" Tess asked.

"Close—Madeira, from Portugal, 1600s I think, and quite untampered with." She held out the bottle for Tess to inspect, but Tess pushed it back toward her.

"That's okay," Tess mumbled. "I don't have to look. I believe you."

"Hey." Flora caught Tess's eye for a moment. "Don't be ashamed to ask for what you need."

Tess closed her eyes—the familiar images flashed before her: Snowfall over the Hudson. A rocks glass full of whiskey. The pile of clothes on the floor.

But none of that was here. She smiled and thanked Flora as she poured two small glasses of the thick, garnet-red liquid. They clinked glasses and drank—the flavor exploded in Tess's mouth, nutty and rich with caramel, blackberries, and figs.

"Oh my god." Tess turned to Flora, who was grinning.

"Right? I wouldn't do you wrong." She pulled up a stool on her side of the bar and took a seat, leaning closer to Tess. "So tell me, Tess. Where would you like to go?"

"To the Isle. I need to deliver a message," Tess said carefully, her pulse speeding up.

"The Isle!" Flora beamed. "And you're not worried about being killed by vampires? Oh, you are a little, but you're also super excited, which I take it means you're a big fan of a certain series of novels?"

"Guilty as charged!" Tess grinned. "I'm a total Feudie, I love those books so much."

"Me toooo," Flora half sung. "You know, we've always had this policy that any human who made their way into Bar Between could visit the Isle at their own risk, and once the books got big I was a little worried we'd be, like, overrun with fans?? But you're the first one who's actually made it here."

"Wow, a dubious honor!" Tess laughed, and Flora did too.

"So which book is your favorite?" Flora asked. "Who's your favorite character? Oh my god, are you a total Callum girl?? You seem like a complete and utter Callum girl."

"Seriously? Ew."

"What, you're too good for a hot vampire?"

"No, nothing like that!" Tess laughed and took another sip of the incredible wine. "He just seems like—I don't know. Like you can't trust him. Like he would just . . . take what he wanted. No matter what you said."

Flora tilted her head, giving Tess a long, appraising look. "And you want someone who'll always listen to you."

"Right." Tess blushed, feeling like she'd shared too much. "Anyway, it's Felix for me! Classic romantic, love and devotion, blah blah blah."

"Eh, he's not as great as you think." Flora groused. "He dated my sister for a minute, like fifteen years ago? Before the Isle. He was super romantic and everything, but at some point it's like oh my god, stop reciting poetry and pick a fucking restaurant."

"Fern *dated* him?!" Tess was utterly agape. She leaned in, conspiratorial. "So can I ask, whoever August Lirio is, they'd have to be magical, right? To have a way of knowing what's happening on the Isle? Like, do you think they've been in here??"

Flora shrugged. "To be honest, *everyone* comes through here at some time or another. I've thought about it, but we get so many people, from so many different worlds, there's no way to know." She took a sip of her wine and smiled. "It's pretty cool, though. August Lirio could have been in *my bar*. I could have served them a drink! And since it's my job to keep an eye on the Isle with vision portals, sometimes I try to see if I can figure out what's gonna happen next in the books, but it's never worked."

"I'm sorry, vision portals?" Tess frowned.

"Oh—like this." Flora moved her hands, and a little circle appeared in the air between her and Tess—like a small floating screen rimmed in blue light, showing the street in Vinegar Hill where Tess had just been standing. "I can see what's happening in any world connected to the bar. Cool, right?"

"So you'll be able to see me?" Tess asked, her voice small. "On the Isle?"

Flora nodded. "But I can't actually *do* anything there. So if anything goes wrong, I won't be able to help. You'll just have to get to the crystal bridge as fast as you can and come straight back here, okay?"

"Oh." Tess swallowed. "Of course."

"Okay then!" Flora laid her hands over Tess's, and Tess felt suffused with warm energy. "Let's read your tarot and get you on your way."

"My tarot?" Tess was confused. "What does that have to do with anything?"

"You're embarking on a journey," Flora said matter-of-factly. "We need to find out what you're seeking."

"No." Tess disagreed. "I'm just delivering a message. I'll probably be right back here in an hour."

Flora looked at Tess for a long moment but said nothing. Then she smiled.

"Let's just see what the cards say, okay?"

Flora opened a drawer beneath the bar and took out a gorgeous deck. The cards looked at least a hundred years old, ornate illustrations printed on thick stock, accented with foil that caught the light as Flora shuffled, the cards flying through her fingers so quickly they looked like one big blur.

"Have you had a reading before?" Flora asked, her eyes never leaving the cards.

"Only with friends, like at parties and stuff," Tess murmured. "Never with an actual witch."

"That you know of." Flora winked. She put the deck of cards down in front of Tess. "Okay, they're warm—I need you to cut the deck twice, with your left hand. Think about where you're going. Think about what you're leaving behind. And think about what you need."

Tess tried to do what Flora said, but in truth, her mind was a swirling mess. The past twelve hours had completely flipped around her understanding of reality, and she wasn't sure how to locate herself in it at all, let alone what she needed to get out of it. She thought about Joni, and the hope she felt when she opened the email from Dr. Vázquez asking if she wanted to come back to Columbia, and the smell of antique books. She thought about the shock of watching Octavia feed, the revulsion of Rick's hand on her shoulder, about a doorway appearing in the wall of this strange bar, a flash of blue light, a chance to be free. She cut the deck twice with her left hand and looked at Flora.

"Good," Flora said. "Now restack the deck with the same hand— put whatever pile you want on top. And draw a card."

"Just one?" Tess asked, and Flora nodded. Tess considered the piles for a moment; Tess's left hand had faltered when cutting the second pile, the one now in the center, so it held only a few cards. For some reason, Tess felt that she ought to draw the card from this pile instead of the others. She restacked the deck accordingly and flipped over the card on top.

"The eight of swords," Flora nodded. "Tell me what you see."

Tess peered at the card—it didn't seem like a good one. It showed a woman tied up and blindfolded, surrounded by a circle of eight swords sticking out of the ground.

"She's in trouble," Tess said softly. "She knows she's about to die—or worse. She's trapped, and there's nothing she can do."

Flora put her hand over Tess's, and Tess felt another surge of energy pass through her.

"Look again," Flora urged. "Is anyone guarding the woman?"

Tess looked closely. "No. And—actually, there's an open space in the circle of swords. She could walk away if only she'd take off the blindfold and see the path in front of her."

"What does that tell you?" Flora asked.

Tess considered this for a long moment. "She thinks no one will help rescue her. But that doesn't matter. Because really, she has everything she needs to rescue herself. She just needs to open her eyes."

Flora picked up the card and handed it to Tess.

"Take this with you to the Isle," she instructed. "Deliver your message. But don't come back until you've done what the cards have asked."

Tess looked down at the card—and almost dropped it in surprise. The woman was gone from the illustration. Her blindfold and the ropes that had bound her lay in a pile in the center of the now-empty circle of swords. Tess stared at the empty space where the woman had been. Was this a simple magic trick? Or something more?

When she looked back up to ask, Flora was gone.

"What the actual fuck?" she exclaimed, loud enough that the other customers stopped what they were doing to look.

"Sorry," Tess apologized. "I didn't mean to—sorry."

They went back to what they were doing, and Tess slipped the tarot card into a little zippered pocket in her purse. She looked over toward the wall where Fern had walked through her portal, but there wasn't any door there. She was confused—was she just supposed to go out the main hallway, the way she came in? But as she surveyed the room, she saw a door in the corner, with the word "Exit" painted in black across its center.

That hadn't been there when Tess walked in, had it?

She walked over to the door, and she could hear something like white noise, or a whisper. She couldn't explain how, but she knew, as strongly as she'd ever known anything in her life, that she was supposed to walk through this door.

When she opened it, everything was dark and musty—she thought vaguely that it smelled exactly like her memory of the antique books—but in an instant, there was a buzz, a blip, a blackness. And then, a flash of blue light.

Chapter 5

Excerpt from *Blood Feud*
(book one, chapter twenty-two)
BY AUGUST LIRIO

Isobel paced her bedroom furiously, clutching the intricately carved dagger Felix had given her for protection. Why wasn't he home yet? He was only supposed to talk to Callum and Octavia, and that shouldn't have taken long . . .

Unless something had gone terribly, terribly wrong.

She snapped to attention with every noise, each rush of wind or snapping twig interrupting the eerily silent evening, waiting for any sound of Felix returning. When she heard footfalls pounding up the tower stairway, she flew to her door, her heart in her throat: Was it Felix, or was it someone else coming to say that her lover had died?

Her whole body pooled with relief when she saw him, his pale skin gleaming in the moonlight streaming through her doorway.

But then she saw his clothes were soaked with blood.

"Are you all right?" she cried, rushing to him. He pulled her in and kissed her, his touch shockingly gentle given the urgency of his manner.

"They're brutes," he whispered. "Barbarians."

"What happened?" Isobel cradled his beautiful face as they sat on her bed.

"It was a trap, a vicious fight. We barely made it out alive—and we wouldn't have at all if it hadn't been for the poison daggers you made. All I wanted was for them to join our clan, to see that we're safer together than we are apart."

"You're right," Isobel reassured him softly. "Of course you're right."

"Callum doesn't think so." Felix laughed bitterly. "He said he'd rather risk death every single day than take orders from me. He said . . ."

Felix's voice caught in his throat, and Isobel ached with sympathy.

"What, my love?" she asked softly. "What did he say to you?"

"He said Konstantin never took me seriously. And that Callum never would, either."

Felix looked down, his face flushed with shame.

"Oh, you can't listen to that!" Isobel cried out. "I know you were loyal to Konstantin, but he's dead now, Felix. You have to make your *own* way, do what *you* think is right."

"But how?" Felix looked bereft. "How can we go on when that clan is out to obliterate us? Not just Callum and Octavia—all of them. Tristan is a vicious killer, and Hamish is just as cunning as he is deadly. Antoinette and Angelique look like sweet teenage girls, but I saw them tear off a grown man's arm and drink blood from his mangled flesh. And Nantale . . ."

He trailed off. The mere mention of Nantale's name sent a chill down Isobel's spine. Nantale was the leader of Callum and Octavia's clan, rumored to be the oldest vampire on the Isle and the strongest as well, capable of murdering anyone she chose. And Isobel knew that if Nantale got the chance, she'd end Felix's immortal life without a second thought.

"How did you escape?" Isobel's voice was tender, but her need was primal. She had to know that Felix could hold his own against this beastly clan, could keep himself safe. Nothing could happen to Felix. She couldn't go on without him.

"We ran." Felix shook his head with disgust. "We had no other choice."

"I'm glad." Isobel's heart swelled. She climbed into his lap, straddling him—and even though his face was lined with humiliation, she could feel his desire straining against his breeches.

"How can you be glad?" he whispered. "How can you feel anything but embarrassment to be with a coward?"

"You're *not* a coward," she assured him, squeezing her thighs against his. He pulled her closer, his hands warm and firm at the small of her back. "It's no mark of humiliation that you're nothing like Nantale and her ghouls. Felix, it's a badge of honor."

❧

TRANSCRIPT OF *HERE TO SLAY* PODCAST, EPISODE 87

Cat: Hey, this is Cat!

Ruby: And this is Ruby. We have some very exciting news today— Cat, do you want to tell them?

Cat: I'M READING *BLOOD FEUD*!

Ruby: Yeah, you are!!!

Cat: Only took you four years to drag me onto this train, kicking and screaming, but now I am fully on board and basically the conductor.

Ruby: Okay, Shining Time Station.

Cat: Wow, deep cut.

Ruby: PBS millennials rise. How are you liking the books so far, Cat?

Cat: As my grandma always says: I don't like them. I *love* them.

Ruby: Your grandma loves sexy vampire novels?

Cat: You know that's not what I meant, but as a matter of fact, she does. Shout-out to Grandma Vidya!

Ruby: So today, in the interest of furthering Cat's *Blood Feud* education and appreciation, we're going to get into the differences between the two main tribes in the novels.

Cat: Two vampire clans, both alike in dignity.

Ruby: Precisely. So the simplest way to break this down is that on the Isle, the heroes live on the east side and the villains live on the west side.

Cat: Joke's on the heroes, the villains get better bagels. Okay, so the east side is Felix and Isobel?

Ruby: Exactly. This clan is all about order—that's like Felix's whole thing. He wants there to be a vampire hierarchy with sheriffs and accountability to stop indiscriminate violence.

Cat: And the west side? Callum and Octavia's clan?

Ruby: They looooove indiscriminate violence. Clan of chaos!!!

Cat: Maybe they get to this later in the books, but like *why* did the two clans form? Why do they hate each other so much?

Ruby: This is gonna sound a little reductive, but it's basically sibling rivalry? I know you just referenced *Romeo and Juliet,* but the story is actually closer to *King Lear.* Before the Isle, Felix, Callum, and Octavia all worked for a big bad vampire named Konstantin. And Konstantin was, like, a super villain. Think Thanos, Voldemort without the transphobia, whatever.

Cat: Wait, but I thought Felix was a good guy?

Ruby: He is! Felix always believed he could bring Konstantin to the side of good, could use his influence to help create more order in the vampire community. But Felix wasn't sired by Konstantin—

Cat: Meaning Konstantin didn't make him a vampire with his own blood?

Ruby: Exactly. But Konstantin *did* sire Callum and Octavia—in fact, they're the only two vampires he ever sired. And Felix was always pretty butt-hurt that Konstantin favored Callum and Octavia over him, no matter how hard he worked for Konstantin's approval.

Cat: Woooooooow, huge Kendall Roy vibes. Who are Callum and Octavia? Roman and Shiv?

Ruby: They're certainly not Connor.

Cat: America's first pancake, gone but not forgotten. Okay, so this actually makes a ton of sense to me! Because Konstantin died right before everyone was sent to the Isle, right? So now there's a power vacuum, with Felix on one side, and Callum and Octavia on the other?

Ruby: You got it! On the east side you have Team Felix, where everything's nice and organized and kinda noble but also occasionally verging on boring? On the west side you have Callum and Octavia, and it's all about hedonism—they do whatever they want, whenever they want, without sparing a thought for any possible consequences. This clan is a lot more dangerous than Felix's clan, but they're also a lot more exciting. That's why fans love them so much.

Cat: Well, Ruby, if you want more danger and excitement in *your* life, you may want to consider trapeze lessons—and luckily, we have a discount code for you to do just that!

Ruby: Really, Cat?

Cat: It's been kind of a slow month for ads.

Tess barely had time to register her journey through Flora's portal, but she felt it in her stomach—a lurch like a too-fast elevator, except instead of just going up, it seemed to move her body in every possible direction simultaneously. She doubled over, bracing herself against her knees so as not to topple sideways.

"Fucking hell," she whispered. She inhaled deeply, and the air felt cool and clean.

After a few big breaths, her stomach began to settle, and Tess straightened up and took stock of her surroundings. It was a grove of trees, misty but not gloomy, thickly populated with young-growth evergreens that made the whole place smell like Christmas. The light was dim and pleasing—a mix of orange, pink, and lavender, like the first minutes after sunset. Behind her was another silver birch tree and a little igloo like the one she'd used to enter Bar Between, except this one was made of dark petrified wood that blended seamlessly with its surroundings.

Okay, she thought, *so far, so good.* She'd come through the bar unscathed, she had a way to get back home, and beyond the trees, she could see the outline of the crystal bridge, mammoth and steeped in sunlight. There was a path through the grove, and Tess hurried down it so she could get a better look. She'd read about the bridge in the *Blood Feud* novels, of course, but that was nothing like seeing it hulking before her, glittering in the light, refracting thousands of rainbows over the sparkling iridescent waters of the lilac river below it.

"It's like I walked into a fever dream of Lisa fucking Frank," Tess muttered, gaping at the sheer size of the bridge, the intensity of the colors.

As Tess got closer to the bridge, she was able to see the silhouettes of buildings on the Isle beyond. It was darker there, but Tess could make out what had to be enormous homes—towering gables, flying buttresses, and even a turreted palace. She felt a small twinge of regret that she'd never fully get to experience it, this place she'd spent so many hours reading about, imagining, visiting in her dreams. But it was exhilarating just to see it, to know it was real, that she might be the only human ever to have gotten this close.

Tess felt a reassuring surge of warmth as she stepped into the sunlight at the foot of the bridge, and her rushing pulse slowed enough that she could take a moment to appreciate the staggering beauty of this place. The glimmer of the water, the sparkle of the cut crystal, all of it was beyond anything she'd ever seen on Earth—and, Tess realized, maybe that was the point. If the vampires were lulled into complacency by a beautiful prison, they might not fight as hard to get out.

As Tess walked closer to the Isle, the buildings came into sharper focus, but she didn't see any movement at all. It was pretty dark outside the bridge's banner of sunshine—was this their nighttime? Maybe all the vampires were asleep? Or maybe this part of the Isle wasn't very populated? As best as she could tell, the crystal bridge approximated the location of the Brooklyn Bridge, and she was near the Isle's southern tip. Tess knew from *Blood Feud* that most of the vampires on the Isle lived on one side or the other of the forest at the Isle's center, which served as a sort of neutral zone in the ongoing conflict between the Isle's two main clans. So it stood to reason that this part of the Isle would be empty.

At least, that's what Tess was telling herself as she stepped off the bridge and into the final stripe of sunlight that offered any sort of protection. The Isle was as silent as the forest on the other side of the bridge had been, but the silence felt different here—charged, somehow. Alive with the possibility of danger.

Quickly, her movements jittery, Tess reached into the neckline of her dress and extracted Octavia's scent vial. Her hands shook as she unscrewed the little cap, but she was flooded with relief as the heady smell of Octavia's perfume filled her nostrils: smoke and musk, leather and rose, overwhelmingly and unmistakably the same as the woman Tess had met in New York. This was going to work. All she had to do was wait.

How long would it take Callum to get here? A minute? Five? Tess took out her phone to see what time it was (did they even have time zones on the Isle?), but it wouldn't turn on. She wondered if the entire dimension was some kind of technological dead zone—or possibly she was just out of battery.

After several minutes, Tess started to get antsy. Octavia hadn't prepared her for this possibility. What should Tess do?

"Callum," Tess whispered. "*Callum.*"

Her heart was pounding so loudly she could hear it—if any vampire was nearby, there was no doubt in her mind that they could too. But as she got closer and closer to the place where the bridge's hot sunshine melted abruptly into darkness, she still couldn't sense any movement, even as she was just inches away . . .

No. This was too crazy. She couldn't step across that line—she had to go back. She'd just tell Octavia what happened, and maybe they could try again? Or figure something else out? It was time to get the hell out of here.

Except that the second she turned her back on the darkness, she felt a blunt object crack across the back of her head—like a thick stick, or a baseball bat. Stars exploded into her vision and she staggered from the pain, stepping out of the safety of the sunshine—and as soon as she did, she felt an arm around her neck and heard a low voice in her ear.

"Aren't you a long way from home?"

She tried to answer—or fight, or do anything useful—but her body went rigid in a state of absolute terror and panic. There was too much pressure against her throat. She felt her consciousness slipping away, and then everything went black.

The first thing Tess registered was the sound of voices, hushed and arguing—arguing about her, she realized quickly. She heard the sound of rushing water, but she had the distinct impression she wasn't outside. She was sitting, and her wrists and ankles were bound with rope. All around her were the most mouthwateringly delicious smells, roast meats and fragrant stews. Tess was desperate to open her eyes and see what was going on, but given the conversation, she thought it might be wise to play dead a little longer.

"I know you're joking right now." A man sighed dramatically. "We're all starving, and you're not going to let us feed?! You're doing us dirtier than Charles did Lady Di, and you know I don't say that lightly."

"You are not starving—you're literally attending a feast," a woman replied wearily. "You do not like the food you have. There is a difference."

The woman's voice lilted with an accent Tess couldn't quite place, though it sounded African. Was that Nantale, the leader of Callum and Octavia's clan? Was Callum here too?

"If we keep her alive, we can feed on her indefinitely," a man with a cold voice interjected—Tess was almost certain this was the same man who'd grabbed her from the bridge. A shiver ran down Tess's spine. She knew there was a chance that she'd be killed on this island, but to be held captive and used as a human blood bag for months, years, even decades on end?

"Fool." The woman with the accent clicked her tongue. "Thinking only of your most base desires."

"I'm a vampire," the cold-voiced man replied unapologetically. "My desires are what define me."

"And do you not desire to leave this isle, Tristan?" The woman was dangerously quiet. "Did it not occur to you that the sudden arrival of a human from our old world might herald an opportunity to return there? Or would you rather drink from just one neck for as long as she lives, waiting your turn like a pauper on a bread line?"

Tess tried to be still, but her pulse was thrumming beneath her skin. In *Blood Feud,* Tristan was known as the most violent member of Callum and Octavia's clan—if he was the one who grabbed her, she was lucky she wasn't dead already. But if Nantale wanted Tess alive, then Tess had a fighting chance.

"What if we, like, used a syringe?" a girl asked. "To portion out the blood."

"Omg, that's so smart," another girl agreed. "That way everyone gets a little! So balanced, you're such a Libra."

Tess clenched her jaw to stop herself from reacting—that was Antoinette and Angelique, the rude teen girl vampires! Tess *loved* them!! She was dying to open her eyes and get a look at everyone— but not if doing so would lead to her literal death, which still seemed very much on the table.

"Come on, Nantale," the dramatic man wheedled—Tess was pretty sure he was Hamish, a fabulous queer vampire who loved pop culture. "You don't really think she knows a way off the Isle, do you? And even if she does, what's the harm in us having a little teacup full of blood while she tells us?"

"Why don't we ask her right now?" Nantale suggested casually. "She's been conscious for several minutes."

Fuck! Tess thought. *Fuck! Fuck fuck fuck!!!!!!*

In the silence that followed, Tess could almost feel everyone in the room turning toward her. She summoned every shred of courage in her body, every memory of standing on the subway telling some drunk guy to fuck off, and opened her eyes.

There was so much to take in, it was hard not to gasp. The room was spectacular, just as it had been described in *Blood Feud*—a cavernous, circular great room with turquoise stone walls inlaid with gold, a paneled glass ceiling, and intricate white marble flooring forming a latticework over water thick with bulrushes and lotus flowers.

But nothing was more overwhelming than the other people in the room. Because Tess was seated at a banquet table with at least a dozen vampires.

They were all ages, races, and sizes, and dressed in all different manners—but they all had that same look as Octavia—the otherworldly glow to their complexions, the self-possession, the unmissable, confident air of stone-cold killers. And despite the table laid with all manner of decadent foods, they were looking at Tess like she was dinner.

Say something, Tess urged herself. *Say anything!*

"Hi," she managed weakly.

Motherfucker. She was surrounded by vicious monsters and all she could say was hi?!

"Hello." Nantale offered a small smile. She was exactly how Tess had pictured her from *Blood Feud,* elegant and statuesque, with dark skin and black hair twisted back in an elaborate series of braids. Her exploits were the stuff of legend: As a human, she had been a gender-fluid spiritual medium, one of the most powerful in the history of the Lugbara people. In modern times, she'd be called trans, but that term didn't exist in her culture and time; the duality of her identity was believed to be the source of her power to walk in both the human and spirit worlds. As a vampire, she was one of the greatest warriors the world had ever known—she was arguably the strongest vampire on the Isle, the commander of this clan. And now she was eyeing Tess with a sort of . . . bemusement?

"I take it you're not a witch," Nantale said.

"Oh, no." Tess nodded with understanding. "Just a regular human. That's why you bound my hands?"

"I'm sure you'll forgive the precaution." Nantale folded her arms. She wore simple, flowing pants and a sleeveless top made of crimson silk, which emphasized the warm glow of her skin in the room's dim lighting. For having been dead nearly six hundred years, she looked exceptionally good.

"Of course," Tess said softly. "Of all the precautions you could have taken, this one seems pretty measured."

Nantale laughed softly as she approached Tess, and some of the other vampires joined in.

"So tell us, human," Nantale intoned. "Who are you? What is your purpose here?"

"And what's been going on for the last eleven years?" Hamish folded his arms. He had a flaming ginger beard, a pudgy belly, and an effete manner. "Did Kristen Stewart and Robert Pattinson get back together, or did the cheating ruin them forever?"

"Hamish, not now!" Nantale snapped.

"You have your priorities, I have mine," Hamish retorted.

"Um, Kristen Stewart's actually gay now?" Tess offered. "Total lesbian icon."

Hamish approached Tess, his face lined with grave concern, and knelt before her.

"I need you to tell me everything."

But before Tess could say anything, a desperate voice rang through the hall, deep and gravelly, with a crisp British accent.

"Octavia? Octavia, is that you?!"

Callum Yoo stood in the great room's doorway. Tess could immediately see he was Octavia's twin: He was tall and gorgeous like her, but where she was sharp and delicate, he was thick and muscular. It was obvious why everyone in *Blood Feud* was terrified of him—Tess didn't know if she'd ever seen so much raw power emanate from a person.

Until he took one step forward and stumbled, grabbing a nearby column to stay standing. A few of the vampires rolled their eyes.

Was Callum Yoo . . . *drunk*?

"Callum, you're wasted." Antoinette sighed. "Octavia died, remember?"

Tess inhaled sharply. So Octavia was right: Callum *had* assumed her disappearance meant she was dead—and apparently he'd told the whole clan his suspicions.

"Of course he remembers, he's refused to leave his rooms since it happened," Angelique responded.

"Then why did he think she was here?" Antoinette asked.

"Who cares? This is boring." Angelique turned to Nantale. "Can we drink some blood now?"

"I thought I smelled Octavia . . ." Callum shook his head, looking confused and devastated.

"As you may have noticed, that's a literal human," Hamish said.

Callum turned toward Tess in shock—the rest of the room looked at her too.

"Um, you're right, you do smell Octavia," Tess said, her heart pounding. "Because I have her scent vial."

In a flash, Callum was right beside Tess—he moved faster than any creature Tess had ever seen, and he stared at Tess with a terrifying intensity. She was taken aback by how attractive he was—high cheekbones, gray eyes, curved nose, strong jaw covered in stubble, full lips pursed in a knowing smile. He ran a finger along Tess's neck, and she tensed with fear—

"Callum," Nantale warned, "what exactly do you think you're doing?"

"I'm not going to hurt her." Callum's voice was gruff and low, and his scent reminded Tess of Octavia: pine and smoke and leather. He looped his finger inside the chain around Tess's neck, slowly drawing the scent vial out of her cleavage. "I just want to know where she got this."

"Octavia gave it to me," Tess said with as much confidence as she could muster. "Because she's not dead—she's in New York City."

"You're lying," he whispered. There was desperation behind his eyes, raw and vulnerable—it was obvious to Tess that he was in agony. He jerked on the chain and it snapped easily, ripping it right off Tess's neck—she yelped in surprise and pain. "Did someone glamour this for you? Did Felix put you up to this?"

"Callum!" Nantale said sharply. "You haven't wanted to discuss details, so I haven't pressed. But now I must ask: Did you actually *see* your sister die?"

"No." Callum gritted his teeth, and there were shocked reactions from the other vampires. "But I know exactly what happened. I *know* she's dead."

"She isn't!" Tess protested. "I was just with her—she's the one who took me to Bar Between and told me how to get to you. I work at a hotel in Brooklyn, she found me there and asked me to come here to tell you how she escaped the Isle. I was only supposed to go to the foot of the crystal bridge, she thought you'd smell the scent vial and come meet me there. Except . . . you didn't. And someone grabbed me and brought me here."

"Is this true?" Nantale demanded. "You know how to leave the Isle?"

"Yes, human. Tell us how to leave this island." Tristan stepped toward them; Tess could see now he was tall and slender, with angular features and golden hair pulled back in a bun. "If it works, we go home. If it doesn't, we feed on you. Either way, we get our first good meal in a decade."

He gave her a chilling smile, and Tess's pulse raced as the other vampires murmured in agreement.

"Silence." Nantale held out her hand, and the vampires fell quiet. "Girl, tell us what you know."

"Octavia doesn't know exactly how she got back," Tess explained, though she was so afraid, it was a struggle to keep her voice from shaking: "She told me as much as she could remember about where she was and exactly what happened, that she was in the graveyard in the forest when she was transported back to Central Park, but there's no way to guarantee it would work the same way again."

"When did she go back to New York?" Callum asked. "Did she tell you?"

"Eight nights ago—maybe nine now, I'm not really sure what day it is," Tess answered.

"The same night you said she died," Nantale said.

"She's making this up." Callum shook his head. "This could be a trap—"

"Callum, please. This island is the trap." Nantale folded her arms. "We have to investigate the possibility that the girl is telling the truth, that there's a way out of here for all of us. Do all of you agree?"

The vampires nodded, and Nantale turned to Callum. "Your sister spent years researching potential ways off the Isle, didn't she?"

Callum nodded.

"Good," Nantale went on. "Then you'll work with the human—what's your name?"

"It's Tess."

"Fine. Callum, you'll work with Tess to determine how Octavia left the Isle and whether we can follow. And Tess, as long as you help us, I will personally assure your protection. No one in this clan will harm you, and no one outside this room will know a human has come to the Isle, understood?" She looked sharply at the group gathered around.

"Protect a human?!" Tristan spat. "If we feed on her, that's not even harming her! There's no reason to deny us blood."

"Think, Tristan." Nantale's patience was wearing thin. "We have more than a hundred vampires living in this compound, and none of you has tasted human blood in more than a decade. If just one of you went too far, drank too much, our first real chance to leave this place could be over in an instant. Do you really think it's worth the risk?"

Tess could see plainly that Tristan thought it was very much worth the risk.

"You've lost your judgment, Nantale," he said quietly. "And if you aren't careful, you'll lose control of your clan."

Nantale stood evenly, appraising Tristan.

"Perhaps you wish to challenge me right here?"

Tristan snarled, baring his teeth at Nantale. But he folded his arms and stepped back—the moment finished, at least for now.

"Good." Nantale's lips curved into the smallest smile. She waved her hand at a vampire standing in the shadows alongside the great room's walls. "Sylvie? Untie our guest."

An older woman whom Tess hadn't noticed hurried forward to untie the ropes binding Tess's wrists and ankles (she was older in human appearance, anyway—who knew how ancient any of these creatures actually was). Tess was relieved to be free of the ropes, but the whole time Sylvie was untying them, Callum never took his gaze off her.

"You really think this is a good idea?" Callum asked Nantale. "Letting a stranger into our compound?"

Nantale stood close to Callum.

"You are the only one I trust to do this," she said, her voice so low that only he and Tess could hear it. "You saved us once before. Now you must do it again."

Tess frowned—what did Nantale mean Callum had saved them?

There was nothing like that in *Blood Feud*. If anything, Nantale's clan were the aggressors, and Callum was the worst of the bunch.

"Do you want to eat?" Nantale touched Callum's arm gently. "We've missed you at Sunday dinner. You'd be welcome company."

"Think I'll pass." Callum eyed the rest of the vampires at the table, who'd mostly returned to their own conversations. Then he leaned down to murmur directly into Tess's ear. "If I find out you're lying about my sister, I'll be eating well soon enough."

Chapter 6

If one wishes to understand the intricacies of the most heated vampire controversy of our times, one need only look at the fan cams.

On TikTok, they number in the thousands, with view counts in the millions. Video after video with titles like "POV: Your summer romance with Felix," and "Toxic, chaotic, tantalizing Callum." They refer, of course, to the two main love interests in the *Blood Feud* series by August Lirio: Felix Hawthorn, the gallant romantic hero, and Callum Yoo, the devastatingly attractive bad boy. Both teams offer photo montages and video clips set over romantic music, but the tone and timbre could hardly be more different.

On #TeamFelix, the colors are soft and the music is dreamy. Fans imagine Felix taking them for a post-sunset picnic (not pre-, lest the object of their desire burst into flames and perish), a moonlit swim, a ride on horseback under the stars. They wear flowing gowns and flower crowns, and Felix gently grazes his fingers against their cheeks. In the videos, Felix is usually portrayed by male models with Raphaelite features—Timothée Chalamet has featured prominently since news broke that he'll be playing the character onscreen. Felix fans are self-designated "soft girls," and they long for a man as sweetly sensitive as they are.

The Callum girlies, not so much.

The #TeamCallum cams are grittier stuff, underscored with aching rock music, set in dark alleyways and moody hotels, featuring players clad in mesh and leather. There's no need for an itinerary of romantic activities in these cams; one gets the sense that there's really only one activity on the menu, and all it requires is a bed (or a chair, or a desk, or a wall).

An easy way to summarize the teams would be to say that #TeamFelix wants to be loved, while #TeamCallum wants to get fucked. But this reporter thinks there's something slightly more interesting at play: #TeamFelix wants permission to experience every emotion in the world. But #TeamCallum? They don't want to feel anything at all—except ecstasy. But hey, doesn't everyone want to feel that?

TRANSCRIPT OF UNHEARD VOICEMAILS FROM THE INBOX OF TESS ROSENBLOOM

Voicemail from Joni Chaudhari [August 11, 11:24 a.m.]: Hey, it's me. I figured you wouldn't pick up, and I guess you're never gonna respond to my texts, so I'm just trying this because . . . I don't know! Because you showed up at my birthday party after not seeing you for three years, and then just ghosted again? Why did you come at all? And why won't you tell me what's going on? I hate this, Tess. I can't believe you're doing this again. Please just call me, okay?

Voicemail from Mika Cox [August 11, 9:41 p.m.]: Hey, hope you're feeling better! I'm calling because Taylor said you haven't been answering your texts—I covered for you, but do you know when you'll be back? Not that I think they'd really fire you or anything, but like, you know, probably a good idea to keep in touch? Hope you're doing okay, babe!!

As a rule, Octavia Yoo did not care for human men. She detested their natural stench almost as much as the noxious products they used to mask it (she felt so-called body sprays ought to be banned as an act of law or god, whichever went higher), she found their opinions on politics and literature to be reductive and dull, and their utter lack of emotional awareness (and tendency to turn to acts of violence rather than identify one feeling) was tedious in the extreme. Octavia had always avoided men whenever possible—unless she needed something from them. Which was the only reason, at this particularly strange and lonely moment of her life, Octavia's favorite person in the world was a human man named Nicky Galanis.

Nicky was a night watchman at Bergdorf Goodman, and he gave Octavia everything she needed.

The problem with having lost her powers in the dead of summer was that the sun set too late for Octavia to visit most of her favorite stores. On the rare occasion that she could make it in somewhere by eight, the places were usually pretty empty, making it much more difficult to slip into a fitting room and steal anything she fancied—a process she disliked in the best of circumstances. Octavia had hoped Tess would be back with Callum within a few hours of having gone into Bar Between, but it had been an entire day, and Octavia was getting restless. What was she supposed to do, hole up in that hotel forever? Repeat outfits? Certainly not!

So Octavia went to Bergdorf's just after sunset and watched who came and went. When she saw Nicky, middle-aged and pudgy with a kind face and a hip flask, she knew she'd struck gold. She sold him some sob story about having lost her grandmother's necklace in the fitting room a couple of hours earlier, and he let her right in to try to find it.

"Oh, sir—what was your name?" Octavia asked, smiling through her tears.

"It's Nicky, Nicky Galanis." He doffed his little night watchman cap like a character in a Frank Capra movie. His face was flushed and he smelled like cinnamon and rye—as far as male scents went, not bad at all.

"Thank you, Nicky." Octavia took his hands. "You have no idea what this means to me—oh, I could just kiss you!"

And then, without waiting for any sort of a response, she leaned down and did exactly that. It wasn't a fast kiss, either; Octavia had seduced thousands of lovers, and she knew exactly how to make someone's knees weak. When she felt Nicky go woozy beneath her touch, she moved to his neck and sunk her fangs into his flesh.

It wasn't the best blood she'd tasted—it didn't even come close— but after a decade of animal blood, the warm stuff in Nicky's veins might as well have been the steak omakase at COTE. Octavia drank deeply, indulgently, until Nicky lost consciousness. She didn't want to kill him; he'd wake up later with a bit of a headache and probably think he drank too much, maybe wonder if Octavia had been real at all, convince himself the wound on his neck was a spider bite. By then, she'd be long gone, and the empty shopping bags she'd brought with her would be filled with dozens of gorgeous new outfits— enough to last at least a week, maybe even two? Surely Tess would be back by then. How long could it possibly take to deliver one simple message?

"I just can't figure it out. It doesn't make any sense!"

Joni was pacing her living room, which still bore some scars of the previous night's party—a cigarette burn here, a sticky patch there—but was mostly back to normal.

"No, *this* doesn't make any sense." Nasser flopped back onto the couch and gestured toward Joni's outfit. He looked fabulous in a purple silk caftan; she was still in her cutoffs and a threadbare Columbia tee she often slept in. "The concert starts at midnight, it's after eleven, and you look like you got in a fight with your closet and lost."

"I can't dress up twice in one weekend, it's against dyke code," Joni grumbled. "Give me some of that."

Nasser handed over his joint, and Joni inhaled deeply.

"Okay," she said, trying to let the pot open her mind, to invite new possibilities she hadn't yet considered. "Let's think this through. Why would Tess come to my party?"

"Because she loves you, stupid," Nasser replied, his voice thin as he held in a hit of his own.

"But then why would she leave so quickly?!" Joni could hear her voice edge into whining, but she didn't care. "Why reappear just to ditch me all over again?"

Nasser sighed. "You have to ask her."

"I tried! I called, I texted, I DMed, I'd stand outside her apartment with a damn boom box if I knew her address, but nothing's working." Joni's voice hitched in her throat. Damn it. Wasn't it bad enough that she'd gotten too drunk at the party and ended up spending an hour in the bathroom, crying and puking and wishing Tess were there to laugh their way through it? Why couldn't she brush this off, put it all behind her as easily as Tess could?

"Okay, first of all, Lloyd Dobler was a total stalker, and if you did the boom box thing you would be too."

"Rude." Joni nudged Nasser's leg with her knee.

"I know Tess showing up totally spun you out, but then, I have to ask . . . why did you invite her?"

"I don't know." Joni sighed. "I guess I assumed she wouldn't come."

"And you could add that to your little list of grievances against her?"

"Ouch." Joni leaned her head onto Nasser's shoulder. "Not wrong, though."

"I'm not saying you don't have a right to be mad at her," Nasser said gently. "But if you really do want to repair the friendship, you might need to try a different approach. Maybe see it from her side? She came all the way up here and left after twenty minutes. Something probably upset her."

Joni frowned. "Like what?"

"I have no idea." Nasser took another hit. "But she's not in Siberia, she's at a hotel in Brooklyn. Maybe get on the subway and ask her?"

"You think I should just like . . . show up at her job? How is *that* not a stalker move?"

"They have security, don't they?" Nasser shrugged. "If she asks you to leave, you'll just leave. But I bet it'll mean something to her that you cared enough to go all the way down there."

"Maybe . . ." Joni considered it. It certainly sounded better than sending angry texts and leaving desperate voicemails for the rest of time.

"You know my favorite thing about this plan?" Nasser asked.

"What?"

Nasser kissed Joni on the tip of her nose, then stood up and headed toward the door.

"Once you actually start talking with Tess, this won't be my problem anymore."

The Georgia lobby was mostly empty by the time Octavia got back from her shopping excursion; the lobby bar closed at midnight, and it was getting close to one A.M. Octavia really wanted a cocktail—it wasn't too late to put on one of her lovely new dresses, head to a bar in the neighborhood, and find someone to feed on. Or sleep with. Or both! Octavia glanced at the front desk as she passed by, hoping Tess would be there with good news to report. But the desk worker was the same woman who'd been there the last two nights, with black hair in a bun, a disaffected air, and a name tag that read Mika. She was talking to a tall, bedraggled girl in a Columbia hoodie and frayed cutoffs who seemed agitated for some reason. Maybe she was on drugs? Hmm, maybe she had something fun to share with Octavia.

"Please," the hoodie girl pleaded, "I know it sounds crazy, but we used to be best friends."

"I'm sure you understand why we can't give employees' home addresses out to strangers." Mika the desk worker spoke with the practiced patience of a person who handled unreasonable requests for a living.

"Yeah, I'm really sorry." Hoodie girl looked close to tears. "I didn't mean to put you in a bad position or anything. I just thought, if I could see Tess, you know? If I could just talk to her."

Octavia froze at the mention of Tess's name. Who was this girl? If she knew Tess, was there any way she could know about Octavia? No, there couldn't be—Octavia had been with Tess the whole time between leaving the hotel and going to Bar Between. Even so, Octavia wondered if she should leave the lobby right away, or if that would just draw more attention. But before she could decide, the girl turned around and almost smacked dead into her.

"Oh shoot, sorry, I'm so sorry." She shook her head.

"It's just a bump, I'm sure we'll both recover," Octavia clipped. "If you'll excuse me . . ."

But the girl was staring straight at her, transfixed with wonder.

"Oh my god," she whispered. "Octavia?"

Damn.

"Sorry." Octavia smiled calmly. "Must have me confused with someone else."

She pushed past the girl and toward the elevators, sharing a conspiratorial glance with Mika along the way. This was good—if the desk worker thought hoodie girl was out of her mind, then there was very little chance of her saying anything that could blow Octavia's cover.

But when she pressed the button to call the elevator, the girl in the hoodie was holding up her phone right in Octavia's face.

"This is you, right?"

Octavia gaped—it was a photo of her and Callum at Truman Capote's black-and-white ball.

"That's . . . not . . ." she started, but the girl swiped on her phone to show another photo, this time of Octavia and Callum hanging out with Josephine Baker in Paris in the 1920s.

"This is you too." Hoodie girl swiped again: Callum and Octavia in the background of a tourist's vacation photo from Jeju Island. Octavia had seen that one during the brief flurry of *Blood Feud*-truther research that led her to Tess—it made her heart ache to remember the years she'd spent traveling around Korea with Callum, finally connecting with their culture after so many years denying it.

The elevator doors slid open with a ding. Octavia could brush off this girl, get in, and pretend this never happened. But the girl had a hungry look about her; there was always the chance she'd keep at this, come back to the hotel, raise exactly the kind of attention that could get Octavia kicked out of her suite (which was, disappointingly, in Brooklyn, but which was still quite comfortable and extremely free). She turned to the girl and sighed.

"What's your name?" she asked.

"Uh, Joni. Joni Chaudhari," she responded, her tone suspect.

"I'm Octavia Yoo." Octavia held out her hand to shake. "It's a pleasure to make your acquaintance."

The blood drained from Joni's face. "You mean—you're really? I mean. No. You can't possibly—you're not really . . ."

"Really, with all the shock and awe?" Octavia exhaled heavily. "You were so certain it was me a second ago."

"I just can't believe—you're really a vampire?!?"

"Keep your voice down," Octavia hissed.

"Oh my god, and you're in Tess's hotel. Does that mean Tess knows?! And what about the Isle? Is that real too?!"

Octavia patted Joni gently on the shoulder.

"Why don't you come up to my room and we can talk? There's a lot to fill you in on."

"Really??" Joni's eyes lit up, but then she frowned. "Wait. You're not gonna kill me, are you?"

"I'm glad you think so little of my intelligence as to imagine I'd murder someone I was seen with on camera in the lobby of my own hotel mere minutes beforehand."

"Of course not!" Joni let out a trill of anxious laughter. "That'd be so stupid. Duh. Sorry."

As they stepped into the elevator, Octavia was unnerved by the way Joni wouldn't stop staring at her.

"Could you ease up on the gawking? It's rude."

"Sorry, it's just that you're so beautiful," Joni murmured. "Um, and an immortal demon from hell or whatever."

Octavia hit the button for the pool deck and said a silent goodbye to the dancing, the blood, and the sex she wouldn't be having tonight. But as the elevator began to rise, so did her spirits. It would be nice to have a devoted little minion who could run errands in the daylight.

Octavia flashed Joni a dazzling smile, and Joni moon-eyed right back at her.

Perhaps this night wasn't a total loss after all.

Chapter 7

Excerpt from *Blood Feud*
(book one, chapter seven)
BY AUGUST LIRIO

allum and Octavia Yoo were two of the most vicious—and virulently feared—vampires on the Isle.

But they were nothing compared to their sire.

Born in ancient Greece a thousand years before Jesus Christ walked the Earth, Konstantin Adamos stood well over six feet tall, broadly muscled with olive skin, sleek black hair, and features chiseled more finely than any marble statue. During his millennia on Earth, Konstantin enjoyed enormous influence: Some say Konstantin fed his blood to the Holy Father during the Crusades, controlling him in a perpetual blood thrall; others insist Konstantin spent the last fifty years of his life as an arms dealer in Shanghai. All that is known for sure is that Konstantin died shortly before the Isle was created.

Throughout his expansive life span, Konstantin was never more powerful—or more violent—than during the years he spent in Victorian England. During that time, Konstantin was a titan of industry, the shadowy owner of more than a dozen dirty factories that churned through workers at an alarming pace—especially the orphans whose little fingers stitched lace doilies for the ladies of London. Of course, back then, if a poor factory worker went missing, no one batted an eye. So it was that Konstantin had a constant supply of victims, gorging himself on the fresh blood of children, knowing the pipeline would never run dry. In all that time, Konstantin spared only two children that crossed his path:

Callum and Octavia Yoo.

Callum and Octavia's father was a Korean ship worker who may or may not have known they ever existed. Their mother, a British seamstress, died when the twins were only a few years old, probably of cholera or typhoid. Like so many other children of that time, Callum and Octavia were sent to various orphanages in appalling disrepair, but since they had each other—and a remarkable aptitude for mischief—they always figured out a way to survive. By the time they were twelve and wound up in one of Konstantin's factories, they'd started a full-on gambling ring for the adults who worked there.

When an ornery guard found them out and brought them to Konstantin for discipline, no one expected ever to see them again. But something in the twins' nature must have impressed Konstantin, because instead of killing them, he decided to take them on as wards. Throughout their adolescence, they had only the most luxurious clothes, the most lavish trips around the world, the finest tutors. By the time they reached adulthood, they were known throughout London as two of the most charming, witty, and attractive people in the city—but Konstantin forbade them to marry. This suited them fine; they lived such carefree, extravagant lives that they had no wish to take on the burden of spouses or children of their own. But they did find Konstantin's mandate curious—after all, why should he care whether the twins ever married?

On their twenty-ninth birthday, they found out. That was the night he turned them both into vampires.

Twin sires are exceedingly rare, because almost no vampire is strong enough to use their own blood to sire two new vampires in the same night—and on top of that, the two new vampires must also be biological twins. This combination of twindoms, human and vampire, creates a bond so magically powerful, it imbues the twin sires with strength that would normally take them centuries to build.

Callum and Octavia were the only vampires Konstantin ever sired, and he valued them above any other vampires in his employ.

And he never let his most loyal servant, Felix Hawthorn, forget it.

Tess woke up groggy and disoriented—she was still in the black silk dress she'd worn to Joni's party. It was pitch dark in the room where she was sleeping; after the tense events in Nantale's great room, she'd been so tired she'd gone straight to bed without bothering to take in her surroundings. But now she realized she had no idea where she was. She was stricken with a pang of hunger—when was the last time she ate?

She rolled over in bed, edging a foot over the side. Something about this place felt familiar. She reached out and felt a night table, a little desk lamp with a nubby glass shade, just like the one in her old apartment with Joni on 112th Street. She flipped on the lamp— she *was* in that bedroom. What the fuck?? But then she heard a sound—footsteps outside her door. She shrank back on the bed.

"Joni?" she whispered. But she knew it wasn't Joni. The footfalls were too heavy. It wasn't Rick. It couldn't be Rick—

The door swung open, and there was Callum, his tall frame cast in shadow. His face was backlit in profile, and she could make out his curved nose and full lips, the stubble that lined his strong jaw. And that look in his eyes . . .

It was desire. She was sure of it.

"Why did you wear that dress?" he asked, his smooth British accent at odds with his low, dangerous voice.

"This?" Tess gripped the dress, the silk pooling between her fingers. "There was a party, I didn't—"

She hurried to stand, and in an instant Callum was beside her.

"Why did you dress like Isobel?" His voice was strained.

"So you would want me," Tess whispered. "As much as you wanted her."

He wrapped his arms around her waist, drawing her close—god, he was strong. Tess looked up at him. His eyes were gray, with flecks of amber and gold.

"You're so beautiful." Tess ran her fingers across his cheek. "Are you going to kill me?"

"We're all dead here," he breathed. "Is that all right?"

She nodded, and then he was kissing her, and she was kissing him back, and his body was cold, but he felt so *alive* against her. His hands moved down the silk of her dress as he drew her closer to him. She heard a moan escape her as his lips found her neck.

"How did you find me?" she asked, digging her fingers into his shoulders as he kissed down her chest, his mouth moving toward her breasts. "I haven't lived here for years."

He stood up straight then, cupping her face in his hands, his touch surprisingly gentle.

"Don't lie to yourself, Tess." His face turned hard, his eyes blank and empty. "You never left this place. You never will."

And with that, he wrapped his hands around her neck and started to squeeze.

Tess woke gasping for air—she was soaked in sweat, and tears were rolling down her face. She hadn't had a nightmare like that in months. God, it felt so vivid—just like the dreams after Rick, back when she couldn't stay asleep for longer than an hour or two, when exhaustion and delirium and constant terror made it almost impossible to discern what was real.

She slid out of bed and pulled open the heavy jacquard curtains—

it was dusk, the sky pale and purple as stars began to appear. Dim light spilled into the room, illuminating walls made of enormous slabs of black marble shot through with veins that shimmered gold. The floors were smooth, polished wood, light with an almost pinkish hue, like maple. The furnishings were simple and elegant: black wooden dressers that seemed to melt into the walls, plush patterned rugs in soft grays, and the enormous bed Tess had slept in—a soft, thick mattress on a low platform, covered in silk sheets and woven blankets and scattered furs in various grays and blacks.

It was the most luxurious room Tess had ever slept in by several orders of magnitude, and she had a feeling it was far from the most impressive suite in Nantale's compound.

"I thought I heard you wake up!" Tess whipped toward the door, immediately on edge, but it was the stout older woman who'd untied her the night before. She looked to be in her sixties, with frizzy silver hair that flowed past her shoulders, crinkly white skin, and an infectious energy. She wore an oversized button-down and soft linen slacks, and big eyeglasses with purple frames that kept sliding down her nose. She reminded Tess of her favorite librarian at Columbia, a woman who'd once literally jumped for joy upon receiving a box of rare science fiction magazines from the 1950s.

"How'd you sleep?" she asked. "Are you hungry? How about some coffee?"

"Good morning—I mean, um . . ." Tess trailed, not knowing exactly what to say. The woman laughed.

"That's the Isle for you, hon." She smiled warmly. "Good luck knowing what time of day it is, let alone the week or month or year. It's just night for a while, then gray and cloudy like a stormy day, then night again. Who knows for how long!"

"So there aren't seasons?" Tess asked.

"What you see is what we've got! I'm Sylvie, by the way. Are you sure you don't want coffee? How about something to wear? Did you sleep in that dress you came in? Good lord, vampires make the worst hosts."

Tess looked down at her dress, which was clinging to her body and sticky with sweat from her nightmare. Sylvie was right—it would be nice to change.

"Maybe a robe?" she asked. "And a shower would be lovely. And then I guess, something to wear afterward, if it's not too much trouble?"

Tess watched Sylvie's eyes change—they seemed to glow with a golden intensity as she placed her hand on the wooden dresser. After a moment, Sylvie stepped back and motioned for Tess to open the drawer: It was filled with pajamas, jeans, tees, sweaters, and dresses, all of which looked to be exactly Tess's size. When Tess looked up from the drawer, Sylvie was holding out a thick terry robe, which Tess gratefully took and wrapped around her body.

"Now, how about that coffee?" Sylvie grinned, but Tess was dumbfounded. She knew from *Blood Feud* that vampires could glamour their surroundings on the Isle—it's how they made places like this compound. But it was one thing to have read about it, and quite another to see Sylvie casually whip up an entire wardrobe.

"You can really?? Did you just glamour—how did you *do* that??"

Sylvie shrugged. "We're not sure how it works. On Earth, we can look into the eyes of a human and bend them to our will. Here, we can do the same thing—except instead of humans, it's objects. See?"

She put her hands on an armoire, and when she opened the doors, it contained a fully stocked kitchenette, including a small silver coffee maker, a platter of buttery pastries and loaves of hearty brown bread, and an ice chest filled with cheeses, cold cuts, fruit, and cream.

"We can make you anything you want, of course." Sylvie nodded toward the food. "But this way you'll always have a little nosh on hand if you're in your room. Speaking of which—how do you like the room?"

"Are you serious?" Tess held in a laugh. "It's unbelievable."

"Sure, sure, but is it *you*? It doesn't really seem like you."

"But it's beautiful! And really, you've done too much already, I couldn't ask you—"

"Oh, pssh," Sylvie scoffed. "I had seven children back in my human days. I love taking care of people."

"Wow, seven." Tess took this in. "And are they—here? I mean, are they . . ."

"Vampires? No. I met Alberto when I was in college, and we fell madly in love, but I knew I wanted a family—and he couldn't give that to me. Forty years later, when my kids were grown and their dad had passed, he came back for me. Said he didn't want to spend eternity without me. So here I am!" She laughed and shrugged a little.

"And Alberto?" Tess asked. "He's here too?"

Sylvie shook her head. "No, he was killed about a year after we came to the Isle."

"I'm so sorry," Tess murmured, but Sylvie just shrugged, the way you do when a wound is old.

"There was a lot of fighting in those days, people scared, confused about how we ended up here, how long we'd be here, blaming each other for what happened," she explained. "This was before we formed the clans and started living together for protection. I'm pretty young for a vampire—Alberto turned me only a few years before we came to the Isle. Once he was gone, I was vulnerable, to say the least."

"So how did you survive?" Tess asked, spellbound.

"I spent a long time hiding at the northern end of the Isle," Sylvie said. "There's not much population up there, so it was safer—lonelier too. But after a year or so, one of Nantale's clan members ran into me hunting up there, saw how hungry and afraid I was. They offered me company—and security—if I moved in here. Nantale was good to take me in and look after me. So I try to look after everyone around here in return. Including you. Which means it'll be just fine for you to tell me how you'd like to decorate your bedroom."

Tess frowned—Nantale and her hunting party helping a vulnerable old woman? That didn't track with the vicious murderers August Lirio described them as in *Blood Feud*. Tess gazed at Sylvie, taking in the meaning behind her story. If she'd only become a vampire a few years before coming to the Isle, that meant her children—and, presumably, grandchildren—were still alive back home. And she was trapped here, without them, without the man who'd loved her so much he'd waited forty years to be with her, taking care of a compound full of vampires instead of her own family. Tess had to suppress a strong urge to rush over and hug her fiercely.

"Maybe this is silly," Tess started, "but I've always wanted a bedroom that was green?"

An hour later, the entire room had transformed under Sylvie's touch: dark green walls patterned with delicately painted chinoiserie, soaring arched windows with sprawling views of the forest below, a gargantuan mahogany sleigh bed, floor-to-ceiling shelves stuffed with books, and a squashy leather armchair and a velvet settee beside a stone hearth that housed a crackling fire. Sylvie left Tess to shower and change (though not before upgrading Tess's bathroom with shiny penny tile, a rough-hewn teak vanity, and an oversized copper soaking tub that Tess was dying to try). Tess stood under a steaming shower, feeling the vestiges of her nightmare rinse away. She pulled on her new robe and enjoyed a delicious cup of coffee and a perfectly crisp croissant that rivaled the best Tess had ever had, the way she dreamed they tasted in Paris. Tess had always wanted to visit Europe, but her family only ever went wherever there was a free place to stay. They never had money for vacations, so books had been Tess's escape. It made her smile to think that not even her richest, snobbiest classmates had ever been to a place like this.

She put on a ribbed black turtleneck and tucked it into a pair of faded, high-waisted blue jeans that hugged her hips and legs. She opened a drawer of her bathroom vanity to discover Sylvie had thought to stock it with all manner of creams, serums, and makeup; it made her feel more human to put on a coat of mascara and some cheery red lipstick.

She heard her bedroom door creak open—Sylvie must be back.

"I'll be right there!" she called.

"By all means, take your time," a smug voice replied. "Your life will end eventually. Who cares how much of it you waste?"

Callum. The moment he spoke, Tess's dream came rushing back and her heart started pounding; she could feel his tongue in her mouth, his hands on her throat. She squeezed her eyes shut to force out the image—*no.* She had to stay grounded, stay present. No matter what protections Nantale had ordered, if Tess made one wrong move, she was certain Callum would kill her without a second thought. If she wanted to live through this adventure, she had to keep her wits about her. She couldn't show him even a modicum of fear.

"I'm sorry," Tess said crisply as she walked into the bedroom. "I didn't realize you were waiting."

He was sitting on the velvet settee, thumbing through one of the books from Tess's lovely new shelves. He was even more handsome than he'd been in Nantale's great room—he looked less rumpled, more alert. He wore gray jeans, brown leather ankle boots, a navy crew-neck sweater, and a buttery chocolate suede jacket; every item fit his body perfectly, because of course everything anyone wore on the Isle was essentially bespoke. His posture was easy but not slack; it was as if his muscles were forever holding tension, ready to lash out and strike.

"I'm an immortal creature trapped on an island." He smiled wryly. "Time is rather a relative concept, wouldn't you say?"

"Must pass slower when you're sober," Tess quipped before she could stop herself, but Callum laughed, then stood and walked toward her.

"Too right." He grinned.

He laid his hands on her armoire, his eyes glowing briefly just as Sylvie's had—but there was something different about how he looked when he performed the glamour. If Sylvie's eyes had been soft and golden, Callum's were hard and fiery, like his glamours were forged in steel. He opened the door of the armoire, where a tray of glass bottles filled with clear and amber liquids had appeared next to Sylvie's little coffee station. He popped the cork out of something brown and took a long draught, then wiped his lips on his sleeve. He held out the bottle and offered it to Tess.

"What do you say, human? Want to pass the day a little faster, or would you rather we take it nice and slow?"

Was he *flirting*? Or just toying with her like a cat teasing a mouse before the fatal claw?

"I think we'd better get going," Tess muttered.

"Oh?" Callum took another drink and gave Tess an amused look. "What's on our itinerary?"

"I thought we could visit the graveyard where Octavia disappeared."

"You want to take me into the deep dark forest, just the two of us?" Callum pursed his lips, mocking her. "Are you sure that's a good idea?"

Tess tamped down her rising fear. "You know, for someone who was convinced his sister was dead until I showed up, you don't seem that invested in getting out of here and actually finding her."

Callum opened his mouth to respond but then seemed to think better of it.

"Fine then," he said smoothly. "Did you want to put on shoes before we trek into the forest, or are you one of those dirty little hippies who prefers to go without?"

"Oh!" Tess flushed with embarrassment. "I don't think Sylvie made any. I have my sandals from yesterday—"

"No need." Callum crouched before Tess, wrapping his hands around her calves; his grip was just as strong as she'd imagined. He moved his fingers firmly against her muscles, slow and rhythmic— she let out a soft, involuntary exhale.

"Everything all right?" He looked up at her, his gray eyes glinting—and in that moment, kneeling in front of her, he was so unbelievably attractive that she forgot to be afraid of him.

"Fine." She breathed.

A slouchy pair of black leather boots formed around Tess's feet, and Callum stood straight up again, towering over her, looking down with a smug smile. Tess refused to give him the satisfaction of showing how much he—and all of this—unmoored her.

"Thanks, that was super helpful." She stepped away from him and turned toward the door. "Shall we go?"

He made a small, displeased *humph* sound and stalked out of the room. Tess felt her stress ease the tiniest bit: She'd survived five minutes alone with Callum Yoo.

Tess knew from *Blood Feud* that Nantale's compound was laid out in a giant triangle, and everything about the building was designed to intimidate and confuse potential intruders: Stairwells jutted off at odd angles, hallways stopped in dead ends, and secret rooms abounded. As Tess followed Callum, she noted intricate gray marble-tiled floors that looked almost braided, high arched ceilings, and an assortment of spectacular paintings hanging from the walls, which were upholstered in dark velvet.

"I'm sorry," she said, "can you walk a little slower? I'm trying to remember some landmarks so I can navigate this place."

"Oh." He paused. "You just have to look at the paintings, see?"

He pointed out the paintings in this hall—a series of wryly surrealist works by Magritte—his hand brushing briefly against Tess's arm.

"What, um"—she cleared her throat—"what about the paintings?"

"They're chronological. If they're getting older, you're moving clockwise. Newer, you're going counterclockwise. So if the paintings are getting more modern, you're heading toward the entry, older, back toward your room. You follow?"

"Oh!" Tess remembered a Botticelli outside her room—so in the space of a few minutes, they'd moved from the Italian Renaissance to the 1920s. Sure enough, she saw some Dalí up ahead. "That's really cool."

"*Cool,*" Callum mocked, and Tess felt annoyed and embarrassed in equal measure.

"Um, who thought of that?" she asked. "It's a really clever system."

Callum didn't answer—great, was he just flat-out ignoring her now? But as they walked into the compound's entry, a grand room with a rotunda-like ceiling, he responded gruffly, "My sister."

"Good, you're here." Nantale stood in the center of the room, looking at them expectantly. She was dressed in a vibrant purple kaftan and holding a perfume atomizer made of carved iridescent glass. "I have something for you, girl."

"What is it?" Tess asked.

"Egyptian musk oil, several thousand years old," Nantale explained. "To mask your human scent. You will wear this anytime you leave your rooms, even inside the compound. Understood?"

"Do you think I need—" Tess swallowed hard. "I mean, am I not safe here?"

"I believe the vampires within these walls will follow my orders," Nantale reassured her. "But I also think temptation is best avoided, do you agree?"

"Absolutely." Tess nodded vigorously. Nantale handed her the bottle, and Tess applied a generous spritz—she noticed Callum's eyes flick to her neck as she did so, and applied two extra sprays for good measure. The scent was deliciously warm and earthy, and Tess was grateful that if she had to smell like this all the time, at least she'd enjoy it.

"I think that's plenty." Nantale smiled. "Give me the bottle, I'll have it sent to your rooms. Callum, may I speak to you for a moment before you go?"

"Of course." He turned and eyed Tess. "Don't move."

"Wouldn't dream of it," Tess clipped.

Callum and Nantale sped down another hall and out of sight. It unnerved Tess, being among creatures that could move so fast—knowing that if she was ever in danger, she had no hope of running away.

And Tess's safety was top of mind in this particular moment—because the second Callum and Nantale disappeared, Tristan strolled into the room, moving slowly, never taking his eyes off Tess. Everything about him was icy, from his pale blond hair to his bone-chilling smile.

"Alone at last," he said quietly.

"Callum will be back any second." Tess's voice came out high and choked.

"You may be right." Tristan approached her, his motions like liquid, footsteps so light she couldn't hear them. "Perhaps I should wait to drink you until we have more time. Can't be sloppy about it."

His voice was quiet, barely more than a whisper—but he was close enough now that Tess could hear every syllable. He inhaled deeply, taking in her scent.

"Musk oil?" He smiled. "Clever. But it won't change the way you taste."

"If you harm me, Nantale will know it." Tess clenched her teeth.

"Do you think?" Tristan cocked his head. "Suppose there's only one way to find out."

His eyes were dark with hunger, and as he smiled, his fangs grew longer, just as Octavia's had back in The Georgia—oh god, should she scream?

But before she had to decide, Callum reappeared in the room, and Tristan was gone so fast it was like he had never been there at all.

"Are you ready?" Callum asked. "Let's go visit a bloody statue."

Chapter 8

MAPPING THE ISLE TO NYC

posted on reddit.com to forum r/BloodFeud

by user GreeneParty

Okay guys, apologies for my photoshop skills, but I *think* this is a definitive map of the Isle??? I looked up every geographic description in the three *Blood Feud* books and cross-referenced them, everything doesn't always match up a hundred percent, but here are the landmarks I'm totally sure about:

- **The forest—Central Park:** Everything on the Isle is centered around the forest. That's where the graveyard is, the milky jade pools where Isobel likes to bathe, the woodlands where a lot of the vampires hunt, etc. This obviously maps to Central Park, which is important because it provides a neutral buffer between the west side (Nantale's territory) and the east side (Felix's territory). Which brings us to:

- **Nantale's compound—Columbus Circle:** It says in the books that Nantale's compound is at the southwestern corner of the forest, so in Manhattan, that would be Columbus Circle.

- **Felix's castle—the Guggenheim Museum:** Felix's castle is on the eastern edge of the forest alongside "the great lake," which I assume corresponds to the Central Park reservoir. Give or take a few blocks, that's exactly where the Guggenheim is, at 88th St. and 5th Ave.

- **The crystal bridge—the Brooklyn Bridge:** Another obvious one! This bridge is near the southern tip of the Isle.

- **The moonflower meadow—East River Park:** The moon-flower meadow is situated along the Isle's southeastern coast, a couple of miles north of the crystal bridge. That's exactly where East River Park is in Manhattan.

- **The northern wilds—Inwood:** The books mention that the northern tip of the Isle is wild and mostly unpopulated, home to a lot of lakes and some notable plant life (like the black jewel-weed lilies Isobel uses as an antidote to her poison daggers). Makes total sense that this would map to the far northern end of Manhattan, which has similar geography.

Okay, I think that's all the major landmarks—did I miss anything? Lmk in the comments and I'll keep updating the map!!

Callum Yoo had only been awake for a few hours, but he already wished this day would fucking end. It was excruciating—inhumane, really—spending every second missing his sister, knowing it was entirely his fault she was gone.

Not gone, he reminded himself. *Dead.* No matter what this human said (or how she'd gotten that scent vial), Callum knew the truth: Octavia wasn't living it up at some posh hotel in New York City. She was a sun-scorched pile of ash blown off the crystal bridge into the churning river below.

Callum glanced over at Tess, who appeared to be having the best day of her life as they took a mundane walk along the western edge of the forest. Erratic, wasn't she? Played it all cool when he came to her room, but was practically shaking with fear after he left her alone for all of two minutes in the compound's entry hall. Now she was gawking at every abandoned mansion they passed, her eyes bright, those annoyingly lush lips parted with wonder.

Callum didn't know why Tess was here or who had sent her, but he had to admit, she didn't seem like much of a threat. Dear god, why was she caressing the bark of a gnarled old tree?

"Birnam Wood," she murmured.

"I think it's an oak, love," he corrected.

"That's not what I mean—Birnam Wood is the forest from *Macbeth*, you know? 'Macbeth shall never vanquished be until Great Birnam Wood to high Dunsinane Hill shall come against him'? It's a real forest in Scotland. It's famous for this massive tree, the Birnam oak. Supposedly Shakespeare was traveling with a band of players and saw it, which partly inspired the play. Anyway, this tree looks just like it."

She was flushed with excitement—Callum hated how pale she was, how easily he could discern the blood moving beneath her skin.

"What are you looking at?" She eyed him with suspicion.

"Nothing," he said lightly. "Just wondering if you worked in a Shakespeare-themed hotel. Give all the guests a little chamber pot, send the luggage to the wrong room to encourage cases of mistaken identity?"

"No." Tess looked down and cleared her throat. "I used to study Shakespeare. I was a PhD student at Columbia."

"Really?" Callum raised an eyebrow. "Have to admit, I never understood the fuss."

"About Shakespeare?" Tess was incredulous. "Seriously?"

"'Shall I compare thee to a summer's day?'" Callum quoted. "Absolute rubbish. What, sticky and full of mosquitoes?"

"That sonnet isn't about summer, it's about mortality," Tess huffed. "But I suppose it's no wonder a vampire wouldn't understand that."

"It's self-important—he's saying *he* gets to be the arbiter of her immortality. Not because of anything she said or did, but because he deigned to write about her beauty."

Tess stopped short, peering at Callum. He was surprised at how much it unnerved him, the way she stared, the naked curiosity.

"What?" he prodded. "You disagree?"

"No, actually. That's exactly what I think too." Tess offered him a small smile—the first time he'd seen her do so. "How do you know the poem so well?"

"Octavia and I had a lot of tutors growing up." Callum shrugged. "Easy to remember the things you hate."

He closed his eyes for a moment, thinking of the endless hours in Konstantin's country manor, Octavia soaking up every bit of knowledge, charming the tutors—charming everyone, really—while all Callum ever wanted to do was get outside and run, hunt, explore the wild countryside that was so utterly different from the smoky streets of London where he'd spent his entire childhood. Everyone loved Octavia. But only Octavia loved Callum.

"So why'd you give up your studies, then?" he asked, trying to force his mind back into the conversation that had distracted him from his grief for all of two minutes. "You left school to work in a hotel?"

"Oh." Tess folded her arms, all evidence of happiness suddenly evaporated. "Just burned out, I guess. You know, academia."

She was clearly finished talking. So now he'd managed to foul up his distraction too—terrific. Luckily, their walk was nearly over: He pointed toward a path up ahead that led into the forest.

"This is the path we take to the graveyard."

Tess pressed her lips together and nodded.

"It's more than likely vampires will be out hunting in the forest," he went on. "It's better if they don't see us at all, and we're only half a mile or so from the graveyard. It'll be much faster if I carry you."

He didn't wait for a reply before he reached for her waist, but she shrunk back in terror, hunching forward and covering her body with her arms.

"Oh, go on, I'm not going to hurt you," he groused. But her whole face had changed, drained of blood, wide-eyed and quivering—she looked even more terrified now than she had in the compound's entry. He felt a sudden need to protect her that he couldn't explain; she wasn't in any danger.

"Hey." His voice was softer, and he approached her slowly. "Really. You don't have to be afraid."

She swallowed and squared her shoulders, her face hardening.

"I'm not afraid," she insisted, though her voice was small. "You just surprised me."

Brave little shit, wasn't she? He extended an arm and waited for her to take his hand. She did so tentatively, and he was overwhelmed by the thrum of her pulse beating in her wrist. He could bring that wrist to his mouth in less than a moment, sink his fangs into her and drink. After a few seconds, she'd even like it—the fear would subside, and she'd give herself over to the pleasure of fuzzy lightheadedness covering her like a warm blanket until she lost consciousness. He imagined her soft body going slack against him, drinking from her pale neck as her head lolled on his shoulder.

"Well?" Tess asked expectantly. He jerked his mind into the present moment.

"Sorry," he muttered. He pulled her toward him, then looped his arm around her waist. Her heart was pounding—he forced himself not to think about the blood whooshing through her body, nor about how soft and warm she felt pressed against him. This would be over quickly. He barely had time to breathe in the scent of her hair—bergamot and violets—before they arrived in the graveyard where Octavia disappeared.

Tess didn't quite have the words to describe how it felt to have Callum carry her half a mile in a matter of seconds. She was still queasy from her encounter with Tristan, and terror had flooded through her when Callum went to grab her without warning. God, she must have looked so stupid to him, so helpless, completely at the mercy of this ornery, judgmental, infuriating creature.

The fact that she *was* completely at his mercy only made this feeling worse.

But then, when she took his hand and he pulled her against him, and she felt the firm grasp of his arms, the broad planes of his chest, he paused for a moment, and she was sure he could feel her heart pounding. She knew she ought to be afraid, but somehow, his hold on her felt safe—even comforting.

Anyway, all that went right out of her head the moment they started moving.

It was like the sound of a machine gun in a movie, except a pounding Tess could feel in her body, the explosive pop of every step Callum took thrumming through her as he sped through the forest so quickly her eyes watered and the trees blurred. When he set her down in the graveyard, her knees buckled and she gasped for breath—she clung to him for a moment so she wouldn't slump to the ground.

"Not your favorite mode of transport?" He smirked at her, and she scowled in return.

"Where's the angel statue?" She stood up straight as her dizziness subsided. The graveyard was large and sprawling; winding paths were shadowed by live oaks draped with Spanish moss, the headstones ancient and crumbling. As a former scholar of the supernatural, Tess usually loved all things old and eerie. But when they presented so many excellent hiding places for creatures who'd drain her blood in an instant if they knew she was human, she wasn't eager to stay here a minute longer than absolutely necessary.

"I think it's in the northeastern part?" Callum scratched at his chin. They scanned the graveyard for a moment, until Callum spotted a pair of wings rising above a headstone. "There."

They approached the statue slowly. It was beautiful and strange, the wings slightly too large to be proportionate to the body, the nose chipped off, the eyes sad and longing, an opening in the trees above positioned just so to cast the angel in a focused beam of silver moonlight.

"Now what?" Callum asked, examining the statue from every angle.

"I'm not sure," Tess admitted. "But I know Octavia was touching the statue when she crossed over—so maybe you have to do that?"

"You honestly expect me to believe that?" Callum pressed. "Eleven years on this island, and all I had to do to leave was touch some bloody statue?"

"If you don't believe me, you don't have to touch it." Tess shrugged.

Callum glared at Tess, then at the statue. He walked over to it, then bowed his head and closed his eyes in a moment that looked almost like prayer. He whispered something Tess couldn't quite catch, but she made out a couple of words: *Octavia* and *please*.

When he opened his eyes, she saw a new expression—his face looked softer, more vulnerable. Tess recognized the mixture of fervent hope and the soul-crushing fear that necessarily accompanies wanting anything so badly. It reminded her of the way she used to look at brochures for Columbia.

He slowly reached out his hands, then laid them on the angel.

They waited for a moment—two—but nothing happened.

"Maybe it's another part of the statue?" Tess suggested.

He put his hands on the angel's face, her head, her body, her wings, her feet, the pedestal below them, moving with increasing urgency and frustration—but each time, nothing happened.

"It's just a fucking statue," he spat, his voice raspy with anger and anguish.

"I'm sorry, Callum." Tess might not enjoy his company, but it was still awful to see anyone so broken.

"It's fine." He set his jaw. "I'm going to hunt. I'll see you back at the compound."

"You can't be serious," Tess sputtered. "You expect me to walk back alone?! You told me it wasn't even safe to walk through the forest with you!"

"Just head straight back and don't talk to anyone," Callum said bluntly. "Think you can manage that?"

She opened her mouth to argue further, but he was gone before she could say a word. She exhaled heavily. Obviously, he'd been uncomfortable to have her witness such a painful moment, and he needed to run away immediately. *Men,* she thought. The same no matter where you found them—or how many centuries old they were.

She looked around the graveyard—spooky, but empty. Annoyingly, Callum seemed right—it shouldn't be that difficult for Tess to get back to the compound from here. She just needed to turn around and head back down the path they'd used to get here until she reached the edge of the forest, which would only take ten minutes or so; then she'd be back in Nantale's territory. If she pushed herself, she could probably be out of here even faster.

She started down the path at a good clip, her ears attuned to any rustle in the leaves that could signal a vampire nearby. She heard a branch snap—was someone there? No—there was nothing. She looked left, then right . . . and then something glimmering in the distance caught her eye.

"What *is* that?" she muttered.

Something was reflecting in the moonlight, pale and minty green, with a shimmering quality that reminded Tess of the lilac waters beneath the crystal bridge. There was a little side path that went straight toward it; it would only take her a few minutes to reach whatever it was. She knew that was a foolish idea, that she should just head back to the compound . . .

But also? Fuck that.

Tess was here, on a magical isle she'd read about for years, and what, she wasn't supposed to explore? To experience any of it for herself? Why? Because someone might kill her? They might do the same in the halls of Nantale's compound—Tristan very nearly had less than an hour ago. So Tess straightened her posture and strode down the side path. She heard the sound of rushing water—she was almost sure she knew what she was about to see—

But her jaw still physically dropped when she saw it.

The milky jade pools were one of Tess's favorite settings in *Blood Feud,* the place where Isobel would sneak away to reflect; supposedly, the waters were a source of everlasting beauty for anyone who bathed there.

"That's easy to believe," Tess murmured.

The water was nearly opaque and palest green—the milky jade color that gave the pools their name. The pools themselves formed a circle, with small waterfalls tumbling over shiny black rocks between them. There was no river to source them—the water came from a natural spring beneath the forest. The ring of pools was surrounded by a grove of weeping cherry trees, graceful boughs laden with soft pink blooms, petals showering into the water with every breeze. It was the most spectacular place Tess had ever seen—and that bar had risen substantially in the past few days.

Tess stayed in the shadows of the trees near the pools for a few minutes, waiting to make sure she was totally alone. But there was no sound, no movement, nothing. So she took off her boots and rolled up her jeans.

Tess gasped when she put her first toe into the water—it was warm and effervescent, pooling around her like the most decadent bubble bath. She'd only meant to wade into the pool, but the water was so delicious, so fizzy with minerals and perfumed with the scent of pink petals, that she couldn't resist stripping off all of her clothes and submerging herself completely.

It was the most amazing feeling, like the water was whispering gentle kisses all over her body. The colors were so beautiful, the breeze so gentle, the water so warm, Tess let out a heady sigh—she felt like she could stay here forever.

"Good, isn't it?"

She froze, panic lacing through her. The man didn't sound threatening—more like mildly amused—but she knew anyone she met on the Isle posed a mortal danger. She looked up, trying to keep her face calm. And there, in the most beautiful place she'd ever been, was the most handsome man she'd ever met.

He wasn't too tall—maybe 5'9" or so? But he was lithe and muscular, with thick golden brown hair that grew past his ears and a face like a Disney prince: straight nose, full lips, bright blue eyes. He was dressed more formally than any of the vampires at Nantale's compound; his billowing white shirt and slim trousers tucked into tall riding boots put Tess in mind of a Jane Austen hero. Something about his face looked familiar—like maybe she'd seen him in an old movie or something? She supposed it was possible; maybe he'd been an actor in one of his many lifetimes.

And she was momentarily too distracted wondering where she'd seen him before to realize she was naked in front of him.

Her hands went automatically to cover her breasts, but he couldn't see them anyway—the water was opaque, and only her head and shoulders were peeking out.

"I didn't mean to startle you." He put out his hands in a gesture of apology. "You just looked so supremely happy, and I thought, it's been a long time since I've seen anyone that joyful on this island."

"It's okay." She cleared her throat and tried to smile. "I've never been here before. It's overwhelming."

The man peered at her. "You've lived here eleven years, and you've never been to these pools?"

Shit shit shit shit shit.

"Oh, um. I mostly stay up north," Tess said quickly, remembering Sylvie's story. "I was only turned a few weeks before we came here, and with all the fighting . . . I just figured it'd be safer."

"That explains why I've never seen you." He took a step toward her. "I thought I knew every face on this island. And I certainly wouldn't have forgotten yours."

He knelt beside the pool. He was still ten feet away, but she started to feel nervous. Would the musk oil be enough to mask her human smell, or had the pools washed it away? Then again, hunting dogs couldn't track their prey in water, right? She was almost certain she'd read that somewhere. Were vampires the same?

"I don't mean to impede on your solitude," he went on. "Would you mind terribly if I joined you?"

"Oh." Tess flushed. "I'm not sure—"

"I'll bathe in another pool, of course." He looked at her earnestly. "But only if it's all right with you."

"I guess that's okay," Tess agreed. "I'll give you some privacy."

She didn't like to turn her back on him, but she supposed he could kill her just as easily whether she was looking or not. She heard the rustle of fabric, then a splash as he sank into the water.

"Ohh, it's as good as I remembered," he groaned, and Tess turned back to face him. He looked even better soaking wet—not to mention shirtless.

"Has it been a long time since you've bathed here?" she asked.

"It has." He waded toward her, the water rippling around his shoulders. "Will you tell me more about yourself? It's been so long since I've met someone new."

"Oh, me?" Tess flushed, her nerves churning. She'd already said one wrong thing; she wasn't sure she'd survive another. "I'm not very interesting."

"You said you've been up north—have you been there this whole time? Living with others?"

"No, just me," Tess answered. "I was afraid, you know? I'm so young compared to all of you, and obviously very weak. I probably shouldn't be telling you that."

He tilted his head with concern. "I'm not going to hurt you. I know some vampires on this island like to prey on the defenseless, but I'm not one of them."

"Oh." Tess nodded. "If you say so."

"Besides, it can't have been easy, being alone all these years, no one to turn to for comfort in your darkest moments," he said softly. "You don't seem weak to me."

"No," Tess agreed, her voice tight. "It hasn't been easy at all."

"So why are you here?" he asked. "I mean, why come to this part of the Isle? Why now?"

"Some vampires found me—a hunting party, from Nantale's clan." Tess regurgitated the rest of Sylvie's story. "They said they'd protect me if I came to live with them. And after all this time . . . I didn't know how much longer I could really stand being on my own. I thought it was worth a try."

His face darkened. "You're living with Nantale?"

"Yes." Tess frowned. "Why?"

"How have they treated you?" he demanded. "Have any of them tried to harm you?"

"No, nothing like that," she assured him—though she was quite sure Tristan *would* harm her given the opportunity.

"Not even Callum Yoo?" The man folded his arms. "I'm sorry, please tell me if I'm overstepping—it's just that I've known that clan a long time, and they're not to be trusted."

"Not at all, you're kind to be concerned. Callum . . ." Tess paused, trying to figure out how to word it. "Honestly, he's mostly just annoyed that there's someone new around. I think he'd rather not speak to me at all if he can avoid it."

"Really? That doesn't sound like Callum."

"Why not?" Tess was puzzled. "Is he usually super friendly or something?"

"No," the man said bluntly. "I don't know—I just don't like the idea of you being with such a dangerous clan after all that time alone. Would you like to stay with my clan instead? We have plenty of room in our palace, and you'd be very welcome."

"Live with you?" Tess laughed. "I don't even know your name."

He shook his head and laughed too. "Of course, you're right. I'm Felix Hawthorn."

Tess dug her nails into her palms under the water—so *that's* why she'd recognized this man, she'd spent hours of her life looking at blurry old photos of his face on fucking Tumblr! Oh god, she was naked in a foaming hot spring not ten feet away from her number one literary crush of all time?! She started to feel lightheaded, and she didn't think it had anything to do with the temperature of the pools.

"I'm Tess Rosenbloom," she replied.

"Pleasure to meet you, Tess." He bowed his head politely. "So, that's enough acquaintance, right? You're ready to move in with me?"

She laughed, and he seemed delighted by the sound.

"You'd love living with my clan," he went on. "Everyone looks after one another, and we throw a ball every full moon. It's a Venetian masque this month, you must join us."

"It's a very nice offer." Tess smiled. "I'll think about it, okay? Where can I find you?"

"Our palace is on the eastern edge of the forest, just alongside the great lake—I'll give the guards your name, come visit anytime. It's beautiful on that side of the forest. Have you been?"

Tess shook her head. "I haven't really seen anything. I've only been down here a few weeks."

"Then we must explore together!" Felix suggested. "You have to see the crystal bridge—and the moonflower meadow! It's exquisitely beautiful, of course, but it's also one of the most powerfully magical places on the Isle."

"How do you mean?" Tess frowned—she'd never read anything in *Blood Feud* about some parts of the Isle being more powerful than others.

"Some places on the Isle just have more magic." Felix shrugged. "A great deal of the Isle's power emanates from this forest—that's why the clans built our homes so close to it. If you were to get farther away—say, very far to the north—you'd have a harder time enacting your glamours. That's why so few vampires live up there. Excepting you, of course."

"I didn't know that." Tess shook her head in wonder. "So this forest has a lot of magic?"

Felix nodded. "Did you see the graveyard just on the other side of those trees?"

"Yes, I was just there."

"That's the epicenter of the forest's power. It's one of the reasons these pools are so . . ."

"Intense?" Tess offered.

"Yes," he agreed. "That's exactly the word for it."

She gazed into his eyes—were they such a vivid shade of blue because he was a vampire, or had they been like that in life as well?

"Wait," she said, a realization dawning. "Is the graveyard the most powerfully magical place on the entire island?"

"Actually, the moonflower meadow is even more acute—because its power isn't diffused over a forest, it's concentrated in a much smaller space."

"Wow." Tess breathed. "I'd love to see it."

An idea was starting to form in Tess's mind—if the graveyard was a center of magical power, could that be the reason Octavia was able to cross back to New York from there? And if the moonflower meadow held an even stronger power, was it possible that could be harnessed to create another portal?

"I could take you there now, if you'd like?"

He was standing next to the natural stone barrier that separated his pool from hers—as close as he could get to her without crossing it. She knew she shouldn't move toward him, but her body seemed to be drifting of its own volition, the current pushing her nearer . . .

"I can't," she said quietly. "I should be getting back."

"Okay." He leaned toward her, resting his arms on the stones between them. "Another time."

"Soon, I hope."

"Can I . . ." He hesitated. "Would it be an imposition if I told you something personal?"

"Not at all," Tess breathed.

"It's just—when you asked me if I bathe here often. I actually haven't been here in years, since my lover died. This was one of her favorite places on the island."

"I'm so sorry," Tess murmured, her mind flashing instantly to Isobel's shocking death scene. Tess didn't need Felix to tell her about it. She'd read it dozens of times.

"Thank you." Felix nodded. "It's strange, isn't it? The night I finally come here just happens to be your first time at these pools. It reminds me of Virgil: 'Wherever the fates lead us, let us follow.'"

Tess smiled, remembering Flora's complaint about Felix quoting poetry instead of choosing a restaurant. She had to admit, it didn't seem so bad to her.

"'Our remedies oft in ourselves do lie, which we ascribe to heaven: the fated sky,'" Tess replied.

"Shakespeare!" Felix's eyes lit up. "So you don't believe in fate? You think us meeting here is just coincidence?"

"I'm not honestly sure." Tess laughed. "But if it's a coincidence, it's a happy one."

Felix gazed at her, but then his face turned more serious. "Promise me you'll look out for yourself back at Nantale's? Stay safe?"

"I'll do my best," Tess promised.

"Good." He smiled. "Because I'd really like to see you again."

Chapter 9

Joni [7:23 AM]: TESS TESS OH MY GOD TESS

Joni [7:24 AM]: Okay so I understand that you're probably not getting these because you're on an island in another dimension and whatnot But JUST IN CASE here is the deal:

Joni [7:26 AM]: I went to your hotel last night to try to talk to you and INSTEAD I met OCTAVIA FREAKING YOO and we HUNG OUT and she told me EVERYTHING well maybe not like everything everything, she was reallll glib and did not care for my questions, but I feel like I have a pretty basic understanding of what's going on.

Joni [7:28 AM]: ps she's ridiculously hot??? Idk what I expected but truly wow

Joni [7:29 AM]: Anyway, I'm just leaving the hotel now, I'm gonna go home and crash and then meet back up with Octavia tonight. I want to take her to Central Park to check out the spot where she crossed over, see if anything weird happens!! Maybe we'll be able to communicate with you somehow??

Joni [7:31 AM]: (And for the record, she's worried you might be dead. Well, not worried, exactly, but she lists it as a thing that could possibly be true. But I don't. Because I can't. Please don't be dead, okay? I need you to come home so I can yell at you about my birthday.)

✌

"What in the name of god is all of this?" Octavia guffawed.

She wasn't surprised to see Joni wearing sweatpants, a plain tee, and rubber Birkenstocks—in Octavia's experience, most humans lacked even a modicum of shame. But the girl was carrying a huge backpack plus a couple of shopping bags, and Octavia couldn't begin to fathom why.

"I had an idea about how to find the portal that got you off the Isle!" Joni said brightly.

"You understand I spent years researching that very topic to no avail?" Octavia sniffed. "I've delved further into interdimensional portal theory than you could possibly grasp. Magical history, physics, geography—"

"Totally—it says so in *Blood Feud*." Joni nodded. "But you were kind of flying blind, right? I mean, all that research was theoretical, you didn't have any hard data points to work with. But now we do—we know where you crossed over. So I was thinking maybe we could spend the night at Bethesda Fountain? See if the portal that brought you here is some kind of nightly recurring thing?"

Octavia peered at Joni—she hadn't imagined the girl was capable of this much rational thought.

"Fine," Octavia conceded. "I suppose that's not a terrible idea."

"Yeah? Okay great! And I brought provisions!" Joni nodded toward her shopping bags. "I have snacks, games, an iPad loaded with vampire movies—sorry, is that too on the nose?"

"And the backpack?" Octavia asked, already weary.

"Pillows and sleeping bags! I know you're nocturnal, but I'm not, and anyway it's always nice to be cozy."

"You think I'm getting into a sleeping bag in a public park," Octavia deadpanned. "This dress is MINJUKIM."

"Your body, your choice." Joni shrugged. "Should we head to the subway?"

"Subway?" Octavia's shoulders sank. "Surely you have one of those apps to order a black car?"

"Are you serious? An Uber Black to Manhattan would be a hundred bucks at least. The subway costs three dollars and will probably be faster."

"But . . . you attend an Ivy League school. I assumed you'd have . . ."

"Money?" Joni snorted. "Dude, I'm a grad student. I bet your dress costs more than I make in a month. Come on, we're burning moonlight. Let's go!"

Octavia sighed heavily. Would the indignities of her current situation never cease?

They took the L to the C to the Upper West Side, and the whole way Joni prattled about portals and *Blood Feud* and how cool it would be to find a secret route to the Isle.

"Of course, there's always a chance the portal correlates with the cycle of the moon or the placement of Cassiopeia in the sky or whatever. I bet we can figure out if there were any big planetary movements the night you crossed over on the Chani app."

"The what?"

"Omg, Chani is my favorite astrologer!" Joni exclaimed. "Hey, when's your birthday?"

"June fifth," Octavia answered dryly.

"Shut the fuck up, twins born in Gemini?" Joni squealed. "No wonder you love fashion. And gossip. And Callum's personality turns on a dime, this all makes so much sense."

"I beg you to stop talking," Octavia muttered, but she knew there was very little chance of Joni's compliance.

It was fully dark by the time they walked out of the subway at 72nd and Central Park West, across from the Dakota and Strawberry Fields. Octavia hadn't been to this neighborhood since she'd come back from the Isle, and she felt a distinct unease as soon as she and Joni stepped into the warm night air. This was the area where she'd spent most of her time on the Isle, west of the forest where she and Callum and the rest of Nantale's clan protected the territory. Being here in Manhattan, the grid of the streets the same but the contents completely different, the endless mundanity of the buildings and cabs and pedestrians, filled Octavia with the strangest sense of déjà vu. It was the same, but it wasn't. The Isle was real, but it wasn't.

"Did you spend a lot of time in the forest?" Joni asked. "On the Isle, I mean."

"Not really. Callum did—he was always spoiling for a fight. But I tried to avoid the violence as best I could. I didn't want to die in that place."

"The books made it seem like you hated it there."

"That's an understatement," Octavia said bitterly. "Years feeling like a rat trapped in a cage, researching any possible way to get out of there, but nothing worked. I got so desperate, it started to feel . . ."

She trailed off.

"Feel like what?" Joni prompted.

"It doesn't matter," Octavia clipped. "Let's just get to the fountain."

It was a beautiful night, warm but not too humid, with a bit of a breeze; it only took about ten minutes to get to Bethesda Fountain. Octavia felt tense as the hulking angel statue came into view. She was flooded with the memory of arriving here, the confusion, gasping for air, not understanding what had happened, the realization she'd lost her powers, that she was totally alone—

"Hey, are you okay?" Joni asked. Octavia hadn't even realized she'd stopped walking. Joni was so earnest, eyes brimming with concern, so overloaded with her stupid backpack and grocery bags. It was all a little touching, really. Octavia didn't care for it.

"I'm fine," Octavia said smoothly. "Where did you want to sit?"

"Oh, over on one of these benches?" Joni led Octavia to an L-shaped seating area carved into a corner of stone. She took the sleeping bags out of her backpack and started to lay them out on the two benches—

"I told you, I am *not* getting inside one of those," Octavia insisted.

"It's just for a little cushion! But if you'd rather be uncomfortable, suit yourself."

"Oh, I see." Octavia walked over to the bench and gave the sleeping bag a little pat, like she was testing a mattress in a store. "That's very thoughtful."

She sat, grateful not just for the softness, but also to have something between her lovely new clothes and whatever grime existed on that bench. Joni pulled a thermos out of one of her grocery bags, along with a couple of plastic cups.

"Do you want some wine?" she asked.

"I don't know. How much did it cost?"

"Man, you really are a snob." Joni smiled good-naturedly. "Not much, but it's really good—it's a fizzy red from Languedoc, kinda fresh, kinda messy? Try it."

Joni handed Octavia her wine; they clinked cups and took a sip. The wine was lovely—juicy and tart on Octavia's palate, bright and herbaceous with an undercurrent of something darker. It tasted like being in France, moody and alive.

"Good, right?" Joni was grinning at Octavia's obviously positive reaction.

"It is." Octavia rewarded the girl with the barest hint of a smile. "I like it quite a bit."

"I love a sparkling red, how they get all frothy in the glass, kinda makes me feel like I'm a vampire." Joni laughed. "Not that it's the same as blood, obviously—oh shit, are you hungry? Should I have like gone to a blood bank or a butcher or something? I'm not really familiar with vampire etiquette."

"I'm perfectly capable of securing my own meals, thanks." Octavia gave Joni a pointed look and took another sip of wine.

"Oh. Does that mean, like—are you expecting that *we*, I mean—"

Octavia looked at the poor bumbling girl and repressed a smile. She considered toying with her a bit, letting Joni think Octavia really did plan on drinking her blood. And come to think of it, she was so young, so eager, she'd probably let Octavia feed, and it would probably be delicious . . .

"No." Octavia cleared her throat. "You're helping me, and I don't feed on people I plan to see again."

"Really?" Joni looked surprised. "I thought that feeding was like . . . intimate?"

"It can be." Octavia shrugged. "Some vampires choose to have close relationships with humans, and feeding can factor in to that. But I've never seen the point. I never stay in one place long, humans age and I don't, they have needs I can't meet and vice versa."

"Couldn't you make a human into a vampire though? Like not even for romantic reasons, just if you liked them and cared about them and wanted them to stick around?"

"No," Octavia said flatly. "Callum and I don't sire new vampires."

"I'm sorry." Joni sat back against the bench. "I didn't mean to upset you."

"You didn't." Octavia forced her tone into something lighter. "It's just that we didn't have a choice in becoming vampires, and our sire was . . ."

"Konstantin." Joni finished the sentence.

"Those damn books," Octavia muttered. "You probably know more about my life than I do."

"No, come on," Joni demurred. "First of all, the books only

cover six years on the Isle, and you've been alive for more than a century. And second, they're just one author's opinion about you, not the totality of who you are."

"One author whose work you've read over, and over, and over—"

"They're really good books!" Joni gave an exasperated little sigh, and Octavia felt a twist of pleasure at having riled her.

"Who's your favorite character?" Octavia asked with genuine curiosity. "Don't say me, I'll know you're lying."

Joni flushed red. "Ugh, it *is* you."

"No, it's not," Octavia needled.

"It is!" Joni protested. "I even wrote a damn paper about you. It helped form the foundation of my dissertation about feminine qualities in hero archetypes."

"Really?" Octavia raised an eyebrow. "What did you write about me?"

Joni looked excited, but also a little embarrassed. "How you have these very feminine markers, namely the focus on fashion. But how that doesn't deter from your strength at all? Like just because you wanted to wear an ostrich feather minidress didn't mean you wouldn't kick the shit out of some guy while wearing it, you know?"

Octavia smiled—she remembered the dress in question. She'd glamoured it for herself on the Isle, inspired by a Saint Laurent mini with a feathered bust and a scalloped hem that she'd once bought in Milan. She'd been stuck wearing it when Callum got them into a drunken brawl with a few of Felix's henchmen—as she recalled, she'd kicked her stiletto heel directly through one of their eyes.

Octavia looked at Joni with interest. "What else did you write?"

"I thought it was interesting that the books frame you as a villain." Joni looked a little uncomfortable. "And I wrote about how often that happens with strong feminine characters, dating back to Medusa, and even farther than that. The idea that you would take such pleasure in your femininity, and that even the way you dress is for you, and not to please men—"

"Obviously not, who cares what men think?" Octavia interjected.

"Exactly!" Joni grinned. "The whole idea of a 'hero' is so complicated, because heroes put other people before themselves, which is actually a very feminine quality. But heroes are usually men who wouldn't be able to pull off their heroic feats if it weren't for the support and sacrifices of women. And when a woman prioritizes herself in that way, she tends to be portrayed as a villain. So if you're a woman reader who's interested in strong female characters . . ."

"You tend to get stuck rooting for the villain," Octavia completed the thought.

"Not just rooting for." Joni leaned in. "But like, identifying with. If you don't want to organize your whole life around ending up with some man, rooting for the villain is the only way you can aspire to have that much power, that kind of independence."

Octavia swallowed a long drink of wine, letting the fine bubbles prickle on her tongue and down her throat. "Then you must find the real me terribly disappointing."

"What?!" Joni almost spilled her wine. "Why?"

"Because here I am, utterly powerless without my brother." She drained her wine and set down the empty cup. "Ironic, no?"

"You're not powerless." Joni's voice was low, but her tone was firm. "You showed up in the middle of New York City with no money, no friends, no ability to be outside during daylight, and within two weeks you're living in a posh hotel suite with a wardrobe Carrie Bradshaw would kill for? You're a fucking force of nature."

Octavia gazed at Joni. She was so passionate, so sweetly intense, with her wide eyes and thick dark hair. It would be stupid to kiss her. As much as Octavia hated to admit it, she needed Joni's help, and there was nothing more self-destructive than getting romantically involved with someone you actually needed. Still, Octavia was tempted by the idea of pulling her close, kissing just the right spot between her jaw and her ear that would make her writhe in Octavia's arms, taking her back to the hotel—

"Oh shit," Joni muttered. She was looking at an email on her phone.

Octavia cleared her throat. "Did something happen?"

"No, our department chair just called a meeting for tomorrow morning. I would skip it, except I'm applying for this job, and everyone on the hiring committee will be there. I don't want to look irresponsible, you know? My interview is next week."

A job interview. Octavia smiled. How totally pedestrian. How utterly human.

"And you're worried that if you stay out here with me all night, you'll be exhausted and they'll notice?"

"Oh." Joni flushed. "Yeah, kinda?"

Octavia waved her hand. "You should absolutely go home and get some sleep. I'm sure a police officer or two will come through after the park closes, they'll be easier to handle if you're not here."

"I'm so stupid, I didn't even think of that." Joni looked worried. "Are you sure?"

"Of course. I'll just hide if I feel like it, or have a little snack if I don't." She grinned. "I'm a force of nature, remember?"

"Okay, but I'm leaving you one of the sleeping bags. And the wine. Ooh, and the iPad! You can watch *Buffy*!"

"I don't want to watch *Buffy*—" Octavia started, but Joni was having none of it.

"You absolutely do. Oh my god, start with 'The Wish,' you're going to love Vampire Willow. And Cordelia! And Anya! And obviously if you see the portal, don't worry about the stuff, and I'll come to the hotel tomorrow to hear what happened?? Okay, have fun, bye!!"

Octavia watched as Joni scurried off. She poured herself some more wine and opened the iPad—if she was going to sit here alone all night staring at a fountain, she supposed she might as well have some entertainment to pass the time. As the hard-rock theme song of *Buffy the Vampire Slayer* emanated from the device's tinny speakers, Octavia made a promise to herself that she would go out and find a woman to fuck tomorrow night. It had been too long—she must be terribly hard up if she was fantasizing about Joni.

Chapter 10

Excerpt from *Blood Feud*
(book three, chapter fifty-four)
by August Lirio

allum glared at Isobel, his eyes cold with fury.

"Do you think I don't know?" he spat.

"Know what?" Isobel tried to keep her tone casual, but she was inwardly quaking with fear.

"About your betrayal." He grabbed her dress and yanked her close—even through her terror, she could sense desire pulsing through him, and she felt her own respond in kind.

"You know every detail of my betrayal." She snaked her arms around his neck, and though his skin was icy as always, his breath was hot. "Because you've been here for every second of it."

He kissed her deeply, pressing his body against hers, and she cried out with pleasure from the feel of him, the endless torment of wanting him so badly—no matter how much he gave her, she always wanted more. He dragged his fingers through her hair, twisting it into a rope at the base of her skull, pulling her head backward to expose her neck.

"Yes," she breathed. She wanted to feel his mouth against her skin, to give herself over to his most savage desires. But he just leaned in and whispered in her ear . . .

"I don't mean your betrayal of Felix," he snarled. "I mean your betrayal of me."

Isobel went absolutely still. It wasn't possible. There was no way he could know that she was the one who'd overheard his plans and shared them with Felix, who'd sentenced his clan to a humiliating and bloody defeat in their latest battle. She'd been so careful to cover her tracks, to tell Callum it was Felix himself who'd overheard Callum and Nantale discussing strategy in the forest. Callum had seemed to believe her at the time . . . but the way he was looking at her now, she knew she'd been a fool. He knew the truth, and he was going to punish her for it.

"Please," she whispered. "Callum, I do care for you, really—"

"I don't need you to care for me." He pulled her hair tighter. "This thing with us—it isn't *love*. I've never needed that from you—I've certainly never asked you for it. But ten members of my clan are dead because of you. What would you do if the situation was reversed, Isobel? What would you do if your friends were dead because of me?"

"My friends *are* dead because of you!" Isobel snapped. "How many members of my clan have you killed, ripped apart with your bare hands?"

"Didn't stop you from getting into my bed," Callum growled. "Where, as I recall, you had no complaints about what I can do with my hands."

He kept her hair firmly gripped in one hand, then ran the other down her side, moving it dangerously close to her center.

"Do you regret me?" she asked him. "Because I don't regret you. Even with the deaths. Even with the betrayal. I would do it all again, because it felt so fucking good."

"Sweet Isobel," he exhaled, and he wrapped his arms around her, pulling her close. She sighed into his embrace, a sigh of deep relief—for how good it felt to have his body pressed against hers, for how lucky she was to be able to live one more day while double-crossing the two most powerful men on this island.

"I don't regret you." He kissed her softly. "But I also don't regret this."

And then, without warning or ceremony, Callum Yoo snapped Isobel's neck so hard that her head broke clean off her body, ending her immortal life for good.

It took Callum hours of hunting to shake off the feelings of anger and humiliation that lingered on his skin like a palpable stench after his outing to the graveyard with Tess. Usually, hunting was when he felt most himself: attuned to every sound and movement, the thrill of stalking his prey, the indulgence of sinking his fangs into a living creature's neck, feeling the fresh blood slide down his throat and course through his body with a fizzy, powerful sensation. But today, everything felt fucking wrong.

He couldn't shake how *stupid* he'd felt laying his hands on that damn statue. As if Octavia were playing some kind of joke, laughing at his expense from wherever she was. Back in New York, as Tess claimed? Maybe, though Callum doubted it. It struck him as a bit too convenient that the sister he missed so desperately would send a messenger to his doorstep, especially considering how badly they'd parted.

He didn't want to think about that—not the fight that had driven his sister away, not the fact that she was probably dead, not the human who'd arrived out of nowhere to toy with his hopes, and certainly not the sweet fragrance of that human's auburn hair. He just wanted to hunt the fastest animals the Isle had to offer. But no matter how many hares streaking through the forest Callum caught and sank his teeth into, he didn't feel satisfied.

By the time he stalked back into Nantale's compound, hours after leaving Tess in the graveyard, he was exhausted, vexed, and in absolutely no mood to see anyone. But Nantale had instructed him to report back the instant he returned, and his loyalty to her ran deeper than his foul mood.

"So?" Nantale looked up from her desk as he trudged through the door to her private chambers. "How did it go?"

Nantale kept her rooms simple—wooden furniture, clay walls—in stark contrast to the rest of the compound's grandeur. She said they reminded her of her childhood, of home. Nantale rarely allowed anyone into her rooms, and Callum never took the privilege of being invited for granted.

"My liege, it wasn't good." He poured himself a glass of whiskey from one of her bottles. "We went to the graveyard, I put my hands all over a statue like a fucking idiot, absolutely nothing happened, and we're no closer to getting off this island than we were two days ago. Cheers."

He drained the glass and poured himself another.

"Slow down." Nantale put a hand on his arm.

"What for?" He shrugged her off. "Why are you so keen for me to have hope?"

"Why are *you* so keen to refuse?" She narrowed her eyes. "It was your hope that brought this clan together in the first place. Your hope that saved my life. And now, when there's an actual *reason* for hope, you want to ignore it?"

"I didn't save your life," Callum grumbled.

"Felix and his goons would have killed all of us who refused to join his idiotic vampire hierarchy if we'd stayed living on our own," she chided. "You convinced me to form this clan, and you convinced the others to follow me."

"Not like I had much choice." He took another swig. "It was that or wait around for the day when Felix finally got his wish to kill my sister and me, wasn't it?"

"That is the part I do not understand," Nantale said. "I have known you for decades, and in all that time, your motivation to protect your sister has been the single most predictable element of your character. Until yesterday. When a human arrived bearing a message from Octavia, whom we have all presumed dead for days, instead of leaving your grief in elation, you chose to sink further down. Why? Do you really believe the girl is lying?"

Nantale looked at Callum with her piercing gaze. Even in a simple cotton robe and head wrap, sitting perfectly calmly, the woman was downright terrifying.

"Maybe."

"And what cause would she have to risk her life to lie to you? To me?"

"She's human." Callum closed his eyes. "Who knows why these desperate mortals do what they do?"

Nantale gestured for Callum to take the seat opposite hers.

"Before the girl arrived, what did you think had happened to Octavia?"

"I thought . . ." Callum sank into the chair. "I thought she'd finally had enough. She told me she had. I tried to stop her, but she wouldn't listen."

"She was depressed for a long time," Nantale said gently.

"And I couldn't do a damn thing to fix it." Callum shoved away his empty glass. "I would have given my arm to get her off this island, but I couldn't, could I? I couldn't save the one person I cared about most, and now you think I'm this clan's bloody salvation? Sounds a bit deluded, doesn't it?"

"Perhaps. Then again, perhaps your sister is trapped in New York, waiting for you to help her while you throw a tantrum instead."

"Trapped?" Callum laughed. "She's not trapped—she's free."

"You don't think she feels as bereft without you as you do without her?" Nantale raised an eyebrow.

Callum stared at the bottom of his whiskey glass. Even if what Tess said was true, and Octavia really was alive and well in New

York . . . Callum didn't see why she should want him there. In fact, he was pretty sure she was better off without him.

Callum stood. "Look, I appreciate the pep talk, but the only idea the girl had was to go to the graveyard. Seeing as that didn't work, I think we're about done with this adventure, don't you?"

Nantale looked at Callum for a long moment, then turned back to the papers on her desk.

"You are finished with this 'adventure' when I say so. And not one second before."

After he left Nantale's quarters, Callum was truly looking forward to getting back to his rooms and taking a long, hot shower. He wanted nothing more than to rinse off the dirt and sweat of his hunt, the endless frustration of this stupid, interminable day.

Until he found Tess waiting outside his door.

"Why am I not surprised?" he muttered. Clearly *she'd* had time to shower—she was wearing cozy sweats and her eyes were bright with excitement.

"Good, you're here!" She stepped aside to let him open the door. "We have so much to talk about—"

"Haven't we talked enough for one day?" He pushed past her into his rooms, which he'd fashioned after his memories of Konstantin's London townhouse: dark, creaky wood-paneled rooms glowing with warm fires and stuffed with books and curios.

"Seriously?" Tess followed him inside without waiting for an invitation. "You ditched *me* in the middle of a forest filled with deadly vampires, and you want to act like you're the one who has the right to be annoyed right now?"

"I don't know about the right, but I do know about the annoyance," Callum quipped. "Do you want a drink?"

"No, thank you," she said quickly, her body tensing.

"Do you not drink?" He peered at her.

"I do drink, I just don't want a drink right now. I want to talk about—"

"What?" Callum flopped down into a leather armchair. "Another brilliant theory from the world's leading Isle expert who's been here all of thirty-six hours? That graveyard idea worked out so well, I just can't *wait* to hear about our next escapade."

"Does this get you a lot of friends, usually?" Tess waved her hand in his general direction. "This whole snide sarcasm thing, do people find it charming?"

"Why, did you want me to try to charm you? Sounds a lot more fun than feeling up some bloody statue, I'll give you that."

"No! I just—ugh! You're so—"

He couldn't conceal how much he enjoyed watching her squirm. The way her face flushed, how hard she tried not to ball up her little fists—honestly, it was the best part of his day.

"All right, all right, out with it then." He'd better put the poor thing out of her misery. "What's your grand idea?"

"I think we should go to the moonflower meadow."

Great, another of Octavia's favorite places. This girl really knew how to twist a knife.

"Why would we go there?" he asked gruffly. "Where did you even hear about it?"

"Sylvie told me," Tess said hurriedly. "She said it's a source of magic on the Isle—maybe even more powerful than the graveyard in the forest. What if Octavia's crossing wasn't about the statue—what if it was about accessing that magic?"

"That's brilliant," Callum jeered. "Or at least, it would be if we had the first fucking idea of *how* to harness that magic."

"What about desire?" Tess asked.

"Now you're on to my area of expertise," Callum teased, and Tess rolled her eyes.

"No, I mean—portals. I met a portal witch at Bar Between, and she told me creating portals was all about desire. Being in one place, needing to be in another. Maybe Octavia's desire to get off the Isle was so strong, and she was experiencing it in such a specifically magically powerful place, that she was able to create the portal? Even though she didn't know it? So if the moonflower meadow is even more powerful than the graveyard, maybe your desire to get back to your sister combined with the magic there would be enough."

He thought about what Nantale had said—about having hope, about how much Octavia needed him. Unfortunately, none of it was enough to supersede the fact that everything Tess was saying was really, really stupid.

"Mate, do you honestly think this is like a children's story and fairy dust? Just think lovely thoughts, and you'll be able to fly?"

Her face fell. "I don't hear you offering any better ideas."

"Because there aren't any better ideas." He exhaled with frustration. "My sister spent *years* trying to figure out how to get out of here and got absolutely nowhere—"

"That's not true!" Tess interjected. "She got back to New York, she's there right now—"

"Says you!" Callum thundered.

"Is that why you don't want to go to the moonflower meadow?" Tess pressed. "Because you don't believe me?"

"There's a difference between disbelieving you and thinking your ideas are a waste of time," Callum explained. "In this case, it's both."

"It's like you don't even *want* to leave the Isle," Tess snapped. "Don't you want to see your sister again? She's all alone, she doesn't have her powers—"

"What?" Callum interrupted. "She doesn't?"

"Oh." Tess stopped, apologetic. "Sorry, I should have said. Since she got back to New York, she can't glamour anymore, and her strength and speed are mostly gone too. So she's just kind of stuck there, you know? She thinks it's because her power is tied to you, and you've never been so far apart."

"And that's why she wants me back in New York." Callum sighed, everything making sense for the first time since this girl appeared. "Not because she misses her dear old brother."

"What? No," Tess pushed back. "She misses you badly, she told me—"

"Cleverer people than you have fallen victim to my sister's lies, believe me," Callum said, rising to usher Tess out of the room. "I think it's time you stop speculating on matters you don't understand, and time for both of us to abandon this inane little group project Nantale assigned us."

"Are you serious?" Tess snapped. "You're just going to give up on escaping the Isle? What about everyone else?"

"What about them?" Callum asked.

"Sylvie has grandchildren back home—alive, human grandchildren who miss her! And I thought Nantale was your friend? But I guess that doesn't matter to you at all. God. No wonder you're the fucking villain."

"What?" Callum turned to Tess. "What does that mean?"

"Nothing." Tess shook her head. "Just . . . Octavia made it sound like you would care that she needed you. But I guess she was wrong about you. I wish I could say I was surprised."

With that, Tess turned and flounced out of the room, finally leaving Callum alone with the silence he'd been craving for the last hour. Except now, he found it didn't sit quite as well as he had hoped.

❧

Tess stormed down the hall toward her bedroom. What had she been *thinking,* coming to this place to help Callum Yoo of all people? Did she imagine she'd be welcomed as some kind of rescuer princess, showered with gifts and praise? No, of course not! But Felix had seemed genuinely concerned for Tess's well-being within minutes of meeting her—was it entirely unreasonable to expect Callum might be at least a *little* bit thankful that Tess was risking her life to help him? That after eleven years trapped on this island, when she arrived with news that he might be able to get back home, he might not be boozy and mean, pretending not to care about anything when it was so deeply obvious how badly he missed his sister?

I wonder if he misses Octavia as much as I miss Joni.

The thought flashed through Tess's mind, but she shoved it quickly away—the situations weren't remotely the same. Tess moved out of the apartment to *protect* Joni, to make sure Tess's ruined life didn't poison Joni's too. Octavia needed Callum, was powerless without him, and he was refusing to find a way back to her because he was . . . what? Scared? Selfish? Obstinate? An infuriating combination of all three?

Tess thought back to the tarot card Flora had given her, the instruction to rescue herself. She supposed she could go to the moonflower meadow on her own, maybe find something to prove to stupid Callum that she did have value here. But the moonflower meadow was miles away—how could Tess get there without help? It's not like she had a car, or the subway, or—

"Hey!"

She looked up—she'd almost plowed straight into Antoinette and Angelique, who were both dressed in full equestrian regalia: tall boots, dark tights, and velvet jackets, their hair twisted back in elaborate braids, riding crops in their hands.

"Watch where you're going." Angelique sniffed.

"God, humans are so annoying," Antoinette agreed.

"Especially when you can't feed on them." Angelique gazed longingly at Tess.

"Sorry, I didn't see you," Tess mumbled, backing away. It was unclear whether the pair was more terrifying because they were deadly vampires or because they were just really mean teenagers.

"Obviously." Angelique rolled her eyes.

"Where did you get those clothes?" Antoinette giggled, and the two walked off down the hall, arm in arm, clearly laughing at Tess.

As if this day could get any worse.

Except—wait a minute. They were both in riding gear. Did that mean this place had horses?

• • •

It turned out the compound had two horses and two ponies, all kept in a small stable on the grounds next to a meadow where they could roam and feed. After Tess slept for a few hours, she put on leggings, a warm sweater, and another generous douse of Nantale's musk oil. It only took her about twenty minutes of exploring to find the stable, and she was grateful not to run into any vampires along the way. Tess didn't ride with any regularity growing up, but her family did spend a month on some distant cousin's ranch one summer when Tess was ten or eleven. One of the stable grooms was kind to Tess and gave her a few riding lessons; she was sure she could manage a simple journey.

The compound's stable lay just outside one of the side entrances: It was small and practical, a simple wooden structure with four horse stalls, each labeled with the horses' names. The first stall, labeled BESSIE, had a door that went all the way up to the ceiling, and Tess could hear snorting and stomping behind it.

"Absolutely not," Tess muttered. The second two stalls, labeled SALOME and SERAPHINA, had traditional half-doors and held two nearly identical pretty white ponies with elaborately curled hair— Tess was certain these two belonged to Antoinette and Angelique, and they looked just as mean and devious as the girls who rode them. Another no.

So Tess moved on to the fourth and final stall, which was labeled ARISTOTLE—but the nickname "Artie" was scrawled in white chalk below it. Artie exhaled softly as he padded over to the edge of the stall to see who'd come to visit; he was giant and brown with a gleaming black mane and a beautiful white stripe down his nose.

"Hi, Artie," Tess said softly, approaching him slowly from the side. "Are you a philosopher? Did you invent the dramatic unities and virtue ethics? Was Plato your mentor?" She stroked his neck to say hello, and Artie sighed happily. "What do you think? Should we go for a ride?"

Artie's ears pricked up immediately and he snorted with excitement. It took Tess a minute to remember how to properly affix his saddle, but since she'd fed him a couple of carrots from a basket full of them, he was munching happily and largely unbothered. Once he was ready, Tess climbed on a little step stool to mount him, and after a few awkward turns around the meadow, they trotted through the gate and out into the Isle's misty evening.

And it was wonderful. Oh, Tess loved it, feeling like she could finally explore this magical place without fear—or without Callum's ornery attitude killing the vibe. They flew down the Isle's avenues, passing fabulous mansions and wild ruins, stretches blanketed thickly with trees and craggy rocks, silver streams where Artie could dip for a drink, fallen trunks he leapt with ease, giving Tess a jolt of adrenaline. A few times, Artie tensed as he heard a noise nearby, and Tess was terrified he sensed a vampire. But it was only ever a bird or a rabbit, and the longer they rode, the more secure Tess started to feel. They were moving so quickly, a vampire would have to be really invested in picking a fight to get close enough to figure out Tess was human. And they hadn't seen anyone out at all, anyway. After an easy ride of half an hour or so, the sky was fully dark, and the towering moonflowers came into view.

They were even more spectacular than Tess had imagined, so named because they stretched and sank with the phases of the moon, rising like ocean tides. With the full moon coming next week, they were nearly their full height, almost twenty feet tall. They looked sort of like sunflowers, but instead of yellow and black, they were all shades of purples and blues—and of course, absolutely gargantuan by comparison—glowing vividly in the silver light of the Isle's rising moon.

Tess slowed Artie to a walk as they approached the meadow, then dismounted and looped his reins around a thick moonflower stalk. She gave the reins a tug to make sure her knot was secure—she didn't want the horse to bolt if a gopher happened to scurry by— then began to walk deeper into the field of flowers.

It was strange and beautiful walking through the giant flowers, like Tess was Alice in Wonderland, experiencing life on an entirely different scale. She wasn't sure exactly what she was looking for, or how she might even be able to tell if the magic of this place might be useful to escape the Isle. She thought again about Flora's explanation of portals, the essential component of desire.

Please, Tess thought, trying to let the desire fill her completely. *Show me the portal. Show me something. Show me anything.*

She paused for a moment, waiting—but of course nothing happened. Tess felt so silly; what had she expected? She couldn't sense Bar Between with Octavia, nor had she felt anything especially magical about the graveyard in the forest—did she really think she was going to come to this grove of massive flowers and find a secret doorway back to New York? Maybe Callum was right about her being useless.

She was about to let out a huge sigh and proclaim this entire outing a bust, but she stopped dead when she heard footsteps—and voices.

"This is a waste of time," a man grumbled.

"That's not for you to say," a woman snapped in response.

Tess's blood went cold—those were two vampires. Were they out hunting? Tess had gotten lucky the last time she ran into a strange vampire, but she was pretty sure that wouldn't happen twice. If they found out she was here—and that she was human—she didn't know if she'd leave this grove alive.

Chapter 11

Excerpt from *Blood Feud*
(book one, chapter four)
BY AUGUST LIRIO

"I don't understand why you need a clan of your own," Felix pleaded with Octavia. "You're like a sister to me—surely we should be fighting on the same side?"

"You're not my brother, and you never have been," Octavia spat.

"We spent a hundred years together!" Felix insisted.

"Worst century of our lives, to be fair." Callum rolled his eyes. "You were always going on about rules and regulations—"

"To keep us safe!" Felix shouted. "I know the two of you just did whatever you liked, traveling the world for Konstantin's most secret missions, killing anyone who got in your way without a second thought because you enjoyed his unconditional protection."

"He's dead now." Octavia narrowed her eyes. "He can't protect anyone anymore."

"But that's exactly my point, don't you see?" Felix didn't understand why they were making this so difficult—though he supposed it might simply be habit. "We can only count on each other for protection now. If you join my clan, we can keep each other safe."

"But we don't *need* you to keep us safe," Callum hissed. "Who knows how long we're going to be trapped on this island? We're certainly not going to spend our time here taking orders from you."

"Can't you picture it?" Octavia smirked. "Felix is our boss, making us punch our little vampire time cards, do our little vampire jobs in our vampire prison. Ooh, is it laundry duty today?"

"It wouldn't be like that," Felix insisted. "More than a thousand vampires trapped together on an island with no humans, no sunlight, no structure of any kind to keep us in check? It's pure chaos. We *need* a clear-cut hierarchy to keep us civilized—sheriffs, deputies. Leadership. Accountability."

"Vampire cops?!" Callum was incredulous. "That's worse than laundry."

"And I'll thank you not to presume to tell *me* how to be civilized." Octavia looked down her nose at Felix. "Who do you think taught Grace Kelly how to hold her pinky during tea?"

Felix sighed with frustration. "I know you two can protect yourselves without a system like this, but what about the vampires who can't? Don't you care about them? Or is it fine for all of them to die as long as you get to live, and never mind what that means for the future of our species?"

"So you're the savior of our *species* now, is it?" Callum laughed bitterly. "So sorry, mate, didn't realize we were in the presence of vampire Jesus."

"He'll call himself anything he likes, so long as he gets more power," Octavia observed.

"You'd rather see that power in the hands of murderers like Nantale? Vicious criminals like Tristan?" Felix felt like he was going mad. "Do you really hate me that much?"

"It's not about hate." Callum folded his arms. "Vee and I? We don't answer to anyone—not since Konstantin died. And we're certainly not going to let a pretender like you take his seat."

"So that's it then?" Felix's heart sank. "There's no chance of us cooperating, bringing some kind of order to the Isle?"

"Sorry about that, mate." Callum had a twinkle in his eye, the same way he always did before a fight. "But sparring sounds a hell of a lot more fun than surrender, don't you think?"

Tess went perfectly still, straining to hear what the vampires were saying, but they were moving farther away. She had to figure out a way back to Artie—if she could just get to him, and if they could move quietly enough, she could ride out of here. Oh, *why* had she thought it would be a good idea to leave on her own, to prove to Callum how useful and independent she could be? Why did she care what he thought of her, anyway? *He* certainly wasn't going to care when these vampires shredded her flesh into ribbons—if he did, he'd probably just be disappointed that they got to drink Tess's blood before he did.

Tess tried to stay focused, but her panic was rising. She felt like every inch of ground around her was covered in dried leaves and twigs crunching underfoot, like she couldn't take a single step without alerting the vampires to her presence. There were a few moon-flowers growing very close together just a few feet from where Tess was standing—if Tess could slip between them, maybe she could stay hidden in the darkness, wait the vampires out? Hope they moved before they found her—or saw the horse tethered nearby? She wasn't at all sure it would work, but it was the least risky option she could think of.

She took one very careful step in the direction of the moonflower formation. Then another. So far, so good—no noise, no movement.

But before she could take a third step, she felt one hand close around her wrist as another moved over her mouth.

"Don't scream," came a whisper. "Don't move at all."

Was that—

"Callum?" She turned, and there he was, wearing a grin tinged with violence. "How did you find me? How did you even know I was here? And who are those vampires—"

"Afraid we don't have time for chitchat, love. One of us needs to kill a couple of vampires, and the other needs to run to her horse and trot on home. I trust you can figure out which is which?"

Tess rolled her eyes. Leave it to Callum Yoo to come to her literal rescue and still manage to annoy the absolute hell out of her.

"Fine." Tess sighed. "What's the plan?"

"I kill," he said slowly. "You run. Do you need me to use smaller words?"

"No, I think I've got it."

"Good."

And with that, he left her and raced toward the two vampires, who were now less than forty feet away.

"Thomas, Althea," he greeted them coolly. "Lovely weather we've been having."

"Callum. You're far from home," the woman vampire said.

"I could say the same of you," Callum replied, his tone casual—but Tess could hear the edge of a threat.

"You're on our side of the Isle," said Thomas.

Did that mean they were part of Felix's clan? Tess assumed they had to be, given how chilly the vampires and Callum were being with one another.

"South of the forest is fair game," Callum countered. "Which means you are too."

"Is that a threat?" Althea hissed.

"Doesn't have to be." Callum shrugged. "You could go home to your shiny castle, knit some little mittens, maybe do a puzzle? We go our separate ways, everyone lives through the night. How's that suit you?"

"You're our sworn enemy, Yoo. Why would we show you mercy?" Thomas sneered.

"Oh, was I not clear?" Callum was toying with them now, Tess could feel it. "I'm not the one at risk of dying."

He moved so quickly she could barely track him, but she heard a terrible scream and a sickening crunch. She couldn't be sure, but it looked like Callum had torn Thomas in half and thrown his mangled corpse to the ground.

"You evil bastard," Althea roared as she leapt toward Callum with such speed and force that it looked to Tess like she was flying. Callum dropped into a deft roll to avoid her, but she caught hold of one of his feet. Her forward momentum propelled them both in Tess's direction—Althea hoisted him off the ground and launched him into the air like a shot put. Tess covered her mouth to suppress a gasp. Callum tumbled to the ground not fifteen feet away from her.

Tess wanted to run to the horse, but they were too close—she'd certainly be seen if she moved now. Callum sprang back onto his feet as the woman sped toward him; he stopped her with a vicious punch to the throat, and she bent over, gasping for air.

"What's the matter, Althea?" he needled. "Cat got your tongue?"

"You won't best me," she wheezed, her windpipe clearly broken. "I'm stronger than you."

"God, you're so boring. Just throw a bloody punch already."

He dove for her knees, knocking her to the ground with a hard thud. She kicked his head upward, sending his body reeling backward, but he was strong enough to plant his feet firmly and end up standing. She leapt up, and the hand-to-hand combat was brutal and intense. Callum was a magnificent fighter, nimble and graceful as he ducked punches and twirled into devastating kicks. But Althea was right—she was stronger than he was. And she was driving Callum closer to Tess with every landed blow.

They were just a few feet away now, and Tess could see Althea clearly: She was nearly as tall as Callum, broadly muscled with dirty-blond hair pulled back in a braid, wearing form-fitting black clothes that looked made for combat. She went to kick Callum again, but he grabbed her leg and twisted it to a sickening angle, and Althea yowled in pain. Callum pounced on her and sent them both hurtling to the ground. They landed with Callum on top—he wrapped his hands around her throat and squeezed.

"Pity you have to die this way," Callum clucked. "I thought you'd know better than to pick a fight you can't win."

Althea's eyes bulged outward. She swatted and clawed at Callum, but he was too tall; he had her pinned down with one knee, and she couldn't reach his face. Tess looked away—she had no particular desire to see Callum kill this woman. But Tess turned back when she heard Callum yell—Althea had stabbed him in the thigh with a dagger! She must have pulled it from some pocket; Callum was shaking with pain. Althea got on top of him and held the knife against his throat.

"You don't have to die, Callum." She smiled, then leaned down close to him. "Just tell me where she is."

He gasped and sputtered, laboring for breath. Tess couldn't understand why he wasn't fighting back—his leg wound should be healing quickly.

"Tess?" Althea called. "Tess, if you can hear me, it's safe to come out, okay? Callum's not in charge of you anymore."

Tess froze. Who the hell was this woman, and how did she know Tess's name? Had Felix sent her—and if so, was she there to protect Tess or harm her? Tess's instinct was to stay hidden, but if she did, would Althea kill Callum? And what then? If she knew Tess was nearby, surely it wouldn't take long for Althea to find her. Whether or not Althea was theoretically there to help Tess, she would certainly drain her blood once she realized Tess was human.

Which meant Tess really only had one choice: She had to figure out a way to save Callum's life.

Tess looked around for anything that could be used as a weapon—

there was a thick stick on the ground with a fairly sharp end. It was far from a proper stake, but it was the best she had on hand. And come to think of it, she didn't even know whether a stake would really kill a vampire—that question had never come up. But she was out of time. If she didn't act now, Callum was dead, and possibly so was she.

"Okay," Tess called, slipping the stick into the waistband of her leggings. "I'm coming out."

She stepped out from behind the moonflowers with her hands in the air.

"Are you here to help me?" she asked Althea, her voice shaking. "I've been so afraid of Callum."

Althea rose and looked at Tess with a satisfied smile. Callum stayed on the ground, obviously still in significant pain—but he threw Tess a sideways glance.

Tess took a step toward the pair of them, then stumbled, bracing her ankle.

"I'm sorry," she said, gasping for breath. "He keeps breaking my ankles, trying to get me to talk. He's convinced I know something about what happened to his sister. He won't believe me no matter what I tell him. Can you help me?"

As Althea sped toward her, Tess made her move—she grabbed the stick and thrust it forward, hoping Althea's momentum would do most of the work to drive the stake through her heart. Tess felt the stake pierce the vampire's flesh and heard a disgusting squelch as Althea staggered backward—

"You fucking *bitch*," she seethed, yanking the stick out of her gut.

"Fuck," Tess breathed—she hadn't hit the heart. Not even close.

Althea stalked toward her, and Tess steeled herself for the inevitable moment when Althea figured out that she was human.

"I'm sorry, Callum," she whispered, but she'd barely gotten the words out before she saw that Callum had staggered to his feet, and he was racing toward her—

Except then Althea whirled around and saw him too, and the knife was in her hand, and Tess was screaming—

But then they were all thrown off their feet by a sudden flash of ice-blue light—the same light Tess had seen when she crossed over from Bar Between. Tess threw up her hands to shield her eyes from the blinding brightness, but it was gone as quickly as it came.

She looked from Callum to Althea, unsure what to do—but they both looked just as confused as she did. And then, without another word, Althea sprinted off into the night.

"What the fuck?!" Tess asked Callum, but his knees were buckling, and Tess rushed over to help him stand. "Callum? Are you okay?"

He clearly wasn't—he couldn't support his own weight, and he was too heavy for Tess to hold him up. She helped him sink to the ground—he was breathing hard, his gaze unfocused.

"Octavia?" he mumbled.

"She's not here," Tess entreated. "It's me, it's Tess. Can you hear me, Callum?"

"She was right there." Callum blinked. "Like the other side of a curtain."

"I think that light was a portal," Tess explained.

"So she really is alive?" He looked at Tess with desperation. "The portal, New York—it's all true?"

Tess nodded, grateful that Callum finally believed her—but worry took hold of her again when he groaned with pain.

"Oh god, your leg." Tess knelt to examine it—it was still bleeding badly. Why wasn't he healing? "I need to make a tourniquet."

"Afraid I'm fresh out of medical supplies, love," he gritted.

"We can use your shirt. Can you sit up?"

He tried to oblige, but he didn't get more than a couple of inches off the ground before he grimaced in pain and fell back, panting.

"It's okay, I'll help," Tess said gently. "Can you lift your arms for me?"

He did, and she started to pull off the Henley he was wearing. It took a good bit of effort; he was heavy, and she worked slowly and carefully, trying not to cause him any unnecessary pain.

"So you're a combat medic in addition to a horse thief and amateur vampire slayer?" Callum's tone was wry, but his breath was uneven. "Where'd you pick that up?"

"First-aid training at the hotel. The owners made the whole staff go to this kooky woman's loft in Bushwick, there's no way she had proper accreditation."

"You're instilling deep confidence."

"I can tie a shirt in a knot." Tess shot him a look, and he met her gaze with a rakish smile.

"Good with your hands, eh? I suspected as much."

Tess rolled her eyes and started to ease his shirt over his shoulders. As she pushed the neckline over his face, he winced.

"I'm so sorry," she murmured. "I'll be done in just a second."

He clenched his jaw and nodded as she pulled the shirt off his arms, leaving him naked from the waist up. His body was thick with muscle and gleaming with sweat, reflecting soft blue and purple light from the moonflowers glowing above.

As Tess tied his shirt around his thigh, she couldn't help thinking of the scene in *Blood Feud* when Callum and Isobel first had sex— right here, in this meadow. Tess had read the scene so many times she could practically recite it from memory: how it started off slow and tender, then built to a feverish pitch, Isobel grabbing a moonflower stalk for purchase as Callum took her from behind, stars exploding into her vision as the pressure grew and grew—

"Everything all right?" Callum put a hand on Tess's thigh, startling the crap out of her.

"Fine!" she squeaked, her voice an octave higher than normal. "I'm fine! I mean, you're fine. The tourniquet is working, the bleeding is slowing down."

"Good." Callum nodded, exhaling heavily.

"Are you in a lot of pain?" Tess bit her lip.

He smiled sadly. "See? This is why I don't go in for all that hero nonsense. Someone always ends up maimed."

Tess felt a wave of guilt—it was her dumb idea to come to this meadow in the first place, her hotheaded plan to do it on her own after he said no, putting them both at risk.

"This is all my fault," she mumbled.

"Pretty sure it was the blonde with the big knife, but you're sweet to worry."

"I *am* worried," she insisted. "You're clammy, I think you're running a fever."

She leaned over to feel his forehead—it didn't seem hot, but she couldn't be sure when his skin was so cool to begin with.

"Tess," he whispered, looking up at her. He brought his hand to hers, holding it against his face—her whole body started to feel warm. They were so close together; if she moved forward, even a few inches, her mouth would be on his. Was that what he wanted? Or was he remembering his exploits with Isobel too? Had he known, even back then, that he was going to destroy Isobel one day? Had Rick always known that he was going to destroy Tess? No, *fuck,* she couldn't think about any of this—

"We need to get back to the compound," Tess said, sitting up straight and shoving Callum's hand away—it thudded to the ground, and he didn't respond at all.

"Callum?" she asked, but he didn't move. "Callum?"

She gave his shoulder a little shove; he was really out of it, eyes closed and mumbling something incoherent. She tried to regulate her breathing—she had to figure out a way back to Nantale's. But how was she supposed to lift Callum onto the horse? What would she do if Althea came back and Callum wasn't conscious, let alone able to fight to protect her? And even if she got him safely back to the compound, what would the rest of the clan do when they saw he was injured? Would they accept her word for what happened, or would they hold her accountable—and punish her accordingly? She was only supposed to be here to deliver a fucking *message,* and now it felt like absolutely anything she did would probably lead to her death. How had this spiraled so out of hand so quickly?

Panic clouded Tess's senses. Every nerve in her body was screaming that there was only one reasonable thing to do in this moment, that she needed to stop thinking and *do it,* right fucking now.

She found Artie in a matter of seconds, and soon they were flying down the Isle's eastern coast, jagged cliffs dropping off to her left as bright sunshine spilled over the churning lilac river. It didn't take long for the hulking mass of the crystal bridge to come into view, and Tess urged Artie to canter even faster, to get there sooner, to get the hell off this island and out of danger. Callum was going to be fine—he was literally immortal—and he wasn't her damn responsibility anyway, she'd already done more than enough to help him.

Except . . .

The closer she got to the bridge, the more Tess's panic cleared, and her stomach roiled in knots of uncertainty. They were almost there—if she kept Artie going at this speed, she'd be across the bridge and back inside Bar Between in just a few minutes. And maybe Callum would be okay. Or maybe something was really wrong, and he'd die in that meadow. Or the other vampires would return to finish what they started, and it would be all Tess's fault that Octavia and her brother were never reunited again.

Goddamn it.

Tess tugged gently on Artie's reins, and he pulled to a stop.

"Come on, boy," she whispered. "We need to go back."

She pulled to turn him around, and they started galloping back the way they came. Tess hoped they'd get there fast enough, that Callum would be safe and just as she left him when they returned. Somehow, she'd get Callum onto Artie and back to the compound; Nantale trusted her (she thought), and hopefully she'd believe the truth about what happened. And if Tess still didn't feel safe, she could always head straight back to the crystal bridge, her conscience clear. She could take Artie and leave tomorrow, or any day she liked, once she got Callum safely home. The longer she rode, the more strongly she felt that this was the right thing to do.

Until they were almost back to the meadow, and a boom like a crack of thunder rang out—except it was louder, closer, and a thousand times more terrifying than any thunder Tess had ever heard.

Artie whinnied and bucked into the air, and Tess clutched the reins to keep her seat—he wanted to take off running, but she turned him around to see what had caused the boom—it sounded like it came from somewhere near the crystal bridge—

Except when they turned around, she saw the bridge was no longer there—at least, not in any state where she could cross it.

Something—*someone*—had set off an explosion at the foot of the bridge. An entire section of it was gone—the crystal broken off in jagged splinters. Huge chunks of it floated in the churning river, glittering in the bright sunshine.

It was a shocking sight on its own, but even worse as Tess realized what it meant:

Without the bridge, she had no way to get back to Bar Between.

She was trapped on this island, just like the vampires.

Chapter 12

Excerpt from Octavia Yoo's notes, kept on the Isle

Can't sleep again, brain won't stop turning. When K. came to Seoul, C. was so sure standing up to him was the right thing. But I can't stop thinking—what if that's what landed us here? (I don't mean literally. I know K. is dead, C. was there. Hates talking about it, goes all silent on me. Understandable, I suppose.)

Still, it's strange. Makes me think of ghosts and after-lives—something to do with River Styx? The waters of the river would destroy any ships except ones made of bone. Maybe a ship of bone would get me off this island.

After Joni went back to her apartment, Octavia stayed at Bethesda Fountain until about three A.M. before deciding she absolutely couldn't sit there one more second. She was hungry, uncomfortable, and, most of all, she was bored out of her fucking mind. There hadn't been even a hint of odd light, let alone a full-on portal. But this night didn't have to be a total waste, did it? She was free of the Isle, out in New York City, and she looked fucking good.

She still had the eighty bucks she'd taken from Nicky's wallet the other night; that would definitely be enough to get her down to an after-hours club where she used to party in Alphabet City. She was tempted to leave Joni's things in a bag behind the bench for Joni (or whoever, really) to collect at their leisure, but she was actually enjoying the old episodes of *Buffy,* so she threw the iPad and sleeping bag into Joni's shopping bag to bring back to her hotel.

So much in the city had changed since Octavia's involuntary absence, but the grimy all-night Ukrainian dumpling place by Tompkins Square Park was still there. Octavia was relieved to see that Pavlo, the curmudgeonly old man who was a cross between door guy and security guard and occasional dumpling chef, was there too, sitting at the big table in the window and playing cards with his friends in their frumpy leather jackets, same as always.

"No," he said when he saw her. "After all this time? My Octavia is return?"

"Pavlo, you angel!" she cooed and kissed his cheek. "Can I leave all this with you?"

She held up her shopping bag, he nodded, and she descended the unobtrusive stairway in the back of the restaurant. Octavia had no desire to see what that basement looked like during the day, but in the last hours before dawn, it was dark and hot, bathed in red light, with ice-cold vodka flowing freely and bodies writhing to music with pulsing bass lines. After a couple of shots, Octavia was feeling loose and languid.

She scanned the women in the bar, who were mostly straight (she could work with that if she had to) and very drunk (she refused to work with that, no matter what). Her eyes fell on a woman standing in the corner, scrolling through her phone with a slightly over-it expression on her face. She was tall and curvy, with thick thighs, pouty lips, and shaggy brown hair, wearing ripped black jeans and a faded white tee thin enough that Octavia could make out the lacy green bra beneath it. Octavia snaked her way through the crowd to stand beside her.

"You're too sexy to be in a place like this." She grinned.

The woman rolled her eyes. "What, are you dealing or something?"

Octavia looked at her intensely. "Do you really think you're not so beautiful that I would ignore every other person in here for a chance to talk to you? Because you are. And I did."

This was why Octavia could never understand vampires who glamoured humans into sleeping with them—it was so much more fun, so much more delicious, when they gave themselves over to her willingly, even ravenously, fully of their own volition. The woman's lip gloss tasted like strawberries. Octavia made out with her the whole subway ride back to Brooklyn, and the sex was so good she damn near forgot to draw her suite's blackout curtains before dawn.

"Octavia! Octavia, are you in there?"

Someone was banging on her door—what in the name of god was happening?

"What time is it?" the woman asked. Octavia was pretty sure her name was Rachel. Maybe Roxy?

"No idea." Octavia rubbed her eyes and reached for the black silk robe she'd left draped over the chair next to the bed.

"Octavia? Open the door!"

"Ugh, Joni," Octavia muttered.

"Wait, your name is Octavia?" Roxy/Rachel looked suspicious. "And who's Joni?"

"My . . ." Octavia wasn't sure what word would work here. "Assistant? Kind of? She's helping me with a project."

Octavia opened the door and scowled. "I was sleeping."

"Really? It's after seven." Joni was typically—and annoyingly—in high spirits. "Anyway, I have an idea, it might be nothing but—who's that?"

"Hey, I'm Ruby."

"Ruby!" Octavia whispered.

"Yeah?" Ruby asked. She had the sheets pulled up under her armpits, and otherwise seemed none too fussed that a stranger had just walked into a room where she was naked. God, she was cute.

"Joni, you can see I need a moment—would it be possible for you to meet me at the lobby bar in thirty minutes?"

"Unless you'd rather hang here," Ruby said with a smile.

"No," Octavia and Joni said at the same time.

"Suit yourself." Ruby shrugged. "I'm gonna shower."

She got out of bed and padded over to the bathroom, shutting the door behind her.

"How did you, I mean, is she—did you feed on her?" Joni sputtered.

"Not on her blood." Octavia grinned, and Joni flushed red.

"How was the park?" she stammered. "No portal?"

"Nada." Octavia sighed.

"I figured. But we have other options. That's why I'm here, I think that next we should—"

But Octavia put her hands on Joni's shoulders. "We'll discuss it downstairs. Okay?"

"Oh." Joni nodded. "Sure. See you soon."

❧

TRANSCRIPT OF *HERE TO SLAY* PODCAST, EPISODE 89

Cat: Hey, this is Cat!

Ruby: And this is Ruby. And I feel like before we get into today's show, I should disclose that I'm pretty sure I had sex with a vampire last night.

Cat: Ruby, what the fuck.

❧

Half an hour later later, Octavia and Joni were sitting at The Georgia's lobby bar (a mezcal negroni for Octavia, a fruity IPA for Joni). Octavia was wearing a swishy black jumpsuit with her hair slicked back; even though she had gotten ready in twenty minutes flat, she looked like she'd stepped out of the pages of *Vogue,* as usual. Joni felt respectable in a short navy wrap dress printed with little red flowers, and she wore her hair down in waves instead of in her typical messy bun. She'd sort of thought maybe Octavia would notice how much more effort she'd put into her outfit than usual (granted, not a super high bar), but clearly Octavia had other women on her mind.

It was impossible to sit across from Octavia and not think of her and Ruby in bed all day, of Ruby's casual invitation for Joni to join them, of just how quickly Octavia had refused.

Well, if Joni had ever wondered whether her vampire crush liked her back, she certainly didn't need to wonder anymore!

Joni never legitimately thought anything would happen between her and Octavia, obviously. Octavia was intimidatingly glamorous, and kind of mean besides, and clearly had no interest in some scrubby grad student. And it's not like Joni was trying to sleep with a deadly vampire per se. So it didn't even matter. It was just—the thing that bothered Joni was how *normal* that Ruby girl had seemed. She was hot for sure, but she also just seemed like any girl Joni might know from school, some friend of her roommates or whatever. Not that there was anything wrong with Octavia being into a normal girl like that. Joni just couldn't help but wonder why Octavia was so attracted to Ruby and not at all attracted to Joni.

"Hello?" Octavia prodded. "Didn't you have some big idea you wanted to tell me?"

"Oh, right, sorry." Joni flushed. "I was rereading scenes in *Blood Feud* that take place in the graveyard, and I was thinking about how a cemetery is like, a transitional place. Like a place where the veil is thin between one world and another."

"You think that's why the portal appeared there?" Octavia pursed her lips in concentration. "That's an interesting idea. Some location spells require objects from the person you're trying to locate, so I suppose it's not a complete leap to think a portal spell could make use of a location itself."

"I'd say my thoughts exactly, but I don't really understand what you just said." Joni shrugged. "Anyway, I know it's not much to go on. But since Bethesda Fountain isn't a transitional place, I was trying to think of what might fit the bill here in New York."

"A graveyard in Manhattan doesn't seem right." Octavia set down her cocktail. "It would need to be more of a landmark—what about a bridge?"

"I had the same idea!" Joni gasped. "I was thinking maybe the Brooklyn Bridge? Because it matches up with the crystal bridge on the Isle, right? And it connects the Isle to Bar Between—it's kind of a gateway in both places. What do you think?"

Octavia drained her drink and put the glass down on the bar. "I think it's brilliant. Let's go."

Joni called a rideshare as soon as the sun set, and they arrived at the foot of the bridge not long after. The breeze over the water was cool and refreshing as they walked through the night air toward the glittering Manhattan skyline.

"Why don't I do this more?" Joni mused.

"Walk over random bridges?" Octavia frowned. "Why would you?"

"I don't know." Joni smiled. "It's romantic, isn't it?"

"You could bring your boyfriend," Octavia said agreeably.

"Uhhhh, what?" Joni laughed uncomfortably. "I don't have a boyfriend. I'm gay. Oh god, I don't look straight, do I?"

Octavia shrugged. "Bring your girlfriend then."

Joni peered at Octavia. She was breezier than the damn wind over the bridge—but was Joni crazy, or was Octavia trying to suss out whether Joni was single?

"I don't have a girlfriend either," Joni said.

"Probably because all the dykes think you're straight."

"Hey!" Joni gave Octavia's arm a playful slap.

"Just kidding." Octavia grinned. "No straight girl would wear sweats out of the house as much as you do."

"What about you?" Joni asked.

"The whole world knows I'm not straight. As you may recall, there's a series of highly popular novels about it."

"No, I mean—do you have a girlfriend?" Joni suddenly felt shy. "Like, back on the Isle or something?"

"Never been my thing." Octavia wrinkled her nose. "Everyone on the Isle was so incestuous, I didn't want any part of that. And Callum and I have always felt it was simpler if our primary loyalties were to each other—even when we were human, Konstantin forbid us to marry. Of course, it turned out that was because he wanted to make it easier to turn us into vampires. But it really didn't matter to me, since, you know."

"Being gay in the 1900s wasn't really an out and proud kind of time?"

"To put it mildly. If anyone had found out what I was back then . . ." Octavia shook her head. "But I suppose that's still true for some. For you, maybe?"

"Oh, me? No—well, actually I thought my parents might have a problem, but they were really cool about it." She smiled at the memory. "I was so stressed to tell them, senior year of high school, I sat them down all serious. When I said I was gay, my mom let out this huge sigh of relief and goes, 'I thought you were going to say you totaled the car.'"

Octavia laughed appreciatively. "You're close with your parents?"

"Oh definitely, super tight. With my little brothers too, even though they're assholes who always steal my shit." She grinned.

Octavia looked at Joni for a moment, her face pained. "I didn't know you had brothers."

"Hey," Joni said quietly. "We're gonna find Callum, okay?"

"Maybe." Octavia nodded. But she didn't seem to want to talk anymore.

As they neared the end of the bridge and it became clear that no portal was going to appear, Joni stole a few sideways glances at Octavia. She looked cool and detached as always, but Joni noticed her breathing was shallow, not quite even.

"I'm sorry," Joni said when they stepped off the bridge and onto Frankfort Street. "It was a stupid idea."

"At least you're trying," Octavia muttered. "I researched ways to get off the Isle for years, and I only managed it by sheer coincidence. And now that I'm back here, I can't make myself spend any time thinking about that damn portal—all I want to do is go to bars and buy clothes and forget that any of this ever happened."

"First of all, that makes total sense," Joni reassured her. "You went through something horrible, of course you want to put it out of your mind! And second . . . you know. They're really, really good clothes."

Octavia smiled sadly, then nodded toward Joni's dress. "You've made a bit of a sartorial upgrade yourself tonight."

"Oh." Joni flushed with pleasure. "Yeah, well, you were making me feel like a fucking schlub. Had to prove I own some actual nice clothing."

Octavia stepped behind Joni and pulled the label out of the dress's neckline.

"Oh, Joni. Poly-rayon blend?" Octavia wrinkled her nose.

"Is that bad? Why is that bad?!" Joni gesticulated broadly, and they both laughed.

Octavia held Joni's gaze for a moment. "Do you want to walk a little more? There's a park I used to like a bit north of here, by the river."

"Sure." Joni nodded. "That sounds good."

• • •

The East River Greenway was mostly empty as they headed north. Joni asked Octavia about her favorite designers, and Octavia told wild stories about the time she spent as a muse to Cristóbal Balenciaga in the '50s and Mary Quant in the '60s, her friendships with iconic Korean designers like Park Youn Soo and Lee Young-hee in the '90s.

"The fuss they made over Mary's miniskirts, my god." Octavia laughed as they walked into a big green meadow. "As if a woman showing her thighs could bring the world to a grinding halt."

"That's still a thing!" Joni blustered. "School dress codes, making girls cover their legs and shoulders so boys can learn, never mind what the fucking girls want. It's all a bullshit way of policing women's bodies, and I for one—"

But before Joni could finish her sentence, there was a loud cracking sound and a blinding flash of icy blue light. Octavia looked at Joni in shock, then sprinted toward the light.

"Octavia, *wait*!" Joni called, but it didn't matter, Octavia was flying through the meadow, she was almost at the light—

And then it was gone. It had only lasted a couple of seconds. Octavia was spinning wildly, heaving for breath.

"What happened?" She was flailing in panic. "Where did it go?!"

"I don't know!" Joni rushed over. "Did you see anything?"

"Callum." Octavia was shaking now, and tears were rolling down her face. She sank to her knees in the soft grass, and Joni crouched beside her.

"Callum!" she screamed, her voice raspy with emotion. "Callum, can you hear me?!"

But nothing happened—they were still alone in the empty meadow.

"Could you see Callum in the light?" Joni asked.

"No." Octavia covered her face with her hands. "I could feel him. He was right there."

"What did it feel like?" Joni asked quietly.

"Like I was whole again." Octavia shook with tears. "And then I wasn't."

She turned to Joni, her face streaked with black stains from her previously perfect cat eye.

"Am I ever going to see him again?" Octavia's face crumpled. "I don't want to spend eternity alone."

"Hey, no, that's *not* going to happen." Joni threw her arms around Octavia. Octavia was tense at first, but then let it go, crying softly into Joni's shoulder.

"I finally wear a nice dress, and you get mascara all over it," Joni teased.

"It's not that nice a dress." Octavia sniffled, and Joni laughed.

"This is good news, okay?" Joni comforted Octavia, rubbing gentle circles on her back. "I low-key thought we were just gonna wander around Manhattan forever and never see a portal, but we saw one! We must be doing something right."

"But it's so random," Octavia fretted. "We lucked into it this time, but if the portal showed up once in Central Park, then here—how are we supposed to know where to find it? And what does it matter if we can't get through it even when we do?"

"What if it's not random?" Joni sat up straight, something clicking in her mind. "What's here on the Isle?"

"What do you mean?" Octavia sat up too, wiping her eyes.

"Like how Bethesda Fountain matched up with the angel statue in that graveyard," Joni explained. "What matches up with where we are now?"

Octavia thought for a moment, then her eyes lit up. "The moonflower meadow! It's one of my favorite places on the Isle."

"Is it possible Callum is there right now?" Joni asked. "Or at least, that he was a few minutes ago when the portal opened?"

"He definitely could be." Octavia nodded, getting excited.

"But that wasn't enough to open the portal long enough for either of you to cross through," Joni spoke slowly, thinking it over. "Which means we have two questions to answer."

"How to keep the portal open longer, obviously," Octavia agreed.

"And once we have that part, we'll need to figure out—"

"How do we get Callum and me in the same place at the same time?"

Chapter 13

BREAKING: FIRE IN PRAGUE NIGHTCLUB KILLS DOZENS

posted by the Associated Press

eleven years ago

PRAGUE (AP)—Fire broke out in the early hours of Sunday morning at one of Prague's most popular nightclubs, trapping dozens inside. A spokesman for the city's fire department said the total death count is not yet known, and rescue efforts remain ongoing. In a peculiar detail, many of those who escaped the club appeared to have severe puncture wounds in their wrists and necks; at least eight such persons required hospitalization. In a press conference, officers from Prague's Regional Police Directorate did not comment on whether these injuries were connected with the fire, nor on any possibility of arson. There was some speculation that a rabid animal had somehow gotten loose inside the club and that the fire began during the ensuing panic. However, no officials have yet confirmed this theory. This report will be updated as more details become public.

Callum wasn't sure how long he was in the darkness.

He could smell smoke, hear screams—the music was still pounding, people hearing the yells too late to run, get out, save themselves. There was nothing Callum could do. None of this was supposed to happen.

Callum, what's wrong? Where's Konstantin?

The look on Octavia's face when Callum told her their sire was dead. He couldn't bring himself to confess that it was all his fault.

Callum? Callum?

That wasn't Octavia—it was Tess. Were they still in the meadow? She was leaning over him, the neckline of her shirt dipping low. *Yes,* he thought, *be close to me.* He ran his hand over her thigh, feeling how soft she was, how strong. The moonflowers glowed so brightly they burst into flames—god, it was so warm, and Tess was dripping with sweat, peeling off her shirt so he could finally see her luscious body. Her hair was soaking wet, and she flipped it forward, dragging it over his chest, the water scalding and sizzling as it burned his skin. The pain was so pleasurable, so addictive, he wanted to flip her on her back and move against her, to feel her slick body pressed to his—

"Callum!"

Someone slapped him—hard—and his eyes fluttered open.

"There," Nantale clipped, looking stern but also a little worried. "Took you long enough."

It took him a second to get his bearings—he was lying on a couch in his rooms back at Nantale's compound. Nantale and Sylvie were there, and so was Tess—she was wringing out a wet cloth, dripping cool water onto his forehead.

"Are you okay?" Tess looked even paler than usual.

He felt a lurch in his body, an involuntary desire to comfort her, to show her she didn't need to worry. But when he tried to move, his head swam again, and he felt like he might be sick.

"Easy, easy." Sylvie stepped in front of Tess and Nantale. "You two, give him space. And you—don't try to move yet. Here. Drink."

She had filled a whiskey glass with warm rabbit's blood, and he sipped it slowly. The sustenance felt medicinal and right, and he felt a bit less woozy with each sip; everything around him came into clearer focus.

"What happened?" he asked.

"You were stabbed," Tess said gently. "Sylvie thinks the dagger must have been poisoned."

"The wound should be healing, but it isn't." Sylvie looked concerned. "I don't know exactly what's causing it, but it's in your bloodstream. Did you hallucinate when you were passed out?"

Callum avoided eye contact with the others. "Erm. Yes."

"That's what I thought." Sylvie nodded. "We need to figure out what kind of poison it is so we can find an antidote. I have a book in my room that might help—I'll go get it."

She sped off, leaving Callum alone with Tess and Nantale.

"How are you feeling?" Tess asked. "Do you remember what happened in the meadow?"

His mind immediately flashed to his hallucination, but he knew that wasn't what she meant. She looked squirrelly—was she hiding something?

"Not really," Callum admitted. "How did I get back here? Nantale, did you come for me?"

Nantale nodded toward Tess. "The girl brought you."

"On the horse," Tess clarified. "You were half-conscious, we rode back together. You don't remember that at all?"

"I don't." Callum peered at Tess. "Why?"

Tess looked down, and her cheeks warmed. Now Callum was *sure* there was something she wasn't saying.

Sylvie rushed into the room with a thick leather-bound book and laid it on Callum's table with a thwack. Tess frowned as she read over Sylvie's shoulder.

"Henbane?" Tess asked. "You think that's what poisoned Callum?"

"Maybe." Sylvie frowned. "But these effects seem awfully severe for henbane."

"Felix's clan has used poisoned blades against us before." Nantale shook her head. "But we've never been able to identify the poison—or find a cure."

"Oh!" Tess's eyes lit up with recognition—but then she bit her lip, looking worried. "Do you think it could possibly be Datura?"

"Datura?" Callum looked puzzled.

"Devil's trumpets—of course." Sylvie flipped pages in her book. "Highly toxic, hallucinogenic, can cause fevers, delirium, psychosis, and death."

Nantale looked gravely from Sylvie to Callum. "But there is no cure for Datura."

"That's true," Sylvie confirmed, shutting her book with a dreadful finality.

Everyone looked crestfallen, but Callum had to repress an urge to laugh. After all his lifetimes, was this really the end? Some stupid little leg wound with a dirty knife?

But then Tess cleared her throat.

"What is it, girl?" Nantale asked, eyes narrowing.

"So that's not, um—I mean, that's not strictly correct. About there being no cure." Tess looked deeply uncomfortable—even nervous. "You know the black jewel-weed lilies? That grow in the north? You can use them to make . . . um, a poultice? I think that will cure the wound."

They all looked at Tess, absolutely dumbstruck.

"How can you possibly know that?" Callum asked, but Sylvie waved her arms at him as if to shoo the question away.

"Who cares how she knows it! If she's right, it could save your life. Isn't that good enough for you?"

"It's not good enough for me." Nantale folded her arms. "It

would take days to travel north to retrieve those flowers. We'd need to send a hunting party, which would risk valuable members of the clan and leave us vulnerable to attack here at the compound. If we're going to take your word, I want to know the source of your information."

"Wait." Callum shook his head, his memory jogging. "Sylvie, did you tell Tess about the moonflower meadow?"

Tess gave Sylvie a panicked look, and Sylvie stuttered, "I— probably, if she says I did, I'm sure I did! My memory isn't what it used to be—well, look who I'm telling, yours must be even worse, no?"

"I recall perfectly clearly," Callum growled. "Tess said you told her about the meadow, she led me there, and then I was attacked. So if you didn't tell her, a vampire outside this clan did."

"They didn't," Tess insisted. "Callum, I swear."

"Then how do you know about the antidote?" Nantale reiterated. "No one in our clan has ever discovered it. You must have been speaking to someone else."

"Was it Felix?" Callum turned to Tess, furious.

"No!" Tess blurted, but Callum felt certain she was lying.

"It explains *everything*," he fumed. "He brought you here to cause chaos in our clan, to make me think Octavia was alive, to lure me to the meadow—"

"And how would he have done that, exactly?" Tess countered. "I live in New York, remember? How the hell is Felix Hawthorn going to communicate with me and bring me here?"

"You know his *name*?" Callum seethed. "How do you know his name if you haven't talked to him?"

"Because I've read about him!" Tess exploded. "The same way I've read about all of you, because you're all characters in a goddamn novel!"

There was a moment of stunned silence, then Nantale spoke.

"Explain yourself. Right now."

Tess dug in her bag and extracted a worn paperback, which she handed to Nantale.

"*Blood Feud?*" Nantale asked. "What is this?"

"It's the first in a series," Tess explained. "Three novels about the Isle—about all of you. Obviously they're fiction, because most people don't think vampires are real, except some of us do—I mean, some Feudies do—sorry, that's what the fandom is called, Feudies, like *Blood Feud,* see?"

Callum felt woozy. "Am I hallucinating again?"

"No—well, maybe, but not about the books." Tess sighed. "Anyway, so some of us Feudies, we would, like, find pictures of you and Octavia, or Felix, or Konstantin, and get all into these conspiracy theories of how you were all real vampires and the Isle must actually exist too. That's how Octavia found me—she read some dumb essay I wrote on *BuzzFeed*—"

"On what?" Nantale interrupted.

"It's a website, it doesn't matter. I wrote this essay about how the Isle was real, and Octavia saw that I lived in New York, so she came to me for help. And she told me not to tell you about the novels because she thought you might think I was crazy, and looking at your faces now, maybe she was right. But anyway, that's how I knew about the Datura and the black jewel-weed lilies, because I read about them in book one when Isobel gave Felix a poisoned dagger to use in a fight against you."

"You know about Isobel?" Callum was taken aback.

"When I came here I was *dressed* as Isobel!" Tess confessed. "Because I had been at my former best friend's *Blood Feud*–themed birthday party!"

"So when you said I was a villain . . ." Callum thought back to that moment, the context suddenly clicking into place. "It was because I'm a villain in that book?"

"This whole clan kind of is?" Tess said apologetically. "And no offense, but the way every vampire here looks at me like they have murder in their hearts hasn't done much to disabuse me of that opinion."

"And the moonflower meadow?" Callum asked. "You knew about its source of magic from your books too?"

Tess paused for a moment, then nodded. Callum's instincts prickled again—he still had the distinct sense she wasn't being entirely truthful.

"But who is writing these things about us?" Nantale asked, pointing to the cover of the book. "Who is August Lirio?"

"No one knows." Tess shrugged. "It's a pseudonym—we have no idea who the author really is."

"Excuse me," Sylvie butted in, "but can we focus? Whoever wrote those books, whatever they know and however they know it, we have a chance to save Callum's life here. Don't you think we should take it?"

"Yes," Nantale answered. "Sylvie, you know the north best. I'll give you a hunting party to gather the lilies, and we'll increase security here in their absence. Tess, you'll stay with Callum at all times to monitor his health and bring him anything he needs. I can't spare anyone else to do it, I hope you understand."

"Of course." Tess nodded.

"Hold on," Callum objected. "I don't need a babysitter."

"Yes you do, you can barely move," Nantale said dismissively. "Tess, after all you have seen, you must be eager to leave this island, and I don't blame you. But given what you know from these books—not just how to cure Callum, but potentially how we might all escape—I must require you to stay with our clan a little longer. Is that acceptable?"

Callum expected Tess to argue, but she just nodded, looking defeated. Strange—that wasn't like her.

"Sylvie, come," Nantale commanded. "We must move swiftly."

Sylvie hurried out of the room. Nantale turned to follow, but then paused and picked up Tess's copy of *Blood Feud*. As she held the book, her eyes glowed a deep and vivid scarlet—and suddenly, she was holding two copies instead of one. She handed the original book back to Tess and swept out of the room with the newly glamoured copy, leaving Callum and Tess alone for the first time since Callum had regained consciousness.

"So, um." Tess folded her arms, uncomfortable. "Do you need anything?"

"Will you pass me that?" he asked, nodding toward the book. "I think I'd like to read."

Chapter 14

Excerpt from *Blood Feud*
(book one, chapter eight)
BY AUGUST LIRIO

Callum heard a twig snap—he was certain someone was following him through the forest.

"Who's there?" he snarled. "If you want to fight, don't be a cowardly little shit about it. Show yourself."

He was expecting to see Felix or one of his many henchmen, but instead, a girl Callum had never met peeked out from behind a nearby tree. She wore a simple white linen dress and looked to be in her early twenties, young and afraid—but Callum wasn't stupid enough to judge any vampire based on appearances. Still, he found her wide eyes, rosy cheeks, and ample curves extremely appealing, so he strode toward her.

"Out for a walk, love?" He gave her a charming smile.

"I know who you are." Her voice was light and breathy.

"Oh?" He raised an eyebrow. "Who am I?"

"You're the most dangerous man on the Isle." She took one step closer. "You've killed dozens of vampires, hundreds of humans. Felix says—"

She stopped talking. Callum narrowed his eyes.

"What does that jealous little prig say about me? Go on."

She bit her lip, and Callum felt his desire building—he wanted to take that lip between his own teeth, to suck on it until it was bruised and purpled. He was a creature of voracious and insatiable appetites, and he had little inclination toward restraint.

"I shouldn't say," she whispered. "He told me not to."

"Let me guess." Callum closed the distance between them in half a moment. "He said I'm a vicious beast who can't be trusted, who'll rip you apart just to amuse myself—or toy with his mind."

Her voice was strained and full of lust. "Something like that."

"And instead of staying away from me, that made you curious." Callum's voice was low. "What a dirty little bird you are. Wanted to meet the monster and judge for yourself?"

She nodded. Callum ran a finger along her jaw, and she shivered with anticipation. His icy blood grew hot as he imagined all the pleasures that lay before him—he was going to fuck this girl until her legs shook and she begged for more. And then, just as Felix predicted, Callum was going to kill her to send Felix's clan a message: If they weren't afraid of him yet, they should be.

"Can I tell you a secret?" he whispered into the girl's ear, then sharply nipped her earlobe.

"Oh!" she gasped. "*Yes,* please."

"Everything Felix said was true."

The kitchen at Nantale's compound was, as one might expect, more like a blood bank: a long row of glass-doored refrigerators stocked with different sorts of animal blood, as well as several industrial stoves to heat the blood to a vampire's preferred temperature. Most of the vampires hunted their own food, but since Callum was still too weak to leave the compound, Tess was warming up his breakfast. He'd mostly been asleep for the past two days; she thought it was a good sign that he wanted a hot meal.

"Don't tell me you've gone native." Hamish swanned into the kitchen wearing a black yoga onesie and a silky floral robe that billowed behind him. "You're drinking blood now?"

"It's for Callum." Tess exhaled with relief that Hamish was alone. Of all the vampires here, he seemed the least interested in killing her—and since the crystal bridge was destroyed and Tess was now trapped on this island indefinitely, she was grateful for any scrap of safety she could find.

Hamish grabbed a bottle of blood out of the fridge, popped the top, and took a deep drink.

"*So* good. Goose blood." He indicated the bottle. "Can't compare to human, but at least it's got foie vibes. What's Callum having?"

"Pig's blood. So more like *Carrie* vibes."

"What I wouldn't give for a little telekinesis just to pass the time." Hamish sighed. "So how's it going with you two?"

"Me and Callum?" Tess asked. "Not great—we still haven't found a way off the Isle."

"Ugh, who cares, I want to know what's happening with you and the hottest vampire alive! All those hours alone in the forest, him wanting your blood, you wanting his body? Are you two doing that sweet human-vampire nasty?! It's been so long since I've had hot tea, please, you have to tell me."

"What?! No! Nobody wants anybody's anything." Tess flushed, her mind lurching to the moment in the moonflower meadow when Callum put his hand on her thigh. Ugh, that was nothing—and besides, she didn't have time to think about it. She needed to focus on helping Callum get healthy and finding a way back to New York.

"It's so stupid he doesn't sleep with men," Hamish groused. "It's like, hello, we're immortal, maybe live a little?"

Hamish gestured broadly, and the bottle of goose blood slipped out of his hand—it shattered on the kitchen's immaculate white floor.

"For fuck's sake." He grabbed a kitchen towel to mop up the mess.

"Let me help you," Tess offered. She knelt to pick up some glass that had landed near her feet but yelped in pain when she pricked her finger.

"Fuck! We're a couple of klutzes, huh?" She turned to Hamish and smiled, but his whole face had gone dark—his eyes were practically black.

"Hamish?" Tess asked quietly. "Are you okay?"

"You're bleeding." His voice was strained.

"Oh." Tess looked down—the cut was tiny, but the smallest droplet of blood was visible at the surface of her skin.

"Go," he ordered. His jaw was clenched, his hands balled into fists.

"Hamish—"

"Get out of here. Right now."

Tess grabbed the pot of pig's blood off the stove and bolted into the Isle's art-covered hallways. Was this what the rest of her life was going to be? Living in constant fear that at any moment, some stupid cut would spell her death? What the hell was she supposed to do when she got her period?

The walk to Callum's rooms helped Tess feel calmer, but her hands were still shaking as she opened his door.

"What's wrong?" Callum sat up in bed, then sniffed the air twice. "You cut yourself? Are you all right?"

"You can smell it?" she whispered, terror flooding through her. "I stopped bleeding, I thought—I'm sorry, I'll leave right now."

"Why?" He frowned. "You have the pig's blood, don't you?"

"I mean, with my cut. Should I really be here . . . with you?"

"You think I can't control myself?" He raised an eyebrow. "Just because a certain book describes me as 'a creature of voracious and insatiable appetites'?"

"Wow, you're already on chapter eight?"

"You know exactly where some arbitrary line is from?" He peered at her. "How many times have you read these books?"

"That's a really famous passage." Tess blushed. "It's Callum's first—I mean your first—I mean—"

"The first sex scene in the book? Yeah, I noticed. Do you mind pouring the pig's blood into one of those bowls by the fireplace?"

He nodded toward a sideboard filled with celadon bowls and teacups, all glazed a vivid dusky blue and inlaid with a pattern that reminded Tess of ocean waves.

"These are beautiful," Tess remarked.

"Glamoured them after a set Octavia found in Busan."

Tess filled a bowl with pig's blood, and he laid his hands on it, his eyes glowing fiery amber. The bowl started steaming, and Tess saw the blood had morphed into a hearty soup; it smelled delicious.

"Soondae guk—blood sausage soup," he explained, then lifted the bowl to his mouth and drank. "Glamour works a lot better when you have fresh blood. Thanks for that."

"I live to be a good babysitter." Tess grinned.

"God, that bit. You really don't have to stay."

"I have a feeling Nantale's protection is contingent on obeying her orders," Tess pointed out. "But anyway, we have a lot to discuss—if you're up for it, I mean."

"Do we?" Callum looked at Tess with interest.

"We still haven't talked about the portal we saw in the meadow."

He leaned back against a pile of pillows. "What did you make of it? Did it remind you of anything from your books?"

"I was obviously wrong about desire being what summons it." Tess sighed. "It appeared in the middle of the fight. Neither of us was thinking about conjuring a portal to New York. Or at least, I wasn't. Were you?"

"My thoughts were somewhere along the lines of 'Ow, fuck, my leg, ow, that fucking cunt.' Sorry."

"Thank you for apologizing. As a meek and proper lady I'd never heard the word 'cunt' until just now and I'm very offended," Tess deadpanned, and Callum chuckled softly.

"Delicate little flower, that's you," he teased, and her cheeks warmed.

"So if it wasn't desire—uh, I mean, if it wasn't, you know, a strong will to create a portal, why do you think the light appeared?" she asked. "Just dumb luck?"

"I have no idea." Callum tilted his head, considering something. "But I know someone who might."

Octavia's rooms were just down the hall from Callum's, but it still took them several minutes to get there, Callum walking with a cane to support his injured leg. From her brief encounter with Octavia, Tess expected her rooms to be sleek and organized, but they were just the opposite: a riot of colors, fabulous dresses and furs strewn everywhere, mammoth reproductions of striking modernist paintings hung on walls already covered in patterned wallpaper, extravagant oversized furniture upholstered in velvet and silk.

"Wow," Tess said.

"My sister." Callum's tone was terse—Tess noticed he seemed more tense the second they walked into the room. He pointed toward a massive drafting desk made of iron and glass, covered in notes and drawings. There were books piled around it, most of them ancient-looking and leather-bound, written in languages Tess couldn't identify, let alone read.

"What is all this?" Tess asked, walking over to the desk. There was a stack of faded watercolor paintings atop one of the piles: an old-fashioned sewing machine, an icy blue tunnel, a large gold pendant in the shape of a medieval cross set with a glowing ruby.

"Octavia was . . . a bit obsessed with finding a way off the Isle," Callum explained. "She'd hole up for weeks researching, then get demoralized and abandon the whole endeavor. She'd try to make the most of living on the Isle, but that never lasted long. The longer we were here, the more time she spent in this room, looking through . . . all of this."

Beneath the watercolors, Tess noticed a book open to a page with a drawing of an angel. Tess held it up. "Callum, look."

He walked slowly toward her, leaning heavily on the cane. Tess slid the book across the desk toward Callum. His jaw twitched as he ran his fingers over the drawing.

"Do you think this is why Octavia went to the angel statue the night she left?" Tess asked. She peered at the caption beneath the drawing, but it was written in an alphabet Tess couldn't recognize.

"No." Callum's voice was cold. "I don't."

"What is it?" Tess frowned. "What aren't you telling me?"

"Octavia and I . . . we had a fight that night," Callum said. He sat down slowly in her desk chair and groaned with relief as he removed the pressure from his leg. "She was, um. Pretty angry with me."

"What about?" Tess asked. She pulled over another chair to sit beside Callum.

"She was in one of her states, really obsessive." He shook his head, the memory obviously painful. "And she was convinced she could glamour a suit that would let her walk across the crystal bridge without being harmed by the sun. I told her she'd lost her mind, that nothing glamoured could get you across the bridge or the river, that everyone who'd ever tried it burned to death. But she was consumed, she kept saying over and over that I had to trust her, that she knew it would work. She finally went to bed—at least, I thought she did. But the next morning, when I couldn't find her . . ."

"You assumed she tried it." Tess closed her eyes. "And that she died."

Callum's face looked stony, his expression distant. "Yeah. And it was my fault."

"But why?! You tried to stop her."

"At first, I did," Callum acknowledged. "But when she wouldn't give it up, I told her to go ahead and do it. I said she was as good to me dead as alive, that she was so far gone I couldn't even recognize my own sister."

"Oh." Tess wasn't sure if she was more shocked by what he'd told her or the fact that he'd admitted it at all.

"Pretty despicable, eh?"

"I don't know," Tess said sadly. "It sounds like you were both incredibly desperate. She was going through something terrible, and you were trying to shake her out of it. It makes sense you would snap in a situation that intense."

"Maybe." Callum shrugged. "Or maybe it's like your books say. And I really am a monster."

Tess felt a twist of sadness for him; she didn't know what to say.

"Do you . . ." He looked up at her, and she was shocked by how vulnerable his face seemed, how open. "Do you think it's true? What Lirio wrote about me?"

"I don't know," Tess answered honestly. "Is it true that you've killed hundreds of humans?"

"No." Callum sighed. "I've killed forty-three. Not sure if that's better."

"You know the exact number?" Tess frowned.

"Not something you tend to forget," he said quietly. "Especially when you didn't want to kill them."

Tess peered at him. "How could you murder someone against your will?"

"Guess I could have given up my life to save theirs, but it wouldn't have done much good." Callum shrugged. "If Konstantin wanted someone dead, they ended up dead."

"Wait." Tess was confused. "You're saying you only ever killed humans when Konstantin made you? The books make it sound like—I don't know, like you enjoy killing."

"I enjoy killing *vampires*," Callum corrected. "That's who we are, it's what we're supposed to do. Natural order of things, isn't it? If we didn't kill each other, we'd all live forever, and that's no good for anyone. But killing humans? There's no challenge to that, it's not sporting. It's just . . . mean."

"Doesn't stop most vampires, does it?" Tess asked. "I mean—sorry, you guys aren't exactly known for your strict codes of morality."

"Do you know about Konstantin's factory? Is that in the books?"

"I know you and Octavia worked there when you were kids. You ran a gambling ring, right?"

"The gambling ring." Callum laughed. "I forgot that. We rigged it too."

"Why am I not surprised?" Tess smiled despite herself.

"We'd let one poor soul a day win big, so everyone wanted to gamble with us, they all thought they'd be the lucky one. Little did they know we were stealing from everyone else. It was more money than we'd ever seen—it was nothing of course. Enough to eat, buy candies from street carts."

"It sounds fun," Tess said gently.

"It was, yeah." Callum was wistful, but then his face hardened. "Anyway, kids went missing all the time there. We figured some died in the machines, some got sick, some ran off. But when Konstantin turned us into vampires, we realized what was really going on."

"You mean . . ."

"That the man who rescued us from poverty was the one killing all our friends, stealing them from their beds and draining their blood?" Callum folded his arms. "Yeah. That's exactly what I mean. Kinda put us off the idea of killing humans."

"And then he made you do the same thing to other humans that he'd done to your friends," Tess said. "That must have been awful."

"It was a nightmare." Callum set his jaw. "One I couldn't wake up from for a hundred years."

"Was it . . . easier, being here?" Tess asked carefully. "Like, you were somewhere new, away from him—like you could close that old chapter of your life, finally be free of it?"

Callum didn't answer—just looked at Tess with a kind of awe.

"I'm sorry," she said, "did I say something wrong?"

"No." He shook his head. "It's just—you're the first person to notice I felt that way."

"Oh." Tess looked down at Octavia's watercolors. "I guess I've felt that way too."

"When you left school?" he asked. She looked up sharply.

"How did you . . ."

"Not every day you hear about someone dropping out of a PhD program to work in a hotel. Figured there was more to the story."

All this time, Tess had been studying Callum, paying careful attention to see how this person matched up—or didn't—with a character she felt like she'd known for years. It had never occurred to her until this moment that he might be paying the same kind of attention to her.

"Can I ask you a question?" she asked, and he nodded. "Why did you come to the moonflower meadow?"

"Worried about you getting captured, wasn't I?" he said casually. "Couldn't very well have Felix using you for information on our clan."

"Oh," Tess said, unsure why she suddenly felt so disappointed. "That makes sense."

"Speaking of information." Callum nodded toward the stacks of notebooks on Octavia's desk. "You take half, I'll take half?"

Tess and Callum started paging through Octavia's piles of notebooks, and soon the only sound in the room was the shuffling of papers. Trying to follow Octavia's train of thought was a challenge—sentence fragments didn't match up, one thought about Konstantin would bleed into a paragraph about the River Styx and ships made of bone. Even when Octavia's writing was more cogent, Tess found her own thoughts kept slipping back to Callum: the feeling of his hand on her thigh, the notion that he cared at all what she thought of him, the revelation that he'd never kill a human by choice. At every turn he was subverting her expectations—but did that even matter? It didn't change the fact that she was trapped on this island, and that this stack of papers hadn't given her a single idea of what to do about it. She glanced over at Callum, but he looked equally frustrated—he set his notebook down with a *thwack*.

"Going that well?" she asked.

"I've got bloody nothing," he grumbled. "You?"

"Same." Tess sighed. She was starting to wonder if Callum was right—maybe Octavia's research really had been a waste of time. "How are you feeling? Do you want some more blood?"

"I'm fine," he demurred, but she noticed him wince when he shifted in his seat.

"You're not," she said. "Why don't you head back to your rooms and lie down? I'll get some cloves from the orchard to make you a tea. Sylvie said that would help with the pain."

"You shouldn't go alone." Callum sat up straight, clenching his teeth. "I'll come with you."

"Please, don't be ridiculous," she said. "I'm not even leaving the compound. I'll be fine."

Tess didn't wait to see if he'd argue more. A walk in the fresh air was exactly what she needed—plus, she could pick some apples to bring to Artie. The compound's hallways were blessedly empty, and Tess made it outside without incident. The day was cool and windy, with purple-hued clouds swirling above, threatening to open up and unleash a storm. Tess had no idea if it ever actually rained on the Isle—the place was so lush, she thought it probably must, but then again, anything was possible here. Still, she heard an ominous rumble of thunder in the distance, so she figured she'd better not waste too much time finding the trees she needed.

The orchard was lovely and sprawling, with uneven paths wending through trees from all different places and seasons—olives and almonds, pears and peaches, all growing in haphazard harmony. Tess found the apples first, threw a few into a basket for Artie and ate one herself—it was crisp and tart, and it made Tess wish Sylvie were around to glamour up a strudel. But another crack of thunder (this one sounding much closer) kept Tess moving. Sylvie had told her the clove tree would be one of the tallest in the orchard, bearing red fruit—after a few moments, Tess spotted it and hurried in that direction. She was almost there when someone stepped from behind a tree and startled her—

She stopped cold.

What the hell was Felix Hawthorn doing at Nantale's compound?

Chapter 15

Felix rushed toward Tess but stopped short of hugging her; Tess felt a sudden wave of gratitude that her large basket of apples stayed between them. She was wearing her musk oil as always, but she was sure that if Felix felt the warmth of her skin, she was done for. He was as handsome as she remembered, full-tilt Mr. Darcy in loose brown trousers tucked into tall boots, a white shirt unbuttoned over his broad chest, and a long dark overcoat. His golden-brown hair was disheveled from his run through the forest, and he was looking at Tess with deep concern.

"What are you doing here?" Tess rasped, gesturing for him to follow her behind a thick group of trees. "If anyone from the clan sees you—"

"I know, but I was so worried after what happened in the moon-flower meadow—"

"You know about that?" Tess gawked.

"Know about it? It was all my fault." Felix looked stricken. "I asked Thomas and Althea to stop by the meadow if they were in the area—in case you showed up, just to make sure you were doing okay."

Tess was stunned. "I thought those vampires were going to kidnap me. Or possibly kill me."

"*What?*" Felix's face fell. "God, I should have known. You saw two strangers get in a violent fight, what else would you think? I thought you'd be on your own, and they'd be able to explain."

"I was alone. But then Callum came . . ." *To rescue me,* Tess thought. Except he just told her that wasn't true—he showed up to stop her from telling Felix what she knows.

"Of course he came," Felix fumed. "He wanted to make sure you couldn't leave his clan. And then he killed Thomas, all because I wasn't there myself. Tess, I never meant for them to frighten you—that's the last thing I wanted."

"So then, what *did* you want?" Tess pressed. "I was on my own when we met in the forest, wasn't I? Why would you need to send some minions to keep tabs on me when you know I'm perfectly capable of taking care of myself?"

"You remind me so much of her." Felix smiled sadly.

"Who?" Tess frowned.

"Isobel." Felix sighed. "My lover, who died five years ago. You would have no way of knowing this, but . . . Callum's the one who killed her."

Actually, millions of people know that, Tess thought, but she didn't think it would be wise to say so.

"He did?"

"Yes." Felix took a step toward her. "She was like you, always wanting to see the good in people. I think that's why she underestimated how violent Callum is. But I never have, because I know Callum better than almost anyone alive. We worked for the same vampire back on Earth, and Callum was always sent to do his most violent, dangerous bidding. Torture, murder, stuff that would turn your stomach. And he *loved it.* He can be charming when he wants to be, but Tess, I swear to you, if you should be afraid of anyone, it's him."

Tess bit her lip. Callum had seemed so genuine with her up in Octavia's rooms—but what if he was simply ensuring Tess's loyalty, to stop her from running away to join Felix's clan instead?

"Look," Felix went on, "I'm sorry for sending Thomas and Althea to check on you. But Isobel died because I wasn't there to save her, and when I thought about the same thing happening to you . . . I couldn't stand it. I needed to know you were safe. I needed to *keep* you safe."

Tess felt dazed. "This is a lot for me to take in."

"I know, I come on too strong." Felix smiled sheepishly. "Isobel always said so. Her first birthday we were together, I got her this red diamond ring—rarest stone in the world because she was the rarest woman I'd ever met. She loved me for being so over the top, and I loved her for letting me. Now that ring is just sitting in her empty room, with all the other things that used to be hers."

"It must be terrible for you," Tess said. "Stuck on this island with all your memories of her."

"It is," Felix agreed. "But that's true for all of us, isn't it? I mean, we've all had terrible things happen to us here, and none of us can escape them. Not yet, anyway."

Tess narrowed her eyes. "What do you mean, 'not yet'? Are you working on a way off this island?"

"I can't tell you that," Felix said earnestly. "I'm sworn to tell only members of my own clan. But if you join us . . . Tess, I can show you."

Tess's heart sped up—was it really possible that this man she'd dreamed of, this gentle hero, was here to offer her a way home?

"What's wrong?" he asked softly.

"I'm afraid," she answered honestly.

"You should be," a low voice growled behind her.

Tess's stomach dropped. She whipped around to see Callum leaning on his cane, his fists clenched, his face lined with anger.

"Stay out of this, Yoo," Felix warned. He moved in front of Tess, blocking Callum's path.

"Me stay out?" Callum laughed coldly. "Mate, I think you've forgotten whose land you're on. See, one word from me, and the entire clan will be out here to rip you apart. Might leave enough of you intact for your little friends back east to recognize you. But I doubt it."

"Callum, please," Tess implored, but he wouldn't even look at her.

"Not one word," Callum gritted. "I'll deal with you when he's gone."

"Don't you see how he is?" Felix turned to Tess. "This is why I've been so worried—"

"Worried about *me*?" Callum scowled. "That's rich, coming from a sadistic little fuck like you."

"I'm not the instigator of violence on this island, and you know that," Felix said calmly. He turned to Tess, a pained look in his eye. "Please, Tess. You don't have to stay with him. We can leave right now."

Tess looked from Felix to Callum, utterly unsure whom to believe. Felix certainly seemed more trustworthy than Callum—but he had no idea Tess was human, and Tess had no idea what he would do if and when he found out.

"Just go, Felix," she whispered.

"You want me to leave?" He looked hurt.

"I want us both to live," she clarified.

"Listen to your girlfriend," Callum taunted. "Be a good lad and run along."

Felix looked pained—Tess felt a sudden wave of doubt. Was she an idiot to turn down a chance to go with him, and potentially to escape this island?

"All right, I'll go," Felix said to Tess. "Just . . . please, stay safe."

Tess nodded once, then watched as Felix sped away, easily hopping the orchard wall, then streaking into the distance.

"How long?" Callum asked, his voice low.

"What do you mean?" Tess asked, though she had a feeling she knew exactly.

"For fuck's sake," Callum fumed. "How long have you been talking with Felix Hawthorn behind my back? Or was I right all along that he's the one who sent you here in the first place? Did he kill Octavia—then give you her necklace?"

"What? No!" Tess huffed. "I met Felix the other day, after you left me in the forest."

"Oh, that's perfect." Callum laughed meanly. "All alone in the moonlight, abandoned by the big bad, who should show up but your handsome hero? Bet you thought he was gallant."

"I don't know how gallant he is," Tess sputtered, "I don't actually know him at all."

"You're right about that part," Callum seethed. "Your precious book has him all wrong."

"Why?" Tess scoffed. "Because it says you're a monster? You killed Isobel, didn't you? You don't think Felix has a right to be angry about that?"

Callum frowned in confusion. "Bloody hell do you mean? I didn't kill Isobel—no idea who did."

"You expect me to believe that?" Tess guffawed. "It's awfully convenient, the way you have an explanation for every negative thing the books say about you—and every positive thing the books say about him."

"So that's it, is it? You wanted to be with your hero, so you hatched a little plan?"

Callum stalked toward Tess. He was leaning heavily on his cane, and she could see sweat beading at his hairline—he looked feverish and sick, far worse than he'd been even an hour before.

"You're not making sense. There isn't any plan—"

"You wanted to go with him, but you knew I'd come after you if you did. It's clever, really. Lure me to the moonflower meadow, Felix's goons at the wait, two against one, just a quick stab to the leg and then goodbye, Callum."

"Are you fucking kidding me?!" Tess swore. "I staked Althea, I got you back to the compound, and I told Nantale and Sylvie how to cure you! If I wanted you dead, why would I have done any of that? I gave up my last chance to get off this island to save your stupid life!"

"What are you talking about?" Callum frowned. "You can leave this island whenever you like."

"No, I can't!" Tess exploded. "When you passed out in the meadow, I left. I was terrified, and I just wanted to go home. Except when I got to the crystal bridge, and I thought of you lying there unconscious, where anyone could kill you . . ."

Tess's voice caught in her throat—why the fuck was she getting emotional over this man who'd shown again and again how little he cared about her?

"What?" Callum pressed. "What happened?"

"I couldn't leave you there." Tess swallowed hard, keeping her voice dull. "So I turned around. But when I was almost back to the meadow, I heard this massive explosion—half of the bridge blew up and fell into the river. No one can cross it now."

"*What?!*" Callum looked genuinely shocked.

"If I hadn't come back for you, I could have gotten across the bridge before it happened, and I'd be back in New York right now," Tess spat. "So don't you dare say I'm a threat—not when I traded my safety for yours. And not when it's members of *your* clan who keep threatening me!"

"Rubbish. Nantale forbid anyone to touch you." Callum dismissed her.

"Oh please, you're deluded," Tess retorted. "Hamish could barely restrain himself when I cut my finger, the twins look at me like I'm a snack their mom put on a high shelf, and Tristan straight-up told me he plans to murder me the second he thinks he can get away with it."

"When did he say that?" Callum demanded. "Why didn't you tell me?"

"Because you're just like the rest of them!" Tess fumed. "In fact, you know what? I bet Tristan blew up the bridge! Trapped me here so he could drain my blood like he's been wanting to do since the night I got here, when he knocked me unconscious and dragged me to this godforsaken compound because you were too drunk to come meet me like Octavia promised."

"Tristan's a nasty twat, but how thick are you? You want to know who blew up the bridge? It's obviously Felix!"

"What?! Why would he do that?"

"Because that's what he does." Callum seethed. "He cozies up to people, makes them think he's on their side, and they don't realize until it's too late that he's trapped them like a rat in a cage. It's exactly what he did to me—why shouldn't he do it to you?"

"When?" Tess demanded. "When did he do that to you?"

"What does it matter?" Callum laughed coldly. "If it's not in your precious books, you won't believe it anyway."

"I'm trying to believe you, Callum." Tess's voice broke. "I want to."

"I haven't lied to you once," he said flatly. "But you've lied to me every day since we met. Different set of rules, eh, Tess? To think I came down here to make sure *you* were okay."

With that, he turned and walked back toward the compound, his movements slow and ginger as he put weight on his injured leg, leaving Tess alone in the orchard.

Even when he had every right to be furious with her, she realized, he'd never laid a hand on her—never even threatened to. Was it possible that *Blood Feud* had him all wrong, that he really was the man he claimed to be?

In her entire life, Tess had never been less sure of what was fact and what was fiction.

Chapter 16

WHO IS AUGUST LIRIO—MASTERPOST

posted on BloodFeudEvidence.com/masterposts/lirio/UPDATED/truth/

Okay guys, SO MANY OF YOU have asked for this post, but the truth is we really don't know that much about Lirio??? I don't really feel comfortable calling this a "masterpost" because I have a higher standard for what that entails, but whatever, here's what we DO know all in one place:

- **Lirio got their start writing fan fiction.** The first record we have of Felix, Callum, Octavia, and the rest of the BF characters is on AO3, where Lirio wrote fics for years. (Though not under the name August Lirio; back then they wrote as username DarkAura1213.) The fics gained popularity on Tumblr, especially in the Twilight/Buffy/Vampire Diaries fandoms, and the stories started getting longer. Eventually, a full novel-length fic called *Blood Feud* gained more than 83,000 hits.

- **Lirio self-published *Blood Feud* before getting a traditional publishing deal.** After *Blood Feud* went viral on AO3, the same work was self-published as an ebook—that was the first time we saw the name August Lirio. In an interview, literary agent John Betherton said he saw that ebook had sold more than 20,000 copies, read it himself, and reached out to represent August Lirio. *Blood Feud* came out as a traditionally published novel one year later.

- **There is no longer any way to contact August Lirio.** Lirio used to have a contact form on their website back when *Blood Feud* was self-published, but that came down before the traditional book came out.

- **Lirio is now the biggest-selling author on the planet with a secret identity.** With almost ten million books in the *Blood Feud* series sold, Lirio is certainly in rare company. Very few authors can sell those kinds of numbers, and all the ones who do have, you know, names and faces.

- **A fourth book is coming (we hope?????).** Lirio's original book sale was a four-book deal. Three *Blood Feud* books are out already, so theoretically they're under contract for one more??? But it's been five years since book three came out, and there's no news at all about whether they've even started book four, let alone a publication date, so we all just have to wait in pain!!!!

   . . . annnnnd that's what we know about August Lirio. Did you find this post helpful? Lmk in the comments!

Comment from user KStan88971: Post was ok but can you please post more info about Konstantin he is my DARK KING DADDY

"Dark King Daddy?" Octavia put down her wine and peered skeptically at Joni.

"I didn't write it!" Joni protested.

"But you agree?"

"Octavia, please, I'm literally gay." Joni cringed. "Cate Blanchett is the only Dark King Daddy I acknowledge."

"She is *fun*," Octavia agreed.

"Stop. You know her?"

"Not like *know*-know, but we've hung out." Octavia shrugged and sipped her wine. "When you've been alive as long as I have, you run into everyone eventually."

"God, your life is cool."

"It used to be." Octavia sighed.

Joni refilled Octavia's glass of Pineau d'Aunis, another quirky little bottle from Joni's favorite wine shop—Octavia was pleasantly surprised that the girl had interesting, sophisticated taste. They were spending the evening in Octavia's hotel room, trying to figure out how to track Callum's movements on the Isle so they could attempt to reopen the portal they saw on the Lower East Side.

"It still seems simplest to me that you should just go to the Isle and tell Callum where to meet me," Octavia said.

"Yeah, except for the part where Tess has been there for days and we have no idea if she's dead or alive," Joni countered. "I mean, I'm sure she's fine, right? She has to be fine."

"There's an easy way to find out for sure," Octavia needled.

"No—you tried that plan, now we're doing mine. We're finding August Lirio," Joni insisted. "They *have* to know what's happening on the Isle—how else could they write about it?"

"I don't see why the person who spends their career lying about my brother and me should want to help, but we can try." Octavia sniffed. "I suppose we'll start with their literary agent? They'll have Lirio's address on file."

Octavia googled "John Betherton," but the results were page after page of articles and fan posts about *Blood Feud*.

"Let me do the internet, please." Joni held out her hand, and Octavia grudgingly gave her the laptop. "Just gotta log in to the Columbia library search engine, and—okay, here we go. John Betherton is the founder of and only agent at the Betherton Agency. Now we just do a search of recent hits, and . . . hey, this actually looks promising! He's on the host committee of some foundation that's having a gala fundraiser this weekend at the Met. He'll probably be there."

"Well, that's two pieces of good news." Octavia grinned.

"Two?" Joni looked puzzled.

"One: We can make some progress toward helping my brother. And two: I get to wear a proper dress."

✑

Joni didn't know why she was so nervous about some stupid gala. Yes, okay, she was still mildly traumatized about the time she'd attended her rich cousin's black-tie wedding and knocked over an entire tray of champagne, which made the loudest clanging sound anyone had ever heard and soaked her most obnoxious aunt, who'd never let her live it down and still said, "Have you got a firm grip on that?" to this day anytime she saw Joni holding a drink. Joni was fairly certain if she did anything even a fraction that embarrassing in front of Octavia, she would die on the spot.

Of course, just *existing* in front of Octavia was embarrassing. She was so languid and cool, so totally chic and put-together—well, except for those seconds after they saw the flash of blue light when she lost her shit slightly, which was actually kind of reassuring from Joni's perspective. There was still something human inside that tough (ridiculously attractive) glamazon exterior.

Joni knew she had a lot to focus on in her academic life: She needed to finish her dissertation, prepare for—and subsequently crush—her interview for the job she desperately wanted as an assistant professor at Columbia, not to mention apply for a whole host of backup jobs in case the Columbia thing didn't work out. But whenever she tried to focus on any of that, she always found her thoughts drifting back to Octavia. Which was understandable—how often did you meet an unbelievably beautiful vampire who needed your help with a quest where your ex–best friend's life potentially hung in the balance?

Even so, none of that felt like the real reason Joni was so nervous when she arrived at Octavia's hotel room at six P.M. Saturday night and knocked on her door.

"Good, at least you're on time." Octavia exhaled as she opened the door to let Joni in. She was already dressed in a black column gown with glittering crystal-studded ties at the back, her hair pinned up in a chignon, her lips painted vivid red.

"Wow," Joni breathed.

"Oh this?" Octavia smiled. "I grabbed an elegant little Tanya Taylor from Bergdorf's, didn't want to draw too much attention since we're crashing the party. Go on and change—your dress is in the bathroom."

Joni had been relieved when Octavia insisted on picking out her dress for the gala—Joni didn't have anything nearly fancy enough to wear, and she certainly couldn't afford anything new. But when she saw a Tom Ford gown hanging from the bathroom door, her breath hitched in her throat. It had a sporty racerback neckline, was slinky and floor length and covered in deep purple sequins that glimmered like oozing liquid. It was tight on Joni, but in that way that was kind of perfect. The dress hugged her angular frame and made her feel like a badass bitch—but when she opened the door of the bathroom, Octavia just stared at her.

"What? Is it bad?" Joni asked, suddenly doubting how hot she'd felt in the bathroom mirror.

"No," Octavia said quickly. "No, it's perfect. As I suspected. Come on, let's do your makeup."

Joni sat in a desk chair, and Octavia instructed her to close her eyes. Her touch was feather-light as she swept brushes over Joni's skin, occasionally smoothing things out with her fingers.

"Okay," Octavia said softly. "Look at me?"

Joni opened her eyes, and Octavia's face was so close—if either of them leaned forward, they'd be kissing. Octavia inspected Joni's face slowly, gently tapping glimmering highlighter along Joni's cheekbones, pushing back a lock of her dark hair.

"Open your mouth," Octavia instructed.

"Sure," Joni whispered, trying to keep herself from breathing heavily. Octavia applied rosy lipstick, then held up a tissue.

"Blot," she said. Joni pressed her lips into the tissue, which was draped over Octavia's palm, wishing that thin layer of paper wasn't there. Octavia held the tissue for longer than she needed to, and Joni kept pressing her lips against it, wondering if something was really about to happen—

"All done!" Octavia stood up abruptly. "Looks good."

"Great." Joni cleared her throat. "I'll call a car?"

Forty minutes later, they arrived at the Met in a sleek black SUV. There was a line of black cars outside the Met's main entrance with its iconic stairs, but Octavia had their car pull into the parking structure off 80th Street.

"This way, we go directly into the museum and hopefully avoid security," Octavia explained.

"And what if we don't?" Joni asked. As a kid, she'd never so much as stolen a candy bar—she wondered what her parents would say about her gate-crashing a charity gala with a vampire. To be honest, they'd probably be less upset about the vampire than the fact that Joni was blowing off her dissertation to hang out with her.

"If we have to deal with security, we'll deal with them." Octavia shrugged. "One way or another."

Joni hoped none of the ways was murder, but she didn't entirely want to ask.

It turned out Octavia's plan worked like a charm. They made their way through the lower level of the museum, past the costume institute, and up a fire stairwell at the north end of the museum that dumped them in the middle of eighteenth-century American furniture. From there, it was a quick walk to the rear entrance of the room that housed the Temple of Dendur, where the gala was taking place. There was a guard stationed at the door, but one giggle from Octavia and an "Oh my word, we got lost coming back from the loo!" in her crisp British accent was all it took to get by him.

"How many times have you done that?" Joni said under her breath.

"Honestly? Almost never." Octavia grinned. "I'm so used to glamouring people, it's kind of fun to manipulate them the old-fashioned way."

"Very analog," Joni deadpanned. "Super retro."

"I'm a hundred and thirty years old. Everything I do is retro," Octavia murmured in Joni's ear. Joni felt the warm tickle of Octavia's breath, inhaled the smoky scent of her perfume. They hadn't had a drop to drink, and it was a good thing too, because Joni was already feeling intoxicated.

The gala was a beautiful event: The temple was surrounded by trees made of glass, lit from within by thousands of twinkle lights. Round tables were set with candelabras and sprays of orchids, and there was a dance floor by the fountain filled with bulrushes, though no one was on it yet. The moneyed East Side crowd out in their Barney's best chatted to the music of a jazz ensemble while drinking ice-cold cocktails.

"I miss being rich." Octavia looked wistful. "All right, shall we find Betherton?"

Joni had a picture of Betherton from an interview in his college magazine, and she showed it to Octavia on her phone. "Do you see him anywhere?"

"How can you tell the difference?" Octavia muttered as she scanned the crowd. "All these people look copy-pasted from the same Yale yearbook."

"Ooh! There!" Joni said too loudly, and Octavia shot her a look. "Sorry, sorry. He's waiting in line at the bar."

"Trapped and alone," Octavia intoned. "It's perfect. Let's go."

Octavia strode over like she wanted a drink, Joni trailing close behind. She went right up to the bar but then stopped as if only just realizing that people were waiting.

"Oh, I'm sorry," she said to John Betherton. "Is there a line?"

"There is," he said curtly—but when he turned and saw Octavia, his manner softened considerably. "Would you like to wait with me? It'd be a delight to pass the time together."

It took all of Joni's self-restraint not to roll her eyes, but she kept her cool and stepped into line with John and Octavia. He was in his fifties, with the trim physique of someone who probably had insufferable opinions about macro-grains and the oily smile of a guy who regularly cheated on his wife. It lessened Joni's opinion of August Lirio somewhat to know they'd chosen a man like this to represent them. But Octavia was looking at him with a mix of shock and delight.

"Oh my god." She gasped. "John? John Betherton, is that you?!"

"It is." He smiled with confusion. "I can't believe I'm saying this given a face like yours, but I can't place how I know you?"

"It was one of these tedious dinners, who knows how long ago." Octavia waved her hand dismissively. "I introduced myself because I'm such an admirer, but you had to duck out before we could chat."

"I'm certain no dinner spent with you could be described as tedious." He smiled. "Are you in the literary world, Ms. . . . ?"

"Parker." Octavia smiled. "Julia Parker. And actually, it's funny you should ask, because I've just accepted a position with *The Paris Review*. I wonder . . . you wouldn't be interested in a profile, would you?"

"You're not serious?"

"Dead serious." She grinned. "In fact—could we discuss it right now? Maybe somewhere a little more private? My friend can grab our drinks."

John looked over at Joni as if realizing for the first time that a third person was standing in their group. "If you don't mind? Scotch, rocks."

But he didn't wait to see whether Joni actually did mind before he and Octavia walked off.

Joni wasn't sure what to do next. She supposed it was a good thing that Octavia didn't need her at all for their little mission (other than as a placeholder in a drink line), but she wished she'd had a chance to be more useful. She was still several places from the front of the line; she guessed she'd just wait around until Octavia came back. Might as well get herself a cocktail.

"What do you think they're up to?"

Joni looked up to see a reedy woman with a dark pixie cut and a tailored black pantsuit; she didn't look familiar to Joni in the slightest.

"I'm sorry?" Joni tilted her head.

"Your boss just walked out with my boss."

Joni tried to suppress the sudden leaps her heart was doing. This woman worked for Betherton!

"I'm Fern," she said, extending a hand to shake.

"Hey, I'm Joni. You work for John?"

"Yeah, I'm an assistant at his agency," Fern said with an exasperated exhale. "I was so excited to work for him because I love *Blood Feud* so much, but he's kind of a nightmare."

Joni's pulse sped up even more—there was no way she could make herself be cool, so she decided to lean in to the fact that she wasn't.

"No fucking way, the *Blood Feud* books are my favorite," Joni effused. She could have sworn she saw Fern sneer in response—but a millisecond later, Fern was smiling again. "And my boss is a nightmare too. I'm her personal assistant, just dealing with all her bullshit so I can help pay for grad school."

"Pretty nice dress for a personal assistant," Fern observed.

"One of my boss's cast-offs, obvi," Joni said conspiratorially. "Anyway! So Betherton's a jerk, huh? I'm really sorry. Do you at least get to read Lirio's new stuff before everyone else? Do you know if another *Blood Feud* book is happening?!"

"I can't say for sure"—Fern dropped her voice—"but John went to Lirio's townhouse downtown a couple of months ago, and it definitely wasn't a social call. I kind of get the sense that Lirio hates him?"

"I *knew* it," Joni muttered, and Fern laughed. "Sorry—I just couldn't believe August Lirio would hire a guy like that. Or whatever Lirio's real name is. Oh my god, do you know who Lirio really is?! And wait—they have a place in New York?! Aaaahhhh, your job is so cool!!"

Joni hoped she was selling her part as a random fangirl and not as someone asking really pointed and specific questions. The intel that Lirio had a townhouse in Manhattan was already a huge win—maybe that combined with whatever Octavia had learned would be enough to get them a real lead.

"I wish I knew their name. Or anything about them—John keeps all that under lock and key."

"Understandably." Joni sighed. They'd reached the front of the line, so Joni ordered two glasses of champagne and a scotch.

"For John?" Fern pointed at the scotch, and Joni nodded. "Fuck him, I'll drink it. And you should down one of those champagnes and keep the other. Live a little!"

Joni laughed and clinked glasses with Fern, and they both took deep drinks as they wandered away from the bar.

"Hey, would it be crazy if we exchanged numbers or emails or something?" Joni asked, hoping she wasn't pushing this too far too fast. "It'd be nice to get drinks and gush about *Blood Feud* and bitch about work sometime."

Fern smiled. "Give me your phone."

Joni did, and Fern sent herself a text—but as she handed the phone back to Joni, she got distracted.

"Oh shit, there's your boss coming back," she said. "And John's not with her. Probably getting coked up in the bathroom."

"Really?" Joni frowned. "He's too old for that to be cute."

"Tell me about it." Fern rolled her eyes. "I'd better go babysit his wife before she realizes what he's up to. Nice to meet you!"

She was off before Octavia returned—Joni rushed over to her.

"So??" Joni asked. "How did it go? Did Betherton know anything?"

"Mm, he was fairly useless." Octavia shrugged. "A solid meal, though. Tasted like pheasant."

"You *fed* on him?" Joni whispered.

"Does that shock you?" Octavia whispered back. She pulled Joni close to her, her hands gripping Joni's waist. "I am a vampire, you know."

Joni hadn't seen Octavia like this before—there was something wild in her eyes, something dangerous. She looked like she wanted to devour Joni, maybe in more ways than one.

And Joni really fucking wanted her to.

"I know exactly what you are." Joni looked Octavia dead in the eye.

"Who was that girl you were talking to, with the unfortunate suit?" Octavia didn't break eye contact. "Were you ignoring our mission to flirt?"

"Mission?" Joni snorted. "Okay, James Bond. And what do you care if I was flirting?"

"Finish your champagne," Octavia instructed.

"Why?"

Octavia pulled her even closer. "So you can dance with me."

If this was Octavia at her weakest, Joni couldn't imagine what she'd be like with her powers fully restored. Joni had never in her life felt more powerless to resist someone.

Joni drank the rest of the champagne—her second glass—it was fizzy and cold, and the bubbles went straight to her head. And then Octavia's fingers were laced through hers, and she was leading her to the dance floor. The jazz band was playing a slow, sultry cover of "I Put a Spell on You," and the dance floor was completely empty.

"I thought you didn't want to draw too much attention," Joni teased.

"Don't you know me at all?" Octavia smirked. "I always want attention."

Octavia circled her fingers around Joni's wrists, then moved them behind her neck. She put her own hands at the small of Joni's back, and slowly, rippling like water, they started to dance. Joni could feel the eyes on them, see the people craning to get a look. And she loved it.

"Don't you want to know who the girl was?" Joni said softly.

"You're thinking about some other girl while you dance with me?" Octavia raised an eyebrow.

Joni moved even closer to Octavia, their bodies brushing against each other for an aching half a second.

"She's Betherton's assistant," Joni intoned. "And she told me where Lirio lives."

Octavia stared into Joni's eyes for a fleeting moment, her gaze full of fire, and then they were kissing, so fast Joni couldn't have stopped it, but she'd never wanted anything more. Octavia's lips were soft, but her bite was sharp, their hands were grasping at each other, all those people were staring—

"What now?" Joni broke away and gasped for air.

Octavia ran her tongue along the spot where Joni's jaw met her neck, then grinned like she was the best, most wicked thing in the world.

"Come on, Joni. Haven't you always wanted to know what it's like to fuck a vampire?"

Chapter 17

"Come on, Callum. We've got too much to do for you to sleep all night."

Callum's eyes creaked open. He had a vile hangover, a splitting headache that felt like an ice pick jabbed somewhere through his brain. He needed blood—and he needed someone to bring it to him.

"Tess?" he croaked, his voice still scratchy from sleep.

"Is that who you fucked all day? She left hours ago, and we should have too. Let's *go*."

Octavia snatched the blankets off of him, and he looked up in shock—his vision was cloudy, but there she was, wearing wide-slung trousers, a silk shirt, slouchy overcoat, and a soft cloche hat. How did she get here? Or did he get back to New York somehow?

"Did the blue light come again?" he asked, confused.

"Oh God, don't tell me you took absinthe." She sighed and put her hands on her hips. "Do you know what year it is?"

He shook his head; he really didn't. Where was he? The bedroom looked familiar—he could make out the burgundy jacquard of the bed curtains, a series of clumsy charcoal drawings tacked to the wall.

"Are we in Paris?" he asked.

"*Oui, bien.*" She rolled her eyes. "We're meant to return to London tomorrow with a package for Konstantin. I can't get it on my own, and you're utterly useless."

Now he remembered—he'd kept this place for a while in the '20s, up near Montmartre, where it was dark and easy and the streets overflowed with women and wine. He relaxed at the realization, happy to be able to place himself, but something was still bothering him.

"What's in the package?" Callum asked, suddenly desperate to know what object was so important to Konstantin he'd send his two most trusted lieutenants across the English Channel to retrieve it.

"Ugh, who *cares?*" Octavia flopped on the bed. "A long-lost vial of the blood of Cleopatra, stored for centuries in a golden box."

"That's not it." Callum bit his lip.

"Of course that's not it, I just made that up!" Octavia's exasperation only grew with each passing moment.

"That's the package we need," Callum told her. "We have to steal it, and then we have to run. We can go live in Seoul, like we always wanted."

"My sweet, stupid brother." Octavia leaned down beside him. "He found us in Seoul, remember? He can always find us."

Callum closed his eyes, and it was dark again. His head was still pounding—no, that was the music. The nightclub in Prague, eleven years ago. It was dark and hot and stank of cigarettes.

"Callum." Konstantin looked pleased. "I'm glad you came."

Konstantin wore all black, like he always did, like an absolute cliché. Callum stood six feet tall, but his sire still towered over him, his expression set firm, his eyes glittering with anticipation.

"Couldn't miss this, could I?" Callum laughed uncomfortably.

"I know how much you've struggled to control your true nature." Konstantin put a hand on Callum's shoulder. "After tonight, you won't have to anymore."

Callum nodded tightly. Ever since Callum was a boy, Konstantin had always told him that they were just alike: powerful, unapologetic, brutally violent. *That's why I chose you,* Konstantin told him. *Because I saw myself in you.*

Callum knew how much he owed to his sire—his wealth, his immortality, his salvation from an impoverished childhood he might not have survived. But he didn't *want* to be like Konstantin. And even more—he felt a compulsion to protect Konstantin from his own darkest desires. That was why Callum had to do this—had to stop Konstantin from setting in motion a course of events that could never be undone. It was one thing for Konstantin to be the most powerful vampire alive, but entirely another for him to murder humans en masse with no attempt to hide his identity and no fear of repercussion.

Callum had a plan. He separated from Konstantin and the others and made his way down a back hall toward the club's storage room, away from the humans mindlessly dancing with no idea of what was about to happen.

Strange bedfellows, Callum thought as he picked up the jug of kerosene and pile of rags Felix had left for him. He hated Felix Hawthorn, the smug little killjoy—but in this case, they wanted the same thing.

"Konstantin didn't ask me to come to the club—if I show up there, he'll know something is off," Felix had pleaded. "You have to do this, Callum. You're the only one who can stop him."

All Callum had to do was start a small fire, set off the club's sprinklers, and this whole mess would be over before it started. The humans would file into the street, clothes wet and cigarettes lit, and Konstantin and his followers would be robbed of the darkness and tight quarters they needed for their attack.

Callum soaked a few of the rags in kerosene, then pulled a silver lighter out of his pocket. Click, spark, and that's the end of all this.

But the second the flames went up, Callum knew something was wrong. It was like the whole place was a tinderbox, the walls crackling, the wires sizzling within, the fire moving through the ancient electrical system too fast for anything to stop it.

The smoke was black and thick—Callum's eyes teared and his throat burned as he tore through the club, telling people to leave, trying to find Konstantin—but it was too late, too late for everything: the vampires already attacking, the fire roaring all around them, and Callum's sire nowhere to be found.

"Konstantin!" he screamed, over and over, his voice parched and raw. The smoke couldn't kill a vampire, but the fire would—if Konstantin had passed out from smoke inhalation somewhere in this building, his body would burn to ash.

Callum searched as long as he could—until the walls started crumbling and the blaze was too hot to bear. But he couldn't go, he had to find Konstantin—he couldn't let him die, because if he did, it would be all his fault—

"Callum—"

Was that Konstantin? No, a woman. Octavia?

"Callum, can you hear me? Callum!"

Callum forced his eyes open—he was in his rooms at Nantale's compound, his vision bleary, his body slick with sweat. Tess was there, looking as worried as he'd ever seen her. Why was she worried? She didn't care if he died.

"Oh god, you have a fever, you're burning up," Tess fretted. She rushed over to his bath and ran cold water over a cloth, which she laid across his forehead—it felt cool and smelled of eucalyptus.

"What are you doing . . . here?" he asked weakly. His dreams—hallucinations?—had been so vivid, he'd felt the fire all around him, the choking stench of the smoke, the panic as he searched for his sire.

"Nantale said I had to take care of you, remember?" Tess looked worried. "Do you want me to go?"

He looked up at her with confusion. His whole body felt swollen and wrong, like the poison was liquefying him from the inside out, heating him until he boiled and burst.

"I feel hot," he slurred. "Too hot."

"Okay," Tess said, as if steeling herself. "Okay, here's what we're going to do. I'm going to draw you a hot bath—I know, it sounds awful, but it will help break the fever—and I'll make you that clove tea."

He shook his head. "You don't—have to."

"Don't be silly," she clipped, already in motion. "I can't just leave you like this."

"You should have left me when you had the chance," Callum mumbled, his mouth dry and thick. "Then neither of us would have to be here."

Tess looked back at him for a long moment, but she didn't respond. Maybe she hadn't heard him over the water from the bath.

❧

"How is he?" Nantale was stately and reserved as always, but Tess could sense she was deeply worried. They were standing in the hallway outside Callum's rooms, speaking in hushed tones while he slept.

"I don't know," Tess answered. "The fever got a little better after a hot bath, but he seemed very weak. Do you know when Sylvie and the others will be back?"

"Tomorrow, I hope?" Nantale folded her arms. "Unless something has happened to delay them."

Tess nodded, a knot of dread taking hold in her stomach. She was afraid for Callum, but also for herself—if he died, would Nantale assign someone else to work with Tess to figure out a way off the Isle? Or would she give up hope—and give her clan the green light to use Tess's blood to sate their hunger? Maybe she'd allow Tess to leave the compound and go home—except the crystal bridge was gone, so Tess couldn't go anywhere. Tess imagined living out her mortal life in this place, subsisting on whatever food she could find in the northern woods, hoping no vampire came across her. A quick death would probably be preferable.

"I know Callum can be difficult," Nantale said quietly. "But you must understand, he is my most trusted ally in this clan."

"He's a brilliant fighter," Tess murmured.

"It's more than that. Do you know what it was like in the early days on the Isle? Does it say this in your books?"

"I know there was a lot of violence, but not much more than that."

Nantale nodded. "That's true. Felix and his clan made clear rules in this place: Join or die. If we didn't like them or what they stood for, they killed us off one by one."

Tess frowned—that didn't track with the Felix she knew from *Blood Feud,* nor with the man she'd met.

"Callum is the one who came to me to suggest we form a clan, who convinced the rest of the group to follow me—and as you may have noticed, this is not a group who likes to do what they're told."

"Why didn't you want to join Felix?" Tess asked.

"Those robots?" Nantale wrinkled her nose. "I never took orders from men as a mortal—I'm certainly not going to start in my sixth century of life. Felix claims to want to protect vampires, but isn't that what autocrats always say? 'Only I can keep you safe.'"

That's exactly what he told me, Tess thought.

"But . . ." Tess suddenly felt nauseous. "If Felix isn't trying to keep his clan safe, why does he need a clan at all? What's the point?"

"*Power* is the point." Nantale gave Tess a sharp look. "Don't tell me you haven't seen this, girl, even in your short life. A man who thinks his desires are the only desires, who'll justify taking what he wants by any means necessary?"

Tess nodded numbly. "I've seen it."

"Felix is drunk with it. If Callum hadn't been brave enough to try to stop him . . ." Nantale's expression was dark. "I owe Callum a debt of gratitude to protect his life with mine. I appreciate you doing what you can to care for him—and I won't forget it."

Nantale took her leave, and Tess quietly went back into Callum's room—he was still sleeping fitfully. Tess didn't know how she was going to keep him alive until Sylvie came back; cool compresses and hot baths and warm rabbit's blood were all well and good, but none of them could stop the poison inside him. And when Tess thought about him dying . . . she was pretty sure it was more than just fear for her own future that made the idea so upsetting.

"Tess?" Callum's voice was hoarse.

"What is it?" She rushed to his bedside. He looked wan and exhausted, and she had to suppress an urge to brush his hair back from his forehead. "Do you need another compress? More blood?"

"Maybe some water?"

She grabbed a glass from his cupboard and filled it from the tap, then brought it over to him. He struggled to sit up, then drank deeply—he exhaled hard, coughing.

"Take your time," she said gently.

He nodded, then took a smaller sip.

"I need to tell you something." Tess shifted uncomfortably in the chair next to his bed.

"Christ, Tess. Another secret?" he grumbled. "It's like Pandora's bloody box every time you open your mouth." Tess felt a surge of affection for him—even at death's doorstep, he was adorably ornery.

"Not a secret." She bit her lip. "An apology."

Callum's face turned more serious. "Go on."

"I should have told you about Felix. It's just—I've been confused. With what *Blood Feud* says about you, what *he* said about you . . . I didn't know if I could trust you, if I was stupid not to trust him instead. But I believe you've been honest with me. And I'm sorry I lied to you."

"I understand why you lied." Callum looked up at her. "The way

I'm portrayed in your books . . . A lot of it's wrong, but a lot of it isn't. I can see how you wouldn't trust a man like me."

There was a heaviness in his voice, a sadness Tess wanted desperately to ease.

"It's not just you," Tess said softly. "I, um. I'm not really a trusting person."

"Yeah, but at least you tried to give me a chance, which is more than I did for you." Callum looked down in disgust. "Leaving you alone in that forest? That was shameful. Especially when I think of what Felix could have done to you."

"You don't really think he'd hurt me, do you?" Tess frowned. Even if Nantale was right that Felix was drunk with power, Tess still had a hard time believing he'd harm an innocent.

"He would if it served him. If he knew you were valuable to me, to our clan? He'd torture you to death just to cause me pain."

Tess's breath caught in her throat—Callum would be in pain if she was harmed?

"What is it with you and Felix?" Tess asked. "Why do you hate each other so much?"

"What do your books say about it?"

"Not much. Just that Konstantin preferred you and Octavia, that you were his only sires, his favorites. The books make it seem like Felix was trying to protect the vampires on the Isle from you."

Callum sighed. "The first bit is right—Konstantin did prefer us. To be honest, we never paid Felix much thought. He was always trying to push his agenda on Konstantin: his idea for a vampire hierarchy, sheriffs, order, that whole scheme. Felix said it was a way to expand Konstantin's power, but Konstantin never wanted that. He liked to keep a lean operation, move in the shadows, do what he pleased."

"And make *you* do what he pleased," Tess pointed out.

"True," Callum acknowledged. "As long as Octavia and I did what Konstantin wanted, there was no question about the pecking order—it was us first, then Felix far behind. No matter how hard he worked, he wasn't as powerful as us, and he wasn't Konstantin's blood sire, either."

"That must have driven him crazy."

"Expect it did, poor lad." Callum smiled grimly. "But things changed when Vee and I fell out with Konstantin."

"Wait, did that happen in Korea? In Seoul?" Tess asked.

"Yes." Callum looked alarmed. "Was that in *Blood Feud,* or did Felix tell you?"

"No, neither," Tess assured him. "Octavia mentioned it in one of her notes. But it didn't seem relevant to getting off the Isle, so I didn't think anything of it."

"It was her idea to go to Korea, back in the late nineties," Callum said. "Nineteen nineties, that is."

"Thank you for clarifying." Tess smiled. "You'd never been?"

"It was easier to stay close to Europe, in case Konstantin needed us. Longer flights are hard to navigate with daylight—especially before you could just look up a flight schedule online," Callum explained. "And our father . . ."

"He was Korean, right?" Tess asked. "A ship worker?"

Callum nodded. "We knew nothing about him, and the name Yoo was far too common to track. We looked different from every other kid in the orphanages, every worker at the factories, every aristocrat Konstantin introduced us to, and none of them let us forget it. We found the best way to deal with the looks and the comments was just to ignore them, act like we were exactly the same as everyone else, even though of course we weren't. We felt like our father abandoned us, left us to the care of strangers with nothing but a target on our faces."

"What a horrible feeling," Tess murmured. "What changed? What made you want to go to Korea?"

"Do you know about the Hallyu?" he asked. "The Korean wave?"

"Vaguely," Tess answered. "This one girl I knew in college was super into K-pop."

"Korean culture was exploding, reaching us in Europe far more than ever before. Vee and I started watching K-dramas, then we met a Korean expat in Paris who introduced us to Korean music—and we loved it. We felt like we had to be a part of it. So we figured out a series of night flights, and we just went."

"What was it like?" Tess asked.

A hazy pleasure fell over Callum's face—Tess had never seen him look so relaxed.

"Every place we went, we felt like we belonged. Vee made friends with designers, musicians, artists, like she always did. Eating the food, traveling the country, meeting all these people, even a few vampires—we couldn't get enough. We started coming back more and more, staying for longer periods of time. And being so far from Konstantin . . ."

"He didn't have so much power over you," Tess said quietly. "The distance gave you freedom."

"Precisely." Callum eyed her. "It was the first time we felt like we could be ourselves, make our own choices instead of only ever obeying him. So around ten years after that first visit, he asked us to come to London to do something for him, and we just . . . didn't."

"I bet he loved that," Tess muttered.

"Yeah, hardly. He turned up in Seoul a few days later, told us he'd never been so disappointed in anyone, to have his own sires turn our backs when he needed us most."

"Needed you?" Tess was puzzled. "What for?"

Callum sighed. "He said he was working on something big—biggest thing he'd ever planned. Said he couldn't do it without me, that I owed him for all he'd done for me and Vee. So I agreed to go with him, but only if Vee could stay in Seoul."

"You protected her." Tess shook her head with wonder. "Of course you did."

Callum looked up at Tess—there was an intensity in his gaze she couldn't quite read, but it made her whole body feel warm.

"So, um." She swallowed hard. "So what happened next?"

"Oh." He looked down, breaking the moment. "Turned out Konstantin's big idea was to attack a nightclub."

"The one in Prague?" Tess frowned.

"You know about it?" Callum raised his eyebrows, and she nodded. "Of course you do. Anyway, Konstantin meant it as a coming-out party of sorts. A statement to let humans know vampires exist, to be afraid. I was furious with him—*this* was why he dragged me back from Korea? To murder dozens of helpless humans for some harebrained show of force? I decided I had to stop him, to foil the plan somehow. Then Felix came to me with an idea."

Tess narrowed her eyes. "Out of the blue?"

"Too convenient by half, wasn't it?" Callum laughed, but the sound was dark and hollow. "Should have known it'd go sideways, but it seemed simple enough at the time. He suggested I start a small fire in the back of the club, set off the alarms to derail the attack and keep everyone safe. It made sense to me, so I went along and did it. Except . . ."

Tess already knew what happened next—she'd read at least a dozen articles about it in her Feudie days, looking for clues of vampire involvement.

"The club burned to the ground," she said softly. "Did Konstantin die inside?"

"Konstantin, a few other vampires, half a dozen humans." Callum grimaced. "Once they got the fire out, I stayed searching for him as long as I could, until dawn. Even afterward, I combed the city for days, desperate for any sign of him. For all he was a terrible man, for all the times I hated him . . . he still saved me, you know? He picked me and Octavia, gave us this whole other life."

"Oh god," Tess said, realizing. "So when you felt relieved about being here on the Isle, being out from under Konstantin's thumb—you must have felt so guilty too."

"And that was Felix's plan all along." Callum gritted. "With Konstantin dead, he could finally take over, claim all that power for himself. He blamed me for the catastrophe at the nightclub, made sure Konstantin's whole crew stayed loyal to him. That's how he started his clan. And he thought I'd feel too guilty about what I'd done to fight him."

"Except you did." Tess clenched her fists. "Nantale told me—you were the one who rallied this clan to follow her and fight back."

"Couldn't bloody well let him win, could I? Not after what he did."

"And then you saw him with me in the orchard." Tess exhaled heavily. "No wonder you were furious."

"I thought it was the same bit again," Callum mumbled, his words starting to slur again—Tess could see he was fading. "Using my emotions against me."

"What emotions?" Tess asked.

Callum closed his eyes—he was clearly in pain. "I didn't want you to leave."

"But you didn't try to stop me." Tess shook her head, trying to make sense of what he was saying.

" 'Course not. Your decision."

He opened his eyes, and Tess was struck, not for the first time, by how extraordinarily handsome he was. She thought about Felix, how he'd pushed her from their first meeting to move into his castle. Callum had never pushed her once—never put the slightest pressure on her to do anything she didn't want to do. Callum gazed at her with his striking gray eyes, and Tess felt so pulled to him, so close to him.

Was she afraid of him because of everything she'd read in *Blood Feud*? Or was she afraid because it was becoming impossible to ignore how she felt about him?

"You must be tired." Tess cleared her throat. "I shouldn't have made you talk so long. You should get some rest."

"You're not the boss of me." He grinned through his exhaustion. "You can't make me do anything."

"Wanna bet?" She swallowed her emotions and smiled. "I'm making you go to sleep right now."

"Will you stay?" he asked softly. "I don't want to be alone."

"Of course," Tess said, her voice tender. "If you need anything, I'll be right here in this chair, okay? I promise."

He propped himself up slowly, sliding over to the far side of the bed.

"Don't be thick." His breath was labored. "You can't sleep in a chair."

"Oh." Tess felt suddenly tense—she hadn't shared a bed in years, not since Columbia. "No, no, um—that's okay. I wouldn't want to disturb you."

He smiled sadly, like he could see right through her. "Still lying to me, love?"

"Yeah." Tess nodded. "I am."

"I don't want you to be afraid of me," he murmured.

Tess's chest felt tight. "Me neither."

"It's your choice," he said again. "It's whatever helps you sleep."

Tess thought of all the nights she'd lain awake, at war with her memories, praying for sleep—an hour, twenty minutes, anything at all.

Callum didn't want to hurt her. He just wanted her to rest.

"Okay," she whispered.

She climbed into bed beside him, relaxing into the soft mattress, pulling the heavy covers over her body. He settled down on his side, facing her, and she did the same. Callum blinked heavily—once, twice—his thick lashes fluttering in the moonlight. It was marvelously strange, sharing a bed with a vampire from her favorite story. But the weirdest part about it was that, for the first time since arriving on this island—and maybe for a good deal longer than that—Tess didn't feel afraid.

Chapter 18

When Tess woke up, the light was soft and white, like the prettiest morning sunlight filtered through the finest silk.

"Where are we?" She stretched in bed luxuriously, like a cat. The bed was all white too; the sheets were crisp and cotton.

"You've been here before." Callum rolled over and smiled at her—not his usual teasing smirk, something sweeter. "Don't you remember?"

"I don't know this place," Tess murmured. She was confused, but she also knew he wasn't wrong.

"You could," he said. "You just have to walk through that door."

Tess looked behind her—he was right, there was a doorway. The door was made of white marble, patterned with the same ancient runes she'd seen on the door to Bar Between back in Vinegar Hill.

"There's no silver tree with yellow leaves." Tess was worried. "How do I know this is the right door?"

"The same way you know everything."

He took her hand, and his skin was warmer than she'd ever felt it.

"The light," she realized. "It's safe for you?"

"It's safe for both of us." He kissed her palm. "I promise."

"Come with me," she urged, and he nodded. He didn't need convincing.

She wore a nightshirt and he wore pajamas, the same cool cotton as their bedsheets.

"I'm so nervous," she told him as they approached the door.

"You don't have to be." He squeezed her hand. "Everyone's waiting."

Slowly, she pulled open the white marble door, and when she saw what was behind it, she was so happy she nearly cried.

It was the library at Columbia, her favorite round room, an oak table piled high with books and a picture window overlooking a cluster of trees.

"Is this really happening?" Tess whispered. "How did we get here?"

"You found the answer," he told her. "You brought us home."

His smile was so beautiful, so kind—she felt like her joy was so powerful it couldn't possibly be contained within one person's body. She threw her arms around his neck, and he drew her close, holding her in his strong arms.

"Are you going to kiss me now?" She beamed at him.

"Word of warning, love." He grinned. "Once I start, I'm not likely to stop."

He leaned toward her, but they were interrupted by a banging on the door.

"What is that?" she asked him.

He shook his head—he didn't know.

The banging grew louder—someone was shouting her name.

"Who's there?" she called. She took a step toward the door—when she turned back, Callum was gone, and the room had gone pitch black.

"Callum?!" she screamed in a panic. "*Callum!*"

• • •

"Tess, open the door!"

Tess woke with a shot—oh god, what was happening—she never slept long anywhere. How was it possible she'd fallen dead asleep sharing a bed with a fucking vampire?! Callum was out cold, curled on his side—was he okay?

"Callum," Tess croaked, her voice thick with sleep. "Wake up, someone's here."

But he didn't move—a sickening wave of dread took hold of Tess. She shook him, but he didn't respond—oh god, was he dead? She rolled him onto his back and saw that he was breathing—oh, thank god. The knocking was getting louder. She flew to the door and pulled it open. Sylvie and Nantale were there. Sylvie was holding a large pot full of something that smelled sour and herbaceous.

"Come quickly," Tess panted. "He fell asleep. I can't wake him."

"Move," Nantale said firmly, and Tess did. Nantale and Sylvie sped across the room to Callum—Sylvie stripped off the bedding as Nantale laid him out flat.

"You found the lilies?" Tess asked, trying to keep the panic out of her voice. "Did everything go okay?"

"Quiet, girl," Nantale ordered.

"Tess, will you get me some fresh water?" Sylvie asked, her voice calm but urgent.

Tess rushed to the sink as Sylvie removed the dressing from Callum's wound. Tess gasped when she saw how bad Callum's leg looked—the wound had festered, the veins around it were black.

"He's still breathing," Sylvie reassured her. "That means we can still save him."

Tess nodded, hoping fervently that she was right. Sylvie cleaned the wound with the water and a white cloth, then dipped a wooden rod into the poultice.

"This is going to hurt," Sylvie said to Tess and Nantale. "I need you to keep him still."

Nantale nodded, then placed one hand on each of Callum's ankles—she was strong enough to keep him from kicking. Tess climbed back into the bed and took his hand.

Sylvie used the rod to spread the poultice across Callum's wound, and he woke with a shot.

"Fuck! What the bloody fuck—"

"It's okay." Tess clasped Callum's hand as hard as she could. "Sylvie's putting on the poultice. She's going to cure you. That's just the medicine working, you're okay. Try to stay still if you can."

Callum looked up at Tess, tears streaming from his eyes. She knew he was more than a century old, but he looked so young to her then, like a little boy in terror.

"It's okay," she said again, removing one of her hands from his so she could brush the hair back from his forehead. "We're going to get you better, and then we're going to get you home to your sister, okay? Everything's going to be okay."

Tess realized that she was crying too. She tried to blink back the tears, but Nantale was already eyeing her. Nantale didn't say anything, though—she just held down Callum's legs as Sylvie finished applying the poultice and redressing the wound.

"There," Sylvie said. "It's done."

Callum's eyes were closed; he was breathing heavily, but the pain seemed to be much less than it had been even a few moments before.

"How long will it take to work?" Nantale snapped at Sylvie.

"I've never done this before," Sylvie replied evenly. "We'll just have to wait."

"Fine," Nantale said curtly, removing her hands from Callum's ankles and standing up. "Alert me when something changes."

Nantale looked down at Callum once more, her hands clasped tightly together, before she turned and swept out of the room.

"Tess?" Callum asked softly.

His eyes fluttered open, his thick lashes wet with sweat and tears.

"I'm here," she whispered. She squeezed his hand, and he looked into her eyes. "What do you need?"

"I need . . ." His eyelids were heavy; he was struggling to stay awake. "I need . . ."

"You need to rest." Sylvie put one hand on Callum's shoulder and the other on Tess's back. "And Tess probably needs to eat something, am I right?"

"Oh." Tess looked up at Sylvie. "No, I'm fine. I can stay here."

"I know you want to, mamaleh." Sylvie rubbed Tess's back gently. "But he needs to sleep, let the medicine work. And you'll feel so much better after a meal and a shower. I'll watch him, I promise."

"Is that okay, Callum?" Tess turned to Callum.

"'Course." He nodded—his breath already seemed easier, and he looked more relaxed.

"See?" Sylvie smiled at Tess. "Go ahead, we'll be fine. Do you need anything? Do you want me to make you some food?"

"No, there's plenty in my room," Tess said—then something occurred to her. "Actually, I have a question. Does this compound have a library?"

⁊

After Tess left, Callum asked Sylvie for some more clove tea, so she put on a kettle.

"So," she said, her voice a little too casual. "Tess spent the night here?"

"*Sleeping,*" Callum emphasized. "Do I look like I'm in any fit state to do more than that?"

"Not really," Sylvie conceded. "But you want to?"

Callum laughed softly. Just hours ago, he hadn't thought he'd live through the night. The pain of Sylvie applying the poultice was excruciating, but it was already dulling, and he could feel the antidote working within him. He knew it wouldn't be long until his strength returned—and all he could fucking think about was getting that woman back in his bed. God, he was so predictable.

"Doesn't matter what I want," he said gruffly. "She's afraid of me."

Sylvie's face softened. "If that were true, she wouldn't have shared a bed with you."

"Sure, when I could barely move." Callum sighed. Sylvie looked at him shrewdly.

"Is she afraid, or are you?"

"Me?" Callum scoffed. "Afraid of her? What, you think she's gonna stake me when I'm all postcoital and glowy? She just saved my life."

"And have you ever stopped to wonder why she did that?" Sylvie rolled her eyes. "Do you think it's possible the two of you might need each other, and that's why you're both so scared?"

"I know you look like a wise grandma, but I'm actually much, much older than you."

"Doesn't mean you're not an idiot," Sylvie said frankly.

"Well—what do I do then?" His tone was grumpy, but he still felt vulnerable.

"Feh, what do I know?" The kettle whistled, and Sylvie poured some steaming water into a mug. "If it was me, I'd show her you're not afraid and she doesn't have to be."

After a couple of wrong turns—one down a trick passageway with doors that all led back to each other and took Tess the better part of an hour to get out of, another into a room that looked like an operating theater but was lavishly appointed in brocade and velvet and definitely seemed like an *Eyes Wide Shut* situation—Tess finally found what she was looking for.

The compound's library wasn't a room, exactly—more like a giant glass terrarium that housed an elaborate treehouse. Except "treehouse" was far too reductive: This was a self-contained tree city, with at least twenty towering oaks whose long boughs twisted and intertwined to provide a kind of webbing, on which there were dozens of wooden platforms, each about the size of a small room, filled with bookshelves and tables and comfortable chairs. An intricate system of stairways and ladders connected the various platforms; it would take hours to explore them all. The whole place had a twinkle-lit glow—there were fairy lights strung through the branches and lamps with jewel-bright stained glass shades on every table—all of which reflected in the glass enclosing the library and the trees outside the room.

"Oh my god," Tess said aloud. She quickly looked to see if anyone else was here—the last thing she wanted was to be trapped in a labyrinth fifty feet off the ground with a vampire who fancied a snack. But the library was totally silent except for the soft rustle of leaves.

Tess wasn't sure how she could possibly navigate all these books—finding one that had the exact information she needed seemed utterly improbable. But when she ascended the staircase to the first platform, just a few feet off the ground, she discovered it held several plush wingback chairs and a card catalogue. She opened a few drawers at random to see what topics they held, including "Crusades, role of vampires in" and "Garlic, common myths regarding," before she found the card for "Portals, properties of." On the card's back side, there was a whole list of books, many of which were in languages Tess couldn't understand. She decided to start with a philosophical text on dimensional theory, a memoir of a time traveler, and a compendium of gems that could be used to enhance other forms of magic (which she didn't expect to be all that useful, but it sounded fun). Each book listed on the card had a corresponding platform number. The platforms were arranged in a haphazard spiral pattern, and each platform had a small wooden post with a gold plaque engraved with its respective number. So Tess took her card and got to climbing.

As breathtaking as the library was when she walked through the door, it was somehow even better once she started making her way up the platforms. Each one was different, reflective of the books it housed: The carved wooden chairs in the Egyptology section were inlaid with gold hieroglyphics, while the section on common remedies for vampire ailments was its own small greenhouse filled with herbs for various tinctures. The gemology section felt like being inside a giant geode, every surface spiky with glittering crystals. And all of it felt like floating through a forest, rich with the scents of pine, soft leather, and ancient books.

It was Tess's idea of heaven—and it made her miss Columbia so badly her chest throbbed with a dull ache.

She remembered how it felt those first few weeks at school, the outrageous notion of being paid (an absolute pittance, but paid nevertheless) to spend her days surrounded by scholarship on all her favorite topics. It was ironic that she was in this library trying to figure out how to get back to New York when she'd come to the Isle in the first place because she was desperate to escape. She'd been terrified when she saw Rick at Joni's party—but was he scarier than the vampires in this place? More frightening than standing up to Tristan or staking Althea in the gut? Was some golden boy with a rich dad enough of a threat to keep Tess from living the life she'd worked so hard for, the future she'd dreamed of?

After hours in the library, Tess found all the books she was looking for, but she didn't feel any closer to understanding the portal she'd seen in the moonflower meadow (let alone how to re-create it). The philosophical text was too dense to parse; the time-traveling memoirist used objects from the past to create his portals, which was interesting—maybe something Tess had brought with her from New York could help to create a portal to get back there? She'd have to see if she could find another book to confirm that theory. The compendium of gems was, as expected, more fun than it was useful.

It had gorgeous illustrations of fabulous jewels that could be used to enhance all kinds of spells, but the only one it mentioned for portal magic was a rare snowflake obsidian mined exclusively in Antarctica, which reminded Tess of the dome she'd walked through back in Brooklyn to get to Bar Between. But Tess thought it rather unlikely they'd find any on the Isle. (Glamoured or otherwise man-made stones, Tess learned from the book, were of no use for magic, because they lacked the inherent properties of the places from which they were mined.)

Tess's stomach growled—Sylvie's pastries were delicious, but she needed a proper meal. She carried her books to Callum's rooms, feeling increasingly nervous as she walked down the compound's empty hallways. She wanted so badly for him to be better. She wanted herself to be better too.

But when she knocked on his door, no one answered.

"Sylvie?" she called softly, not wanting to wake Callum if he was sleeping. "Callum, are you in there?"

When there was no response, she gently tried the door handle, and it opened right up. The room was empty, but there was a note on the desk scrawled in Callum's slapdash writing:

Tess—Meet us in the great room. C.

Tess knew that vampires made fast recoveries, but had Callum really gotten better so quickly that he could already leave his room? She hurried down the hall, hoping everything was all right. She wondered if Nantale had called a clan meeting, and if so, what it was about—maybe news had spread about the crystal bridge? But when Tess made it to the great room, she saw something different entirely.

Two dozen vampires were there, all yelling at one another.

"I am not *rude!*" Angelique huffed. "I'm *truthful,* god, there's a difference!"

"At least you're described at all!" Hamish looked on the brink of tears. "I'm only mentioned in an aside, Angelique. An aside!!"

Every single one of the vampires was holding a copy of *Blood Feud*.

"Oh my god." Tess had to stifle a laugh. "Are they—is this—?"

"Welcome to vampire book club." Callum appeared beside her, a snide grin playing on his lips. "Shall I fetch you a chardonnay?"

Chapter 19

Zoe: Omg what's going on with Prof. Chaudhari

Rebecca: Is she sick???? She looks DEAD

Rob: Dude she's been out of it for like a week
Rob: She has a new boyfriend, bet

Jessica: Ok in the first place are you blind she's g-a-y
Jessica: Second place yeah she's down bad for someone

Rob: So you're saying I was right??

Jessica: I would never say that

Zoe: Did you see her get all misty-eyed when she was talking about Eros and how physically passionate love doesn't necessarily translate to long-term partnership, but you just have to enjoy and accept it for what it is??? You guys it was so CUTE

Rebecca: All I know is if she doesn't grade our papers soon I'm filing a complaint

—Forwarded Message—
From: Professor Lareina Vázquez <lv553@columbia.edu>
To: Joni Chaudhari <jc718@columbia.edu>
Sent: August 20 11:24 AM
Subject: Interview prep?

> Hi, Joni. I heard you have your first interview with the search committee this Friday, and I'm wondering if you'd like to do some prep. I've been meaning to catch you around the department, but haven't seen you at all the past week—have you been sick? I have office hours Wednesday from 2–4 p.m. if you'd like to drop by. Hope to see you there. LV

"Who are you texting?" Octavia rolled over in bed, her fingers grazing Joni's arm.

Since their kiss at the Met, they'd spent most of the last few days in bed. Joni had picked up some cow's blood from a butcher for Octavia (not Octavia's favorite, but it was convenient to keep it in the hotel room's little fridge), and went out every so often to get food for herself, mostly boxes of cereal and bodega sandwiches. After weeks of being alone and powerless in New York, Octavia relished the constant companionship more than she imagined possible. Joni was overly enthusiastic and a bit of a weirdo, sure—but she was also funny and empathetic and had an endless appetite to talk with Octavia about absolutely any topic Octavia found interesting.

And Joni's enthusiasm, Octavia found, was a highly useful quality in someone with whom you were having quite a lot of sex.

"Just checking my email." Joni shoved her phone over on the nightstand and rolled over to face Octavia. "I thought you were asleep."

"So you're not texting another woman?" Octavia needled.

"What?" Joni laughed—then peered at Octavia. "Why? Do you, like, not want me to text other people?"

"No, you can talk to anyone you want," Octavia said quickly. She lightly kissed the spot at the edge of Joni's jaw, just below her ear. Joni squirmed against her, and the frisson was delicious. "I just want to make sure you're not distracted when I have so many occupations for you right here."

"Oh yeah?" Joni's breath was hot on Octavia's neck. "What kinds of occupations did you have in mind?"

Octavia raked her fingers through Joni's hair—it was so thick, so easy to grab in decadent fistfuls. Joni gasped softly, a high-pitched little noise that made Octavia feel deliciously in control.

"You're going to do exactly what I tell you, do you understand?"

"Yes." Joni nodded, eager as always.

"Good girl." Octavia nipped at Joni's earlobe, and Joni writhed again, wrapping both of her legs around one of Octavia's.

"Did I say you could do that?" Octavia teased her.

"Do you want me to stop?" Joni slid her body up Octavia's thigh, so that now Joni's thigh was pressed against Octavia too—Octavia moaned despite herself.

"You wicked little thing." Octavia grinned.

Even without her powers, Octavia was still stronger than Joni—much stronger. In an instant, Octavia had Joni on her back, her thigh pressed between the girl's legs—Joni instantly arched her back, desperate to create more friction.

"You want me, don't you?" Octavia leaned down, her face close to Joni's.

"I always want you," Joni murmured. She tipped her chin upward—she obviously wanted to kiss Octavia, but Octavia leaned back, out of Joni's reach.

"Good," Octavia said softly. "Now lie back and close your eyes."

Joni did as she was told. Octavia slid her hand between Joni's legs, working her fingers in slow circles, moving firmer and faster until Joni's hips jerked and bucked and she screamed out Octavia's name.

There, Octavia thought as Joni fell back against the mattress, breathing hard. *Let's see her think about some other girl now.*

⁓

It was well and good for Octavia to sleep all day after having sex all night, but Joni had class, and she was fucking exhausted.

"Don't go." Octavia pouted as Joni threw the last of her stuff into her backpack. "It's raining. Wouldn't you rather stay here in a nice hot bath?"

"That does sound substantially better than teaching undergrads about modern interpretations of Greek tragedies," Joni acknowledged. "But if I want to keep collecting my meager stipend, they like for me to show up."

"It's cruel, is what it is." Octavia draped her hands around Joni's neck. "What are you doing after?"

"I have to meet with my adviser to talk about my job interview."

"And then?" Octavia raised an eyebrow.

"Umm, home, I guess? Shower, do some laundry, sleep in my own bed? At night?"

The excuse sounded flimsy coming out of Joni's mouth, but she really did need to get some sleep and prep for her interview—and if past was prologue, she knew she wouldn't be doing either in this hotel room.

"Good." Octavia's tone was chilly. She picked up a champagne coupe filled with blood and took a sip.

"What are you going to do?" Joni asked nervously. "Just hang here?"

"All this rain, I was thinking I might get outside for a bit."

Octavia gestured toward the suite's window, where the curtains were uncharacteristically open. The Manhattan skyline looked smeared and dismal in the storm; the view was so romantic Joni thought for a moment about blowing off everything she had to do and spending another day with Octavia. But she couldn't ditch class . . . and as nervous as she was to talk with Dr. Vázquez about a job she was certain she wouldn't get, she knew her adviser was generous to offer to help her prep—and Joni really needed the advice.

"Cool," Joni said brightly, even though she suddenly felt like crap. "I'll call you if I hear anything on Lirio?"

"Sounds good." Octavia got up and wandered toward the bathroom, not bothering to turn around as Joni left. "See you when I see you."

"Joni, you're going to be *fine,*" Dr. Vázquez insisted.

"But what if the committee doesn't take my work seriously?" Joni wrung her hands. "I mean, I study a lot of pop culture—"

"You study modern interpretations of ancient archetypes," Dr. Vázquez corrected. "The undergrads love you, you get amazing teaching ratings, and you've been published in a major journal."

"As the second author," Joni grumbled. She was still salty that Rick Keeton had demoted her on the article they co-wrote three years ago, but she knew they never would have been published in the first place if it wasn't for his family connections at the journal. So she didn't complain. It was good for her to get the publication, and Rick was a nice guy who could definitely help her career in the future. It didn't seem worth picking a fight about credit—even if he was probably about to get her dream job over her. He was the undisputed star of the department, even without that article. He probably would have gotten the job anyway.

"You're right—this hiring process is going to be extremely competitive," Dr. Vázquez said bluntly. "And frankly, if you don't believe you deserve to win the job, I don't see how you're going to convince the committee. Our department already has plenty of pretentious blowhards who study so-called serious literature, and of course there's value in that. But I also believe there's value in studying popular writing—work that affects millions of people. Don't you believe that too? Isn't that why you're dedicating your career to that pursuit?"

Joni's cheeks felt hot. Obviously she agreed with Dr. Vázquez—she'd made a version of that same impassioned speech on multiple occasions (usually following three or more glasses of wine).

"You're right." Joni sighed. "Of course you're right. I guess, I don't know—I guess if I kind of quit on myself before I even apply for the job, it won't hurt as much when I inevitably don't get it?"

"No shit." Dr. Vázquez smiled wryly. "But if you want something in this life, you have to sack up and be vulnerable and fucking go for it. So quit whining and do it already, okay?"

Joni nodded. "I will. I promise."

She was feeling a lot better when she walked out of Dr. Vázquez's office—she had a lot of work to do before her interview, but she had almost two full days. All she had to do was stay out of Octavia Yoo's hotel room.

"Joni, hey!"

Joni looked up to see Rick waiting on a bench outside Dr. Vázquez's office.

"Oh, hi." Joni forced a smile. "You're not waiting for me, are you?"

"Nah, here to talk to Dr. Vázquez about my interview." He flashed her an easy smile.

"Wait, what? But she's not even your adviser."

"Oh, I'm talking to every professor in the department—aren't you?" He looked at her earnestly.

"Right." Joni pressed her lips together. "Of course. That makes sense."

Dr. Vázquez poked her head out of her door. "Rick? I'm ready for you."

"Cool." He stood up and grabbed his backpack. "Nice to see you, Joni. And hey, good luck on Friday!"

He gave her an affable pat on the shoulder as he went into the office. Joni tried to shake off what felt like a cross between nausea and white-hot fury, but she was entirely distracted when she saw a tall, gorgeous woman leaning against the wall a few feet away.

"*Octavia?*" She gasped and rushed over to her. "It's daylight! What are you doing here?"

"Still raining." Octavia grinned. "And I was bored! Wanted to see where you're always running off to. Sat in on a lecture about the long-term ramifications of the Chinese Exclusion Act—someone should tell Professor Chang-Reitman he's missing a lot of crucial details. And I should know. I was there."

Joni closed her eyes; she felt a tension headache coming on. "Please do not tell the history professors that you're a vampire."

"Wouldn't dream of it!" Octavia breezed. "Unless they're cute enough to feed on. Anyway, now that I'm here, what should we do with our afternoon? I could fancy a museum, or maybe an early supper—"

"I can't, I told you." Joni sighed. Her phone was buzzing in her bag, and she reached in to grab it.

"Oh, blow off work," Octavia wheedled. "When you're as old as I am, you realize how silly all those mortal concerns really are—"

But Joni wasn't listening to Octavia—she was wide-eyed, staring at her phone.

"What is it now?" Octavia huffed.

Joni looked up, her eyes wide. "It's Betherton's assistant. She found an address for Lirio, and she wants me to meet her there tomorrow."

Joni held out her phone, and Octavia quickly scrolled the messages from Fern.

"This is *brilliant,*" she breathed.

"No it isn't!" Joni protested. "My interview is Friday, and I so need to prep. Maybe Fern can reschedule?"

"To introduce you to a notorious recluse?" Octavia looked flabbergasted. "This is the break we've been wanting for days, this is exactly what we need to get my brother home, my entire future depends on this!"

"Then go yourself!" Joni burst out. "If you can make it to my campus, you can make it to some townhouse in Gramercy Park."

"She wants to meet you at two P.M." Octavia tapped on Joni's phone. "Is it supposed to rain again tomorrow?"

Joni pulled up her weather app and sighed. "No. Hot and sunny."

"See?" Octavia took Joni's hand. "I know your other obligations are important, but this is my whole life we're talking about. Please, Joni, do this one thing for me—once Callum comes back, I promise I'll be out of your hair forever."

"Oh." Joni was taken aback. "Really?"

Octavia threaded her fingers through Joni's. "I mean, you have your life, I'll have mine. No more imposing on your busy schedule. That's what you want too, right?"

Joni felt a tightness in her chest. What had Dr. Vázquez just said about being vulnerable and going for what you want? It suddenly seemed unbelievably stupid. Because it didn't matter how much Joni might want something real with Octavia—Octavia would never want it back.

"Right," Joni mumbled.

"What do you say, then?" Octavia pulled Joni close and kissed her cheek. "Will you meet Fern tomorrow?"

"Sure." Joni swallowed hard and her voice was flat. "No problem."

TEXT MESSAGE TRANSCRIPT:
JONI CHAUDHARI AND TESS ROSENBLOOM

Joni [1:07 PM]: I know I've told you a lot of crazy things in the past few days, but this might top them all?

Joni [1:08 PM]: I am leaving my apartment right now to get on a subway to Gramercy Park, theoretically to go meet August Lirio

Joni [1:08 PM]: Needless to say, I am absolutely losing my shit

Joni [1:09 PM]: I really, really, really wish you were here

Chapter 20

"Callum." Tess's breath caught in her throat. "You're—I mean, you look . . ."

He looked *good,* was how he looked. Healthy and strong, his color returned—well, what little of it he had to begin with—wearing faded jeans and a soft flannel shirt, the sleeves rolled up over his forearms. It wasn't just that he looked miraculously recovered . . . there was something else too. Maybe it was that, for the first time since Tess had met him, he looked genuinely happy.

"All better? That poultice was just the ticket." He grinned again, then leaned close to murmur in Tess's ear; his cool breath made the hairs on her neck prickle. "Thanks again for saving me."

"Oh." Tess's heart raced; she was suddenly very aware that she'd spent the last twenty minutes rushing through the compound carrying three heavy books. She cleared her throat. "Good. I'm glad."

"I want you to know . . ." He kept his voice low, so only she could hear it. "All the things you've told me over the past few days, I've been listening. So there's something we need to do, all right?"

He looked at her meaningfully, then took her by the arm—her stomach instantly tightened.

"What?" she asked. "Where are we . . ."

"Trust me," he assured her. But then she saw they were heading straight toward Tristan.

"Absolutely not," Tess hissed. "I don't want to talk to him."

"You don't need to talk," he replied. "Just listen."

"Well, well," Tristan sneered when he saw them approaching. "Look who's made it out of Callum's bedroom. Tell me, Tess, is he as good as it says in the book?"

He waved his copy of *Blood Feud* and gave them a sickening grin.

"Tess and I have been talking. A lot." Callum's eyes glinted dangerously. "As a matter of fact, she's told me some pretty interesting things about you."

Tristan glared at Tess, his expression dark. "I don't know what this *human* said—"

"Save it." Callum put his hands on Tristan's shoulders—a friendly gesture with a menacing effect. "She has no reason to lie, and I have no reason to disbelieve her. So what do you say you and I make a deal?"

"What deal?" Tristan growled.

"It's simple." Callum leaned closer to Tristan, bearing down on him. "You stay away from Tess, you get to live. But if anything happens to her—and I mean if anyone drinks one drop of blood, if she gets one cut, one bruise, at someone else's hand—then I give you the most painful death I can imagine. And I have a very, very good imagination. So not only are you not going to touch her, and I mean *ever*—you'd better hope no one else does either. Because even if I see another vamp attack her with my own eyes, I'm still going to hold you accountable. We clear?"

Tristan glowered at Callum with seething hatred, but Tess knew he didn't dare argue.

"Crystal," he agreed, his voice oily and calm.

"Good." Callum relaxed into an easy posture and released his grip on Tristan, affably clapping him on the shoulders. "Glad we got that sorted. Tess, you want something to eat?"

Tess nodded, feeling stunned, as she followed Callum toward the banquet table.

"You shouldn't have done that." She shook her head. "What if he comes after you? What if he comes after me?"

"Like to see him try," Callum scoffed. "Little twat can't fight worth a damn."

"But, Callum—"

"Listen to me." Callum whirled around to face Tess. "I can't control what happens outside this compound. And I know how afraid you must be, with the bridge gone and all—if you want to leave this compound and hide somewhere, even from me, I'll understand. But if you choose to stay here, I'll do everything I can to protect you, okay? I promise."

Tess felt a lump in her throat, a tightness in her chest—goddamn it, she was dangerously close to tears.

"What is it?" He looked worried. "What's wrong?"

She reached for his hand—but then thought better of it, that would be a stupid thing to do in front of half the clan. So she let her fingers brush his, and even though it was just for the briefest moment, it made every part of her body feel warm.

"I really am hungry." She smiled.

He grinned back at her, his expression tender and joyful—like he was proud to stand by her side. Tess's emotions flared; she felt exactly the same way.

The banquet table was piled with all kinds of food glamoured by different vampires to suit their own tastes: platters of Chinese lacquered pork, tender braised lamb shanks, steaming pots of Indian stews, bowls of fluffy whipped potatoes, and gorgeous leafy salads with bright lemon dressing. Tess grinned as she filled her plate; this had to be the best—and weirdest—book club pot luck dinner in history.

"Are we ready to begin?" Nantale clinked her glass as the vampires took their seats. There were a few smaller tables set up so the vampires could eat while they talked; Callum and Tess sat at a table with Sylvie and Hamish.

"Did you try some brisket?" Sylvie nudged Tess. "I glamoured that."

"It's so good!" Tess raved. Her own parents had never bothered to celebrate Jewish holidays or cook traditional Jewish foods; Sylvie was starting to feel like the bubbe she'd never had.

"Okay, in the first place," Angelique was addressing the group, "I don't know how we're supposed to form an opinion with just *one* book. What do they say about us in the sequels?!"

"Ask the human." Antoinette pointed at Tess. "She's obsessed with them, right? Isn't that her whole thing? She's like our fangirl."

"It's not my *whole* thing," Tess muttered.

"Tess, tell me the truth." Hamish reached across the table and put his hand gently on hers. "Do I have a bigger role in the sequels? How would you characterize my dramatic arc?"

"Um . . ." Tess bit her lip. "You're kind of a side character?"

Hamish's expression turned dark. "What did you just say?"

"If we can all please focus for a moment." Nantale closed her eyes. "I think we can agree that the most pressing matter is to discover August Lirio's true identity."

"Yeah, so I can kill them." Hamish sniffed.

"No," Nantale said coolly. "Because that person clearly knows intimate details of events that transpire on the Isle—which means it's possible they live here. And if someone on this island has a way to communicate with people back in our world, that's something we should know about."

"Isn't it obvious?" Sylvie cut herself another piece of brisket. "August Lirio is Felix Hawthorn."

A stunned silence fell over the room—Tess turned to Sylvie.

"Why do you think that?"

"Because he made himself the hero," she said, as if any kindergartner should have reached this conclusion. "You all hate how you were portrayed in the book, right? You think it's unfair? None of it was true? Ask yourselves who thinks of you that way—and who thinks Felix is a hero. Felix does."

Tess gazed at Sylvie with wonder. She had to admit, it was a pretty solid theory—it definitely made more sense than any vague ideas Tess had considered.

"Hold on." Callum rubbed his temples. "If Felix had a way to communicate with people back home, wouldn't we know about it? Be hard to keep a secret that big on an island this small."

"Oh," Tess blurted out. "Actually—Felix did tell me he had a secret, something only his clan was allowed to know about."

"You're talking to Felix too?" Hamish's eyes went wide. "You are *messy.*"

Callum turned to Tess, a tamped-down fury building behind his eyes. "Did you think it might be a good idea to tell me about this?"

"I'm sorry, it was in the orchard," Tess said quickly. "And then you and I fought and then you almost died and then Sylvie cured you and here we are and I'm telling you now, okay?"

Callum looked like he wanted to say more, but Nantale interrupted.

"Tess, what did Felix say?"

"Um, nothing specific." Every vampire in the room was staring at Tess; her skin was crawling. "He just mentioned that at his castle—he said they were working on a way off the Isle. And I wonder—I mean, if he'd figured out a way to communicate with people back home, that would be a big step, right?"

"This is it." Callum looked at Tess with a burning intensity. "This could be our way home."

"No, it couldn't." Nantale sighed.

"What?" Callum whipped around to look at her. "Why not?"

"Because how are we going to find out what's happening in Felix's castle?"

"We could send spies, or we could bloody torch the place, fight our way in with brute force—"

"Or I could just ask him," Tess interjected.

"No," Callum snapped.

"Callum—"

"It's out of the question."

"But Felix likes me!" Tess insisted. "We can find the safest possible way for me to see him, but this is too big a lead not to pursue it."

"I agree," Callum said. "I just think there are much less stupid ways to pursue it than putting your mortal life in danger."

"Mortals' lives are *always* in danger." Angelique rolled her eyes. "That's the literal definition of mortality."

"Yeah, she could just as easily fall off a horse and snap her neck, and what good would that do us?" Antoinette sniffed.

"If she snapped her neck, at least we could drink her blood," Tristan sulked.

"Wait." Nantale held out her hands, and the room fell silent. "Callum, what if the girl drinks *your* blood?"

Tess's throat suddenly felt dry, her breath was like sandpaper scraping against it.

Callum looked at Nantale for a long moment, then nodded slowly.

"Why?" Tess couldn't think of the right words; she felt woozy. "Why would I—what would that do?"

"It'd make you a lot faster and stronger, for one." Callum was leaning toward her now, excitement building. "Make it a lot easier for you to escape if something went wrong."

"But . . ." Tess couldn't breathe. She could explain if she could just breathe. "Your blood, the poison."

"Oh, hmm," Callum considered. "I think it should be all right, now that I'm better? Sylvie, what do you think?"

Callum turned to Sylvie, but she clocked Tess's discomfort and shrugged noncommittally.

"But listen," Callum went on, "if you want to wait we can wait, certainly I'm in no rush for you to talk to Felix. This would just be a safeguard—"

"We don't have to talk about it now." Tess stood abruptly, her chair screeching against the marble floor. Everyone in the room looked at her like she was losing her mind—and maybe she was, she felt like she was, but if she didn't get out of this room right now, she was going to pass out.

"Tess—" Callum reached for her arm, but she jerked it back.

"It's fine," she squeaked, her voice high and ragged. "You're having your book club, I've already read the books, I should go, it's time for me to go."

And before he could respond, before any of the vampires could say a single thing, she grabbed her books and rushed out of the room. The images were already coming—the snowfall, the whiskey, the pile of clothes. It didn't matter what dimension you were in, you couldn't let your guard down for a single second. Tess wasn't going to drink Callum Yoo's blood. And she was a fucking idiot to believe him when he said she could ever be safe, on this island or anywhere else.

Chapter 21

QUIZ: WHICH *BLOOD FEUD* VAMPIRE SHOULD BE YOUR VALENTINE?

by Amy Bello, posted on buzzfeed.com

Dear reader, are you single on V-Day? Well, never fear, because the hot vampires of *Blood Feud* are WAY sexier than any of the losers you've been swiping on Hinge (so sad, but you know it's true). The only question is: Which one will give you the best Valentine's Day of your life? Take this quiz to find out!

1) Where is your valentine taking you for your big date?
   a) A private candlelit dinner with a table strewn with rose petals where you'll drink expensive wine and be serenaded by violinists—you like it romantic!
   b) The hottest club in downtown Manhattan, where you'll have bottle service at a center table and be the envy of all who see you—you like attention!
   c) Why go out at all when you could stay home, lock the door,

have sex all night, and not have to interact with anyone besides your hottie? You like it dirty (and a little bit misanthropic)!

2) Surprise! They have a private jet all fueled up. Where are you heading?
   a) Paris, *mais bien sur*! The city of love!
   b) Tokyo for fashion week and twenty-course omakases
   c) A ruggedly gorgeous castle in Scotland

3) When you arrive, there's a wrapped present waiting for you. What's inside?
   a) A book of poems they wrote about you
   b) Insanely expensive lingerie
   c) A very large box of condoms

4) Your valentine is drinking blood, obvi—but what are YOU drinking?
   a) Vintage champagne
   b) A mezcal cocktail
   c) Whiskey, neat

5) You're both exhausted from all your V-Day ~activities~; time to curl up and watch some TV. What are you watching?
   a) It's Valentine's Day—a freaking rom-com, duh!
   b) A sexy thriller, to get you in the mood to start kissing again.
   c) You're finished having sexy times, and now you're "exhausted" and "want to watch TV"? Bad news, sweetie, you're about to get drained by a vampire.

If you got mostly A's: Your valentine is Felix Hawthorn! You're the most romantic person in your friend group (or possibly in anyone's friend group), so of COURSE you're spending the most romantic day of the year with the most romantic vamp on the planet: Felix will whisk you off your feet and shower you with flowers, poetry, gems, champagne, and all the romance you crave and deserve.

If you got mostly B's: Your valentine is Octavia Yoo! You're incredibly chic and not afraid of a little danger, so you're going to love being in Octavia's orbit, jet-setting the globe in search of power and pleasure, seeing the most beautiful art and tasting the most delicious food the world has to offer while gazing into her hypnotic eyes.

If you got mostly C's: Your valentine is Callum Yoo! There's a reason so many readers are gaga about Callum—he's gruff, he's powerful, he's mysterious, he's so good in bed that his partners regularly lose consciousness. And so what if he usually kills his paramours when he's finished with them? At least you'll know your last Valentine's Day on earth was also your very best.

Tess tore through the compound, her pulse pounding in her ears. She needed her copy of *Blood Feud*—shit, she'd loaned it to Callum. It was probably still in his room.

Everything felt blurry, like it was all happening too fast, like she wasn't really here. She was picking up her clothes off Rick's bedroom floor, careful not to wake him. She was crying on the subway, she was having a panic attack in the bathroom on the first floor of the CompLit building, she wasn't asleep, she wasn't awake, she was some unholy something in between.

Callum made it seem like it was no big deal, like she could just drink his blood, be altered by some chemical fucking compound, when she couldn't even drink a cup of punch at a party. He acted so altruistic, so heroic and protective, but she knew men were all the fucking same.

She felt like the air was pressing in against her temples as she stepped through the door of his rooms, but she had to stay focused. Her copy of *Blood Feud* was still on the table next to Callum's bed, the same bed where she'd slept beside him just last night. *Stupid,* she admonished herself as she flipped through the novel, a physical red flag, right there in her hands. When would Tess learn that she couldn't trust anyone—and that if she did, she deserved whatever she got?

It was a passage about Konstantin, she was almost sure—she just couldn't remember the exact language. She flipped through pages, desperately scanning paragraphs until she found the one she was looking for, wedged in an exposition dump in chapter seven:

> *During his millennia on earth, Konstantin enjoyed enormous influence: Some say Konstantin fed his blood to the Holy Father during the Crusades, controlling him in a perpetual blood thrall . . .*

There it was, in black and white. If Callum thought Tess was going to drink some unknown substance and turn into his puppet, he was out of his fucking mind.

That had happened to Tess once before. She would never let it happen again.

Callum couldn't understand why Tess had run out of the great room like that. Had he done something wrong? Should he ask her? Or would that be read as needy—or worse, aggressive—and was it better to give her space?

"Fucking hell," he swore under his breath as he stormed down the hall back to his rooms.

He'd never felt so unlike himself—first the injury, now the girl? He'd never cared about a human's opinion before; he didn't see why he should start now. And so what if the best part of being injured was the night she spent in his bed—smelling her hair, the tantalizing feeling of her body only inches from his, the soothing comfort of her warmth, her steady breath, her living pulse? He was attracted to her, fine. And grateful to her for saving his life—sensible enough. But the only woman he'd ever really cared about was his sister, and he barely knew Tess. Let her be angry. It made absolutely no difference to him.

Except when he opened his door and saw her standing inside, he sped toward her faster than he imagined possible given how badly his leg had been injured only a few hours before.

"Tess!" he exclaimed. "Are you all right? What's happened?"

He'd never seen her like this before—her expression was ragged and wild, like she'd gone feral in the twenty minutes since she'd left the great room.

"What's a blood thrall?" she demanded.

"What? Why do you want to know about—"

"Just tell me," she spat. "Right now."

"Erm." He mussed his hair anxiously. "So you know what a glamour is, yeah? Vampire looks in your eyes, you do whatever they say, only lasts as long as they maintain eye contact?"

"I'm familiar," Tess bristled.

"Right. Glamours are dead useful for little things like booking in hotel rooms or bank transfers, but if you really want to control someone . . ."

He trailed off.

"Go on." Tears were streaming down Tess's face. "Say it."

"You feed them your blood. And then the glamour can last for days, or if you keep feeding them and keep glamouring them . . ."

"It can go on forever." Tess slammed her copy of *Blood Feud* down on Callum's desk. "That's what Konstantin used to do, right? It's how he amassed so much power? You said you weren't like him, you fucking liar."

Hot shame roiled through Callum's body—oh god, it wasn't possible—there was no way she could honestly think—

"Tess, I would *never* do that to you." He moved to comfort her, but she shrank back from him in horror. He felt desperate with worry—how could he have fucked up this badly, just when she'd finally started to trust him? "Please, you have to believe me—"

"Why should I?" She folded her arms tighter. "You told me to drink your blood, but you didn't tell me what it would do—why would you do that unless you wanted to make me some kind of hostage? To control my mind, my body, to have complete power over me? Why, Callum?! Why would you do that to me?"

She was shaking now, tears spilling down her cheeks. He rushed over to her, reached to hold her, but she shoved him away.

"Don't you touch me!" she shrieked. "I never said you could touch me!"

"Please," he begged, "I swear to you, I never meant to use my blood that way."

"Then how were you going to use it?" she demanded. "Why did you want me to drink your blood?"

"Because the idea of Felix hurting you was fucking unbearable!" he swore. "Tess, I would never hurt you. To make you do anything you didn't want to do—that's the last thing I could do. Your strong will, your stubborn determination, this fierceness about you—how could I ever change the thing that made me want you in the first place?"

Tess sank down in his favorite leather armchair, looking dazed. "That made you . . . I don't understand."

"I don't either." Callum fell to his knees before her. "None of it makes sense. I've been trapped on this island eleven years. After Octavia left . . . I didn't know how I'd go on. If I even could. And then to meet you . . ."

Tess buried her head in her hands. "You're saying . . . what are you saying?"

Callum sighed. It was time to stop lying—to Tess, and to himself.

"I'm saying I haven't stopped thinking about you since the first time we went into that forest. I'm saying I would lay down my own life to protect yours if it came to that. I'm saying I could never hurt you, because any wound to you is a wound to me, sweet girl."

Tess looked down at him, scanning his face as if to discern whether he was lying. She pushed out of the chair and stood up—he did the same.

"And you didn't want . . ." She spoke quietly and clasped her hands together, her knuckles were white. "I mean, if I drank your blood. It wasn't to—to make me do things?"

"What?!" He felt a physical pain in his chest as realization thundered down on him. Her obvious terror when he tried to carry her into the forest, her fear of sharing a bed, the way she bolted tonight—all of it suddenly made the most horrible sense. It wasn't only about whether she was afraid of him. It was about something that had happened to her.

"Tess, I've never done that. I would *never* do that," he promised. "How could I do something like that to someone I care about?"

"I don't know." Tess was crying in earnest now. She felt the fog of her panic dissipating, the anxiety attack sparked by Nantale's suggestion that Tess drink Callum's blood was finally ending. Tess felt completely exhausted—not just from the last twenty minutes but the last three years of constantly being on guard, forever trying to discern whether any man she met might secretly be a monster. She looked at Callum—he looked so upset, so absolutely bereft by her obvious pain. He wasn't Rick. His blood wasn't that fucking whiskey laced with god knows what. She had a sudden urge to let Callum hold her, to cry in his arms, to finally feel, after all this time, like she didn't have to carry this horrible burden alone.

She thought back to sitting across from Flora at Bar Between, the witch putting her hands over Tess's. *Don't be ashamed to ask for what you need.*

Callum stepped toward her—tentatively, not too fast, like she was a creature he didn't want to spook. But she was done with questions—done running, done overthinking, done stopping herself from having a single thing she wanted because every last one caused too much pain.

"Callum," she croaked, her voice hoarse from crying. She hurtled toward him and threw her arms around his neck, burying her face in his chest as he pulled her close. He was so strong, and it was such a fucking relief just to be in his arms, just to let herself believe that he might not wish her harm.

"You have to know I'll always protect you," he whispered into her hair. "I won't let anything happen to you."

"Something did," she said, her voice breaking.

He pulled back far enough so he could look at her, his face lined with concern. "At Columbia?"

She nodded, the tears coming back again. She leaned into him, and he held her softly. He moved his hands gently across her back, and she let the slow rhythm of his movements and his heartbeat lull her into something like calm.

She'd never told anyone about Rick—not Joni, not anyone at school, not her new friends at the hotel. After all the years of Rick infesting her brain, not talking about him felt like some kind of victory. Like she could make him go away by pretending he didn't exist, by never telling anyone her secret.

No. Not her secret. *His.*

"I want to tell you," she said, the need suddenly desperate.

"I want to hear anything you want to say," he said softly. "Should we sit down?"

She nodded, and he led her to a comfortable brown leather chesterfield situated opposite a small fire burning in a stone hearth, which lit the room with an amber glow. Tess kicked off her boots and curled her legs beneath her, leaning against Callum. He rubbed her shoulder reassuringly.

"Okay." She took a deep breath. "It, um . . . It happened on Valentine's Day, three years ago."

"Stupid holiday, making people buy chocolate to honor some murdered priest," Callum muttered, and Tess smiled through her nerves. "Go on."

"I was in our department's lounge with Joni—she was my best friend. And actually, we had just taken a quiz about *Blood Feud*."

"Like trivia?"

"No." Tess smiled. "A personality quiz. About which vampire would be your perfect valentine."

"Really?" Callum looked at Tess with interest. "At least tell me you got me."

∽

Tess got exactly who she knew she would get, the same character she always got after taking dozens of variations of this exact quiz.

"Felix." Tess breathed out the name with a little sigh.

"Ugh, of course you did." Joni rolled her eyes. "Do you ever get bored of being a straight-girl-romance cliché?"

Tess hit Joni with one of the CompLit lounge couch's micro-suede pillows. "I want a man to touch my hair gently and read me a fucking sonnet, asshole."

It was a long-standing joke that Tess was basic for having a literary crush on the romantic hero of the *Blood Feud* books when there were so many morally complex side characters, but she couldn't help herself. Felix Hawthorn was gallant and brave, the polar opposite of every self-obsessed New York guy Tess had gone out with whose boundless interest in his own opinions made it impossible to sit through dinner, let alone form a lasting relationship. Of course Tess loved Felix. Who wouldn't?

"Who'd you get?" Tess asked.

"Octavia!" Joni proclaimed in a loud singsong voice, like she was a horn at a medieval court.

"How is that possible??"

"Because she's my destiny, duh."

"You hate fashion," Tess pointed out.

Joni nodded. "It's a construct of gender performance designed to deplete women's time, energy, and money."

"You don't drink mezcal." Tess referenced another of the questions on the quiz.

"Because it tastes like smoky spit."

"And you won't watch thrillers!"

"To be fair, I won't watch movies with any kind of stakes. Too stressful!!" Joni got up to refill her coffee from the ancient pot.

"What's wrong with Felix, anyway?" Tess turned back to her phone, skimming her fingers over her quiz results. "He's sensitive, and intuitive, and actually values the opinions of women, and has great hair—"

"You talking about me?" Tess looked up in shock to see Rick Keeton, who was, undoubtedly, the Felix Hawthorn of the Columbia Department of Comparative Literature. Tess had thought he was cute since they started the program, but she'd seen a lot more of him recently, now that he and Joni were working on an article together—and Tess's affections had developed into a full-blown crush. Their article, which compared archetypes in epic poetry (Rick's specialty) to contemporary hero portrayals in pop culture (Joni's area of expertise) was a really big deal for Joni. Rick was sure it was going to land in a major publication, the first serious byline of Joni's career.

"Nah, your hair's just okay," Joni deadpanned. Rick laughed heartily and punched her on the arm.

"You guys teaching this afternoon?" he asked, giving Tess a long look. She'd caught him eyeing her on multiple occasions, in lectures, at department meetings. But he was always dating some impossibly beautiful undergrad; Tess figured she must not be his type.

"Shakespeare section," she replied, pulling out her laptop to go over her notes for the afternoon's discussion group.

"Oh yeah?" Rick flopped beside her on the couch. "What play?"

"The sonnets, actually." Tess felt her body heating up with Rick sitting so close. "You know, for, um . . ."

"Valentine's Day." He smiled. "That's just cruel."

She peered at him. "How so?"

He leaned toward her. "I'm sure every guy in your section already has a crush on you—now you're gonna read the world's most romantic poetry on the year's most romantic day?" He shook his head in mock disapproval. "Not cool, Rosie."

She laughed. "If I use my feminine wiles to make the kids appreciate rhythmic subtext in iambic pentameter, would that be so wrong?"

"Sounds more fun than my afternoon with *Anna Karenina,* anyway." Rick sighed. "It's always death with the Russians."

"To be fair, it's pretty often death with Shakespeare," Tess quipped. Rick laughed appreciatively, then stood.

"I'd better get to it—you guys coming to my thing tonight?"

Joni said, "We'll be there!" at the exact moment Tess said, "I'm not sure."

Rick smiled at them both, then looked right at Tess as he said, "I hope you do."

As soon as he left the room, Joni rushed over to Tess. "Oh my god, he *totally* likes you."

"You think?" Tess felt flushed. "No, he was just being nice. He's nice to everyone!"

"He *is* nice, which is the only reason I support this—the window for acceptable straight men is narrow, but he's in there," Joni assured her.

"Okay, but you guys are working together!" Tess protested. "I don't want to make it weird."

"You're not!" Joni insisted. "I really like Rick, and I really love you. What could be bad about you really liking each other? Nothing! So will you just come to the party with me?! I promise, we're going to have an amazing time. Maybe not as amazing as if Octavia were there, but you can't have everything."

"Okay, okay!" Tess laughed. "You convinced me. Let's go to a party."

Here are some of the things Tess remembered from the night of the party:

Choosing her outfit, her favorite black silk wrap dress trimmed with dark fringe and printed with splashy pink peonies.

Pregaming with Joni, cold red wine in mismatched glasses, singing along to Harry Styles.

The February wind accosting them so relentlessly on the walk to Rick's place that Tess suggested they turn back, but Joni insisting that Tess was gonna make out with a hot snob come hell or high blizzard, because this was the Valentine's Day she deserved, goddamn it.

Walking into Rick's building, a sleek high-rise on Riverside Drive with floor-to-ceiling windows overlooking the Hudson, the George Washington Bridge to the north and New Jersey to the west. Joni saying, "Oh shit, this fucker is *rich*."

Nodding along as her classmates debated Joyce and Proust, while thinking inwardly about how much she hated Joyce and Proust. Looking around for Rick, seeing him deep in conversation with a model-thin blonde in a corner across the room. Muttering to Joni that they should leave, Joni responding that she just needed to use the bathroom.

Extracting herself from the Joyce-Proust argument to admire the view; outside, snow had begun to fall against the dark sky. Rick coming up beside her to watch the snow, his arm brushing against hers and resting there, Tess feeling electrified by the contact between them.

"Pretty gross, right?" he deadpanned.

"The view? Oh, terrible. An eyesore. You should see if the building can get you a better one."

She glanced up and saw that he was gazing at her and grinning.

He held two glasses of whiskey on ice; he offered one and she accepted.

"Single malt, from Japan. My dad's favorite." A slight apologetic eye roll as he clinked her glass with his.

"Peaty," Tess remarked, feeling the smoky liquid warm her insides. "Is this your dad's place?"

"He bought it as an 'investment'"—Rick used finger quotes—"which is the most asshole-ish way possible to say I don't pay rent. Don't hate me, okay?"

Tess laughed softly. "Wouldn't dream of it."

She remembered moving to a couch, comparing notes on Shakespeare and their dissertations and favorite poets as the party thinned out. The kind of conversation Tess always fantasized about having with the man she'd someday fall in love with. Wondering if it was possible that Rick could be that man.

Joni stopping by to say she was leaving, Tess saying she would see her at home. Joni kissing her cheek and whispering, "Have fun, hottie." A classmate with curly hair giving Tess a dirty look, Tess wondering if it was envy.

Rick refilling her whiskey; once, twice. Not more than twice.

The room tilting. Was she drunk? It had been hours. She shouldn't be this drunk.

Asking him, "Is Rick short for Richard?"

Him smiling. "Frederick."

"Like Felix," she breathed, sinking deeper into the velvet cushions.

Her head going foggy, a dull pain seeping in.

Rick's voice, muffled. "Are you okay? Tess?"

Nodding, trying to nod. Everything feeling heavy.

"Do you want to lie down?"

A bed. His bed?

The sound of heavy breathing. Then darkness. Then nothing at all.

Gray dawn light through his giant window, the curtains only partly drawn. Splitting pain—her head throbbing. Rick, asleep beside her.

Realizing she was naked.

Confusion, panic. Quietly pulling on her clothes and rushing out of the apartment, terrified he might wake up.

A knowing smile from the doorman. Feeling like she might vomit.

Stumbling into the subway, unsteady on her feet. Wishing she had sunglasses so no one on the train could see that she was crying. If anyone noticed Tess's tears, they looked away.

"Oh my god, how was it?"

A few hours later, Joni bounded into Tess's room and leapt on top of her crinkly green comforter, wrapping Tess in her arms with absolutely no concern for whether she'd been sleeping. She hadn't, of course—every time her eyelids started feeling heavy she was startled awake by a shot of adrenaline, her mouth filling with the putrid taste of acid and bile. Tess went rigid beneath Joni's body; even breathing felt impossible. Joni immediately sensed that something was wrong and moved to a corner of the bed, a reassuring hand on Tess's shoulder.

"Hey, you okay? How was last night?"

"I don't, um . . . I don't really know," Tess said truthfully. "I don't remember."

Joni frowned. "You blacked out? You never black out."

Tess made a tiny shrugging motion with her shoulders. She felt a quivering, shaking feeling pulsing through her blood, an ice-cold feeling like all the heat of being human had leaked out of her.

"Fuck, you must be really hungover." Joni glanced at her watch. "It's almost three. Have you eaten anything today?"

Tess shook her head, and before she knew what was happening,

Joni was gone, banging around in the kitchen, returning minutes later with a steaming bowl of split pea soup and a hunk of brown bread from the nearby co-op.

"Eat," she said, placing the food on Tess's night table.

"I'm too nauseous," Tess protested weakly, but Joni wasn't having it.

"That's because you need food. Eat," she insisted.

Tess brought a steaming spoonful of soup to her lips, worried she would shake and spill it on her bedding. But the second she swallowed the soup, she did start to feel a little better.

"Helps, right?" Joni asked, and Tess forced a small smile. "So what happened after I left? You stayed over? Did you and Rick hook up?!"

"Oh." Tess cleared her throat. "Um, I don't think so. I think I just passed out on the couch."

"Wow, you really were drunk. Are you okay now? Is there anything else you need?"

"Probably just rest." Tess handed the soup bowl back to Joni. "I feel like shit."

"That's a good idea." Joni gave Tess's knee a squeeze. "You'll feel so much better after you get some sleep."

But Tess didn't sleep that night—her body wouldn't allow it. The adrenaline shocks persisted until her body roiled with pinpricks, like the feeling when your foot falls asleep, but across every inch of skin. (An ironic term, Tess thought bitterly, since actually falling asleep had become impossible.) When she did manage to doze for a couple of minutes here and there, she had nightmares of dark shadows looming over her, unfeeling eyes looking down on her, a hand across her mouth.

She woke gasping, terrified, and waited for dawn.

None of it made sense. She had gone to that party wanting Rick, with the express purpose of kissing him, being with him, spending the night in his bed.

And all of that had happened, right? She was pretty sure? Asking him was out of the question. Had he used a condom? She had no idea—she walked to the twenty-four-hour CVS at four-thirty in the morning and bought emergency contraception. She took it with a glass of tap water and said a small prayer of thanks that the pill made her incredibly tired—she'd taken it twice before, though always with firmer information about whether she actually needed it. Around eight A.M., as the cold winter sun filtered through dull gray clouds, she finally fell asleep.

After that first night, the most terrible night, the night when every minute crawled by in nail-screeching agony, Tess thought she'd sleep better. She'd have to eventually, right? Humans weren't built to exist without sleep—and besides, she was fucking exhausted. It was Sunday, and she had classes to teach the following day. So after her few hours of fitful morning rest, Tess forced herself to stay awake through the afternoon and evening, going to a movie with Joni and absorbing none of it, grateful for the noise. She figured if she could just make it until nine or ten, she'd pass out and be functional the next day.

This was a mistake.

The second night wasn't as miserable as the first, mostly because Tess gave up on trying to sleep more quickly and decided distraction was the best strategy. She opened her laptop and watched half an episode of some reality show about a woman looking for love, but it couldn't hold her attention. She grabbed her old paperback copy of *Blood Feud* off her shelf and read a few hundred pages; she eventually slipped out of consciousness at five A.M., and her head pounded when her alarm went off at eight.

She dragged herself through a hot shower and the twenty-minute walk to campus, her mind so foggy she nearly stepped into traffic more than once. Her section that morning was a discussion on the use of prophesy in *Macbeth,* one of Tess's favorite aspects of one of her favorite plays, but she kept forgetting things, misunderstanding her students' points, losing threads of logic in arguments she'd made a thousand times.

"Are you okay? You don't look great," a pretty undergrad observed with concern.

"Just a little under the weather." Tess forced out a smile.

The kids filed out as Tess gathered her notes—she heard a laugh from the hallway and looked up to see Rick talking with one of his friends. The panic flooded through her then, her body screaming at her to run, go, jump out a window, anything to get out of this room, but her muscles were rigid, incapable of motion, even as her breath flamed against her lungs like she'd just sprinted up a mountain.

She knocked into the chair behind her, and Rick turned at the sound. He gave a little nod and a smile—*What's up?*—then went back to his friend, still laughing as they walked off down the hall. Tess felt her knees give way beneath her, and by sheer force of will she managed to collapse into a chair and not onto the floor, her body bathed in sweat, heart pounding, lungs contracting painfully, lightheaded and dizzy as her body's oxygen dwindled.

That was the first panic attack. Tess made it through another dozen or so before she stopped going to campus. Another ten before she decided to drop out of school. When she tried to tell a counselor, she panicked. When she tried to go to campus, she panicked. When she tried to tell Joni, she thought about what would happen if Joni believed her, and it fucked up her article and her future—or worse, if she didn't believe Tess, because Rick really was such a nice guy, and none of this made any sense, and maybe Tess was just crazy to be overreacting like this. When she tried to go to sleep . . . well, eventually she just stopped trying. It wasn't worth it, not at night. She'd get a few hours here and there during the day. It was enough to keep living. Just not enough to stay where she was. So Tess did what she had to do.

She ran.

Chapter 22

Tess didn't know how long she talked about her terrible memories—hours? more?—but Callum listened to every word. When she finished, she felt empty, wrung out—but in a way that felt kind of liberating and revelatory? Like all the shame and self-hatred and anger and fear she'd been carrying for three years was finally leaving her body, leeching out of her pores and vaporizing into the air.

There was something particularly calming about having Callum next to her in this moment—his slow heartbeat, his cool skin.

"How do you feel?" he asked. "What do you need?"

"I feel . . . sleepy." She smiled, and he did too.

"Then I'll let you rest. Should I take you back to your room?"

He rubbed her knee reassuringly, and she sighed as she nestled against him. Tess had been so alone for the past three years; she didn't realize how much she missed the comfort of another person's touch.

"Can I sleep here?" she asked.

"Of course. Do you want me to sleep on the couch?"

Tess looked up at him, and he was so kind, so tentative, she wondered how she ever could have seen him as a threat.

"Stay with me," she whispered.

He took her by the hand, and she followed him back to the same bed where she'd slept beside him only yesterday—but things felt very different now.

Strangely, she wasn't nervous at all tonight, even though Callum had confessed his desire for her. She thought back to Joni's party, to the anxiety she felt when her old classmate Oscar had flirted with her the tiniest bit—she attributed that feeling to not really knowing him, not knowing whether he was the sort of man who would respect her wishes or do whatever he wanted despite them. With Callum, there was no longer any question in Tess's mind that he would never, ever push her into something she didn't want. So she felt easy with him. It was such a fucking relief.

"Do you need anything?" he asked as they both settled under the covers. "Some water?"

"I'm okay." Tess smiled. "What about you? How does your leg feel?"

"I feel like a new man," he said quietly. Tess wondered if he was talking about more than just the leg. Because the truth was, she felt like a new woman too.

Tess woke early the next morning, ravenous with hunger. Callum was asleep, and given that he was recovering from his injury (miraculously quickly, but still), she wanted to let him rest as long as he needed. So she found a scrap of creamy paper and a pen on his desk, and left him a note that she'd gone to eat and shower.

Somehow, everything about her beautiful rooms felt even better this morning; the coffee and pastries Sylvie had left her were divine. (Was Sylvie refilling them, or did they simply have magical properties that kept them from going stale? Because that was magic Tess could get behind: carb-based magic.) After she ate, she finally got into that big copper soaking tub she'd been meaning to try since Sylvie first glamoured it. There was a glass bottle on the rim of the tub labeled blue lotus oil, and Tess tipped a generous amount into her bath—it turned the water a shimmering cobalt and smelled like absolute heaven.

Tess soaked for the better part of an hour, letting the heat and steam unknot her muscles. Her mind wandered through a highlight reel of Callum Yoo: The way his eyes flashed when he teased her. The feel of his strong arms gripping her as he lifted her off the ground. The look on his face when he told her he wanted her.

I haven't stopped thinking about you since the first time we went into that forest.

What was he thinking? She suddenly felt desperate to know.

Tess's skin was hot from the bath and slick from the oil. It was hard to resist imagining what Callum would do if he was in this tub with her, the way the water would slosh as he slid his hands over her body.

She automatically tried to shove her thoughts in another direction—but then she paused to consider why. If he wanted her, and she wanted him, and she trusted him . . . what was stopping her?

When Tess finally dragged herself out of the bath, she was bursting with anticipation for the next time she'd see Callum. As it turned out, she didn't have to wait long: She had just pulled on a buttery dark green wrap dress when she heard a knock at her door—she rushed to open it.

"Hi." She flushed with pleasure at the sight of him. He looked even more handsome than she remembered in another set of his insanely chic dark sweats.

"All right?" he asked. He had a bit of a nervous smile, and she felt a twinge of pleasure that he was anxious to see her too. She opened her arms to hug him, and he beamed as he pulled her close. "God, you smell good."

"I took a bath," Tess murmured, leaning against his chest as he inhaled the scent of her hair.

"I don't think it's the bath," he said, and she could feel the vibrations of his voice against her cheek.

He followed her into the room, and they sat on the little velvet settee Sylvie had glamoured—the same place Tess had found Callum when she emerged from her shower that first morning on the Isle. How long had it been since then? It felt strangely impossible to imagine that there had ever been a time when she didn't know this man.

"How are you, though?" she asked. "Is your leg—are you feeling . . ."

"Good." He swallowed hard. "I feel . . . I'm not quite sure how to describe how I feel, actually."

"Me neither." Tess bit her lip.

"Your heart's racing," Callum said quietly. "Are you afraid?"

"You can hear it?" Tess leaned toward him, and he nodded. He seemed tentative—tense, even. "No, Callum. I'm not afraid."

She looked up at him; his eyes were steady on her as his breath grew shallow.

"I've been thinking . . ." She laid a hand on his arm, and his muscles went rigid beneath her touch.

"Tell me," he urged. His face was open, vulnerable; it reminded her of the way he'd looked just before he laid his hands on the angel statue, the specific pain of allowing yourself to want something so desperately.

She needed him to understand that she wanted him just as much.

She moved her hand down his arm, took his hand, and laced her fingers between his. He looked down at their hands, then met her gaze—she felt like there was a piece of twine connecting her body to his, pulled so taut it might snap if she didn't kiss him right fucking now.

"Tess," he said her name in a way that came out half plea, half moan, and she couldn't take this for one more second—she leaned forward and pressed her lips against his.

He made a noise when she kissed him, a low, guttural sound, and his lips were so soft, his body so thick and strong, she felt like she might break from how badly she wanted him.

"Callum," she breathed. She couldn't take this slowly—her body was screaming for her to give in to everything she wanted, everything she'd denied herself for so many years. She climbed into his lap, raking her fingers through his hair, kissing him hard. The connection felt electric, like he understood her body perfectly, the way he took her bottom lip between his teeth and nipped it gently, his lips moving along her jaw, her neck, the decadent surrender of his tongue in her mouth. Her hips started to rock against him, she wanted to feel his hands pulling at her, grasping her, touching every part of her body, except—

Except, she realized, his hands weren't on her at all. They were balled up in fists, clenched at his sides.

"What is it?" she asked, laying her hands gently over his. "Are you all right?"

"I don't want—I mean, I wouldn't want to . . ." He trailed off.

"Do you not want this?" Tess asked, a pit forming in her stomach. Was it possible she'd somehow read this—and him—completely wrong? "Should I stop? Oh god, it's okay if you want to stop."

"Tess, *no*." He took her hands and held them against his chest. "I want you more than I can remember wanting anyone. I just—after everything you've been through . . . I don't want to do anything you don't want. Not one thing."

Her heart was pounding—with adoration for this man, with adrenaline, with desire—as she placed his hands firmly on her hips.

"Then let me show you what I want," she breathed. "Let me show you how much I want you."

She kissed him again, and she fucking loved the feeling of his fingers digging into her, pulling her closer, her chest pressed to his as his hands roved up her back. She needed to feel him against her skin, needed to get out of this stupid dress—

She went to tear the damn thing off, but he reached up to stop her.

"Hey." He smiled at her. "There's no rush. I'm literally immortal."

"But I'm not." She grinned. "And I've been waiting long enough."

∞

Callum considered it a privilege to sleep with any woman—an opportunity he endeavored to earn through an arduous devotion to all things pleasurable. Before the Isle, Callum had slept with more women than he could possibly count, let alone remember. Women of all ages, races, and sizes, cis and trans, he took joy in all of them and tried his best to give them joy in return. (And in his own humble opinion, he rarely disappointed in that regard.)

Sleeping with Tess was different. Not just because of her past—Callum was no stranger to navigating a woman's triggers, noticing her responses if something he'd done caused discomfort and changing course to give them both a better experience. He'd expected this from Tess; after what she told him, he thought their first time would be stop and start, cautiously moving from one moment to the next, ever watchful for the one where she'd get upset or change her mind.

But Tess was so tender with him, so open. Every new place he kissed her, every new sound she made, new shock of pleasure or gasp of delight, all of it felt like discovering something holy.

He wanted to take this first time slowly, but once she took off her dress, she was tearing at his clothes, then pulling him into her bed, smiling and bright, her pale skin luminescent in the Isle's lavender morning light. He knew she wanted to have sex, but he worried about the pain he might cause—physical or otherwise.

"Are you sure?" he asked, poised above her. She pulled him down to kiss him, and he felt his skin melt against hers, her flesh even warmer and softer than he'd dreamed it.

"I'm ready," she whispered. When he moved inside her, she made the smallest, most exquisite noise; her cheeks were flushed, her hips moved against him, all of it was so tense and perfect he thought he might lose his mind. He made himself go slowly, refusing to prioritize his needs over hers, but when she wrapped her legs around his back and moaned out *more,* he let himself move the way he wanted to, faster, deeper, always closer to her, always together.

He didn't want her to feel pressure to come—and he certainly didn't want her to feel like she was letting him down if she didn't. But when he moved his fingers between her legs as he fucked her and she shook and cried out against him, he felt a surge of gratitude for this woman, how vulnerable she'd been with him, how close he felt to her. He let himself finish too, and they collapsed under the covers, affable and sweaty and cool beneath the heavy blankets.

"Callum, I'm so happy," she murmured. He loved the weight of her head against his chest, the vibration of her voice thrumming through him, his blood still buzzing from the intensity of being together.

"You should always be this happy." He sighed. "The entire bloody world should rearrange itself by any means necessary to accommodate your complete and constant happiness."

"So you're saying we're never leaving this bed?"

"I'm game if you are."

She laughed softly and repositioned herself against him, then let out a little yawn.

"Are you tired, sweet?"

"No," she pouted. "I mean, yeah. Very."

"Then sleep." He kissed her hair and gently rubbed her arm.

Even after a long night's rest, he was tired too. Between the severity of his injury and the relief of the recovery process, the emotional experience of hearing Tess's story, and the incredible release of being with her physically, the last few days had taken a toll on him. But he stayed awake to watch her fall asleep, to feel her breath become heavy as her body rose and fell against his. Her sleeping face looked so peaceful and relaxed, so utterly content. In more than a hundred years, he wasn't sure he'd seen anything so beautiful.

Chapter 23

Octavia [1:49 PM]: Are you at the townhouse yet? How's everything going?

Joni [1:52 PM]: Just got out of the subway, be there in a sec

Octavia [1:53 PM]: What do you see? Spare no detail!

Joni [1:54 PM]: It's just some regular fancy-ass neighborhood! I promise I'll text as soon as I know anything. Don't make me regret getting you a burner.

Octavia [1:55 PM]: Ooh you're being such a top, I love it.
Octavia [1:55 PM]: Pip pip! Radio silence from now on. x

Octavia [2:58 PM]: All right, enough of that, dying for news. Any word? Are you with Lirio?

Octavia [3:27 PM]: Really, still nothing? Just cruel at this point.

Octavia [4:41 PM]: Starting to worry. Pls let me know all is well.

Octavia [5:26 PM]: Just tried calling, straight to voicemail. Did your phone die? What's going on?

By six o'clock, Octavia was becoming seriously concerned. Joni was one of the most communicative people she'd ever met—often annoyingly so. There was no way she'd disappear for an entire afternoon without telling Octavia why. But until the sun set, there wasn't a damn thing Octavia could do about it, so she paced the hotel room and waited, finishing off the cow's blood Joni had brought her, trying to focus on whatever was on TV and largely failing.

Finally, at 6:47, a text came through:

We have Joni. Come to the townhouse.

Octavia's blood ran cold.

Who is this? she typed back.

The burner phone was cheap, not even a smartphone—there was no way to see if the person on the other end was responding. But a few seconds later, another text appeared:

It doesn't matter who I am. It matters who you are, Octavia.

"Fuck!" Octavia yelped. Her phone buzzed again:

If you want Joni to live, come to the townhouse.

Her heart was pounding, and she could feel cold sweat forming along her hairline. She couldn't believe how naïve they'd been, blithely believing the private address of a world-famous recluse had dropped into their laps at the exact moment they needed it as a matter of pure good luck. There was no such fucking thing as good luck—there were only cleverly laid traps, and people stupid enough to walk into them.

But why did they want her to come to the townhouse? If they knew who she was, why weren't they already here at the hotel? She was more or less powerless to fight back, and until sunset, she had no way to escape.

They must not know I'm here, Octavia thought, feeling a surge of affection for Joni—she hadn't told whoever had her captive where Octavia was. Which meant Octavia still had a chance to run.

She didn't *want* to leave Joni behind, of course. But she had to be reasonable: If Octavia took off now, she could be somewhere new by tomorrow. She'd steal cash from somewhere, buy a fake ID off . . . someone. It wouldn't be easy without her powers or anyone to help her, but she'd figure it out; she always did. And as for the threat against Joni's life, Octavia didn't believe it. Joni had friends and family, people who would notice she was gone and fight to find out what happened to her. There was no reason to take the risk. And on the other hand . . . if they *were* the kind of people who would kill Joni, wouldn't they do it anyway when Octavia showed up? What good would it do for both of them to die?

Octavia started throwing clothes into her bag. The sun was almost down, and her best bet was to get as far away from this place as she could. She didn't have much to pack, just the clothes she'd stolen from Bergdorf's: some separates, some negligees, the gown she'd worn to the Met.

Octavia picked up the dress and ran the fabric between her fingers, remembering how excited Joni had been, the pride on her face when she'd announced she'd met Lirio's agent's assistant—the same person who currently had Joni, whoever they were. The hungry look in Joni's eyes when Octavia kissed her on the dance floor . . .

"Goddamn it, Joni," Octavia muttered under her breath. She found the piece of paper where Joni had scrawled the address of the townhouse yesterday and marched down to the lobby.

Octavia was no stranger to obscene wealth, but even she was impressed that August Lirio had snagged one of the last remaining single-family townhomes on Gramercy Park.

Not Lirio, she reminded herself. Who the hell knew who that Fern person really was—all Octavia could assume was that she was extremely dangerous.

The streets around Gramercy Park were mostly empty, and this time of year, the buildings were too—the residents would all be in Southampton or Nantucket or Provence until Labor Day (as Octavia would prefer to be herself—and would be, as soon as she got her powers back). But the townhouse in question was all lit up, and Octavia could see from the street that it was filled with people milling about, maybe for some sort of party. *Shit.* There was a large group here, and she was alone with no powers—should she have tried to buy a gun or something?! Ugh, the last time she had to fire a gun it was really more of a musket, and she hated it even then. Octavia wasn't used to needing a weapon. She was used to *being* a weapon.

Octavia crept down the narrow alleyway beside the building and saw it had a large rear veranda—that was good. It meant there was a crawl space underneath where Octavia could hide, and quite possibly a window where she could wriggle into the basement. Octavia got as near to the windows as she could without leaving the cover of the shadows in the alleyway. As best as she could tell, all the people gathered inside were women, but she didn't see anyone who looked like Joni. She looked up to the second floor—only a couple of rooms were lit up there, and none at all on the third floor. But there was a light on all the way in the slanted attic—Octavia couldn't know for sure that Joni was up there, but it's certainly where Octavia would stow a prisoner. The basement would have multiple routes of egress, but the attic? Getting someone out of there unnoticed would be no easy task.

"Fucking great," Octavia muttered. She looked up as she heard noises inside—the women were gathering around the dining room table, and someone was banging a gavel. Were they having a meeting of some kind? If they were about to quiet down, Octavia needed to move right now.

She sprinted down the rest of the alley, staying as low as she could, until she reached the veranda. There was a little door built in beneath it that she hoped would lead her somewhere useful. The door wasn't locked, but it was pretty well stuck shut; Octavia gave it a good shove, and it creaked loudly as it gave way. Octavia paused, waiting to see if anyone had noticed the sound, but chairs were still scuffling loudly in the house above her. She eased her body through the small space and under the veranda, where everything was, as she'd suspected, absolutely disgusting—filled with cobwebs and who knew what creepy New York creatures, squelchy with mud from the rain the day before.

"The things you do for love," Octavia muttered—then stopped herself. She didn't love Joni, she just owed the girl for all her help. That was plenty good reason to crawl under a porch and risk her life and muck up a perfectly lovely black yoga outfit.

It was difficult to see, but up ahead there was a dim light source coming from the house—yes! It was a window into the basement. Octavia crawled toward it as quietly as she could—it was a double-hung window, cracked slightly open, which meant Octavia could use it to get inside. She marveled at her luck and how easy this had been so far, then reminded herself that there was still an entire group of (potentially deadly) women between her and Joni.

"One step at a time," she told herself as she pushed the window open and slithered through.

The basement was dim and musty, filled with shelves of jars and cans that looked like they'd been there for decades. There was one lit lightbulb near the window, but as Octavia moved deeper into the space, it got much darker. She moved toward the sound of voices coming from the floor above her, slowly taking each step so as not to put too much weight on a creaky floorboard—or, god forbid, jostle the shelves full of metal and glass. Come to think of it, glass might make a good weapon in a pinch—she picked up a wine bottle and held it by its neck, feeling slightly buoyed by the knowledge that she could smash it over someone's head, then slash someone else's throat. She was a vampire, after all. If they saw her feed on someone, if they were terrified enough, she might have a chance.

But the best-case scenario was that none of these women would know she had been here until she was already long gone. So when she found the stairwell up to the first floor, her movements were almost painfully slow, terrified she might make a single sound.

As she neared the top of the stairs, she could hear the voices more clearly—they were still down a hallway, but Octavia could make out what they were saying.

"Something is going on with the portal energy—we've all felt it," came one voice, an older woman with a haughty tone.

"That doesn't necessarily mean there's a rip in the fabric of the shadow dimension," argued a younger woman.

"But it's definitely a problem that they blew up the crystal bridge," a third woman said angrily. "That's a clear act of aggression against us."

Octavia's eyes went wide—they were talking about the Isle! Someone blew up the crystal bridge?! No wonder Tess hadn't come back.

"It's obvious that the vampires are trying to escape." The haughty older woman spoke again. "And we've all heard the rumors that one already has—rumors I can personally corroborate based on the vampire I saw in my hotel room."

Oh shit. They weren't just talking about vampires—they were talking about *her.* That was the old bat Octavia had terrified in the penthouse of The Georgia!

"Please, Mrs. Harriman, what are the odds an escaped vampire showed up in your hotel room of all places?" another woman asked.

"I know what I saw."

"Well—maybe it's time we let them come back," said another woman who sounded considerably kinder than the others.

"You can't be serious, Flora," said Mrs. Harriman.

"I am!" Flora sounded a bit huffy. "We took unprecedented action when we created the Isle and trapped them there, but that was because we had to, because people's lives were in danger—they were too powerful, the natural order was too far out of balance. But now they've been gone eleven years, and it's possible one is back and we haven't heard of a single murder. If not now, when? When will it be long enough to know they've learned their lesson?"

Octavia felt a great deal of kinship for this Flora person, whoever she was.

"Maybe they should never come back," came another voice, stern and prim.

"Give me a break, Fern," Flora muttered.

Fern! That was the woman Joni had been in touch with—she wasn't a literary agent, she was a fucking witch trying to capture Octavia and send her back to the Isle!

"They've been locked away for eleven years," Fern went on. "Do you think they're going to come home quietly? Does that sound like vampires to you? Or do you think they're going to go on an absolute killing spree—starting with seeking revenge on all of us?"

Octavia hated to admit it, but that was a pretty good point. She was sure almost any vampire would kill Fern if they knew she was arguing for their permanent captivity.

"Please, the humans are doing an absolutely fine job of killing each other already!" Flora argued. "And there are far fewer vampires now than there were when we sent them to the Isle—there are only a couple hundred left. And some of them are pretty decent creatures—I'm the one who keeps tabs on them from Bar Between! It's not right that they're all being punished equally for crimes they didn't all commit."

There were murmurs of agreement from the group, and Octavia felt a surge of hope—was it possible that these women were about to end the Isle, and that Callum was about to come home?

"You're being naïve," Fern said coldly. "Our coven is meant to protect order between the mortal and magical realms. The best way we can do that is to shut down the portal to the Isle for good—and trap the vampires there forever."

"I agree," Mrs. Harriman piped in. "Shall we put the matter up for a vote?"

Octavia started to panic—she was out of time. If she had a shot at rescuing Joni, she needed to do it right now. She didn't know if going up to the attic would work—or if Joni was even there—but it was the only plan she had. And if it was really possible that she was about to lose her brother for good, she damn sure wasn't also going to lose the only person on Earth that she still trusted.

She moved quietly up the last few stairs—

But she stopped dead when she heard a noise behind her—was someone there?!

"There you are, Octavia," came a deep, quiet voice. "I wasn't sure you would make it."

Octavia raised the wine bottle to try to fight, but she knew she didn't have a prayer—before she could land a single blow, a dark shadow sped toward her and a hand closed over her mouth.

Chapter 24

Tess knew she and Callum should be focused on figuring out their portal problems, but they just couldn't seem to get out of bed. They'd spend hours talking and having sex, then Callum would glamour up some outrageous food, then they'd sleep, then they'd shower, then they'd have sex again, and it was all a very difficult cycle to break.

"You're turning me into a hermit," Tess joked, luxuriating in her big sleigh bed as Callum grazed his fingers over her body. "I'm the only human ever to visit this magical island, and all I'll ever see is the inside of this bedroom."

"Oh, I'm terribly sorry," Callum teased, leaning over to kiss Tess. "Would you prefer I arranged some sort of historical group tour? A vampire with an umbrella leading us to various spots of interest and giving dry lectures on who was murdered where?"

"Shut up. You know full well I'd fucking love that."

Callum laughed and started kissing her again, and she imagined what the tour guide would say about this particular room.

Now, this is the bedroom of the first and only human who ever visited the

Isle. In this very spot, a woman who thought she might never be happy again realized just how much she'd been missing.

"All right," he said nearly an hour later, reaching for one of Tess's library books. "Let's see what mysteries of the universe we can uncover."

He was sitting up in bed, entirely naked except for a sheet sort of half covering his lower regions. He'd glamoured a platter of charcuterie and cheeses, and Tess was grazing as he opened one of the leather-bound tomes she'd lugged across the compound.

"A compendium of gems with magical properties," he read. "If you want me to scare you up some rubies, all you have to do is ask, love."

"I think emeralds go better with my coloring, don't you?"

"Emeralds it is," he agreed as he flipped through the book. "Blue diamonds for loyalty, yellow for healing, red for blood. That's funny, I had a dream about a red diamond while I was loopy on poison."

"You did? What about?"

"Suppose it was more like a memory." He scratched at his jaw. "This time in the 1920s, Konstantin sent Octavia and me to nick a pendant off some guy in Paris. Thought it would be easy, but he walked in on us mid-heist—about lost his mind when he realized what was happening. Guess it was a family heirloom, worth a fortune even then—can't imagine what it would go for now. He tried to fight us, but obviously that didn't go too well. Fell to his knees weeping, begged us not to take it."

"But you did?" Tess asked.

"Had to." Callum shrugged. "I didn't care about some stupid pendant, but Konstantin wanted it, so. Not worth the trouble to disobey, even if it did ruin some poor sod's life. It was ugly too. Giant stone, all this gold, really gaudy. I thought it was a ruby, but Konstantin said it was a red diamond. Rarest stone on Earth."

"Wait." Tess sat up and looked at Callum, something jogging in her memory. "The pendant—was it a gold cross? A medieval one, like you'd see on a knight of the Crusade?"

"Yes, actually." Callum peered at Tess. "Have you been research-ing telepathy too?"

"The paintings at Octavia's—do you remember, she had those watercolors? One of them was of a gold cross pendant with a giant red stone. I assumed it was a ruby, but it's the same necklace you're talking about, right? It has to be. And if you had a dream about it, and Octavia drew it, then do you think . . ."

"It might have something to do with the portal?" Callum asked.

They looked at each other—had they stumbled upon something real here?

"The book," Tess said hurriedly, flipping through the pages to the one about red diamonds. She scanned the text as quickly as she could: "Red is the rarest color for any diamond—only about fifty red diamonds have ever been found throughout history, and they sell for well over a million dollars per carat. These powerful stones are most commonly used in matters of blood magic, and their pres-ence can immeasurably increase the strength of any existing blood bond."

"Blood magic?" Callum frowned. "That doesn't have anything to do with portals."

"Unless . . ." Tess's brain was spinning as she put the pieces to-gether. "Didn't you say you could feel Octavia on the other side of the portal? Maybe it's not about strengthening the portal itself—but the underlying bond that creates it."

"So all I need to do is glamour a red diamond?" Callum asked.

"Oh." Tess's face fell. "No, a glamoured stone won't work. It says so in the book."

"That's that, then." Callum leaned back against the pillows. "Pretty unlikely one of the fifty red diamonds ever found through-out history is here on this island."

Tess sighed heavily as another memory surfaced. "Actually, one is. And you're not going to believe who has it."

Callum frowned in confusion—then his face turned stony as he figured it out.

"Felix? Really? Really, Tess?"

"Technically it was Isobel who had a red diamond ring," Tess offered. "It's still in her room in his castle, so all I would have to do is go there—"

"We've been through this."

"—and get him to show it to me, then, I don't know, smuggle it out somehow? So we could take it back to the moonflower meadow and try to make a portal last long enough to get back to New York? Callum, please, you know it's the best idea we've had."

"I suppose it's worth it to you, risking your life for a chance to leave this place." Callum sulked.

"Hey." Tess snuggled closer to him, taking his hands in hers. "It's not that I'm not happy here. These last few days, with you—Callum, this is the happiest I've been since I left school. But I think . . . I don't know. I've been having this feeling."

"What kind of feeling?" he asked.

"Like I need to go back. Not just to New York, but—to Columbia, maybe. Three years ago, I quit on my life. But now I'm thinking . . . I don't know. Maybe it's not too late to try again."

Callum bit his lip—which made Tess want to kiss him, but she could sense it wasn't the time.

"I think we have to talk to Nantale."

"What?" Tess was surprised. "Why?"

"Because she's the one who sent us on this wild-goose chase to begin with," Callum said, his expression hard. "And we need to tell her that we're breaking into Felix's castle to get that diamond."

It was common knowledge on the Isle that Felix's clan threw a ball every full moon—and once Tess told Callum that this month's theme was a Venetian masque, he knew it would be the perfect opportunity to slip in and steal the diamond. Callum was somewhat worried that Nantale would declare his plan too risky—after all, aside from Nantale herself, there was no one on the Isle that Felix and his clan wanted dead more than Callum Yoo. Walking directly into their stronghold could be considered suicidal, especially since Callum had every intention of protecting Tess's life above his own (though he wouldn't tell Nantale this). On top of all that, it was a very big risk with no certain reward: Even if they did successfully smuggle Isobel's red diamond out of the castle, they had no way to know for sure whether the diamond would be enough to open a portal back to New York.

But it was the best—and only—idea they had. And Nantale agreed they had no choice but to try.

"I'll come with you," she said, surprising Callum.

"I can't let you do that," he replied, and she gave him a cold look.

"Callum, you don't 'let' me do anything."

"I didn't mean it that way," he blustered. "Look, it's one thing if Felix kills me, but the clan won't survive without you."

"Besides," Tess piped up, "the hope is that they won't even know we're there, right? So the fewer of us that go, the better?"

Nantale tilted her head and appraised Tess. "Fine. You two will go, Sylvie will prepare you a dress. And if you are able to retrieve the diamond, I will consider that the fulfillment of your service to my clan. Even if we cannot use the diamond to create a portal, I will still send a party to take you back to Bar Between so you can return home."

"Actually . . ." Callum said nervously. "I guess I should have told you this sooner, but what with one thing and another . . . someone set off an explosion at the foot of the crystal bridge. So there's no way for Tess to leave the Isle without a portal."

Callum searched Nantale's face for a reaction—shock at the news? Anger at Callum for withholding it? But she remained as unreadable and impassive as ever.

"Well then." She folded her arms. "I suppose you two had better get that diamond."

After that, Tess went to meet with Sylvie to figure out what to wear to the ball, and Callum and Nantale talked through every detail of his plan. Tess would flirt with Felix and try to find out where Isobel's room was, then get away from him as quickly as possible to relay the information to Callum. Callum and Tess would sneak out of the party and go to the room together, counting on the drunken revelry as distraction to give them cover. And if they were found out . . . Callum was a hell of a fighter. He'd do everything he could to get Tess to safety.

He just wished he had more time with Tess before they embarked on a mission that could cost either of them their lives.

She came to his rooms as darkness was falling, by which time he was in bed poring over her copy of *Blood Feud*.

"Hey," she said, pushing open the door to his bedroom. "Still reading that?"

"Seeing if I can find anything about Felix's castle. But this damn Lirio only wants to write about how good I am in bed."

"People need to know that." Tess climbed into bed beside him, kissing him gently.

"So you don't think Lirio oversold my prowess?" He pulled her into his lap.

"Mmm, I don't have enough information," she said. "Maybe if you give me a few more data points."

He laughed—but it caught in his chest.

"Are you okay?" she asked, rubbing his shoulder.

"I don't want this to be our last night together," he said softly.

"You're really worried about tomorrow, huh?"

"Maybe we just skip it." He sighed. "Stay here where it's safe and we're together."

"Glamour ourselves a little cottage in the north, hide out from all the vampires who want to drink my blood?" she suggested.

"I'll spend my nights hunting and my days giving you more data points than you could ever need."

"That sounds nice," Tess said, running her fingers through his hair. He loved the feeling of her nails gently dragging over his scalp; he closed his eyes at the pleasure of it.

"Callum?" Tess asked, and he opened his eyes. Her tone sounded serious. "If we do manage to get back to New York . . . do you think, I mean. Would that be the end of this? Of us?"

"Why? You think a rake like me would move on the second he got back to a city with millions of other women?" He was just teasing, but her face fell.

"I don't know. Maybe?"

"Tess." He drew her close, kissing her hair. "In all my lifetimes, I've never let anyone in—really in—except my sister, and maybe Nantale a bit. But you understand me in this way . . ."

"What way?" She looked up at him.

"It's like your book says—like I'm this villain, right? I always embraced that. When people were afraid of me, I liked it. Because if they were afraid to come after me, it meant I was safer, and so was Vee. But you see this other part of me. This vulnerable part, the part I always thought of as weak. Except with you . . . I feel strong. Like letting you see every side of me, like that's tougher than all that other bit, if that makes sense."

"It absolutely makes sense," Tess said, her voice choked. "I didn't expect you to be so good. After . . . what happened to me. Maybe I never expected anyone to be good again."

"Tess." He felt pained.

"No, it's okay. Because in a way, I think that was easier, you know? To just write everyone off, to never have to risk anyone doing that to me again. But in another way, I was running too. And being with you—it's made me see that maybe I don't want to run anymore."

"I don't want to run from you," Callum whispered.

"I know you don't."

Tess leaned her forehead against his.

"I want to ask you something," she said—and he could sense she was nervous, her pulse was speeding up.

"What is it?" He rubbed the pressure point on her wrist, trying to soothe her.

"You're not back to full strength yet, right? Since your injury?"

"Are you saying you find my current level of strength dissatisfactory?" He raised an eyebrow.

"No." She laughed. "I was thinking, for tomorrow. It would be better if you were stronger, right?"

"Tess, what are you getting at?"

She lifted her soft, fluffy sweater over her head, so that she wore only jeans and a bra.

"Feed on me," she said.

"What?" Callum was so shocked he almost choked. "You're not serious."

"I am."

"But I can't—" he sputtered. "It's too dangerous, I haven't fed in a decade. If I can't stop myself, I could hurt you—or worse."

"But you won't." Tess cradled his face in her hands. "You won't, because I trust you. Callum, you've helped me so much—"

"You've saved my life. Twice," he countered, and Tess laughed.

"Yeah, fair enough. But I want to do this for you, okay?"

He loved the way she looked at him, like he was worthy of her trust. Like despite everything he'd ever done, he was still a good man.

"Tess, are you sure?" he asked.

"I'm sure," she said. She leaned in and kissed him, and he drank in the taste of her, the feel of her warm mouth, her soft body. She leaned her neck to the side for him, but he shook his head.

"Not there," he said.

"Why not?" She looked puzzled.

"Blood moves faster in smaller veins, like the ones in your wrist or your neck," he explained, running a finger over her delicate wrist. "If I drink from your thigh, it will be easier to pace myself."

"Oh," she breathed, and he could feel her pulse pounding—it was hard to ignore his predatory instincts. She undid her fly, arched her back to slide her jeans down over those glorious thighs, the same thighs he'd so enjoyed kissing and teasing over the past days, feeling her writhe and squirm in eager anticipation of his touch.

"Will it hurt?" she asked as he removed his sweatshirt.

"Only for a moment, when I bite you. Which, again, I absolutely do not have to do if you don't want me to."

"No." She took him firmly by his shoulders and moved his body down hers. "I want you to. Now."

It was the most dominant she'd been with him, and he found it excited him just as much as when she was soft and gentle.

"Yes, ma'am." He smiled, and he began to kiss his way down her torso, starting with her neck, letting his lips linger over her décolletage, nipping at her nipples through the slippery silk of her bra. When she moaned at the sensation, he had half a mind to abandon the feeding and go down on her instead—but there'd be time for that afterward. He was going to see to it that this woman had the most pleasurable night of her life.

He lavished kisses on her round belly and wide hips, then used his hands to bend her knee slightly, exposing the soft underside of her thigh.

"Are you ready?" he asked.

"Yes." She was breathing hard.

He extended his fangs and bit her quickly so as not to draw out the anticipation. She gasped at the pain, and he could feel the tension in her. He wanted to tell her to relax, to reassure her that he wouldn't harm her, but her blood had already started flowing, and he couldn't have kept his mouth away from it for anything on Earth. He was so nervous he was shaking, acutely aware of every part of his body, holding his own tension, forcing himself to stay in control as he brought his lips to her thigh and drank.

Her blood tasted like a fresh field of flowers, grassy and bright; drinking it reminded him of childhood, running through a park with Octavia and falling asleep on a soft blanket in the sunlight on a summer afternoon. There was something golden about the taste of her, the feeling of her life force flowing inside of him—and he knew in that moment that there was no danger of hurting her. He felt that he understood her so deeply, that his body was so perfectly in sync with hers, their needs were one and the same.

After a minute or so, he stopped drinking. She looked up at him, a bit dazed—humans always were when they'd lost some blood—but he knew she'd be all right quickly.

"That's all?" she asked.

He nodded, then pricked his own finger and rubbed a couple of drops of blood on the spot where he'd bit her.

"To help the wound heal," he explained, and she nodded, her head lolling gently.

He moved up to lie beside her, and she turned on her side to face him.

"Your eyes," she murmured. "They're so gold."

"Happens sometimes," he smiled. "How do you feel?"

"Oh, I'm fine." She exhaled, already seeming sharper. "How do *you* feel?"

He wanted to tell her exactly how he felt. The buzz of her blood flowing through his veins, his sudden confidence they'd make it through the ball, steal the diamond, and get safely back to New York. But none of that seemed to matter as much as the way he felt about *her*.

Because he was in love with her. He was absolutely certain of it.

But he couldn't tell her that—not when it was entirely possible that either of them could die tomorrow. It would be cruel, would only sharpen both of their regrets.

"I feel better than I have in years," he told her, his voice breaking just a bit.

"Same," she said quietly, and maybe he was wrong, but he thought he understood that one syllable to mean *I love you too*.

He kissed her then, and she kissed him back. And he tried not to think about the ball, what would happen if they succeeded, what would happen if they failed—sacrificing his life for her if it came to it, leaving Octavia trapped in New York, leaving Tess trapped here on the Isle.

He didn't want to think about any of that, not now. He just wanted to be here with Tess, to enjoy his last few hours in bed with the woman he loved.

Chapter 25

Tess was glad to have most of the next day to sleep, since she and Callum were up until almost dawn. When she woke, it was already early afternoon, and Callum had left a note saying he was with Nantale. Tess took a quick rinse in his shower—which was paneled in dark slabs of moss agate and featured a window overlooking the forest, making Tess feel like she was bathing in a canopy of leaves. It was just another casually breathtaking place on the Isle, one more moment of staggering beauty; it gave her a pain in her chest.

It had only been a few days since she first kissed Callum, and she was terrified that if something went wrong tonight, she could lose him forever. Was it foolish to go to this ball? Should they wait until next month—or the month after? There were so many places on this island she'd yet to explore: She imagined lazy days and weeks together, swimming in silver pools under starlit skies, horseback rides along the jagged cliffs of the western coast, visiting magnificent buildings glamoured by vampires who no longer lived there, making love in gorgeous ruins overgrown with ivy.

It was all just a fantasy; Tess knew that. She'd almost been killed more than once on this island, even within the walls of this compound. She knew Callum would do anything to protect her, but she also knew it was unreasonable to believe he always could—especially since Felix's entire clan wanted him dead. The longer she stayed here, the greater the risk that something would go wrong and she would never be able to leave. She knew they had to do this—not just for themselves but for Nantale, Sylvie, and the others too.

Tess threw on clothes and went back to her room—she needed to find Sylvie to finalize her gown for the ball. Since Felix's apparent crush on Tess was crucial to their plan to find out where Isobel's rooms were, it was important that Tess look as beguiling as possible. She and Sylvie had discussed a number of options yesterday, and Sylvie promised that she'd come back with a few finished choices for Tess to try. To Tess's delight, Sylvie was already waiting with the dresses when Tess got back to her room.

"Someone slept in." Sylvie raised an eyebrow—she obviously knew exactly why Tess was so late.

"Sorry," Tess mumbled, though she couldn't suppress a smile.

"Not a problem." Sylvie grinned back at Tess. "Did you eat? Should I make you a little nosh before we get to the gowns?"

"I'm okay—Callum won't stop feeding me." She laughed.

"He likes taking care of you." Sylvie nodded approvingly. "That's how it was with Alberto too."

"Was it very difficult?" Tess asked. "Loving someone whose life was so different than yours?"

"No, bubbeleh." Sylvie rubbed Tess's shoulder affectionately. "He never asked me to give up my priorities. I got to live my life the way I wanted, and at the end of the road, he was always waiting."

Tess nodded tightly. It seemed too hopeful to believe that a future like this could be possible for her and Callum, but at the same time—wasn't it? Wasn't that the point of risking their lives tonight? Tess felt a sudden surge of determination, a belief that they really could do this.

"Okay, Sylvie. Let's try on some gowns."

Sylvie had made a whole variety, from a modern slip dress in forest-green satin to a full-on medieval gown draped in elaborate crimson brocade—which Tess loved, but it was far too heavy to be practical for an event where she might well end up running for her life.

In the end, they settled on a gown made of shimmering champagne lace embellished with tiny crystals. It had a bustier top that fit like a glove and showed off Tess's cleavage, a skirt that was loose enough to move in, and sheer, flowing sleeves that caught the air when Tess walked or twirled, flying behind her like a cape.

"It's perfect," Tess breathed. "I don't know how you did this."

But when she smiled back at Sylvie, she saw Sylvie was on the brink of tears.

"Hey, what's wrong?"

"It's nothing." Sylvie waved her hand. "Just—my daughter, she could never stay out of my closet. And I loved it. Anything I had, I always wanted her to have it, because it made me happier to see it on her. I thought I'd get to do that with my granddaughters too, but now I missed their proms, their graduations . . ."

Tess hugged Sylvie tightly.

"I'll get you back to them," Tess promised. "I swear it."

A few hours later, after Tess set her hair in loose waves, did her face in glowy makeup, and practically doused herself in Nantale's Egyptian musk oil, she stepped back into the gown Sylvie had made her. She grabbed some gold hair clips and earrings from the top shelf of the armoire, and she noticed the purse she'd carried when she came to the Isle. She took it down to examine its contents—no more copy of *Blood Feud* (Callum still had that), but her phone and the tarot card Flora had given her were still inside. She remembered how she'd felt when she'd drawn the card, seeing the blindfolded woman trapped by a circle of swords. Tess identified with that trapped feeling so much when she first saw the card—but strangely, she didn't anymore. She finally felt like she understood some of what Flora had told her: that she was capable of rescuing herself, if only she believed it was possible.

She tucked her phone and the card into a pocket inside the dress and made her way down to the great hall of the compound.

"Wow."

Callum stood in the compound's doorway, wearing high-waisted black trousers along with a crisp black button-down, all beneath a flowing black cape that hit just below his knees. With his hair slicked back and his face shaved clean, he was every bit the dashing rake Tess had imagined for so many years.

"You look incredible," she breathed.

"You're one to talk." He strode toward her and placed his hands at her waist, pulling her in roughly to kiss her. Tess wished at that moment that they didn't have a ball to attend, a red diamond to steal, a stranded sister to rescue. All she wanted was for Callum to take her back to his room and lock the door.

Instead, he glamoured two masks to match their outfits: Tess's was small and sparkly, to be held on a stick and cover only her eyes, since she needed Felix to recognize her. Callum's, on the other hand, was black and covered his entire face, which hopefully would help him avoid detection by anyone from Felix's clan.

"Okay." She exhaled, her nerves starting to roil. "I guess it's time to go?"

"One last thing," Callum said, removing a small black velvet bag from one of his pockets and holding it out to Tess.

"What's this?" she asked.

"Open it," he urged.

It was a necklace, a simple emerald set in gold, hanging from a delicate chain.

"Callum," she gasped, looking up at him.

"May I?"

She nodded and pulled her hair aside as he fastened the necklace. She turned to face him, and he broke into a satisfied smile.

"You were right," he said. "It's perfect with your coloring."

Tess told Callum she was perfectly capable of walking through the forest, and that he should save his strength for the ball, but he insisted on carrying her. The now-familiar pounding of Callum's steps thrummed through Tess's body, the evening air whipping against them, until a couple of minutes later, when they arrived at Felix's castle.

It was more beautiful than Tess could have imagined, even after reading about it so many times in *Blood Feud*. Every part of the building was circular, from the main fortress to the dozens of swirling turrets of all different heights, and every surface was coated in a substance that looked like mother of pearl. There were different shades—pastel rose and lavender and coral and gold—all shimmering as they caught the Isle's waning daylight and the light of the lanterns and torches blazing throughout the courtyard. In a place without sunshine, the castle was the closest thing Tess could imagine to a sunset, and it took her breath away. Dozens of vampires in fantastic suits and gowns were in the courtyard drinking from silver goblets, chatting loudly as lively music played.

Even in this party atmosphere, though, Tess could see that this clan was far more orderly than Nantale's. Guards lined the courtyard's perimeter, keeping a watchful eye on everyone at the party. A chill ran down Tess's spine as she and Callum passed them—but they didn't seem to notice anything unusual.

Callum grabbed a goblet from a tray and swigged, then took another and handed it to Tess.

"Wine, not blood," he whispered, and she smiled appreciatively and took a sip. She wanted to stay sharp, but her nerves were jangling, and a little liquid courage could only help.

The castle's entryway was magnificent, all paneled in a glistening pale golden metal, with floating lanterns that glowed violet and pink. Per their plan, Callum stepped away from Tess as soon as they went in (seemingly to look at a painting), so Tess was on her own as she walked into the main ballroom, where the party was in full swing. Vampires danced to orchestral music that sounded like old-fashioned English country dance melodies, except the scoring was undercut with thrumming bass and pulsing drums, making it all feel much darker and more modern. The lighting was darker in here too—Tess had no idea how she could possibly find Felix in all this mess, so she moved on to the next step of the plan: She put down her mask and poured herself a drink.

She got a couple of strange looks from people who didn't recognize her as she poured a goblet of champagne, and sure enough, Felix was by her side before she'd taken more than a few sips.

"You do know it's a masked ball, right?" He grinned at her and tapped his own mask, which was silver and looked to be encrusted with real diamonds—though not the diamonds Tess needed. He wore black pantaloons and a ruffled shirt along with a waistcoat whose fabric looked like it was sewn from a repurposed tapestry. It was all so over the top—and, Tess kind of hated to admit, he was really pulling it off.

"I have a mask right here!" Tess laughed, lifting it to cover her eyes. "I just couldn't hold it while I got a drink."

"That's my failure as a host for not being here to serve you. But I do appreciate any opportunity to see your face—which looks exceptionally lovely tonight, if I may say."

"Thank you." She bobbed a little curtsy—all the better for Felix to admire her low neckline. "You look amazing. I mean, this is *all* so amazing."

"I'm so glad you're here." He smiled, but then his face turned more serious. "Has everything been okay? Callum seemed so angry when he saw us together."

"He was fine." Tess rolled her eyes. "Just stomped off to his rooms, as if I care whether he wants to be my friend."

"I'd very much like to be your friend. If you're still in the market."

"Good to know." Tess grinned. "I'm still shopping around, mulling my options."

"Excellent—can't settle too quickly," Felix deadpanned. "Have to do your due diligence."

"Exactly! What if your new friend has terrible taste in snacks?"

"Like hamster blood, blech." He grimaced.

"Can't say I've had the pleasure."

"Allow me to save your taste buds—it's thin, grimy, and impossible not to get little bone chunks stuck in your teeth."

"Have you ever considered writing a book on fun conversation topics for parties?" Tess teased, and Felix burst out laughing.

Tess warmed with pleasure at his reaction, then felt a quick twist of guilt when she imagined Callum nearby watching. She knew how much Callum hated Felix—and understood exactly why—but Felix had only ever been kind to Tess. Sometimes it was hard to square the version of Felix she knew (not to mention the hero she'd read about for years) with the sniveling manipulator Callum described.

"All right then, what should we put on the friend-inspection agenda?" he asked genially. "Do you want to meet some of my clan mates? Or we could tour the castle, or dance if you like?"

"Oh, a tour sounds wonderful!" Tess effused. "The castle is so beautiful, I'd love to see more of it."

This wasn't part of the plan—she wasn't supposed to leave the main room with Felix so Callum could stay close by. But meeting other hostile vampires seemed like a bad idea, and letting Felix lay his hands on her long enough to feel her human pulse seemed worse—while a tour could lead Tess directly to Isobel's rooms. She couldn't turn down that opportunity, could she? All she had to do was get back to the ballroom as quickly as possible, and then she could tell Callum exactly where to go to steal the diamond.

Felix led Tess through a labyrinth of hallways, many of them curved and twisting because of the castle's circular shape. Tess could hear footsteps somewhere behind them; she hoped that meant Callum was following. She tried to remember everything they passed on their route: a waterfall running down a wall of crystals here, a larger-than-life mermaid statue made of pure coral there. Before long, they reached a spiral stairway, and Tess followed Felix as they started to climb. After a dizzying number of stairs, they finally arrived at an arched wooden door near the top of the tower. The keyhole had an intricate, octagonal shape, and Felix removed a necklace from beneath his shirt to unlock it—the pendant fit perfectly. He opened the door and held out his arm to welcome Tess inside.

"After you, milady."

"Why, thank you, good sirrah."

The room was like something out of a dream: a circular chamber made of stone, with a mammoth four-poster bed, a writing desk, shelves stuffed with books and boxes and all sorts of treasures, and huge windows and a terrace overlooking the forest, where the sky was almost dark and stars were beginning to appear. Tess recognized a few objects on the shelves from *Blood Feud,* including an intricately carved silver dagger—Tess was almost certain it was the same one Felix gave to Isobel in book one.

"This is so beautiful," Tess said. "Where are we?"

"Isobel's room," Felix confirmed, and Tess got chills. *This was it.* "She loved books, like you. And she kept journals every day of her life—hundreds of years, all documented right here."

Felix led Tess to the shelves that covered nearly half of the room's curving walls. Tess traced her fingers along the books' leather spines; in other circumstances, she could have spent hours in this room, reading Isobel's journals and learning everything she could.

"You must really miss her," Tess observed.

"I do." Felix took a step toward Tess. "Do you mind if I take my mask off?"

"Of course not," she said, but something about his tone was unnerving her. She put her own mask down as he removed his. "It's nice to be able to see you better."

He took a step toward Tess. "Would you like to see Isobel's jewelry?"

Tess fought to remain calm, but something felt terribly off. This was too easy—was it possible he was really just going to hand her the red diamond?

"I'd love to," she choked out. He slipped past her and opened a small wooden chest on the shelves behind her, extracting a worn gold ring with a scuffed red stone.

"It's lovely." Tess kept her voice low to keep it from quivering. "Is that the red diamond you told me about?"

He held up the ring, and even though the room was dim and the stone needed cleaning, it caught the light so brilliantly it looked like it might be possessed of its own inner fire.

"Indeed." His voice was cold. "That's what you came for, right, Tess?"

Tess felt her blood turn to ice water and her stomach dropped. She turned toward the door, but it was too late, Felix was already grabbing at her wrist.

"Stop it!" she shrieked. She tried to pull away, but of course he was so much stronger—

"The fact that you thought I didn't know exactly what you are from the second I met you." He smirked. "How stupid do you think I am?"

"Please, I'm not here to harm you—I—" Tess searched wildly for an excuse, any excuse. "This will sound crazy but there are these novels? They're called *Blood Feud,* and—"

"Tess, please stop embarrassing yourself." Felix ran his thumb over her wrist, massaging her pulse, which was thrumming so fast Tess thought she might be having another panic attack. "I know what *Blood Feud* is, I know that Octavia is back in New York, and I know exactly what you want with my ring."

Tess's head was swimming—was it possible he really *was* August Lirio?? It didn't matter—all of this was a trap—she was going to die in this castle—

"Callum, *run!*" she screamed, but it was too late, he was already in the room wrestling Tess away from Felix.

"Don't you fucking touch her," Callum seethed. "Just give us the ring, and we'll leave without any bloodshed."

"Mm, no. I have a better idea. Hey, guys?" Felix called out to the terrace. "You can come in now."

On Felix's command, a dozen vampires filed into the room—all masked, all huge, hulking men whom Tess felt quite sure could destroy them without a second thought. Maybe Callum would have a chance against one of them, or even two, but twelve?! Callum and Tess moved closer together on instinct, Callum keeping himself between Tess and the other vampires. Tess almost wished he wouldn't; she really, really didn't want to stay alive just long enough to watch him die.

"Now, Tess, since you're such a *Blood Feud* fan, let's play a little game. Do you know who killed Konstantin Adamos?"

Tess pressed her lips together—she wasn't playing any fucking game that Felix Hawthorn was running.

"You don't want to play? Then let's make it interesting. For every question you get wrong, I'll break one of Callum's fingers."

He nodded to one of his goons, who yanked Tess away from Callum—two more grabbed Callum's arms as he lurched forward to try to protect Tess.

"Come on, Tess," Felix goaded. "I know you know the answer. Who killed Konstantin?"

"Callum did." Tess gritted her teeth. "But only because you manipulated him into it."

"Wrong." Felix grinned.

"What?! But, Callum, you said—" Tess turned to Callum. He looked as utterly confused as Tess felt. But Callum's expression changed to agony as one of Felix's goons snapped back Callum's thumb with a sickening crunch—he yelled with pain.

"No!" Tess shouted. She whirled around on Felix. "Why are you doing this?"

"Next question," Felix hissed. "And I'm sure you know this one. Who killed Isobel?"

Tess closed her eyes. "I won't answer."

"Would you rather I break your fingers instead?" Felix stepped toward Tess.

"If you like," Tess said defiantly.

"No," Callum interjected. "Tess, I heal quickly. It's fine. Just answer."

"I can see why you hate Felix so much," Tess said to Callum. "He's not even strong enough to do his own petty torture."

"Are you going to answer the question or not?!" Felix shouted.

"I don't know, okay?" Tess fumed. "*Blood Feud* says it was Callum, but he says—"

"The book says exactly what I wanted the world to believe." Felix's grin was ice-cold. "But alas, I'm the one who killed sweet Isobel."

Tess gasped. "But—"

"Don't tell me you got snowed by a couple of novels, Tess—they're nothing more than fiction. And I'm afraid that means you're wrong again."

Felix walked up to Callum, and Tess's stomach roiled. She felt the most awful fear for her lover, the most terrible guilt for every time she'd doubted him about how much of a monster Felix really was.

"Callum, we should be breaking another of your fingers now—"

"Go ahead." Callum spat right in Felix's face—which didn't seem particularly wise, but Tess couldn't help internally cheering.

"You think you're so much better than I am." Felix wiped his face with a velvet glove. "But you're not good for anything but taking orders—first from Konstantin, now from Nantale. So I have an order for you, Callum. I want you to put on this red diamond ring you've been so keen to steal."

"Or what?" Callum narrowed his eyes.

"You can always refuse me." Felix smiled. "But if you do, I'll chop off both of Tess's hands."

"You're not gonna touch her," Callum growled.

"Callum, it's okay," Tess whispered. "Whatever he wants with that ring, please don't do it."

"He'll just make me wear it anyway," Callum said. "I won't let him hurt you."

Callum held out his hand, and Felix grinned. "Excellent choice."

Then he slipped the ring onto Callum's pinkie, and the entire room flooded with icy blue light.

"What's happening?" Tess called out. She threw up her arms to block the light—it was absolutely blinding. And unlike the light they saw in the meadow, it wasn't going away.

"I don't know," Callum yelled, grabbing for Tess. She clung to him, and he kept his arm around her, even as Felix kept hold of Callum's other hand so he couldn't remove the ring.

After a couple of moments, Tess could make out something in the doorway to the terrace. It was like there was a hole in the light, an archway. But it wasn't leading out to Felix's balcony—it was a window to somewhere else entirely.

To a rooftop in New York City, just after sunset.

Where a tall, terrifying man was standing beside a beautiful woman—a woman wearing a gold Georgian cross set with a mammoth red diamond.

"Octavia!" Callum yelled. "Are you all right? What's happening?!"

"Aw," Felix mocked. "Is Callum sad I'm the one Konstantin chose to confide in?"

"Enough." The tall man's voice was deep and resonant, and everything went silent the second he spoke. Tess squinted to make out his face—she saw Callum's eyes go wide as he recognized him—

"Konstantin?" Callum gasped. "But how—I thought you were—and you were never on the Isle—"

"You thought a little fire would kill me?" Konstantin smiled wide, brute force emanating from his body—Tess had never seen such a terrifying creature in her life. "Felix, no more games. End this now."

With that, Felix's men began filing through the portal, and Felix walked up to Tess and Callum.

"Tess, I want you to know that it was a genuine pleasure to meet you," he said. "And I'm very sorry I never got a chance to drain your blood and leave your mangled corpse on Callum's doorstep to pay him back for sleeping with Isobel, but hey, maybe we'll see each other again sometime, yeah? Then again, my entire clan knows there's a human in the castle, so, you know. Good luck getting out of here. Callum, let's go."

Callum tried to fight, and Tess was screaming and reaching for him, but there was nothing either of them could do. Felix's men dragged him through the portal, and once he was on the other side, the blue light disappeared and the portal closed, leaving Tess utterly alone.

Chapter 26

Tess looked frantically around the room, trying to think of anything that could get her out of this situation, but she just felt . . . numb. She had really believed that Callum would be able to protect her, that they would find some way out of all this. But he was gone, and now she was probably about to die—unless the vampires were planning to keep Tess alive to torture her, drinking her blood over and over until Felix found a way to get them off the Isle too.

She could always leap from the terrace outside Isobel's room. It might be the best available option—the fall was high enough to kill her.

No. She squeezed her eyes shut. She'd fought too hard, clawed her way back from the brink of desperation—she couldn't give up now. She just needed a way out of this castle.

She thought back to that first night at Bar Between, the tarot card Flora had given her. She certainly felt like she was surrounded by a circle of swords now—but she had the strangest sense she just needed to remove her blindfold and the way forward would become clear. What wasn't she seeing?

She took the card out of her dress pocket, held it between her palms.

Come on, she thought. *There has to be a way.*

Suddenly, she felt a shock of heat—she yelped and dropped the card, letting it flutter to the floor. She paused to make sure her yelp hadn't attracted any attention, but she didn't hear anyone coming.

Tess knelt down to examine the card more closely, then gasped—the illustration had changed.

The woman from the original card—the one who'd escaped before Tess's eyes back at the bar—was back in the picture, surrounded by the circle of swords like always, but she wasn't blindfolded anymore. Instead, she was on one knee beside a bed that was pushed at an angle, driving a sword into the space where one of the bedposts used to be.

"Is this—" Tess frowned. "Am I supposed to *do* this?!"

She didn't know who she was asking, or whether she expected a response, but none came. But she certainly didn't have any better ideas, so she set to pushing Isobel's bed so it mimicked the same angle she saw on the card. The bed wasn't too heavy, but it still took a good bit of effort to drag it across the stone flooring—Tess swore under her breath and wished she'd worn a sports bra to this ball instead of a damn gown, but she got the job done.

And there, under the right-hand post at the foot of the bed, was an obvious crack between two of the stones in the floor—a slot exactly the right size for the blade of a sword.

"Okay then." Tess's eyes went wide. She grabbed the silver dagger she'd seen earlier and drove it into the space in the floor. She heard a groan as one of the shelves against the wall swung open, revealing a secret doorway.

"Holy fucking shit," Tess breathed.

She dragged the bed back to its original position, hoping this might prevent any other vampires from figuring out where she'd gone. Then she stepped through the secret doorway into an extremely dark, extremely narrow passageway, and pulled the shelves closed behind her. She took the dagger with her; it seemed like a good idea to have a weapon.

The passageway was dark, cool, and silent. It was sort of like an indoor fire escape, with little landings on each floor and steep stairways-cum-ladders between them. Tess prayed the passage led outside the castle walls, but there was no way to know for sure. It felt like she descended the ladders for hours in the darkness, scraping her body against stone walls, unwieldy in her dress. (Though she was grateful she'd skipped the brocade medieval gown—no way would that have fit through here.) Every so often, she heard shouts and footfalls outside the passageway, and she'd freeze until it was quiet again. Eventually, she made it to the ground floor, where there was a single door—but absolutely no way to tell where it led.

Tess put her ear to the door to try to get any bit of sound, any information at all as to what might lie behind it. But after a few minutes, there was nothing—and it wasn't like she really had any other choice but to keep going. So Tess gripped the dagger in one hand and turned the door handle with the other, pushing it open the tiniest bit—

She immediately smelled cool night air and evergreen trees, and the noise of the party seemed very far away. She pushed the door open a little farther, then almost cried with relief—it was a pathway that led to the forest. She'd have to be lucky to avoid Felix's guards, but maybe she could make it to the compound, find Nantale, and try to figure out what the hell to do next.

As quietly as she could, she stepped through the doorway, pulling the door shut behind her. She looked up—guards were stationed along the castle's battlements, keeping an eye out for possible intruders. She'd just have to try to act as normal as possible and hope she could slip past without notice. She concealed the dagger in the folds of her dress, then cursed herself as she realized she'd left her mask in Isobel's room. Ah, well. She supposed it was probably better to have a knife. She took a deep breath, then set off down the path in a leisurely manner. She took ten paces, then twenty. So far, so good—she was just a few feet from the forest—

"Hey! You there!"

Fuck. She turned to see a guard waving down at her.

"Me?" she asked as innocently as she could.

"Where are you going?"

"Oh, just feeling a bit peckish," she lied quickly. "Thought I'd go find a snack. Thanks for checking on me, though! Can't be too careful!"

She waved goodbye and turned to continue walking, praying that would be the end of it, but in seconds she heard a whoosh of movement, and the guard was right beside her. He was shorter than he'd seemed from high above, and scrawnier too—he was living his immortal life as a pimply teenager, which struck Tess as terribly unfortunate. But he wore the same black robes as Felix's goons who'd taken Callum away, and Tess knew better than to underestimate him.

"What's this about?" she snapped, trying to channel Octavia. Clearly, being friendly hadn't dissuaded him, so maybe this would. "I'm on my way out to hunt, not for idle chitchat with the *help.*"

"I'm sorry to be a nuisance." He took a step back—clearly chastened. "But Felix said there might be intruders tonight."

"If you can use your putrid little brain for just one moment," Tess said coolly, "you might recall that intruders come *in* to the castle, not out. So if you'll step aside and let me be on my way? Or do I need to take this up with Felix? What's your name? I want to tell him exactly which little brat in robes tried to ruin my night."

The guard hesitated, clearly terrified of getting in trouble. Tess could almost feel sorry for him, if she weren't quite sure he would murder her on the spot if he knew she was human.

"I guess it's okay . . ."

"Good." Tess sighed. She set back off toward the forest without waiting for more, but then—

"Hey, is that Isobel's dagger? Why do you have that?"

Fuck, fuck, fuck!!

Tess turned back toward him, trying to think—

But before she could speak, someone rushed past her, so fast they looked like a shadow—and then the guard was on the ground, sliced open from neck to navel, blood spurting out of him, struggling to breathe.

"Come on." Nantale took Tess's arm. "We have to move. Leave the dagger."

Tess dropped it, and then Nantale scooped her up and sped into the forest—and it wasn't like when Callum carried her, because Nantale was even stronger, even faster, she moved so smoothly it felt like flying. They streaked through the forest, then the air was open and they were back in front of the compound, where Artie was tethered and waiting.

"Artie!" Tess exclaimed as she caught her breath, and he nickered happily.

"What happened?" Nantale demanded. "Where's Callum? Did Felix kill him?"

Tess shook her head, not even sure where to start—

"It was a trap, it was all a trap. Felix put the diamond on Callum and used him to open a portal back to New York—Octavia was there with Konstantin, who I guess isn't dead? Felix went through the portal with Callum along with a dozen of his men, and he said the rest of the clan all knew I was human. I thought for sure I was going to die, except then this tarot card I have—"

"Stop, that's enough." Nantale cut her off. "Callum is gone?"

"Yes." Tess's eyes welled with tears. "And the diamond is gone too, so I don't know how any of us can get out of here, especially since someone blew up the crystal bridge—"

"Not 'someone,'" Nantale corrected. "Me."

"*You?*" Tess was flummoxed. "Why?!"

"Did you really think I'd put the future of my clan in the hands of a human without monitoring you?" Nantale raised an eyebrow. "As soon as I learned you'd taken a horse, I assumed you were trying to escape, so I went straight to the bridge to head you off. When I saw you approaching, I did what I had to do. I didn't blame you for wanting to leave, all of us trapped here would do the same. But I am responsible for the safety of my clan, and I knew that your presence here was our best chance to find a way home. So I hope you understand why I couldn't let you go."

Even as Tess was flabbergasted by Nantale's betrayal, she couldn't help but be impressed by her ruthless loyalty to her clan.

"Except now we're *all* trapped here," Tess fumed. "How am I supposed to help you if I can't get back to New York?"

"I am still trapped here," Nantale clarified. "You are not."

"But—the bridge!" Tess sputtered.

"There is another way across the river, a boat. As far as I know, I am the only vampire who ever discovered it. You will find the boat tied to a dock at the base of the cliffs beneath the bridge. There's a stairwell you may walk to reach it."

"So you knew," Tess marveled. "You knew that destroying the bridge would intensify my motivation to find a way off the island, without actually trapping me here."

"I never asked to be a leader. But it's a burden I carry with pride." Nantale lifted her chin, then nodded toward Artie. "Ride quickly. I need to ready the clan in case Felix plans to attack us tonight—that may be part of his strategy. But you must go. Callum is waiting. Do not fail us, girl."

Tess nodded, tears in her eyes. Part of her wanted to go back into the compound, to change her clothes, to say goodbye to Sylvie, but she knew there wasn't time for any of that—she mounted the horse and started riding like hell. Artie was equal to the moment, cantering furiously down the paths they'd trod together weeks ago, before Callum had even been injured, before he'd meant anything more to her than a character in a story. She couldn't believe how listless she'd felt then, how adrift. Now, wearing the dress Sylvie had made her, the necklace Callum had given her, charged with a mission from Nantale, she'd never felt a stronger sense of purpose in her life.

When they reached the bridge, Tess dismounted and looked for the stairway Nantale described—it was carved into the cliffs, nearly invisible if you didn't know where to look. And at the bottom, just as Nantale had said, there was a dock and a rowboat—both made of crystal, of course.

Tess took a deep breath. It felt like everything was happening too quickly; Tess's time on the Isle had transformed her life, and now, in an instant, it would be over.

She stroked Artie's neck. "Thank you for everything," she murmured, and he nuzzled his head against hers. "You know how to get home?"

He looked at her, seeming to understand. She gently slapped his haunch, and he took off into the night.

The top of the stairway was drenched in hot sunshine, at least twenty feet out of the darkness so no vampire could reach it. Tess rushed down the stairs and flew down the dock, climbing carefully into the crystal rowboat.

Tess quickly noticed she had a problem, though: The boat had no oars.

"What do I do?" she muttered. "How do I get to Bar Between?"

As soon as she said the words, the boat set into motion, pulling away from the dock and speeding across the river. The short journey was unbelievably beautiful, the lilac water spraying alongside the boat, the sunlight glittering in rainbows as it refracted through the jagged remnants of the crystal bridge overhead. But Tess couldn't appreciate it—all she could think about was getting back to New York, and to Callum, before it was too late.

The boat docked on the other side, and Tess disembarked and ran through the little forest clearing as fast as she could until she reached the dome made of petrified wood she'd come through what felt like forever ago. She took one moment to turn back and see the Isle—it seemed so small, all the way across the river. Would she ever see it again? It didn't matter now. She walked up to the dome, pushed the door forward, and walked through, off of the Isle and back to the bar between worlds.

Chapter 27

"What happened oh my god that took *forever* I was so *worried* are you okay?!" Flora rushed over to the portal Tess had just walked through. They were in the main bar—the same room Tess had left to walk onto the Isle.

"I—" Tess wasn't sure what to say, but it didn't matter because Flora just kept right on going.

"I mean, I was kind of shipping you and Felix, don't be mad, he can be annoying but he's so cute, you know? And Callum seemed all broken and kind of deranged, but then you really brought him out of his shell—"

"How much of my time on the Isle did you watch, exactly?" Tess broke in.

"Tess, it's literally my job to monitor the vampires! And you were the first human ever to go there, obviously I was gonna keep track of what was happening! When the bridge blew up I was like OH SHIT, but I knew the boat was there, so I was hoping you'd figure it out—and then you didn't, but anyway it was good Nantale knew about it. God, she's iconic, right? *Omg,* and can we even just discuss that Octavia's been back here this whole time? And now Konstantin has her and Callum both? Oh man, what are we gonna do?!"

Tess's face fell. "I was kind of hoping you would know what to do?"

"Me?!"

"Yeah, I mean, you did all that magic with the tarot card, and got me out of the castle—didn't you have some kind of plan?"

"The tarot card?" Flora frowned. "What do you mean?"

"It changed," Tess explained. She took the card out to show Flora what she meant—except now it was back to its original state, with the blindfolded woman in the circle. "When I was in Isobel's room, it showed me how to use the dagger to open a secret door-way."

"That wasn't me." Flora looked impressed. "I told you, I can only watch the Isle—I can't make anything happen there. None of us can."

"So then how . . . I mean, who did it?"

"You, babe." Flora grinned. "The cards told you to rescue your-self. I guess they thought you did a pretty good job."

"Shit." Tess shook her head with wonder. "Now I just need to rescue two vampires from their ancient all-powerful sire—and I don't even know where they are, let alone how to help them. Unless—can you find Konstantin with a spell or something?"

"Not without a possession of his to cast it." Flora took a sip of wine. "You want a drink? Closed bottle, I know—I can open some-thing for you."

"Oh," Tess started. She realized that just hours ago, she'd had a glass of champagne at Felix's ball and hadn't thought twice about it. "That's okay—I don't want a drink. I kind of just want to get out of this dress, and then figure out what to do next?"

"That makes sense." Flora nodded. "Let's go to your place."

"Oh! Great, you're coming too." Tess hadn't expected Flora to come along, but she wasn't going to turn down any sort of help.

Flora cast a portal, and a few seconds later, they were back inside Tess's tiny apartment. Tess suddenly felt ridiculous in her golden gown—as if she were a character in the wrong story, a person without a place. She wasn't some wily heroine; she was just a grad-school dropout in an unkempt studio with a bed in a closet who may well have lost her job since she disappeared for two weeks. Never mind rescuing her vampire lover and his glamorous sister—she wasn't even sure how she was going to make rent.

She started unzipping her gown when something knocked against her leg. Right—her phone. She took it out and stuck it on its charger as a matter of habit. She wasn't expecting many messages from her time away, maybe just a few from people at the hotel asking where she'd been. She threw on some joggers and a cropped hoodie—it was strange wearing regular clothes again rather than some gorgeous bespoke garment made by Sylvie. She went to remove the emerald necklace Callum had given her, then decided to keep it on instead. It made her feel close to him, like there was a chance they could still get out of this okay.

Tess's phone was buzzing nonstop, so she glanced at the screen. She was shocked to see that she had dozens of messages from Joni, maybe even hundreds. She picked them up and started reading as fast as she could—

Joni met Octavia at Tess's hotel?!

The two of them had started hooking up?!?!

She was on her way to Gramercy Park to meet August Lirio—whose agent's assistant was named *Fern*?!

"Flora!!" Tess shouted. "I think I found something!"

Flora rushed into the bedroom. "What is it!?"

Tess shoved her phone into Flora's hands. "My friend Joni met up with Octavia. They've been working together. Joni was in Gramercy Park yesterday, supposedly to meet August Lirio."

"But—that's where the meeting of the witches' council was." Flora's jaw dropped as she scanned Joni's texts. "Fern?! Fern doesn't work for a literary agency, she works for the fucking coven!"

"That's what I'm saying!" Tess said eagerly. "It can't be a coincidence, right? If Joni was meeting Fern yesterday, and Konstantin had Octavia tonight—"

"Fern was working with Konstantin—and probably Felix too—to trap her." Flora gave Tess a dark look.

"Do you think Fern is with them now?" Tess's heart was pounding. "Is there any way to find her?"

"Oh, I can absolutely find Fern." Flora whipped out her own phone.

"With magic?" Tess asked.

"No." Flora held up her phone, which was open to the Find My Friends app. "Fern shared her location so I can always make her a portal."

Damn, Tess thought. *It's good to be home.*

❧

Joni had no idea how she'd ended up trapped in a creepy-ass attic with *Dorian Gray* vibes, but she did not care for it one bit. She'd had a spectacularly crappy twenty-four hours: showing up to meet Fern at a fabulous townhouse where Fern insisted that Joni just *had* to come and see the view from the top floor. At first, Joni thought maybe Fern really was flirting with her, but that went out the window pretty quickly when Fern locked Joni in the attic instead. Joni banged on the doors and yelled and screamed, but no one heard—except for two big men who showed up hours later and tied Joni to a chair, which is where she'd been ever since—meaning she missed her job interview, she was really fucking hungry, and she was, if she was honest, pretty worried about her imminent death.

And what about Octavia? Was she here? Was she even alive? And what was this place, exactly? Who were the people holding Joni? Fern had to be involved, but there were those men around too. Joni had no idea who they were or how Fern was connected to them—nor did she know why they'd kept her alive or how long they planned to continue to do so. She figured they must want some kind of information out of her, maybe about Octavia? But no one had asked her anything yet; in fact, no one had spoken to her at all.

Joni could sometimes hear movement and voices from the floor below her, but it was too muffled to make out anything useful. So she spent hours trying to undo the knots binding her to the chair—she hadn't made major progress, but maybe if they left her alone long enough . . . what? She could try to squeeze herself out of the small attic window? Maybe find a fire escape, or somehow get to the roof of a neighboring building? It wasn't a solid plan per se, but it was all she had. She kept working at the knots, little by little, wondering if they were really getting slightly looser or if that was just wishful thinking.

But she was pretty sure she was actually losing her mind when a circle of icy blue light appeared in the attic and Tess and some goth woman walked through it.

"Tess?!" Joni whispered. "What are you—how did you—what the fuck?!"

"Are you okay? Did anyone hurt you?" Tess knelt beside Joni and started furiously untying the ropes. There was something different about Tess—she seemed more self-assured than Joni ever remembered her being. She always thought of Tess as quiet, a person you were lucky if she let you get to know her. But this person seemed decisive and confident. Had she been like this in all the time since she'd left Joni? Or was the development more recent?

"I'm okay," Joni answered. "Just scared out of my mind. And deeply confused about how the fuck you just walked into this room from a mysterious floating circle?"

"Portal magic," Tess said, as if this meant literally anything to Joni. "Flora's a portal witch."

"Hi!" The goth woman waved. "I'm Flora."

"Okay?" Joni wasn't sure how to react to this, but then she took a closer look at Flora. "Hey, you look kind of like . . ."

"Fern?" Flora tilted her head. "She's my sister."

"I hope you don't mind my saying she's a real bitch." Joni gritted her teeth.

"I don't mind at all," Flora said affably. "Fern's the worst!"

"So obviously she's not some agent's assistant—she's a witch?" Joni asked. "Is that who's holding me? Witches?"

"Vampires," Tess corrected. "Konstantin."

"He's not dead?" Joni's eyes went wide—she was being held captive by one of the most powerful and dangerous vampires who'd ever lived?? "So, what's the plan, we just gonna blue circle our way out of here?"

"Exactly." Tess pulled at a particularly stubborn knot. "But first we have to rescue Callum and Octavia."

"They're here too?! Is Octavia okay?!"

Tess turned to Flora. "Are they?"

Flora nodded. She was moving her hands in a circle over the floor—Joni wondered if she was doing some kind of spell to get them all out of here.

"Finally." Tess exhaled as she got the main knot binding Joni undone, and Joni's arms were free. Joni stretched out her arms, then set about rubbing her wrists and shoulders.

"Fuck, that feels good." Joni sighed.

"I'll have your ankles in a second," Tess promised.

Joni opened her mouth to say thank you but got completely distracted when the floor disappeared beneath Flora's hands, opening a window to the room where Octavia was sitting at a table with two other vampires, drinking red wine. One was a man who looked strikingly like her—that must be Callum. The other was so large and terrifying, there was no question in Joni's mind that he was Konstantin.

"Can they see us?" Joni whispered to Flora.

"No," Flora explained. "It's just a vision portal, like one-way glass."

"If you were alive, why didn't you tell me?" Callum demanded. "I searched Prague for days. You disappeared without a trace."

"I had to." Konstantin's voice was cool and even—not a hint of remorse. "If anyone had known I was alive, I would have been sent to the Isle with the rest of you."

"So you *knew* we were going to be sent to the Isle, and you just let it happen?!" Octavia's voice was more vulnerable than Joni had ever heard it. "Why would you let them trap us in that terrible place?"

"You told me in Seoul that you wanted to be apart from me." Konstantin shrugged. "I simply granted your wish. Do you see now that I was right? That your lives are better when you stay by my side?"

"I don't understand." Octavia shook her head, her voice faint. "How did you know about the Isle in the first place?"

"Fern told me," Konstantin replied. "Useful witch. She wants to be the head of her coven—and she correctly gathered she could get there faster with my help than on her own. Witches and vampires working in tandem, coming out of the shadows, claiming our rightful place as dominant over all other creatures on Earth. An intriguing idea, no?"

"*Fucking Fern,*" Flora whispered.

"So you used me to fake your death in Prague?" Callum set his jaw. "To avoid being sent to the Isle?"

"Exactly." Konstantin nodded. "After you were sent to the Isle, it took Fern and me nearly a decade to work out how to bring you back. My blood bond with Octavia was enough to bring her to New York. But I needed both of you—and two red diamonds—to open a portal strong enough for the others to walk through it. Once we realized your blood bond was the key, it was a simple matter of Fern using her telepathy to communicate with Felix. Felix was meant to bring you to his castle so we could open the portal together, but the arrival of the human complicated things. Fortunately, Felix was able to use her to lure you there."

In the attic, Flora and Joni both looked at Tess. Tess was gripping one of the ropes binding Joni so tightly her hands were shaking.

"Hey," Joni said. "Are you okay?"

Tess shook her head—her eyes were wet.

"But if you needed us, why tell Felix?" Octavia demanded, her voice ragged. "Why didn't you just tell *us*? Why did you let me wander New York without my powers, thinking I was alone?"

"Because I no longer trust you!" Konstantin slammed his hand on the table so hard that everything on it shook. "You betrayed me in Seoul, and again in Prague. You've always been stronger than Felix, smarter, more talented. But my plan required absolute loyalty, and in that, my dear progeny, you are both sorely lacking."

"So what now, then?" Callum set his jaw.

"Now?" Konstantin grinned, and Joni caught a flash of his fangs. "Now's the fun part. The part where you show whose side you're really on. If you choose correctly, we become the three most powerful creatures on Earth, with an army of vampires to do our will."

"And if we refuse?" Callum asked.

"I'll need you nearby to transport vampires to and from the Isle," Konstantin said casually. "All points of entry to the Isle are being permanently closed—even Bar Between. The only way on or off the island will be through the portal you opened tonight. Vampires will have two choices: to be allowed home if they swear to follow me, or to stay trapped on the Isle if they don't."

"You want to use us to trap other vampires, the same way you trapped us?" Octavia said softly. "I'm not doing that."

"Then you're welcome to stay in this townhouse, guarded and bound in chains," Konstantin growled.

Tess whipped around toward Flora. "They're closing the entry to the Isle from Bar Between?!"

Flora nodded gravely. "The coven voted last night. I tried to stop it, but Fern convinced them it was the only way to protect our world."

"But Fern's working for Konstantin!" Joni protested. "She doesn't want to protect humans, she wants to give him limitless power over us!"

"We didn't know that at the time!" Flora huffed. "We should probably have another meeting."

"You think?!" Joni screeched—and then she realized her feet were free. "Oh my god!"

She leapt up out of the chair and took Tess's hands to pull her to her feet as well.

Tess looked at Joni with trepidation. "Joni, I need to say, I mean—"

But Joni didn't need Tess to struggle through all the hard things they had to say to each other—not here, not yet. She threw her arms around Tess and hugged her close.

"I'm so happy to see you," she whispered into Tess's hair.

"Well, yeah, I'm saving your ass." Tess laughed, but her voice was thick with emotion.

"That's not why I'm happy," Joni said, hugging her tighter. "I mean, I'm not not happy you're saving my ass, but—you get it."

"I do." Tess buried her face against Joni's shoulder. And even though this was undoubtedly the strangest day of Joni's life, it felt really fucking good to be hugging her best friend.

"Guys," Flora hissed. "Konstantin just left—this might be our only chance."

Tess and Joni broke their hug, but they stayed clasping hands—Joni had lost Tess too many times before. She wasn't ready to let her go.

Flora moved her hands over the portal on the floor, then slowly pushed it up into the air. Now, instead of looking at Callum and Octavia from above, it was as if they were staring face-to-face—but Callum and Octavia still couldn't see them. Until Flora muttered an incantation and moved her hands again, and the portal sparked and shimmered, icy blue like it had been when Tess and Flora walked into the attic.

Callum and Octavia's eyes went wide as Flora, Tess, and Joni clambered through the portal.

"Are you okay?" Joni rushed over to Octavia. "Did he hurt you?"

"I'm fine." Octavia's tone was blasé, but Joni could see she was really afraid. "What about you? Did anyone hurt you?"

"No, I'm okay." Joni wanted to kiss Octavia, but she thought that would be pretty awkward in front of her brother. But when she turned to look at Callum, he and Tess were kissing passionately.

"Uhhhhh. . . . you guys want to tell us what's going on?" Joni sputtered.

"There's no time," Callum said. "We have to get out of here, right now."

"Good," Tess agreed. "Where are we going?"

Callum and Octavia exchanged a look, and then Callum turned back to Tess.

"Not all of us," Callum said, as gently as he could. "Just Octavia and me."

"*What?*" Tess looked like he'd just slapped her. "You're going to leave us? You're leaving me?"

"I don't want to," Callum pleaded. "Please understand, the things Konstantin will make us do—"

"So fight him!" Tess shot back. "Fight back, take control, do something to stop him!"

"It's not that simple," Octavia said coolly.

"Why not?" asked Joni.

"Because he'll kill you both," Octavia snapped. "Especially if he knows that you matter to us. He doesn't allow us to be loyal to anyone but him."

"I know it doesn't feel this way, but us leaving is to protect you." Callum took Tess's hands. "You're no threat to Konstantin. If we're gone, he'll leave you alone."

"Are you sure about that?" Tess's voice broke. "And what about Nantale, and Sylvie, and everyone else? You're just going to leave them on the Isle forever because you'd rather run away?"

"It's the only way to save ourselves," Callum said. He tried to pull Tess in for a hug, but she shook him off.

"So you're only going to think about yourself? No matter who it hurts?" Tess was holding back tears. "Maybe August Lirio was right about you. You really are the villains."

Callum looked devastated—but Tess did too. It was honestly hard for Joni to tell which of them was feeling worse.

Octavia tugged on Callum's sleeve. "We'd better go before he comes back."

"Do you need me to make you a portal?" Flora asked. "I can send you anywhere you want."

"It's safer for you if you don't know where we're going," Callum responded. "Tess, I . . ."

But Tess just stood there, her arms folded, tears streaming down her face.

"Just go," she said stiffly.

Octavia approached Tess gingerly. "Tess, Callum and I are so grateful for your help—yours and Joni's both. Now that I have my powers back, we'll wire you both some money as soon as we can."

"What?" Tess frowned. "I don't want that—I don't care about that."

"I know." Octavia looked at her sadly. "But right now, it's the most we can do."

Octavia looked at Joni then, and it was awful but predictable. Joni had never really thought Octavia would stick around after she got her powers back. It sucked—it maybe sucked worse than any breakup Joni had ever had. But it wasn't surprising.

"Bye, Octavia," she said quietly. "Stay safe."

It was hardly a satisfactory resolution, but they were out of time—and besides, what else was there to say? So Joni, Tess, and Flora just watched as Callum and Octavia opened the window and easily scaled down the side of the building, their remarkable strength and speed fully restored now that they were back together. Once they hit the ground, they sped off into the dark so quickly that Joni couldn't even watch them disappear.

Chapter 28

"So now what?" Joni asked, looking from Tess to Flora. "We just wait around for Konstantin to kill us?"

"We're not important enough to kill," Tess replied. She tried to say it with as much confidence as possible, but she had no idea whether it was true.

"Did you see that man?!" Joni scoffed. "It doesn't matter if we're important—he'll murder us and care so little he'll forget he did it five minutes later."

"Can I humbly suggest we get the fuck out of here before he gets that chance?" Flora interjected. "We can go to my place if you want?"

"Fern's gonna figure out pretty quick you were involved in the escape," Tess said. "We need a place that isn't tied to any of us. Someplace they won't expect."

"Can that place also serve food?" Joni asked. "I haven't eaten since yesterday."

"Good, fine. Food!" Flora threw her hands up, and an icy blue circle swooped over them—without warning, they were standing in a parking lot of a diner off a suburban highway.

"Where the fuck are we?" Joni asked.

"New Jersey." Flora pointed at the diner's sign, which read *Six Brothers Diner! Best fries in Jersey!* "I used to come here in high school."

Tess and Joni both gaped at Flora, who shrugged. "You think witches don't go to high school? Have you not seen *The Craft*?"

"She makes a point," Joni agreed. "Okay, let's get some fries."

Twenty minutes later, they were jammed into a vinyl-covered booth, Joni inhaling a burger, Tess picking at a tuna melt, and Flora moaning elaborately as she ate a plate of thick-cut fries smothered in gravy and mozzarella cheese.

"*Disco fries.*" Flora caressed the plate. "I missed these so much."

Tess took a bite of one of her own fries, but making herself chew and swallow was a real effort. Her whole body felt tight. Everything was too bright in this diner, the pastel neon lighting and the rotating pastry case with little plastic slices of pie beamed in hot spotlights. Last night, she was in bed with Callum on an island that never saw the sun, and now she was just . . . here? With a witch, and her ex–best friend, eating fries, and possibly running for her life?

"What are we gonna do?" she murmured to no one in particular, but Flora and Joni both stopped eating and looked at her.

"Maybe Callum and Octavia were right?" Flora suggested. "Joni, if you just lie low for a few days, this could blow over? And there's no reason to think he has it out for you, Tess. You might both be safe."

"You don't really believe that, though, right?" Tess said quietly.

Flora waited a long beat, then sighed. "No. I guess I don't."

"So that's it, then," Tess said. "We have to go."

"What, leave New York?" Joni was incredulous. "Uproot our whole lives without even waiting to see if this turns into a problem?"

"Joni, you just spent a day tied up in an attic!" Tess protested. "If that doesn't meet your definition of a problem, what does? Maybe you're okay risking that happening again, but I'm not."

"Yeah, well, I guess it's no surprise you think that." Joni stabbed a fry with her fork. "Kinda tracks with your whole vibe."

"That's not fair," Tess shot back.

"Isn't it?" Joni's voice was too loud, and a few people turned to look. It was ten o'clock on a Friday night, and the diner was crowded with teenagers gossiping and laughing, people stumbling in from nearby bars looking for a snack or to sober up, even a couple of parents out with their insomniac babies. Tess knew this crowd—it was *her* crowd. Nighttime people. The only people she'd seen in years. How could she make Joni understand that none of this was something she chose?

"Oh shit, Fern's calling." Flora cut through the silence. "She'll know something's up if I don't answer. Be right back."

Flora rushed out to the parking lot, leaving Joni and Tess alone in the booth. It was the first time Tess had been alone with Joni in three years—unless you counted that awful moment on the street outside her birthday party. Tess thought of Joni's text from while she was on the Isle, the text she'd first seen just an hour ago.

Please don't be dead. I still want to yell at you about my birthday.

"You can yell at me if you want," Tess said, and Joni looked understandably confused. "About your birthday? That's what you said in your text."

"Oh." Joni looked down at her fries. "Yeah, I was pretty pissed. Like, what was the point of you showing up just to ruin the night?"

"I didn't mean to." Tess closed her eyes. She could still feel Rick's hand on her arm, the nausea that took hold when he smiled at her. "I was really excited to see you."

"So why did you leave?" Joni asked. "Did I—I mean, whatever I did to make you move out, did I do that again?"

"Joni, no." Tess looked at her friend in shock. "How could you think that? I didn't move out because of you."

"I don't know why you're saying that like it's so obvious." Joni shoved a fry into a glob of ketchup on her plate. She didn't pick it up, though, just kind of smushed it around. "When your best friend moves out of your shared home, stops speaking to you, and refuses to return your calls for literal years, you kind of assume you had something to do with it."

Tess took a deep breath. Count five things you can see right now. The insomniac baby lolling off to sleep in his mother's arms. The teen girl in a Weezer shirt drinking a strawberry shake. The green tables. The pink booths. The bored waitress pretending to listen to the ramblings of the older manager. Was there ever a time when Tess slept through the night? Was there ever a time when she was happy?

"I didn't tell you because I didn't want to admit it to myself," Tess said quietly.

"What does that mean?" Joni put down her fry and looked at Tess.

"Every time I thought about it, I would panic. So I just—tried not to think about it. Except being at school, I couldn't not think about it. So the only thing that made sense was not to be at school."

"Tess." Joni leaned forward, her expression intense. "What happened?"

"Rick raped me." The words fell out of Tess's mouth, jagged and impossible, a word she hated to hear or read, let alone speak out loud—let alone apply to herself.

"What?!" Joni's whole body went tense. "When?"

"At his party," Tess said. "On Valentine's Day."

"But." Joni was shaking her head. "I thought you liked him. I thought you went there to . . ."

"I did," Tess nodded. "That's what didn't make sense to me. Why would he put something in my drink when I already wanted to sleep with him?"

"He drugged you?" Joni's face was dark. "Tess, that's like— I mean, that's really fucking serious."

"I know." Tess was crying now, and she felt so stupid—that she'd let this happen at all, that she'd waited so long to tell Joni, that after all these years, even saying Rick's name still flipped a fucking switch that turned her from a confident woman into a blubbering mess.

"Can I sit with you?" Joni asked. "Is that okay?"

Tess nodded, and Joni moved to the same side of the booth so she could put her arms around her.

"Come here," Joni said, and it felt so easy just to be with her best friend, the person who had never let her down a single time, no matter how hard Tess tried to run away.

"I'm so sorry I didn't tell you," Tess sniffled. "I just—it was ruining my life every time I saw him, and I felt so stupid, because like, I wanted it, you know? I didn't understand why I was reacting like I was."

"And you thought I wouldn't understand either?" Joni asked.

"No, that's not it." Tess wiped her eyes. "But you guys were friends, and you were writing that article, it was such a big deal for you—I didn't want to ruin that! Especially not if I was wrong, you know?"

"Wrong?" Joni looked puzzled. "How could you be wrong?"

"I was really confused about all of it. He was such a nice guy—you said so, everyone said so. And it was hard for me to remember what really happened, so, I don't know. I thought maybe I got it wrong."

Joni looked at Tess, her expression ferocious.

"Hey, I believe you, okay? You're my best friend, and I am always gonna believe you, especially over some fucking guy who totally took more credit than he deserved for that article, by the way. He's an asshole, and a monster, and—" Joni stopped mid-sentence and covered her mouth. "Oh my god, Tess. He was at my party."

Tess nodded. "He talked to me, touched my arm. Like none of it even mattered."

"Now we need to get our vampires back so they can fucking murder him," Joni fumed. "Tess, I'm so sorry, I never would have invited him—"

"You didn't know." Tess shook her head. "I never told you."

"You stopped sleeping, right? Before you moved out?" Joni asked. "I used to hear you up all night. Is that why you went to work for the hotel? Because it's a night job?"

Tess nodded. "It's not like I hate it—it's a good job. I like my friends there. It's an okay life, you know?"

"Just not the life you wanted."

Joni's words hung heavily between them.

"I shouldn't have left without telling you why," Tess said. "I'm sorry."

"No, hey, you were going through something awful—"

"Even so." Tess took Joni's hands. "I was just trying to get through each day, each hour. I was doing the best I could. But I still hurt you, and I hate that I did that. And I'm really, really sorry."

"Ugh, you stupid bitch, now I'm gonna cry." Joni pulled Tess into a tight hug, and they both laughed, and they both cried, and it felt so unbelievably good to be back with the person who knew her best in the world, who loved her best in the world.

"What the fuck is going on here?"

They looked up to see Flora, who looked appalled and slightly freaked out by the emotional display unfolding before her.

"Sorry." Tess laughed. "We just had some stuff to talk about."

"I hate to break up what looks like a very fun party, but I have bad news." Flora slid back into her side of the booth. "Fern told me it was super obvious to her and Konstantin exactly who helped Callum and Octavia escape, and now he wants to capture both of you and torture you until Callum and Octavia come back to save you. Ugh, she was so *smug*."

"What about you?" Joni asked Flora. "Will Konstantin come after you too?"

"Oh, he definitely wants me dead, but if he kills me, it's a whole thing with the witches' council." Flora waved her hand dismissively.

Joni turned to Tess. "Okay, I take back all the shit I've said about you running away from your problems. Sounds like a pretty good plan right now?"

"Where would we go?" Tess looked at Joni.

"Octavia said she'd wire us that money." Joni was grasping at straws. "And, um, Flora could make us portals? If we were in danger?"

"So we spend the rest of our lives living off vampire money and running through witch portals until our luck runs out and Konstantin tortures us to death?"

"It doesn't sound that great when you put it like that."

Tess shook her head. "I've spent the last three years organizing my life around not seeing a man who terrifies me. I'm not doing it anymore."

"Babe." Joni put her hand on Tess's. "With all due respect, what other choice do we have? We can't fight an ancient, powerful vampire. We're just regular people, not characters in *Blood Feud*."

"*Blood Feud*," Tess repeated, laughing a little. "Can you imagine what the fandom would think if they knew about this?"

"Stop, they'd lose their shit." Joni laughed. "Hey, maybe that's an option? We can just stay with all different Feudies until the end of time."

"Hide out in basements decked out with vampire posters." Tess snickered.

"Excuse you, I physically live in a basement already." Joni was cracking up now, and Tess was too—god, it felt good to laugh.

"Maybe there is something . . ." Tess bit her lip, the seeds of an idea taking root. "There might be a way we could have a chance. But we'd need Feudies—a lot of them. Preferably in costume."

"Uh . . . where?" Joni looked around. "Here?"

"No, we need a lot more space than that." A light bulb went off in Tess's mind. "The Georgia might work?"

"We could put out asks to the fandom?" Joni suggested. "Post on social?"

"Yeah, but how many people would that really get?" Tess sighed.

Flora sucked down some of her milkshake. "I can help with the Feudies."

"How?" Tess asked. "With magic?"

"No." Flora smiled. "Because I'm August Lirio."

Chapter 29

Tess and Joni looked at each other for a long moment, and then looked back at Flora.

"I'm sorry." Joni spoke slowly. "What the fuck did you just say?"

Flora twisted her straw wrapper around one of her long black fingernails.

"Yeah, so, you know how it was my job to monitor what was happening on the Isle? With the vision portals?"

"Uh huh." Tess felt like her whole brain was on the fritz.

"I mean, you've met those vampires. They were so interesting! And they're always getting in fights, and having sex, and doing betrayal—I got hooked! I couldn't stop watching the portals—they were like the best *Real Housewives* ever, and they were *always on*," Flora explained.

"That actually totally makes sense." Joni nodded.

"Right? Except I had no one to talk to about them." Flora sighed. "And I was always at the bar reading romance novels anyway, so I thought, what if I just write a little about the Isle?"

"That's when you started writing on fanfic sites," Tess said.

"Exactly! I never thought my fics would get so big—because they weren't based on anything."

"They were based on actual vampires," Joni pointed out.

"Right, but not IP," Flora clarified. "But then I got a huge audience, and then I got an agent, and then the novel went crazy . . . I never expected any of that."

"Why would you make Felix the hero, though?" Tess asked. "He's such an asshole!"

"Well, obviously I didn't *know* he was working with Konstantin," Flora huffed. "But that's how it always goes in vampire stories—Edward and Jacob, Bill and Eric, Stefan and Damon, Angel and Spike—some self-serious sap is always the hero. It was way easier to make Felix the hero than Callum."

"Even though Felix is actually the one who killed Isobel?" Tess said pointedly.

"Shut up." Joni gasped. "He *did*?"

"That happened way after I started publishing." Flora shrugged. "At that point it was just about character consistency."

"I can't believe you're August Lirio," Tess marveled. "Wait, what does the name mean?"

"Lirio is the witch in *The Craft*." Flora bit her lip. "And August is my favorite Taylor Swift song?"

"I literally don't know what to do with my body," Joni said. "Too much is happening. I don't know what to do."

"So anyway, I have all of Lirio's accounts on my phone." Flora held up the phone, as if to illustrate what a phone was. "So I could post that I was going to be at The Georgia, and that Feudies should come in costume? As like, my first-ever posts on social media? Do you think that would get it done?"

"Um, yeah." Tess laughed at the absurdity of this entire situation. "I think that might work."

TEXT MESSAGE TRANSCRIPT:
TESS ROSENBLOOM AND TAYLOR LITMAN

Tess [10:14 PM]: Hey Taylor!! Are you at work?

Taylor [10:15 PM]: Hey Taylor?? HEY TAYLOR? ARE YOU KIDDING ME? I thought you were dead! Or that you quit without telling anyone except that REALLY didn't seem like you so I've been covering your ass and working doubles for weeks you owe me SO MANY PAYCHECKS

Tess [10:16 PM]: Taylor I am SO SORRY, and thank you, and I promise I'll explain everything
Tess [10:16 PM]: But first I need to warn you about a tweet that's about to happen

Taylor [10:16 PM]: A tweet? I'm not even on twitter, why do I care about a tweet

Tess [10:17 PM]: Well
Tess [10:17 PM]: You're going to care about this one
Tess [10:18 PM]: Calling you now, please pick up the phone

SIREN EMOJI: *BLOOD FEUD* AUTHOR AUGUST LIRIO
POSTS ON SOCIAL FOR THE VERY FIRST TIME!

by Sunny Burke, posted on vulture.com

Stop the presses, hold the phone, put down your midnight snack, because things are getting CRAZY on these here internets: NOTORIOUSLY RECLUSIVE *BLOOD FEUD* AUTHOR AUGUST LIRIO HAS TWEETED, INSTA'D, AND TUMBLR'D—ALL FOR THE VERY FIRST TIME!!!!!!

This would be big enough news on its own, but the content of the posts themselves was even crazier. All of the posts were text only, all with the same message:

Want to know the truth about Blood Feud? Meet me at The Georgia hotel in Williamsburg at 4:30am. Come in costume.

Okay. So like. WHAT????? Let's break this down:

First of all, freaking what truth about *Blood Feud*???? Obviously everyone hopes this means we're FINALLY getting an announcement about book four, but it could be other things too. Something about the movies? Or could it have to do with the rabid online conspiracies that the vampires from the books actually exist IRL?!

Second, you're telling me August Lirio, THEE August Lirio, literally one of the bestselling authors on planet Earth, is going to make their first ever public appearance at some random hotel in Brooklyn at 4:30 in the goddamn morning?!?! WHAT?!?! WHY?!?! (Side note about The Georgia Hotel—it's owned by lesbians and super gay generally so we have to stan that about Lirio's choice, as weird as the rest of this might be.)

Third, come in costume????? FOR WHAT REASON??????? Like truly what kind of chaos is Lirio trying to wreak right now?!

So, there you have it. *Something* is going down at 4:30 this morning in Williamsburg, and hundreds of lucky NYC-based Feudies have already announced that they'll be there. And even if "there" turns out only to be a wild-ass bacchanal of predawn cosplaying fans getting clowned, this dedicated journalist and faithful Feudie will still be among them.

TEXT MESSAGE TRANSCRIPT:
FLORA CASTILLO AND FERN CASTILLO

Flora [11:04 PM]: Hey, I have a lead for you on Tess Rosenbloom

Fern [11:04 PM]: "A lead"? What are you, a detective on one of those dumb shows you're always watching

Flora [11:05 PM]: Ok first of all you're not besmirching Olivia Benson on my watch and second do you want the information or not

Fern [11:05 PM]: I'm perfectly capable of finding her myself, but sure, let's see if you can save me some time

Flora [11:06 PM]: Can't be nice even when someone is doing you a literal favor

Flora [11:06 PM]: Anyway, Tess works at The Georgia hotel in Brooklyn. Her shift starts at 4:30am

Fern [11:06 PM]: If I'm such an asshole, then why are you telling me this?

Flora [11:06 PM]: Because I don't need to make an enemy of Konstantin Adamos

Fern [11:07 PM]: Smart. I'll let him know

By 4:15 A.M., The Georgia's lobby was more packed than Tess had ever seen it by several orders of magnitude.

"Oh god, we're so over legal capacity." Tess's manager friend Taylor wrung her hands. "Do you think the fire department will come?"

"Probably." Mika the desk worker was filing her nails. "They hate fun."

"It's gonna be fine," Tess reassured Taylor, though her own nerves were buzzing.

"What should I do with all this?" Willie the bellhop wheeled over a giant laundry cart full of linens.

"Take it down to laundry?!" Taylor sputtered. "Honestly, do I have to do everything?"

"I think we're all doing things pretty well outside our job descriptions tonight??" Willie rocked nervously on the balls of his feet.

"Okay, okay, let's go together. Come on." Taylor sighed, and they rolled the cart off toward the service elevator.

Tess understood why everyone was so stressed—and they didn't even know that several absolutely real vampires were on their way to The Georgia (along with the several hundred costumed ones currently present). Tess marveled at how great the crowd looked, especially on such short notice: There were romantic Felixes and gorgeous Isobels, sinister Konstantins of all shapes and sizes, and, of course, dozens and dozens of Callums and Octavias—which wasn't that fun for Tess or Joni, considering they'd been abandoned by those exact vampires just hours beforehand.

"You look amazing," Joni said to one Octavia, a fabulous drag queen decked out in an acid-green sequined minidress Octavia had worn to a party in book three.

"Omg, thank you!" The queen grinned and twirled. "I really connect with how mean she is, like as a character."

"Me too." Joni nodded, looking a little teary. Tess rubbed her arm.

"You okay?" Tess asked Joni as the queen made her way deeper into the crowd.

"Yeah. At least I have you back." Joni looped an arm around Tess's shoulders. "That matters way more than some extremely hot vampire, no matter how good she was in bed."

"That's the ticket." Tess smiled, but her heart caught in her throat when she saw a man whose hair and silhouette looked strikingly like Callum's—until he turned, and their faces were completely different. Her hand went automatically to the necklace Callum had given her before the ball, and she felt a wave of pain. She couldn't believe how much she already missed him.

"If we pull this off . . . do you think they'll come back?" Joni looked at Tess hopefully.

"Maybe," Tess said quietly. She'd had the same thought—and she certainly hoped Callum would want to be with her in New York if Konstantin wasn't an issue. He'd said as much, hadn't he? More than once?

But that wasn't why she was doing this. She wasn't going to spend the rest of her life running from a killer. Her only choice was to step up and kill him first.

"I can't believe we're carrying around all these stakes," Tess said. "I never thought I'd feel this much like Buffy."

"We're putting aside our emotions about being dumped by our vampire lovers to take on the big bad," Joni reasoned. "It's giving season two."

"And season three!" Tess added.

Tess and Joni were both wearing long, hooded black capes, which worked great to conceal their messenger bags filled with sharp wooden stakes. (It turned out Flora's portal magic came in extremely handy when you needed to rob a costume shop and a garden supply store in the middle of the night.) Tess felt pretty good about their plan—but she was incredibly worried that something would go wrong and someone in this crowd would get hurt.

"Oh my god, it took me forever to get to you," Flora huffed as she pushed through the people around Tess and Joni. "Are you ready?"

"I think so." Tess's heart started pounding. She glanced at her phone—it was 4:27. "Where are they?"

"Just a couple of blocks away." Flora held up her Find My Friends app, where a little dot labeled Fern was nearly upon them.

"And you're sure they don't know about . . . all this?" Joni gestured at the crowd, the costumes, the general rumpus.

"Doubt it," Flora answered. "Fern thinks she's too cool for social media, Felix and the other vamps probably don't even have phones, and Konstantin is famously not online."

"Even if they know, it doesn't change the plan," Tess said. "We keep our hoods up, move through the crowd, and stake them before they find us. Joni, are you good?"

Joni nodded, but she looked a bit green. Since she was by far the tallest of the three, it was her job to stake Konstantin.

"I'll just get behind him," she said, gripping a stake tightly. "He can't kill me if he's dead before he realizes I'm even there. And if it looks like he's going to kill me, Flora can always send him through a portal to the Atlantic Ocean or something, right?"

"Not really." Flora shook her head. "Since portals are about desire, it's really hard to send someone through one involuntarily. If I can do it at all, I can probably only send them a couple of blocks away."

"Oh! Cool, cool, that's fine." Joni was jittery—she couldn't stop moving. "It'll probably still be fine."

"Joni, if you feel like you can't kill Konstantin without getting killed yourself, then don't fucking do it, okay?" Tess put her hands over Joni's. "And remember, if things go sideways, just get to the pool deck."

Joni and Flora nodded. They took out their phones and got on a three-way call so they could stay in communication—they each had one earbud in.

"I feel like I'm in a Mission: Impossible movie," Joni joked.

"Yeah?" Tess laughed anxiously. "Which character are you?"

"Tom Cruise, obviously," Joni said. "Because of my unparalleled derring-do and problematic opinions about women. You're Ving Rhames because you're a majestic loyal genius, Flora's Simon Pegg because she's lovable but ultimately useless."

"You'd both be dead if it weren't for me," Flora said dryly.

"Okay, that's your opinion," Joni joked.

Flora rolled her eyes—but then her phone beeped, and her expression hardened. "They're here."

Tess and Joni looked up. There was Konstantin, tall enough that he was easily visible above the packed lobby.

"How many are with him?" Joni asked.

"Eight . . . maybe ten?" Flora exhaled. "Damn."

Tess recognized Fern's pixie cut—and then she saw a mop of curly hair beside Fern.

"Oh shit, Felix is here too," she whispered to Joni.

"No way!" Joni exclaimed. "Felix Hawthorn?!"

"Yes?" A nearby Felix cosplayer turned around—a hot trans man with extremely debonair energy.

"Sorry, not you." Tess smiled. "You look great though."

"Hey, I'm Flora." Flora made her way over to the hot Felix, and Tess rolled her eyes.

"Flora!"

"Sorry, sorry." Flora smiled at not-Felix then turned back to Tess and Joni. "Let's go."

Tess, Joni, and Flora pulled up the hoods on their respective capes and made their way into the crowd, splitting up to stay inconspicuous. Not that it was hard in this group—for all Tess's nerves, she couldn't help feeling a surge of joy being surrounded by all these people who loved *Blood Feud* as much as she did.

"Tess, on your right," Flora's voice came through Tess's earbud.

"Where?" Tess asked, turning slowly so as not to draw attention.

"Two o'clock. Spiky hair, dark turtleneck."

Tess saw him—he was short with a muscled build and shifty eyes darting back and forth, scanning the crowd. He was leaning against the lobby bar, which had no one behind it since it had closed hours before. Tess moved cautiously through the crowd, careful not to jostle anyone too hard, keeping her head low beneath her hood. There was a back entrance to the bar, accessible only through a service hallway. Tess slid her employee ID into the lock, waited for the green light, and slipped inside.

It was empty and echo-y in the dimly lit hallway, which was a stark gray contrast to the decorated lobby. Tess rushed fifty feet down to another doorway, then swiped her ID again, crouching low as she crept into the bar. She opened the door as narrowly as she could, hoping the vampire wouldn't notice the movement behind him.

"I'm behind the bar," she whispered. "Is he still there?"

"Yes," Flora's voice came back. "Move quickly. Drive the stake right between his shoulder blades."

Tess swallowed hard and gripped the stake so tightly she was

afraid she might lose feeling in her fingers. They had practiced staking some sacks of soil at the gardening store, Flora telling them to
throw their hips into the movement. After a dozen or so tries, Tess
felt like she had the hang of it—but then, sacks of soil didn't fight
back.

Slowly, Tess rose to her feet and got into her "staking stance"—
left foot forward, hips open with her body facing slightly to the
right, right hand drawn back and ready to strike.

"Do it, Tess!" Flora hissed.

In the time Tess hesitated, the vamp turned around and saw
her—oh *damn* it—

"What the fuck?" he growled.

Tess didn't think, she just lunged—she drove the stake right into
his heart. At first she wasn't sure if she'd gotten it in far enough—he
staggered, but with the crowd there was nowhere for him to go—
and then she saw his eyes go glassy and the veins in his face turned
black.

"I did it!" she whispered. "I think I staked him!"

"Holy shit, Tess!!!" Joni screeched as quietly as possible.

Tess leaned the dead vamp over the bar. "Where are the others?"
she asked.

"Konstantin is moving toward the front desk," Flora said. "Joni,
can you get there?"

"I'm trying," Joni responded. "There are too many people."

"What about Felix?" Tess asked, her heart beating faster. She
wasn't eager to put herself in harm's way, but when she thought of
Felix's sneering expression while his henchmen dragged Callum
through the portal, she had to admit, she really fucking liked the
idea of watching him die.

"I don't see him," Flora responded. "Joni, do you?"

"Nope."

"Okay," Tess said. "Then where should I go?"

"Elevator bank," Flora said. "There's a vamp trying to get up-
stairs."

"Copy." Tess rushed back into the service hallway and headed toward the elevators—but she only made it halfway there before everything suddenly fell into darkness—she heard cheers and applause rising from the lobby.

"What's going on?" she called.

"The lights went out." Joni sounded worried. "People think Lirio is here."

"Can you get to Konstantin?" Flora asked.

"I don't know." Joni strained. "I can't see anything."

Tess burst through the doors by the elevators—the room was pitch black—with the noise and the crowd, it was absolute pandemonium. Someone started a chant: "LI-RI-O. LI-RI-O."

Then Tess heard a scream—a real one, blood-curdling and terrified.

"What was that?! Are you okay?"

"A vamp is feeding," Flora said. "I can get to him!"

Tess looked around in a panic—

"We can't let anyone get hurt!" she cried. People were starting to shove and get restless—the lights weren't coming back on—

"This isn't working," Tess said. "We have to get these people out of here."

"How?!" Joni asked.

Tess backed against the door she'd just come through, then felt along the wall—

"I know it's here somewhere," she muttered.

"What's here?" came a low voice, and Tess looked up and saw the outline of a man hulking over her.

"Look at your hood." He flicked it. "Little red riding bitch."

He smiled, and she caught a glimpse of his fangs in the dim red light from the exit sign behind her.

"Does that make you the wolf?" Tess hissed. "You know how that story ends, right?"

The vampire moved quickly, a hand around Tess's neck—he was strong, and she couldn't breathe, but she didn't panic—she grabbed a stake from her pouch and jabbed it forward. He was too tall to hit his heart from this angle, but the stake plunged into his stomach, and he staggered back—

"You shouldn't have missed," he snarled. He was about to come for her again, but Tess had enough time to reach for the wall beside the door, and this time she found what she was looking for.

She pulled down hard on the fire alarm, and sirens started blaring as water rained down from the ceiling.

The vampire was momentarily startled by the noise and the sprinklers, and that was all Tess needed—she grabbed another stake and lunged forward, driving it directly into his heart. He seized up and slumped to the ground—there was no bar to prop him against here, so Tess just left him and ran back into the service hallway.

"Tess!" Joni was yelling in Tess's earbud. "Tess, are you okay?!"

"I'm good!" Tess heaved forward, breathing hard, bracing her hands against her thighs. "What's happening out there?"

"People are pissed, but they're leaving," Joni answered.

"Can you get to the pool?" Tess asked.

"I don't know," Joni answered. "There are so many people—"

"Just get to the desk and wait for me," Flora said. "I'll make us a portal. Tess?"

"I'll take the service elevator," Tess said. "See you there."

Tess took a second to collect her breath, but she knew she had to keep moving. She hurried to the service elevator and jammed the up button. Come to think of it, she didn't know whether the elevators would even work once the fire alarm had been pulled—but she breathed an enormous sigh of relief when she heard the elevator cables whirring behind the closed door. Was Taylor okay? And Mika, and Willie, and everyone else? She couldn't think about that now—they had to be.

The elevator door dinged, and Tess rushed in and pressed the button for the pool deck. She hit the door close button over and over, but it didn't do shit. A few seconds later, the doors started closing in their own sweet time—

Except before they could close completely, a hand jammed between the doors and pushed them open with ease.

As the doors spread open, the blood drained from Tess's face.

Because Felix Hawthorn was standing there, a wide, chilling smile on his face.

Chapter 30

"Hello, Tess," Felix said as he stepped into the elevator. "I have to admit, I thought it would take more than a few hours to find you. Perhaps I gave you too much credit."

The elevator doors slid closed, and the car started to rise. Tess kept her mouth shut—she wouldn't give this asshole the satisfaction of knowing how much he scared her.

"Fern?" Felix clipped. "I have Tess. She was on her way to the pool, which I assume means the others are too. Meet you there?"

"You guys doing your fun little telepathy trick?" Tess spat. "How does it feel to be Konstantin's lapdog?"

"Why don't you ask Callum? He has far more experience than I do." Felix sniffed. "Konstantin is so looking forward to meeting you—he thinks torturing you will lure Callum back. But I know Callum. He won't risk his neck for yours. And when he leaves you here to die, I'll be the one who gets to kill you."

Felix leaned in, inhaling Tess's scent—the sound of his breath made her sick. Tess's hand automatically twitched toward her pouch of stakes, but Felix clocked the movement immediately.

"Don't be stupid," he said, his voice low and threatening. "You'd never get there."

"Ask some of your friends how fast I got there," Tess seethed. She knew it wasn't wise to bait him, but maybe if she riled him up, he'd get sloppy, do something she could exploit to her advantage. For a second, Tess saw anger flash behind Felix's eyes—but then he just laughed.

"Do you think you're some kind of hero? You staked a couple of nobodies?"

"*Blood Feud* made me think you were a hero," Tess said quietly. "Now I'm not sure they even exist."

Felix narrowed his eyes as the elevator jerked to a halt and the doors slid open with a ding.

"Come on." Felix stood outside the open doors, glaring at her. "Move."

Tess kept her chin high as she marched down the service hallway and through the door that led to the pool. They walked past the empty cabana suite where Octavia had stayed for weeks, past the bar where Tess used to hole up and read *Blood Feud,* and onto the main pool deck, where Joni and Flora were waiting in the dark gray light before dawn, surrounded by Konstantin, Fern, and half a dozen others. Tess felt a small surge of pride that she'd lessened their number by two—but her heart sank when she saw that Flora's hands were bound. Flora's face was blank and unreadable; Joni was trying to stay tough, but Tess could see that she was terrified. There was no way they could fight this many vampires out in the open—and no way they could escape if Flora couldn't make them a portal.

"You must be Tess," Konstantin said as she approached. "Good of you to join us."

His voice was smooth, and his manner was even, not angry or agitated at all. Unlike Felix, he didn't seem to be acting out of any kind of personal vendetta—he was simply tying up loose ends.

"Thanks for coming all the way to Brooklyn," Tess deadpanned. "Hope you didn't hit too much traffic."

"Very thoughtful," Felix snapped. "Now why don't you tell us where Callum and Octavia went?"

Tess felt an unexpected pang at the mention of Callum's name. He had to know this was a possibility when he left, that Tess would meet some horrible end without him here to fight for her. She squared her shoulders. She could still fight for herself.

"I don't know where they went," she said firmly. "And I wouldn't tell you if I did."

"You wouldn't have a choice," Felix sneered.

"I always have a choice," Tess snarled, but Felix smiled coldly in response.

"Not if I glamour you."

Felix stood directly in front of Tess, locking his eyes on hers.

"Don't try to fight me," he murmured. "It'll only be worse for you if you do."

His eyes changed—they had the same glow she'd seen from Callum's and Sylvie's eyes on the Isle, except Felix's were a terrible green and gold. It was a horrible sensation, like his fingers were all inside her mind, rummaging through the folds of her brain until he found the spot he wanted. She wanted to scream, to cry out, but she couldn't move—her entire body was paralyzed, and everything felt confusing and fuzzy, like she was going to float away. She tried to look over at Joni and Flora, but she couldn't move—

"Focus on me," Felix said. "Focus on the sound of my voice."

Yes, that was better. Her head didn't hurt so much if she just listened to his voice.

"Good." He sighed, clearly taking pleasure in having complete control. "Now tell me. Where are Callum and Octavia?"

"I don't know."

"*Why* don't you know?" he pressed, his voice growing thin with impatience.

"Because they wouldn't tell us." Tess's voice was utterly emotionless, but she could feel the tears burning behind her eyes. "They said it was safer if we didn't know."

"And then what? They just left?" Felix laughed meanly. "Your big strong lover abandoned you to die?"

"Yes." Tess heard the echo of her own voice, and she hated it. "He left me."

"Did he feed you his blood before he left? Are you in his thrall?"

"No." Tess shook her head. "I fed him mine."

"You dirty little slut." Felix's eyes were alive with interest.

"Enough." Konstantin held out his hand. "She doesn't know anything. Let's get them both back to the townhouse."

"Fine," Felix grumbled. "I just want to taste her first."

Tess wanted to run, to fight, to do anything, but she couldn't move, it was like her whole body was suspended in formaldehyde, green and poison.

"Be a good little lamb and bend your neck for me?"

Tess didn't want to do it. He was going to make her do it.

"Leave her alone!" Joni cried. "Get the fuck away from her!"

"Shut up!" Felix shouted at Joni. "Yours is coming next."

It must have been in that moment that Felix broke the glamour—his attention was too focused on Joni to stay completely in control of Tess—because Tess suddenly realized she could move again, and the foggy feeling was gone. As quickly as she could, she grabbed a stake under her cape and got ready.

"Now, where were we?" Felix turned back to Tess. "Oh, right. Dinner."

He swooped in close, but before he could sink his fangs into her, Tess drove the stake into his chest instead.

"You *bitch*," he shrieked, lurching backward. The stake hadn't hit his heart, but he was injured and bleeding badly as he pulled it out. "I'm going to make you regret that."

He looked at Tess for a long moment—then turned and rushed toward Joni instead.

"NO," Tess screamed, and she took off after him, she ran so fast her lungs burned, but it was no use—he was so much faster, she was about to watch a vampire murder her best friend—

"Christ, Felix. Still picking on humans? You're so pathetic."

A woman with a crisp British accent?! It couldn't be—Tess whirled around and so did Felix—

And there they were, Callum and Octavia, standing at the edge of the deck, silhouetted against the Manhattan skyline.

"You came back." Tess's voice was hoarse.

"Tess, get behind us. Right now." Callum was looking past her at Felix and Konstantin—Tess didn't need telling twice. She leapt behind Callum, and he and Octavia charged forward to free Joni and Flora from the henchmen who were guarding them. Tess had seen Callum fight before, but it was nothing like seeing him and Octavia fight together, both at the height of their powers. Their movements were graceful but brutal, and in seconds the guards were so embroiled in the fight that Joni and Flora could slip away, and Tess immediately untied Flora's hands.

"What do we do?!" Joni squeaked.

"Are you kidding?" Tess drew a stake out of her pouch and threw off her cape. "We help!"

She charged forward to where Octavia was taking on three vamps at once, she kicked one square in the gut and sent him reeling backward—when he fell on the ground, Tess hurled her body toward him and shoved a stake through his heart—his eyes glazed over and his veins turned black, just like the vampires downstairs. Another vampire saw and came running toward Tess, but Flora threw up a portal in front of him—he tried to stop himself but he couldn't in time. He ran through the icy blue circle, which reappeared a hundred feet away and sent him straight off the side of the building.

"Nice!" Tess shouted to Flora, who beamed back at her—but then she grabbed her head and screamed in pain.

"What's happening?" Tess rushed toward her. "Are you okay?!"

"Fern," she said weakly. Tess whirled to see Fern in intense concentration, mumbling a stream of incantations under her breath. Tess started toward her, but Joni was already on it—

"You trapped me in a fucking attic!!!!" Joni shrieked as she tackled Fern like an offensive lineman—they both crashed to the ground with a violent thud, and the spell on Flora was broken.

Felix ran to help Fern fend off Joni—Flora threw a portal at him, but he dodged it, so it sent a deck chair soaring into the air and off the building instead. Felix pulled Joni off of Fern and threw her to the ground—hard. Fern started to perform another spell on Flora, but Flora threw up her hands to block it.

"Oh no, you don't," she gritted, and the two of them were locked in battle, whispering words and moving their hands at each other, streams of light and sparks occasionally shooting back and forth. Callum and Octavia had disposed of most of the henchmen, but the last one was giving them trouble: He was huge and strong—and even against both twin sires he was more than holding his own. Konstantin stood back and watched, enjoying the violence playing out before him.

Joni was trying to get up, but she'd hurt her leg when Felix threw her to the ground—she cried out in pain when she tried to put weight on it. Felix was grinning down at Joni—Tess knew she was no match for him, but there was no one else to help—she ran toward him with a stake in hand, hoping at least she could injure him again before he ripped Joni apart—

But before she got to him, Octavia flew in like a bat out of hell, screaming for all she was worth, kicking him square in the face before whirling around and punching him in the gut.

"YES!" Tess screamed, before the giant henchman turned and started stalking toward her. "Ohhhh no. No no no!"

Tess darted behind Octavia to help Joni to her feet. Octavia tried to fight off Felix and the giant henchman at the same time, but it was a lot for her to handle on her own—especially since Flora was still tied up with Fern. Callum sprinted toward them to help, but—

"Where do you think this is going, Callum?"

Konstantin stood in his way, blocking him with a punch that sent him staggering backward.

"You can't kill me if you need me to make portals," Callum snarled. "But I can kill you. And I will."

"Do you think anyone else knows you the way I do?" Konstantin's voice was quiet, calm. Callum drove toward him, trying to land a punch or a kick, but Konstantin simply stepped aside, avoiding every blow. "I'm your sire, Callum. Stop being weak. I'm the only one who really knows who you are—because you're just like me."

"You don't know anything." Callum clenched his jaw.

"I know you'll do anything to protect your sister." Konstantin narrowed his eyes. "Just think how badly I'll torture her to punish you for this."

Callum glanced toward Octavia. Tess was helping Joni to walk, both of them hiding behind Octavia, who was taking on Felix and the giant henchman at the same time. Octavia was holding her own, but the other two were driving her backward—same with Fern and Flora, who were still locked in their witchy standoff. Tess realized they were all being driven toward the cabana suite, which had its glass doors all the way open. Konstantin was moving backward to avoid Callum, but he was moving the same way too. They were only a few feet away from the suite now—if they got inside, they'd be trapped.

"It's an easy choice, Callum," Konstantin went on. "Return to my side, where you belong. Or you can watch your sister suffer the most brutal violence I can imagine."

Tess looked toward Callum—she didn't want to doubt him, but she knew he would do anything to protect Octavia. Callum looked back at Tess, and she caught a hard blaze in his eye, warm and golden—it reminded her of the way he'd looked at her right after he'd drunk her blood. He mouthed three words she couldn't quite make out. But Tess was almost sure she knew what he'd said.

Callum turned back to Konstantin—Callum was the one with the dangerous look now.

"You're never going to hurt my sister again."

He darted forward so quickly Tess could barely make out his movements—she heard a sickening crack and a yowl of pain, and then Konstantin was clutching his arm.

"You'll pay for that." Konstantin stretched his arm, and with a series of pops, his bones began to heal themselves. But if Callum was afraid, he didn't show it. They were almost at the suite now. Tess imagined another world where she was kissing him, where the light was soft and there wasn't any danger.

"Are you ready?" Tess whispered to Joni, who nodded almost imperceptibly.

They crossed inside the suite, and Tess dove for Fern's ankles. Joni grabbed at Octavia's wrist and pulled her out of the suite as Fern crashed to the ground, breaking her hold on Flora. Flora ran out of the suite, and Tess got up and ran after her, screaming Callum's name. He looked up and ran too, and before the others could figure out what was happening, Flora threw up her hands and the glass doors of the cabana suite slammed shut.

"What's going on?" Octavia looked at Joni. "What's happening?"

Konstantin slammed his hand against the glass—it cracked, but didn't shatter, and the cracks shimmered icy blue.

"What's the meaning of this?!" he demanded. He slammed the glass again and again, but Flora's portal held.

"Portal magic, bitch," Flora muttered, a grin spreading across her face.

"So what?" Felix sneered. "You're going to keep us trapped in a hotel room? That's your master plan? How long is that supposed to hold up?"

"Oh, it shouldn't be long now," Tess smiled. "Right, Octavia?"

Octavia looked at the hotel suite and gasped. "The sun."

Callum looked from Octavia to Tess. "What are you talking about?"

"The cabana suite is one of our most beautiful rooms, but not very well suited to vampires," Tess explained. "Because it has glass walls facing east and west. So if you forget to draw the blackout curtains before sunrise . . ."

"You die," Callum murmured with wonder, putting it together. They all looked to the east, where the sky was already turning lavender and pink.

"Draw the curtains!" Konstantin bellowed. The others in the room started looking desperately around, but there were no curtains to be found. In fact, there were no linens at all.

"Yeahhhh, so, funny story." Joni smiled, leaning on Octavia so she didn't have to put weight on her ankle. "Tess had her bellhop friend Willie take down the curtains, along with every single linen in this room. They're all in a big cart in the basement right now. Does that help you?"

"No, that doesn't really help them," Flora said dryly, "since this bitchin' portal means they can't even get to the bathroom or a closet, let alone the basement."

"It *is* a bitchin' portal," Tess affirmed.

"Thanks, babe." Flora threw Tess a smile.

Callum walked over to Tess, his eyes wide. "Is this really happening? Konstantin . . . it's over?"

Tess took his hands, and god it felt good just to touch him again, to feel the particular curves of his palms, his fingers. Callum drew Tess into his arms, and they hugged each other hard.

"It's over," she whispered. "He'll never hurt you again."

"We should get you guys inside," Joni said. "It's almost dawn."

"Callum, you're not going to do this." Konstantin's voice was low, but his face blazed with fury. "You owe me everything you've ever had. I gave you life."

Callum turned to Konstantin, his posture just as strong.

"You gave me life," he said, "but you didn't give me choices. I'm choosing this."

Then Callum took Tess's hand and led her away from the suite.

Felix banged on the glass and screamed Tess's name, but she didn't even bother to turn to look at him. He seemed far away from her now—like the hope he'd once represented, and the terror he'd come to instill, like all of it was part of her past.

Tess, Joni, Callum, and Octavia walked into the hotel, and Tess hit the button for the penthouse. It was empty anyway, so Taylor had reserved it for Tess, Joni, and Flora to recuperate after the long night was over (presuming they lived through it). They walked into the beautiful room and closed the curtains to keep Callum and Octavia safe. Octavia fussed over Joni, taking her into the bathroom to wrap her ankle with a towel to stabilize it before she could get to a doctor—which gave Callum and Tess their first moment alone since his return.

"Hi," he said, taking her into his arms and kissing her. "I missed you."

"I bet I missed you more." She smiled. "Though in fairness, being surrounded by people dressed up as you probably didn't help."

"Excuse me?" He peered at her, and she laughed.

"I'll tell you later." She kissed him again. "How did you know we were here? And why did you come back?"

"It was your blood." Callum took her hands. "I knew feeding you my blood could tie you to me, but I never knew it could work the other way around. Having your blood inside me, when you were in danger—I could feel it. I didn't know exactly where you were, but Octavia suggested we try the hotel. I thought about you, and Konstantin, and what I wanted my life to look like," Callum said. "You made me feel like I could be a hero. I figured I should probably start acting like one."

Tess's throat was tight, and he held her close.

"Joni's the real expert on the topic of heroes," she said. "But I think you did pretty damn good."

"Ow!" Joni yelped from the bathroom. "That's too tight!"

"That's literally the point!" Octavia snapped. "It'll help keep the swelling down!"

"Who died and made you Dr. Quinn!" Joni retorted.

"You're being pretty bitchy to someone who just saved your ass."

"I saved your ass first! *And* I missed my job interview for you!"

"I'm *obviously* going to glamour your department chair so you can reschedule, so stop whining!"

The bathroom door banged open and Octavia huffed out, with Joni hobbling behind her. Tess and Callum caught each other's eyes and grinned.

"Hey, do you guys mind if I go out to the terrace for a minute?" Tess asked. "I want to watch the sunrise."

"I'll come too," Joni piped in, and Octavia exhaled dramatically. Joni rolled her eyes and grabbed Tess's elbow. "Let's go."

Tess and Joni walked onto the terrace, which had a view over the pool and the cabana suite five floors below, where Flora was still holding up the portal. As the rising sun warmed their faces, they saw a blaze inside the suite—the vampires were burning. The pool deck was dotted with the other vampire corpses; Flora would send them through a portal to a crematorium as soon as the others were dead, and she'd leave Fern trapped in the cabana suite until the witches' council could get there. But in the meantime, that was it. It was finally over.

"You know what's funny?" Tess looked toward Joni. "They didn't have sunlight on the Isle. I didn't know if I'd ever see a sunrise again."

"It's pretty good, right?" Joni took Tess's hand and gave it a squeeze.

"Yeah." Tess nodded. "It's really good."

They stood together for a long moment, Tess and her best friend, feeling the ease of each other's company, the breeze off the East River, watching the sun glint rainbows across the Williamsburg Bridge and Manhattan's glittering skyline. The water wasn't lilac and the bridge wasn't crystal, but to Tess, it felt something like a promise, or maybe a new beginning.

Because after three years of darkness, Tess Rosenbloom was finally ready to let in some light.

Epilogue

Dear Ms. Yoo,

Attached please find your itemized final bill, including charges for the various scorch marks and piles of ash that needed to be cleaned upon your departure, as well as the charge to replace the carpeting in the cabana suite, which could not be salvaged. It was our pleasure to host you at The Georgia—and may we say, our staff really appreciated the twenty thousand dollar tip! We certainly hope you'll choose The Georgia for all your future trips to New York.

Have a wonderful day, and let us know if we can be of any further assistance!

Taylor Litman
Manager, The Georgia Hotel

❧

TRANSCRIPT OF *HERE TO SLAY* PODCAST, EPISODE 91

Cat: Hey, this is Cat!

Ruby: And this is Ruby.

Cat: And we have a really fun show today, which I'm affectionately calling, "Who was the best romantic partner for Buffy, and why was it Faith?"

Ruby: This is the homosexual agenda in full force.

Cat: Correct. But first, Ruby, we have a lot of *Blood Feud* updates this week?

Ruby: I'll say! It started when *Blood Feud* author August Lirio announced they were unveiling their identity at four-thirty A.M. at a hotel in Brooklyn.

Cat: Then they didn't even show! And someone pulled a fire alarm and someone *else* insisted there were real vampires at the hotel, and either that's true or this person faked puncture wounds on their neck for attention, which seems, you know.

Ruby: A lot more plausible?

Cat: Tough, but fair.

Ruby: But it turned out Lirio was just whetting our appetite for even *more* exciting news! Three days after the hotel debacle, they announced that we're finally getting a fourth *Blood Feud* novel!!!

Cat: How happy are you right now, Ruby? Scale of one to ten?

Ruby: Thirty million.

Cat: Sounds right! So what do we know so far about the book?

Ruby: We know we're going to see a major shift in who we consider to be the heroes and villains of the series. And we'll meet our first-ever human character—apparently a young woman named Jess.

Cat: Ugh, not a teen though, right?! Not that I hate teen girls, teen girls fucking rule, just enough with teaching them to have crushes on two-hundred-year-old men, you know?

Ruby: Agree!! And no, Jess is a full adult, which is nice. The final thing we know is that this is going to be the last book in the *Blood Feud* series.

Cat: No!!!

Ruby: I know. But August Lirio promises they have other series in mind—including potentially building out Bar Between and showing us other worlds the characters we love can visit.

Cat: I didn't really follow that, but it sounds cool?

Ruby: It's *extremely cool*.

Cat: Okay! Now that we have the big news out of the way, let's take our first break, which is sponsored by Joke TK. You might think that means I just haven't written a joke here yet, but you'd be wrong! Joke TK is actually a service that uses artificial intelligence to steal jokes from the greatest comedy writers of all time, then adapt them slightly for your specific needs. Worried about a wedding toast or company holiday party chitchat? Joke TK has bots at the ready to find the perfect joke for you.

Ruby: Are the jokes . . . funny?

Cat: Um. Sometimes! We'll be back right after this.

—Forwarded Message—
From: Elaine Harriman <eharriman@earthlink.net>
BCC: Undisclosed Recipient List
Sent: September 4, 9:07 PM
Subject: Re: Emergency meeting

Thanks to everyone who made the meeting tonight—I'm glad this mess is finally behind us. For those who missed the meeting, the vote was unanimous to lift the travel ban between the Isle and other dimensions, and those who live on the Isle are free to return through Bar Between after routine questioning via truth serum.

(We don't believe anyone else was aiding Konstantin Adamos, Felix Hawthorn, and Fern Castillo, but it's prudent to be certain.) As for Fern, she'll be dealt with by our council at a trial date TBD. If you have any questions, please ask someone else. I'm getting too old for this.

⁂

TEXT MESSAGE TRANSCRIPT:
JONI CHAUDHARI AND TESS ROSENBLOOM

Joni [10:14 AM]: TESS TESS OH MY GOD TESSSSSSS

Joni [10:14 AM]: Sorry I know you're at the disciplinary hearing, I'm gonna be there to hug your face off when it's over, but I had to tell you about the apartment IMMEDIATELY?!?!

Joni [10:15 AM]: Ok first of all the building has a DOORMAN, who is happy to accept packages and buzz in takeout and also call one of the building's COMPLIMENTARY CARS AND DRIVERS for us any time we need???

Joni [10:16 AM]: There is MAID SERVICE and BUTLER SERVICE (idk what that is) and also a view of the park??? And both our rooms have ensuites?? With massive tubs?!?! Oh my god we have a vampire sugar mama and I've literally never been happier 😭😭

Joni [10:16 AM]: (Also don't worry our rooms are at opposite ends of the floor you will never have to hear it when Octavia comes to town)

Joni [10:17 AM]: Ok I'll see you at 11, hope everything goes great. I'm so proud of you no matter what happens and I love you so so much!!!

Joni [10:26 AM]: OH MY GOD THERE IS A BUILT-IN ESPRESSO MACHINE AND THE BUTLER WILL SOURCE BEANS FOR US THAT IS WHAT HE DOES

TRANSCRIPT OF TESS ROSENBLOOM'S
VICTIM IMPACT STATEMENT AT COLUMBIA UNIVERSITY
DEAN'S DISCIPLINE HEARING

Good morning, and thank you for taking the time to listen to my statement. It's been three years since Rick Keeton drugged and sexually assaulted me, after which I began to experience severe anxiety and panic attacks and dropped out of my PhD program as a result. I'm grateful to have been given the opportunity to return to Columbia this semester, and that I feel strong enough to be on a campus where the man who assaulted me is still a student too. But I don't think I should have to endure any more stress, panic, and terror on his account than I already have—and I think it's appropriate that he experience consequences for his actions. That's why I decided to move forward with disciplinary proceedings against him.

You have a big decision to make today regarding whether Rick will be allowed to remain a PhD candidate on this campus. You may choose to consider leniency, because after all, this happened long ago. And it's often said that young men shouldn't have their whole lives ruined because of one mistake.

But what about *our* lives?

What about all the women who've fallen in love with schools or cities or careers, who've had our futures derailed because we had to make impossible choices to navigate our trauma as best we could, to keep going, to stay alive?

In coming forward, I knew there was a chance I'd be labeled as just "that girl who Rick assaulted." But I know that I'm so much more than what he did to me—I want my life to be bigger, and happier, and more fruitful than the impact of his actions. And I want Columbia to be more than the place where I was assaulted. Years from now, when I look back on my time in graduate school, I want to think of my professors, the sparks of inspiration they engendered in me. I want to recall my fellow students, our long hours laughing and debating literature, their unconditional support when I told them what happened to me, the way they took it upon themselves to make sure I would never again walk anywhere on campus alone.

There is so much good in this place, in these people. I think the way we stay good is by standing up for each other. Finding some small way in our own lives to emulate the heroes we admire in our favorite books. It's probably easier to turn a blind eye, to shut our mouths and move on. But don't we owe each other something more?

No matter what you decide, I want to thank you for giving me the opportunity to speak today. I spent far too long staying silent. It feels really, really good to use my voice.

—Forwarded Message—
From: Professor Lareina Vázquez <lv553@columbia.edu>
To: Joni Chaudhari <jc718@columbia.edu>
Sent: April 3, 10:01 AM
Subject: Congratulations!

Joni, I was so delighted to hear you were appointed as a new assistant professor in our department—congratulations! I don't know if you heard, but you beat out nearly a hundred applicants for the position. I am so proud of you, and I know you deserve this. I hope you know it too.

On a personal note, I want to say how moved I was by your proposal to start a support system for survivors of gender-based violence inside the department. I was horrified to hear about Rick Keeton, and glad the university decided to expel him—but we must do more. I want to help with your proposal in any way I can. Let's have coffee next week to discuss?

Congratulations again. Look forward to speaking soon. LV

TEXT MESSAGE TRANSCRIPT: TESS ROSENBLOOM, NANTALE ANGUYO, HAMISH SHIELDS, AND SYLVIE KAMLER

Sylvie [1:23 PM]: Hello? Is this working?

Hamish [1:23 PM]: Oh my GOD, Sylvie made a group thread?!? I'm LIVING.

Sylvie [1:23 PM]: My son got me this phone, I hate it.
Sylvie [1:24 PM]: But I wanted you all to know we're having seder at my daughter's place on the Upper West Side on Thursday night, and you're welcome to join us.
Sylvie [1:25 PM]: Sunset is at 7:43, so we'll start at 8. Good?

Hamish [1:26 PM]: Is there gonna be brisket???

Sylvie [1:27 PM]: No, we do lamb for passover.

Hamish [1:27 PM]: Ugh, fine. I'll still come.

Tess [1:27 PM]: Hi!! Thursday is great! I'm not sure if Joni and Octavia will be in town, but Callum and I are in!

Nantale [1:37 PM]: Thank you for the invitation. I would be pleased to join you, and I will bring the blood of a virgin for all to enjoy.

Hamish [1:38 PM]: Okay see NOW it's a party

TUMBLR POST FROM USER FEUDERTRUTHER, POSTED MAY 14

This is gonna sound crazy, but I think Callum Yoo is living in Greenwich Village?! I feel like I see him *everywhere* (but never during the day??). I mean maybe it's just some random hot Korean guy, but I swear, he looks EXACTLY like the old photos we used to post of Callum and Octavia. (And bad news, he also has a super cute girlfriend, this auburn-haired chick, they're like obsessed with each other, UGGHHH!!!) But anyway, is he off the Isle?! Does this have to do with Lirio's new book?!? Wtf is happening!!!!!!

⁊

It was a quiet Tuesday night in Greenwich Village. Tess had just finished grading her last papers of the school year a few hours before, and the entire summer was spread before her like a fabulous invitation. Joni and Octavia were off in Paris for a little shopping holiday, but they'd be back in a few days. The two weren't officially together, but they certainly seemed to be enjoying their cycle of bickering, sex, and lavish vacations. Callum wanted to do something extravagant to celebrate Tess finishing her semester, but she was too tired for a Michelin-starred tasting menu or an impromptu night at the opera, so they settled on drinks at a wine bar close to Callum's new townhouse. (Well, his very *old* townhouse, which was dark and creaky and reminded Tess a great deal of his rooms on the Isle.) The bar always had an assortment of bottles open, and Tess loved that they would give you lots of tastes before you chose a glass. She and Callum were sitting at the bar, tipsy on glasses of fizzy rosés and funky chilled reds.

"Come on," he needled her. "Just one?"

"We did one last night," Tess protested coyly.

"But it's so fun when we do it together." He grinned, then leaned in close to murmur in her ear. "And afterward, I have a really good surprise for you at home."

"Oh, yeah?" She laughed. "What kind of surprise?"

"You'll find out when I give it to you, won't you?" Callum winked. "So what do you say—just one?"

"Fine." Tess sighed happily. "A quick one."

A few minutes later, they were strolling through the meatpacking district, eyeing the club-goers and bridge-and-tunnel oglers and finance bros who dropped a grand on bottle service in the middle of the week.

"No, no. Not him, no." Callum was getting antsy—Tess threaded her fingers through his. "Ah. There."

Callum nodded toward a man in a dark suit lurking outside a club entrance. He was handsome and pale, with sharply angled features and a hungry look about him—and talking to a girl in her early twenties who was drunk enough that she teetered on her platform heels.

"Ohh." Tess nodded. "Absolutely."

"Go get him, love," Callum whispered, giving Tess's ass a friendly squeeze as she set off toward the man.

"Ohmigod, girl, what are you doing out here?" Tess put on her own drunken affect as she approached the girl. "Everyone's looking for you!"

"What?" The girl look confused. "Who are you?"

"I'm Zoe's friend," Tess said, as if that explained everything.

"Excuse me," the man broke in. "We're in the middle of a conversation."

But Tess just ignored him—kept her focus on the girl. "Just go inside, okay? Everyone's really worried."

"Cool." The girl nodded and did as Tess said, ambling back toward the club's entrance.

"What was that about?" The man gave Tess a frustrated scowl. "We were just talking."

"Now you can talk to me." Tess smiled viciously, dropping her drunken act.

"And me," Callum said as he appeared beside her.

The man turned and snarled at Callum, baring his fangs—but his expression changed completely when he recognized Callum's face.

"Oh, *fuck,*" he groaned. "Callum Yoo?"

. . .

"Konstantin was right about you," Tess breathed as Callum pushed her up against the wall of the entry to his townhouse, kissing his way down her neck. "You *are* violent."

"But only in the best ways," he growled, nipping at her earlobe.

The worst part about the witches allowing all the vampires to come back from the Isle was that pieces of shit like the one they'd just staked were roaming the streets of New York.

The best part was how much Callum liked killing them—and how much he loved sleeping with Tess after a fight.

"God, you look good." He pushed her hair out of her face. "Why do you look so good?"

"Being in love suits me," she murmured. He kissed her deeper, and his hands started to wander over the contours of her slippery dress . . .

"Hey!" She laughed. "What about my surprise? Or was the surprise just, you know?"

"Sex?" He grinned. "I mean, we're definitely doing that, but I wouldn't call it a surprise. This, on the other hand . . ."

He grabbed a thick envelope off the hall table and handed it to her.

"What is it?" She frowned.

"If I tell you, it's not a surprise."

"Smart ass." She smacked his arm with the envelope.

"Ooh, nice one," he teased. "Do it again. Harder."

"Yeah, you like that?" She laughed. "Okay, let's see what we have here . . ."

The paper of the envelope was thick and creamy. She tore it open and found two plane tickets to London—a night flight, of course.

"A trip?" she asked, her eyes lighting up. "I've never been to Europe."

"I know." He smiled. "But it's actually a bit more than that. Keep going."

She put the tickets down and reached back into the envelope—there was another, smaller envelope inside, letter-sized, embossed with the seal of the Royal Shakespeare Company.

"Callum." Tess inhaled sharply. "What is this?"

"Read it." He grinned. Her hands were shaking as she opened the envelope and removed the letter inside.

"Dear Ms. Rosenbloom," she read aloud, "it is our pleasure to offer you a position as an assistant dramaturg and company researcher on this summer's forthcoming production of *Macbeth*—"

She dropped the letter and leaped into Callum's arms.

"How did you do this?!" she yelped, kissing him again and again.

"Your adviser helped." He laughed, hugging her close. "I knew the right people to call, but she told them how special you are and how lucky they'd be to have you. I thought we could spend the summer together, if you like? I know it'll be harder with the longer days, but you'll be busy with the play, and it'll rain plenty because it's England, and I can show you where I grew up in London—"

"Oh my god, you don't have to sell me! This is the best thing that's ever happened in my entire life."

She kissed him deeply, and he sighed with contentment.

"So you're happy?" he asked.

She nodded, suddenly emotional. "Happier than I thought I'd ever be again."

"I feel the same way," he whispered.

"How soon do we leave?" she asked. "I didn't even look at the date on the tickets."

"Two weeks," he said. "Is that all right?"

"Two weeks is good." Tess nodded. "What are you doing between now and then?"

"Why?" he laughed. "What did you have in mind?"

"Well," Tess said, "I got a text from Flora the other day complaining that we never come to visit her at the bar anymore. There are a lot of worlds we still haven't seen . . ."

"Tess Rosenbloom." Callum grinned. "What precisely are you suggesting?"

She kissed him again, her eyes glinting with excitement.

"Do you want to go have an adventure?"

Acknowledgments

Sometimes, your editor really hates vampires. But sometimes, even then, she is such a wildly passionate, talented, and dedicated professional that she will pace the hallways of a New York City courthouse while on break from jury duty, nailing down the exact rules of a vampiric blood thrall. (I can only guess that this is not the weirdest thing to happen on any given day at jury duty in New York City.) Thank you, Emma Caruso, for that phone call and all the others, for caring about these characters as much as I do, for being the most insightful and supportive editor any author could hope for, and for letting me put back all the questionable jokes you cut. I don't take any of this for granted, and I will never stop being grateful to be able to do this work with you.

This novel exists because on a day when I was having an absolute meltdown about another project, my book agent, Julia Masnik, asked me what I would rather write instead, and I whimpered, through tears, "A girl wakes up in *Buffy*?" "Oh," she replied gently, in a tone I have personally heard her use with her fashionable and spirited toddler, "what would happen next?" J, thank you for your brilliant guidance, for the gossip, for the memes, and for one of the most important friendships of my life. I don't think I could ever write a book without you, but I know for certain I couldn't have written this one.

I love working with the team at the Dial Press, and I am so grateful to all of you for being such fiery champions of books for, by, and about women and queer people. Whitney Frick, thank you for curating this amazing community of bighearted feminists and inviting me to be a part of it. Thank you to all the fantastic members of the *Fang Fiction* team: Melissa Folds (the fanciest Swiftie), Maria Braeckel, Debbie Aroff, Corina Diez, Madison Dettlinger, Avideh Bashirrad, Sarah Horgan, Cindy Berman, Alexis Flynn, Talia Cieslinski, and the incomparable Random House subrights squad. In an industry that can verge on vampiric, I feel beyond lucky to have a place in your fabulous coven. Thanks also to Melissa Yoon for your kind encouragement, extremely sharp suggestions, and commitment to Spuffy.

Thank you to all my wonderful writer friends who took time to read various iterations of this book and give vitally important feedback: Sonia Kharkar, Julia Cox, Sneha Koorse, Morgan Matson, Jeanne Jo, and Nasser Samara (who came up with the title). Thank you to Taylor Salditch for teaching me about horses, and to Tia Subramanian and Michael Cole-Schwartz for your careful consideration of which beverages pair best with the characters in this novel. Thank you to Amanda Litman for reading on behalf of romance enthusiasts and Nick Gaw for reading on behalf of men. Any mistakes in this novel are mine alone, but if you're a man who has a problem, I do encourage you to take it up with Nick.

I am fortunate to have so many wonderful authors and book lovers who have been deeply generous in supporting me and my work. Thank you to Grace Atwood, Eva Chen, Heather Cocks, Rosie Danan, Fiona Davis, KJ Dell'Antonia, Becca Freeman, Kate Goldbeck, Laura Hankin, Lana Harper, Emily Henry, Linda Holmes, Greta Johnsen, Mackenzi Lee, Jenna Levine, Jessica Morgan, Hannah Orenstein, Jo Piazza, Lyla Sage, Amy Spalding, Ashley Spivey, Emma Straub, Elissa Sussman, and especially Jasmine Guillory, whose kindness while I debuted during a pandemic I will absolutely never forget.

I am grateful as ever for my incredibly supportive family, and would like to make particular mention of the fifteen or so Staymans who excitedly passed around one advance copy of *One to Watch*. I will really do my best to get you guys more than one book this time. I love you so much.

Thank you to Adam Klaus for telling me in 2008 that you thought I would like *Buffy the Vampire Slayer* (you were correct), and to Rachel LaBruyere, Amy Beihl, Meg "Jodi the Vampire" Vázquez-Pastrana, Sharon Greene, Trish Welte, Sneha Koorse, Liz Werner, and many more for being fabulous sisters in vampire adoration over the years. Thank you also to Charisma Carpenter and all the courageous people who spoke out about abusive behaviors behind the scenes on *Buffy* and *Angel,* as well as to the many allies from the cast and crew who supported you. I am grateful for your bravery, your talent, and all the time you spent creating a work of art that changed my life.

Thank you to my extremely kind former neighbor Jason Chiang and his dad, Willie, for helping me finally install an air conditioner after ten years in LA. Thank you to Patrick Metz for being the fiercest friend and advocate when I needed one most (and yes, I obviously mean fierce in the RuPaul sense of the word).

I personally have never believed in a wild internet conspiracy for nearly a decade, but if I did, Sonia Kharkar and Keria Madow are the only people who would truly understand. The FeudieTruthers have nothing on us.

Thank you to Corey Ackerman and Katy McCaffrey for fighting so hard for me on the Hollywood side of things, and for being outstanding company at the Taylor Swift picket. While on the subject, it must be said, thank you to Taylor Swift. Thanks also to Krissy Wall for all your support (and excellent taste in baby names).

When I told my therapist, Helen Land, about the topics I planned to address in this novel, she tilted her head in an exasperated way and said, "Oh, Kate. *Really?*" I know, Helen. I know. Thank you for helping me feel strong and happy enough to do this, and everything else.

This book is about so many things, but the most important one is this: The only way to get through the really awful stuff is with the love of your friends. Thank you to Ali, Amanda, Amy, Chase, David, Eleanor, Erin, Franchesca, Jeanne, Jen, Jenna, Jess, Julia, Julia (I'll never say which came first), Kellie, Kent, Keria, Leslie, Lilia, Mark, Meg, Megan, Michael, straight Michael, Mike, Morgan, Nasser, Nichole, Nick, Nora, Patrick, Rachel, Shareeza, Sharon, Sierra, Sneha, Sonia, Steph, Steven, Taylor, Tia, Toni, and Trish. I'm sure I missed someone, this paragraph was a Libra nightmare. Thank you. I love you.

And if you're reading this, and you once helped a friend through something terrible, thank you too. You're a mensch, and the people who love you know it.

FANG
FICTION

Kate Stayman-London

Dial Delights

*Love Stories
for the
Open-Hearted*

Interview with the Vampire Novelist:
Frequently Asked Questions Regarding *Fang Fiction*

Hey! So what's happening here?

We're answering questions about *Fang Fiction*! Thank you so much for reading—I'm so excited to tell you more about the writing process, the vampire stories that inspired me, and, obviously, how this all relates to Taylor Swift.

Amazing! But you know that we know that the questions and answers are both just you, right, Kate?

Bitch, don't break the fourth wall.

Copy that. Okay, let's talk about *Fang Fiction*! Your first novel, *One to Watch,* was set in the world of reality TV—was it a big leap to write about vampires this time around?

In some ways, yes—writing a story with fantasy elements was *way* more complicated than a straightforward contemporary rom-com (although of course writing a romcom with, like, thirty love interests was complex in its own way!). But actually, I think these two books share a very similar DNA: They're both fish-out-of-water stories with elements of wish fulfillment, interrogating the ideas of fandom and escapism and what it feels like when a pop culture fantasy (like starring on a reality show or visiting a magical world filled with vampires) actually comes true.

Did you enjoy writing a novel with fantasy elements? What challenges did you face?

I absolutely *loved* having the opportunity to let my imagination run wild—to make up fabulous places like Bar Between or the library in Nantale's compound (I want to go there). The challenge was how to keep the story feeling grounded among all those fantasy elements. Part of that was keeping every element of the story rooted in the characters' emotions—the library is a great example. I knew I wanted to write that location, but in my first draft, it just felt like a pretty place that didn't serve any purpose. So I thought deeply about what a library would mean to Tess, especially at that point in the narrative, and that's when I came up with the idea that she would have a dream about going to the library at Columbia with Callum. After that change, the library on the Isle wasn't just a beautiful place, it also represented Tess's painful yearning to get back to the life she abandoned.

Writing fantasy elements also requires a lot of technical world-building, creating strict rules of how magic works in this world, who has power and how and why, and making sure the story adheres to those rules. When I was writing the Joni/Octavia chapters, it was like, okay, they want to go to Midtown. They can take the subway or call a car, easy! I know how that works! On the Isle, I had to make deliberate choices about every single element of the world, and whenever I thought I was finished, I'd come across a whole new slew of questions that needed answering. The biggest relief in the entire drafting process was when I realized Tess could have a horse. A horse!! That I didn't have to invent and wasn't magical, just a regular-ass horse! Oh man, I was so happy.

You're a big-time feminist who spent many years working for women's rights as a writer for Hillary Clinton and reproductive justice causes, among others. How did this play into your decision to write a vampire novel?

I love vampire stories and have for a long time—even though they're incredibly problematic! Why is it always some two-hundred-year-old guy seducing a teenager? Characters like Spike from *Buffy* and Damon from *The Vampire Diaries* and Eric from *True Blood/The Southern Vampires Mysteries* are heinous villains, monsters who skulk in the night and commit murder as casually as ordering a cup of coffee. So why do I (and so many other women) find them so attractive? Is it our desire for a protector? The (totally fallacious) notion that we alone are special enough to reform a bad boy? Or maybe it's just that we're all so tired from trying to suss out which men in the real world might secretly be demons, it's a relief to have it right out in the open.

One thing I love about horror is how different kinds of monsters externalize different human fears: Ghosts represent grief, zombies represent death, and vampires represent sex, love, and abandonment—the notion that a lover can take your very life force from you, and then they can either make you immortal or leave you to die. I knew I wanted to write a story about a sexual assault survivor, and my protagonist's core issues would center around trust and bodily autonomy. The more I thought about it, the more I realized that a vampire novel was exactly the right vehicle for the story I wanted to tell.

What was your approach to writing about Tess's trauma? Did you always intend to write a flashback of her experience?

This was really tricky. The flashback sequence was one of the very first things I wrote when I started working on this novel, curled up on a couch in a rental apartment in Annecy, France, as a snowstorm raged outside my window. I felt I couldn't write Tess's story until I knew the details of her experience; it was foundational to understanding her character. I originally had the flashback in Chapter 2, and let me tell you, that was a real bummer of a way to start a novel. At the same time, I did *not* want Tess's trauma to be any kind of surprise or reveal—it was my nightmare that a survivor would be reading this book and having a fun time and suddenly get seriously triggered.

As I went through the writing process, I realized that it made sense to be clear about what happened to Tess from the beginning but also not to get into the details, because Tess is trying so hard not to think about it. Later in the story, as she opens up to Callum and feels safe enough to share her story, that's when we get to see her memories, because she's finally ready to think about them. And, hopefully, by that point in the narrative, so are we.

Fandom is another big element of the novel. Are you part of any fandoms?

Oh boy, am I ever! I'm a huge Swiftie (if you ever bring me a friendship bracelet at a book event, I will absolutely lose my mind). You can definitely see elements of the Swiftie fandom in the Feudies—especially our propensity to hunt for clues, do our research, and dive down potentially unhinged rabbit holes based on the thinnest scraps of "evidence" (RIP Woodvale).

I'm also a more casual member of the *Buffy* fandom, which feels really different because it's so much smaller. Last fall I went to a fan event at Torrance High School, which is where they filmed Sunnydale High—it was a "Homecoming Dance," and I went with friends who love *Buffy* too. We all dressed up as different characters (I went as Buffy, I'm sorry, my Venus is in Leo, I can only be who I am), and it was beyond wonderful to be surrounded by joyful vampire nerds in costume, gawking at locations and getting temporary tattoos and taking photos and dancing. That spirit of community, of people who love the weirdest and most niche parts of you unconditionally—

that's the part of fandom I really wanted to capture in this novel, especially in that climactic scene at The Georgia.

Speaking of _Buffy_, let's say I loved _Fang Fiction_ and I want to read/watch more vampire stories. What do you recommend?

OMG, I'm SO excited for your imminent journey through the wonderful world of vampires! For books, Anne Rice is the ne plus ultra of vampire writers—you can't go wrong starting with _Interview with the Vampire_ (the movie is also iconic; I haven't dipped into the TV series yet but have heard great things!). _Sunshine_ by Robin McKinley is also a fascinating exercise in worldbuilding—it may be the most vividly imagined paranormal story I've ever read. And these aren't vampire stories, but I must recommend everything by my favorite fantasy writer, Leigh Bardugo. Start with the Shadow and Bone series and then read _Six of Crows;_ I promise, you won't regret it.

For TV, _Buffy the Vampire Slayer_ will always be my forever favorite. _Buffy_ uses its monsters of the week to externalize fears faced by your typical teenage girl in ways that are sometimes nothing short of genius. It's also deep and rich and so funny, with an absolutely stacked bench of wonderful characters. (Are Callum and Octavia my spins on Spike and Cordelia? Yes, a bajillion times yes!) If you're new to _Buffy_, I recommend starting with season two—you can always go back and watch season one later. Watch a few standout episodes from the first half of season two to get the lay of the land ("Halloween" and "What's My Line" are bangers), then watch episode thirteen ("Surprise") and buckle up for one of the best storylines in the history of television.

I'm also a huge fan of _The Vampire Diaries_ and _True Blood,_ both of which are based on series of novels! _The Vampire Diaries_ is a pitch-perfect, heightened snarky teen soap (think _Dawson's Creek_ with vampires), and _True Blood_ is a sexy, campy vampire melodrama, where vampires "coming out of the coffin" served as metaphors for queer people coming out of the closet. (The 2000s were wild.) Honestly, there's so much fantastic (*fang*-tastic? ugh) vampire content out there, I hope you have the best time watching and reading!

Last question, and it's an important one. Maybe the most important question anyone has ever asked.

I'm ready.

Which Taylor Swift song best represents each of the main characters in *Fang Fiction*?

Thank god, I've been thinking about this so deeply. Okay, here we go:

Tess: At the beginning of the story, the song I relate most to Tess is "Right Where You Left Me." This is one of Taylor's saddest songs, about a woman who can't move past her worst memory, no matter how hard she tries. Tess thinks she's run away and moved on from Columbia and everything that happened there, but the truth is she's stuck. Stuck reliving her memories, stuck trying to ignore her past because she's not ready to deal with it. Through the course of the novel, though, Tess changes her life, and she changes herself too. She realizes she's strong enough to confront her past and move forward, brave enough to be vulnerable and fall in love. By the end of the book, I think the song that represents Tess is "Fearless." She'll put on her best dress and dance through a storm, because she's weathered more than her fair share and she knows she can do it. *You pull me in and I'm a little more brave. It's the first kiss, it's flawless, really something . . . it's fearless.* That's our girl.

Callum: For a vampire who's deeply worried people will think he's a villain, what song could it be but "Anti-Hero"? Callum does get older but never wiser—he's 135! He wakes up at sunset—midnights are literally his afternoons! The song is glib and pithy, just like Callum, but under the surface, these lyrics get at some heartbreaking fears: that he's a monster unfit for human company, that his true nature is too dark to be confronted, that he deserves to be alone. Luckily, like Taylor, Callum is able to overcome his inner worries to be a global superstar (extremely here for his tortured poet era tbh).

Octavia: There's no one more *Reputation*-coded than Octavia—outside she's hard and glittery, but under that tough exterior she's a puddle of big gay feelings. I could pick any number of *Rep* songs for Octavia, but I went with "I Did Something Bad," because it embodies everything I love about her character: She's unapologetically powerful, deliciously indulgent, and absolutely couldn't give a shit what men think of her. Truly, an example for us all. RATATA-TATATA, bitches!

Joni: Joni! So pure of heart, so bright of spirit, so prepared at all times with snacks and blankets and iPads loaded with old episodes of *Buffy*. She's the kind of best friend who'll hug you tight when things go wrong, then drag you to a disco bar to dance out all your feelings. In other words, she's the epitome of "New Romantics." Rob Sheffield of *Rolling Stone* (a consummate Swiftie) says this song "makes crying in the bathroom sound like a bold spiritual quest," and that's so Joni to me: bighearted, nonjudgmental, and explosively joyful. When the world throws bricks at you, just get a Joni by your side, and you can build a damn castle.

Flora: "August." Duh. ;)

I'm so glad I asked.

Hard same!! And thank *you* for reading the novel and all this bonus content, dear reader. (See what I did there?) I appreciate you more than I can ever express.

The Official
Fang Fiction Annotated Playlist

Music is a super important part of my writing process; I make a playlist for all of my projects to set the mood while I work, adding songs as I go. During the years I spent working on *Fang Fiction,* that playlist ballooned to five hours and seventy-eight songs (it's important to keep a variety so you don't get bored on long writing days!). This playlist only has eighteen songs; some are from that master playlist, and others are songs that are played in the book or reference important ideas or themes from the story. This is also a public playlist on my Spotify called "Fang Fiction," so feel free to add it to your library and throw it on the next time you want to read (or write!) about vampires.

1. **"Seventeen" by Sharon Van Etten**
   This was the very first song I added to my *Fang Fiction* playlist, long before the book had a title. I love the feel of this song, the optimism mixed with a painful twinge of nostalgia. Sharon sings to her younger self, *I see you so uncomfortably alone, I wish I could show you how much you've*

grown. That idea was always the impetus for the story I
wanted to tell, even before I knew what that story was
going to be.

2. **"Golden" by Harry Styles**
Tess and Joni loved having Harry Styles dance parties
when they lived together, and I listened to a ton of Harry
while I was writing. I could have chosen any number of
Harry songs for this playlist, but the lyric *Take me back to
the light* was too on-theme to be ignored!

3. **"Vampire Weeknight" by Jenny Owen Youngs**
Jenny Owen Youngs co-hosts a *Buffy* podcast called
Buffering the Vampire Slayer, where she writes a song about
Buffy every week; she's also a super talented singer-
songwriter. So when I saw she had a song called "Vampire
Weeknight" (so funny), I've never clicked add to playlist so
fast in my life.

4. **"I Can't Sleep" by KEY**
No *Fang Fiction* playlist would be complete without some
K-Pop, and an absolute bop about insomnia?? Fuck yeah!!
*Feeling like a vampire at a dizzying speed . . . go to a world where
there's no morning.* That's the good shit right there.

5. **"Cemetry Gates" by The Smiths**
A cloudy day, the gates of a graveyard; two lovers meet to
talk about the bard. With lyrics in which Keats and Yeats
are quoted, was e'er a song more Tess and Felix coded?
(Yes, those were iambic couplets, idk why I'm like this.)

6. **"If You Want To" by beabadoobee**
Another insomnia bop that's also a low-key consent
anthem? Yeah, it's on the playlist. Also beabadoobee was

one of the openers for the Eras Tour, so you know we like to keep it in the family.

7. **"I Put a Spell on You" by Annie Lennox**
Did you spend a healthy chunk of 2016 listening to the *Fifty Shades of Grey* soundtrack on repeat? No? Not totally sure how you got through that year then! Anyway, this cover is so hot I put it in the scene where Joni and Octavia kiss for the first time, and I had it playing the whole time I wrote it. Warning: If you listen to this song too much, you will be at grave risk of making some very bad, very fun, decisions.

8. **"Virgin State of Mind" by K's Choice**
Buffy fans will know this is an iconic song from the series; the band plays it live during the episode "Doppelgängland" when Vampire Willow visits the Bronze. Joni tells Octavia about a different Vampire Willow episode ("The Wish"), but this one is another absolute banger, and the song is amazing too! This also feels to me like the kind of sexy electronica that was playing when Tess first walked into Bar Between.

9. **"Smooth Operator" by Sade**
Can you tell we're in the slow and sensual portion of the playlist? This is the song playing at the wedding at The Georgia when Tess and Octavia dance. Let's just say I chose it for a reason. :)

10. **"Jade Green" by Kacey Musgraves**
This song is so *Fang Fiction* coded I have to wonder if Kacey got an early copy somehow? *I wanna bathe in the moonlight until I'm fully charged, come into my power and heal the broken parts that I carry.* If this isn't about the milky jade pools, I

don't know what to tell you. The song is also about wearing a piece of green jewelry to remember a loved one is with you—um, hello, the emerald necklace Callum gives Tess much?! Anyway, I kid, but I adore this song, and it will always be special to me because of its connections to the book.

11. **"Nights" by Frank Ocean**
Frank Ocean is another artist I absolutely love, and pretty much all of his work would set an amazing mood for reading *Fang Fiction*. "Nights" is a dense text about a wide range of topics, from handmade project cars to Hurricane Katrina; I love how the song roves freely both musically and lyrically, how it feels like that strange disorientation of working nights and sleeping days.

12. **"Cowboy Like Me" by Taylor Swift**
Okay, you *know* I debated long and hard about which Taylor song to put on this list. But for me, this is one of Taylor's most romantic songs, about a marriage of equals, clear-eyed about their own flaws and each other's even as their eyes are full of stars. My favorite lyric in this song is *Forever is the sweetest con*—and I can think of no better line to encapsulate how it must feel to fall in love with a vampire.

13. **"Heroes" by David Bowie**
So much of *Fang Fiction* is about the idea of what makes a hero, and this is one of my favorite songs ever. It's about two people who can't be together, but they defy the odds to find a perfect moment, kissing as bullets fly over their heads. It reminds me of the scene on the Georgia rooftop when Callum mouths "I love you" to Tess; even as they know they might both be about to die, they still feel connected to each other.

14. **"Always, Joni" by Trousdale**

This is a song about a tough breakup peppered with references to Joni Mitchell. I love how the mood of the song is a soaring sort of melancholy, and with that title, how could I not include it?

15. **"I Will Follow You into the Dark" by Death Cab for Cutie**

This song was a suggestion from, and is a tribute to, my book agent, Julia Masnik, an unfailingly chic New Yorker who can never (and would never) shake the Seattle alt-rock that shaped her childhood and her soul. This is a song about loving someone so much that you'd follow them anywhere. It's incredibly romantic, but for me, it also feels like Tess and Joni's friendship, and their commitment to stay by each other's sides even during the darkest moments of their lives. Always, no matter what. Which is also how I feel about Julia.

16. **"Rainbow" by Kesha**

Kesha's 2017 album *Rainbow* is one of the most important albums of my life, and I considered lots of songs from it for this playlist (obvious choices included "Praying," "Finding You," and "Bastards"). But no song better captures Tess's journey than "Rainbow," which is about stepping out of the darkness and inviting color and light back into your life. *You gotta learn to let go, put the past behind you. Trust me, I know, the ghosts will try to find you, but just put those colors on, girl. Come and paint the world with me tonight.* This album helped me through some very tough moments, and if you're going through something similar, give this song a listen. Even if our hearts are broken, they're still made of gold.

17. **"Run Away with Me" by Carly Rae Jepsen**

    At the beginning of the novel, Tess wants to run away from everything that ever mattered to her and everyone who loves her. But by the end of the book, Tess is back at Columbia, she and Joni are best friends and roommates again, and she and Callum are running into the night together, hand in hand, off to have another adventure. This song is a rush of absolute joy, and at the end of a very emotional playlist (and story!), I hope it's just the catharsis we all need.

18. **"Free" (acoustic version) by Florence + The Machine**

    Every other song on this playlist is about the story of *Fang Fiction,* but this song is about what it meant to me to write it. *Is this how it is? Is this how it's always been? To exist in the face of suffering and death, and somehow still keep singing? . . . But there is nothing else that I know how to do, but to open up my arms and give it all to you.* In the face of overwhelming emotions about my own life and about the world, writing stories is my way through, my path to feeling free. If you've read my work, I can never thank you enough for walking that path by my side.

Listen to the *Fang Fiction* podcast on Spotify: https://open.spotify .com/playlist/1NEXfhB60AipWuuAiLGdme?si=c0f8c714dc8e4219.

KATE STAYMAN-LONDON is a novelist, screenwriter, political strategist, and bisexual double Libra. Her bestselling debut novel, *One to Watch,* was named a best book of the year by *Time,* NPR, *Marie Claire, Mashable,* and more. Stayman-London has written for political icons including Hillary Clinton, Barack Obama, and Cher; she is also a television writer-producer and a proud WGA captain. When not writing, Stayman-London enjoys fabulous trips with friends, rewatching *Buffy the Vampire Slayer,* and fighting for reproductive justice—as well as justice for Speak Now, Evermore, and Reputation. She lives in Los Angeles.

Instagram: @katestaymanlondon
TikTok: @authorkatestaymanlondon

Books Driven by the Heart

Sign up for our newsletter
and find more you'll love:

thedialpress.com

⟲ @THEDIALPRESS

▶ @THEDIALPRESS